Influential Magic

Books by Deanna Chase

The Jade Calhoun Novels
Haunted on Bourbon Street
Witches of Bourbon Street
Demons of Bourbon Street
Angels of Bourbon Street
Shadows of Bourbon Street (March 2014)

The Crescent City Fae Novels
Influential Magic
Irresistible Magic
Book Three in the *Crescent City Fae* series (June 2014)

Other Novels
Defining Destiny (Spring 2014)

Influential Magic

A Crescent City Fae Novel

Deanna Chase

Bayou Moon Publishing

Acknowledgments

A huge thank you to my team: Angie Ramey, Susan Sheehan, Chauntelle Baughman, Anne Victory, Lisa Liddy, and the team at Red Adept. I'd be lost without you. And to my readers, thank you for all your support. You make it all worthwhile.

Chapter 1

The ugly concrete building loomed before us, making my body itch with unease. I gritted my teeth and tried to mentally prepare for the long flight ahead. There was a reason faeries hated airplanes. Metal had an unfortunate way of draining our energy.

"You didn't have to walk me in," I said to Talisen, my brother's best friend and the guy who'd just spent five hours transporting me from Eureka to the Sacramento airport. "I would've been perfectly fine if you'd dropped me off at departures."

"Are you kidding?" Talisen draped a casual arm over my shoulders and made a show of stretching his legs. "One more minute in the truck and my limbs would've seized up."

I eyed his lanky but muscular body. Tall, broad-shouldered, and tan from his long days of working outdoors in my mother's nursery. He'd dressed nicer than usual today. Gone were his faded blue jeans, scuffed work boots, and pop-culture T-shirt, replaced by olive khakis, a short-sleeved, button-down shirt, and black canvas shoes. "I think you could've survived until you hooked up with your lunch date."

He pulled the glass door open for me. "Date?"

"Yeah. Yesterday I heard you tell a client you weren't available this afternoon because you had a date. I assumed that's what this was about." I waved my hand up and down, indicating the change in his wardrobe choice.

He laughed. "I was talking about you, Willow."

"Oh." I smirked. "Sorry excuse for a date. Is dropping your best friend's sister off at the airport the best you can come up with? Maybe you need lessons. Remind me the next time I come home to set you straight on what a normal twenty-four-year-old would consider 'dating.'"

"Ha! Look who's talking. You didn't even so much as look at any other dudes this summer, let alone go out with one. Pathetic, really. No, thanks. I'll get my lessons elsewhere."

His words hit a sore spot in the middle of my chest, and I was grateful we'd reached the ticket counter so I wouldn't have to continue our regular banter. David, my ex back in New Orleans, had dumped me right before I'd left my store, The Fated Cupcake, in the hands of my trusted assistant so I could run my mom's shop while she recovered from an accident. Other than missing New Orleans; my dog, Link; my shop; and my best friend, Phoebe, it had been fun and distracting, hanging out with Talisen nearly every day.

David had become a distant memory. Almost.

I paid the extra fee to check my bag and met Talisen near the security gate.

He held his arms out and sent me a rueful smile.

I tilted my head and eyed him suspiciously. "You don't expect me to fall for that, do you?"

His smile widened. "Get over here."

Wrapping my arms around his waist, I buried my head in his shoulder. "Thank you for this summer," I whispered.

He placed one of his large hands on my head and gently stroked my hair. "There's nothing to thank me for."

Hot tears burned the back of my eyes. I squeezed them shut, forcing the emotion down. "Beau…" My breath caught on a silent sob.

"It's all right, Wil. He's been with us. He's with us every day." Talisen squeezed me harder, and I knew we were both picturing my brother on that fateful day four years ago. He'd been smiling and laughing only a few hours before we'd found him lifeless in my mother's lavender fields.

I pulled back and nodded.

Talisen eased his grip but didn't let go. His deep green eyes bored into mine. "Don't stay away so long this time."

"I already promised Mom I'd be back for Christmas."

"Good." He laced his fingers around a lock of my hair. "Your hair looks nice, lightened by the sun."

Warmth spread to my belly. All the time spent outside this summer had left streaks of gold in my wavy mane. "I'll get highlights for December."

"Don't. Natural's better." Faeries didn't usually mess with chemicals. And I wouldn't, either. But there were natural hair dyes. Still, Tal knew the one quality I really loved about myself was my long, slightly curly auburn hair. "Text me as soon as you get there."

I grimaced and patted my pocket for my phone.

He rolled his eyes. "You didn't leave it at your mom's, did you?"

"Um..." I plunged my hand into my purse, frantically searching for the iPhone I never used. My fingers wrapped around something hard and cool. "Got it."

Talisen took it from my hand and pressed the on button. "Your battery's almost dead. Try to charge it before you get on the plane."

I snatched it out of his hand and tossed it back into my purse. "Yeah, yeah. You're worse than Phoebe."

"She's just given up on your lazy ways. Promise you'll let me know when you land."

I nodded.

"Good." His expression turned serious and he seemed to really look at me. Then he leaned in as if to whisper something, but instead brushed his lips lightly over mine, lingering slightly longer than a casual goodbye kiss. "Stay safe," he said against my lips and then turned and walked out of the airport. I stood still, stunned, my hand against my tingling lips as I watched him go.

Where had that come from? Flustered, I headed for the security gate.

One layover in Houston and seven sleepless hours later, I stumbled off the jet and into Louis Armstrong airport. I'd thought of nothing but Talisen ever since I'd left California. What in damnation was that kiss about? We'd been flirting with each other relentlessly for the past nine years, but because of Beau we'd never acted on anything. Not to mention Talisen's constant stream of revolving-door girlfriends. Now, with Beau gone, if I lost Talisen due to some stupid relationship problem…it was too hard to even think such a thought.

No, we were just friends. More than that. We were family. And that's the way I intended to keep it. I whipped out my phone and powered it on. The tiny red battery light mocked me. So I'd forgotten to charge it. Whatever. I only needed to send one text.

The phone buzzed with an incoming message from Phoebe. *Vampire sighting at Saint Louis Cemetery. Meet me there are soon as you land.*

Dang it all. I hadn't even had time to pee. I sighed and typed out a message to Talisen. Not two seconds after I hit send, the phone died.

Standing in front of New Orleans' Saint Louis Cemetery, I checked my watch. Twenty minutes and no sign of Phoebe. Just perfect. What was I going to do, wait all night? Clutching the handle of my suitcase, I squared my shoulders and strode through the gates, dragging my suitcase behind me. I might've laughed at the absurdity of the situation if it hadn't been for the very real threat I could pass out at any moment. Faeries never—*never*—spent time in cemeteries, and if they did, they sure as hell wouldn't bring half their wardrobe.

The moldy dampness mixed with the stale, rancid stench of decay turned my stomach. I kept my mouth clamped shut. Tasting death would only kill me faster. I scanned the rows of tombs and cursed myself for forgetting to charge my cell…again.

Where the hell was Phoebe?

Darkness swam at the edge of my vision and panic sparked a healthy dose of adrenaline through my veins. Time was up. If I didn't want to check into death's hotel permanently, I had two options: find Phoebe or get my ass out of there. It wasn't much of a choice. If I'd known where the witch was, I would've found her already.

Damn it! I'd never bailed on a job before. With a grunt of disgust, I fled.

My mind turned hazy, my thoughts jumbled. A second later my limbs went ·numb, and I stumbled. Forcing myself up, I struggled to place one foot in front of the other. My eyes never wavered from the exit. If I could just make it to the street, to one of the giant oak trees, everything would be fine.

My head would clear and feeling would creep back into my limbs. Life would flow again. Ten more feet and I'd be free, hugging the old oak, my body sucking up the life force it needed. *Almost there.*

A thick, honey-like sensation skimmed my bare skin. I froze.

Vampire.

Shit! I had to warn Phoebe. It was my job. I turned, intending to run back into the heart of the cemetery. But my feet wouldn't move. The death sealed within the tombs had sucked too much energy from my body, robbing me of the ability to take one more step. I sank to my knees, still clutching my suitcase as I stared at the front gates. Maybe I could crawl my way out.

A shadow fell over me, blocking the moonlight. My breath caught. I didn't need to look up to know what towered over me. Vampire. He was there, inches away, his presence pinning me to the ground. My strange vampire-sensing ability prevented me from moving.

Slowly, I raised my head. My vision swam and all I could make out was a double vision of a tall, dark-haired vampire. This was it. Another moment and either his death energy would suck me dry or his fangs would. I prayed I passed out before I had to endure either one.

A low, vicious growl sounded behind me, followed by a blur of white fur as a wolf leapt over me, landing with his hackles raised and teeth bared. My heart pounded with fear and relief. My mind continued to buzz in confusion, but I knew one thing. Link, my wolf, was there. Maybe I wouldn't die.

Footsteps pounded on the bricks, and a shout rang out, followed by a commotion. A moment later, all the action stopped, and the vampire energy faded. My limbs started to tingle and my mind cleared. "Phoebe?" I asked, glancing around.

"Right here." She appeared by my side and helped me up. "Come on. You need a tree."

The moment she propped me against the large oak, life energy rushed through my veins, clearing all the cobwebs and revitalizing my energy. I sighed in relief and reached a hand out to pet Link.

He licked my hand and then shimmered with gold right before he morphed into his normal Shih Tzu form. He jumped into my arms, lavishing me with tickling kisses.

I laughed. "Link, buddy. I missed you. Thanks for saving my butt."

At the sound of my voice, the Shih Tzu's tongue went into overdrive, licking me everywhere from the neck up. "I'm glad to see you, too, boy." His little body shook and wiggled against my chest as he tried to get as close as possible. Hugging him to me, I buried my face in his fur.

"Welcome home," Phoebe said from somewhere nearby.

I jerked my head up, spotting my roommate leaning against her car a few feet away. Her normally short, spiky hair was concealed by a sleek black wig, styled in a high bun. She wore a belted green tunic over her black leggings. Sensible low-heeled, knee-high boots completed the ensemble. She looked exactly like the free-spirited, hippie-type artists that populated the city. Only they likely didn't have a knife in each boot and magic-wielding stones tucked in their pockets.

"What happened?" I asked.

"What do you think happened? You almost passed out. Would have, too, if Link and I hadn't been there." Phoebe lit a cigarette and took a long drag. "Fuck, Willow, why didn't you wait for me at the gate?"

I scowled. Phoebe knew how much I hated smoking. It wasn't that it was just an annoyance; it made me physically ill. Thankfully she only smoked when she was really stressed. "I did wait! For twenty minutes. What was I supposed to do, stand there all night like bait?"

"It beats checking into the City of the Dead." Phoebe took another long drag. "You could've sent me a text."

I clamped my mouth shut and focused on Link's scruffy coat. He needed a groomer ASAP. Looked as though Phoebe hadn't brushed him once in the two months I'd been gone.

"Wil?" Phoebe prompted, her accusatory tone implying she already knew what I was going to say.

"It's dead." I reluctantly met her gaze.

"Again?" Phoebe narrowed her eyes and shook her head. "One of these days, that lazy habit is going to cost you your life."

"Give me a break. I just got off the freakin' plane. I'm not even supposed to be on duty again until early next week. At least I remembered to turn it back on before it died." The only reason I'd even gotten Phoebe's message was because I'd promised to text Tal as soon as I got off the plane. And for once I hadn't forgotten. How could I? The embrace we'd shared at the Sacramento airport had burned an imprint on my skin.

I shook my head. Tal was a childhood friend, my brother's best friend. It was better not to think about it. I set Link down and leaned against the oak again. "Thanks for getting me out."

Phoebe shrugged. "Not like I could leave you there."

"What are we doing here, anyway? No self-respecting vampire hangs out in a cemetery."

"This one does, apparently," Phoebe said.

"How cliché."

"No shit, right?" Phoebe took one last drag and snuffed out the cigarette. "But he's gone now, so I guess we'll have to try again tomorrow."

"You lost him?" My eyes went wide with shock. Phoebe was one of the best agents in the Void. I couldn't remember the last time she hadn't caught whoever she'd been sent to eliminate.

"It was either you or him." Phoebe grabbed the suitcase. "Come on. It was a mistake to call you out here after you spent hours on a plane."

I lifted one shoulder. It was true. I shouldn't have been working a case after being confined in metal for such a long time.

Living, breathing things filled me up, left me powerful and strong, while metal, concrete, and death sucked me dry. On any other day, the cemetery wouldn't have affected me as fast or as strongly. I would've been weakened by it, but I'd have had plenty of time to find Phoebe, who had the power to shield my energy from being leeched. We'd both been stupid.

"Sorry," she said. "I didn't realize it would be that bad."

I smiled and fell in step beside her. "It's okay. Neither did I. Now, tell me about the case."

"Not much to tell. A cemetery-tour group was attacked last night. The third attack in a week, but this time someone died. The guide identified the attacker as a vampire. So, we've…well, *I've* been dispatched, but you know how I hate to work alone." Phoebe grinned sheepishly.

Yeah. Over the last few years—ever since we'd figured out my unique abilities—Phoebe had stopped running down vampires alone. Who could blame her? My talent was invaluable when dealing with vamps.

"Seems pretty open and shut then," I said.

Phoebe nodded, then heaved the suitcase into the trunk of her green Camry. "Jeez, that's heavy."

The locks clicked, and I reached for the door. Then I went completely still. The heavy, sticky sensation of death settled on my skin, ever so slowly leeching my life energy. Not enough to weaken me. Just enough to put me on high alert.

"Wait," I said before Phoebe could disappear into the car. "Can I get a cigarette first?"

She cast me a questioning glance but passed a cigarette over and held out a lit lighter. I leaned in and mouthed, *He's still here*, then puffed the smoke to life. My eyes watered and my lungs constricted in protest, but I managed to appear cool and collected. Sort of. Until I coughed as I exhaled.

Phoebe, clearly holding back laughter, grabbed the cigarette and took a short drag before crushing it with her shoe. "You don't need any more bad habits."

Ha! As if I would take up smoking. Faeries didn't smoke. At least none I knew. I jerked my head, signaling Phoebe to follow.

"Link," I called. The Shih Tzu bounded up next to me, his normally brown eyes glowing gold. "Keep it together, boy," I soothed. He yelped softly and then put his nose to the ground, intent on the search. "Good boy."

"Jesus," Phoebe said under her breath.

I ignored her. Link had saved Phoebe's ass numerous times. Which more than made up for ruining her favorite ritual robes and her suede boots. Besides, that had been months ago. He was only a puppy, and he *was* learning.

We strolled along the outer wall of the cemetery, quiet and alert. The only sound came from Link's insistent sniffing. I slowed when the sticky sensation intensified; I was swimming in it. Link's nose went into overdrive at the base of a magnolia tree, his tail wagging in excitement. He'd found something.

In unison, we both looked up.

Right there on a lower limb, the vampire sat watching us. I squinted, trying to make out his features, a habit instilled by the Void's training. Eliminators were sent to eliminate. Mistakes were not tolerated. Always identify the perpetrator before the deathblow. Not that I had any idea who we'd been looking for. Phoebe hadn't given me the details.

I took a step back, offering her the stage.

Curious thing about my ability—I could sense a vampire within a mile radius if I concentrated. It was the reason I'd been recruited to the Void branch of the Arcane—the government-sanctioned supernatural authority—two years ago. Prior to that, I'd just been Phoebe's normal faery roommate, spending my days running The Fated Cupcake. Now I was super Willow. Baker by day and badass vampire stalker by night.

Link hovered protectively at my heels. My job was done. Despite having other magical abilities, they weren't ones that could help Phoebe take down a vampire. Not unless he was a diabetic, anyway. Thank the Fae Lords I had Link and his supernatural abilities to protect me, because if anything went wrong, Phoebe would have her hands full.

Link was already trembling and emitting an amber glow. *Uh-oh.*

I crouched, running a soothing hand over his white and gray fur. "It's okay, boy. Phoebe's got this."

"Kind of unoriginal, taking out tourists at Marie Laveau's tomb, don't you think?" Phoebe taunted him, taking a step to her left to get a better view of her suspect. "You vamps, always going after the easy marks. Where's your pride?"

A low chuckle rumbled from the branch.

"Wil, I think our friend finds us amusing." Phoebe gripped her black agate crystal.

"Just you," the vamp replied, his voice as deep and gritty as a thirty-year chain-smoker. "She's interesting, as well as that dog of hers, but I've been looking forward to this matchup for some time."

A grin broke on Phoebe's profile and her eyes glittered. "Oh, good. A challenge."

The hooded figure leapt from the branch a second before Phoebe blasted the spot with her sunlight-infused agate. The branch sizzled and, with a deafening crack, landed inches from where Phoebe had been standing.

"Holy fae," I breathed and took off after Phoebe, who was now sprinting to catch the vampire. She sped up, periodically flashing her agate, trying to stun him. His reflexes proved to be far superior to the average vampire's, and I suspected this one had been around much longer than most. He alternated back and forth from the tree limbs to the cemetery wall in smooth, graceful movements, deliberately waiting for Phoebe to make a move before leaping.

He was playing with her.

At the end of the cemetery, the vampire turned and looked Phoebe in the eye. "What else you got, witch?"

Phoebe stopped yards ahead of me, her tiny, lithe body seeming to grow a few inches. She lifted her left hand straight out, palm up and shouted, "*Siste!*"

Her long, glossy black hair fell from its bun, whipping straight back in the windless night.

The power behind the spell rooted me to the path, frozen in a running pose. Link was a few yards ahead of her, suspended in midair, his face scrunched up in a snarl. The vampire's laughter rang clear as he bounded onto a nearby rooftop and disappeared.

"Fuck!" Phoebe shouted as the power dissipated.

With the spell broken, I lost my balance and fell face-first on the hard brick sidewalk.

Link shot ahead, his little legs never breaking the run. His body shimmered gold before his limbs gave way, expanding until he'd grown to ten times his normal size. Once again in wolf form, he shot out of sight, sprinting after the vampire.

I groaned and rolled over, staring into Phoebe's exhausted face. "You all right?"

She offered me a hand. "Yeah, but shit. I lost him."

"How'd he do that?" I'd never seen a vampire manipulate her magic before. "It's like he blocked it."

"He deflected the spell, and it hit you and Link instead." She rubbed her temple. "I don't know how. I'll need to do some research."

I nodded. "I can't sense him anymore, he must be long gone. We better go find Link before animal control gets him again." The last time they'd picked him up as a wolf, he'd turned back into a Shih Tzu before I could claim him. The paperwork confusion had been a nightmare.

"You go ahead. I'll grab the car and catch up."

"Okay. Be safe. I'll keep an eye out for you." Smiling, I flew to the nearest rooftop.

I spotted Link within moments. He was racing around the corner at the end of the street, his white coat gleaming in the moonlight. Had he picked up the vamp's trail or had Phoebe's magic sent him into a frenzy? I couldn't feel the vampire, so it must have been the magic.

Or could I? My limbs were weighted as if the air was heavy, and my lungs had to work harder for oxygen. Something was off, though. It didn't feel the same as the sticky, swimming death I'd experienced earlier. The sensation pressed lightly and then all at once clung to me.

A vampire was close. Really, really close. But why did it feel so different?

My heart picked up as panic set in. Link was blocks away. Phoebe was in the car somewhere, and I was alone on a roof.

Why had I taken off by myself? *Stupid, stupid, stupid.*

I glanced around at the half-deserted neighborhood. A stone settled in my gut as recognition dawned. I was on vampire property. In the years after hurricane Katrina, the city had swelled with vampires. Drawn to the despair and lawlessness, the vampire population had more than tripled.

At first, they helped the struggling economy by buying up blocks of decimated homes. Unfortunately, they only rebuilt the one they lived in and left the others to rot. The perfect way to discourage neighbors. Vamps had been known to do a lot worse for privacy.

I scanned the streets for Phoebe's car or a glimpse of Link. If I could find either of them I'd be fine. The silence grated. Alone on a roof with no cell phone and a vampire lying in wait. Now what?

I stretched my wings, fluttering a few feet off the rooftop. Flying always gave me a sense of control. I couldn't cover a lot of ground, but I could move pretty quickly if I needed to. Faster than sprinting, anyway.

The sticky sensation stayed with me, but as I flew, the intensity lessened. Maybe he was in the building.

The thought didn't put me at ease one little bit. Vamps were impossibly fast. If one had spotted me...Link reappeared at the end of the block.

"Finally." I flexed my wings and shot toward the edge of the building.

"Willow?"

I spun. My wings stilled mid-flutter as pleasure heated my insides. I knew that voice and missed it more than I cared to admit. Managing to land gracefully on shaky legs, I peered through the moonlight. "David?"

He nodded.

Relief washed through my body at the sight of him, uncurling the knot I'd forgotten existed in my stomach. I took a step closer and froze.

Thick honey vampire energy clung to me and it was coming from my ex.

Chapter 2

Of course, when I'd dated him, he'd been human.

When the hell had he turned vamp? I intended to ask just that but blurted, "Where have you been the last three months?"

Crap. Smooth, Willow, real smooth.

Considering he'd unceremoniously dumped me in a text—after a year-long relationship—the last thing I'd wanted to do was make him think I actually cared about his cold, undead ass. Too bad my mouth forgot to consult my brain.

"Why are you here?" David moved closer, his vampirism making my head swim. Death leeched my life force, but the way he looked right then, his familiar, intense, midnight-blue eyes searching mine, I didn't move back.

"Why are *you* here?" I demanded, struggling to remain calm. "Did you have anything to do with those poor tourists?"

"Tourists? No." His steps slowed when I flinched at his now-alarming proximity. "What's wrong? Are you hurt?"

My chest constricted, making it hard to breathe. The protectiveness in his tone sparked memories I'd just as soon keep buried. Anger quickly filled the ache in my heart. "I'm fine. But you aren't going to be in a few moments if you don't start talking."

"You aren't supposed to be here." His elegant brow furrowed in confusion.

My wings twitched in agitation. "Where the hell am I supposed to be?"

"Not here." He glanced over his shoulder and moved closer.

With one forceful stroke of my wings, I shot straight up out of his path. The cemetery incident had left me too weak to sustain flight, forcing me to land on a nearby dormer. Even though I was above him, I knew I didn't have the advantage. If he wanted to get to me, he could…and I'd be powerless to stop him.

I studied his pale face, the perpetual tan a thing of the past, his tall body much leaner than it had been. Now his muscles would be corded, reminiscent of a chiseled statue. A trait of all vampires. "Why are you here?" I asked again.

"Wil," he said softly. "You've got to get out of here. You're in danger."

"I'm safe enough." Right. Standing ten feet from a vamp on a roof with Link and Phoebe at street level, I'd never been less safe. But I wasn't leaving without answers. Damn it, I deserved them. "Answer my question and I'll go."

"Still stubborn as a wisteria vine, I see." He tried to make his tone light, but the strain in his voice gave him away.

I crossed my arms and waited.

He stalked closer, slowly so as to not frighten me, but I recognized the predator he'd become. The history between us didn't change anything.

"Stop right there." I put my hand out, palm raised, as if that would actually hold him off.

He glanced up with a wry smile, then suddenly appeared inches from me on the dormer. I hadn't even seen him move. The physical effects were instantaneous, leaving me trapped by my unfortunate vampire disability. I couldn't fly in such a weakened condition.

This was bad. Very bad.

"Are you going to answer my question?" I asked, proud my voice held steady.

"So brave," he said, leaning in, his eyes shining in the moonlight. "One of the things I always loved about you."

I bristled. "I'd step back if I were you."

"Or what?" He chuckled. "Gonna force-feed me a Truth Cluster?"

He was making fun of me. Asshole. Heat burned my face, and if I could've lifted my arm, I'd have punched him in the gut. Never mind his vampire physique probably would've broken my hand. "I might, after Phoebe blasts you with her sun agate."

He brushed back a lock of my hair, bringing his lips close to my ear and whispered, "I'm not afraid of the witch."

"You should be," Phoebe said from behind us, steel in her voice.

David vanished and reappeared behind me, his cold arms wrapped around my middle, crushing my wings between us. The impact knocked the air from my lungs, causing a silent cry of pain. Fiery jabs of tiny pinpricks seared my bare arms where his skin touched mine. My knees buckled, and I concentrated on sucking in air, half hoping I'd go ahead and pass out. Anything other than endure a vampire's touch.

"Willow can't protect you from my magic. What I've got for you won't even touch her." Phoebe inched toward us, one hand on her agate, the other one holding an electric stun gun.

I closed my eyes. The gun meant Phoebe was weakened. The combination of her failed spell and however she'd gotten up on the building had taken a toll.

"Calm down, Phoebs." David kept me locked in a tight grip. "I'm not here to start anything."

"Looks like you already have. Let go of Willow, and we'll see if we can sort this out." She stopped a few yards from the dormer. "No need to make this messy."

David's arms relaxed but he didn't let go. The debilitating pain lessened just enough for me to regain my balance.

"You don't have anything on me, witch," he said, his voice hard. "Back off. I came here to deliver a message."

"You're threatening a faery, *vampire*," Phoebe shot back. "I don't need anything else to take you down. This is your last warning. Step away from Willow. Now."

The tension grew as the two held their ground and glared at each other. This would not end well. David and Phoebe hadn't really gotten along when David had been human. And vampire David wasn't scoring himself any points.

A howl rippled through the air, fueling the tension. I lost my cool. "Would you two stop it?" I snapped. "David, let me go."

He didn't move.

"David? Can you step back?" I softened my tone, narrowing my eyes at Phoebe in warning. Threatening him right now wouldn't help. He could crush me in two.

"You need to hear this first," he whispered so quietly I could barely hear him.

"I'm listening," I said. His arms fell from mine. But the fire from his touch still burned. It took every ounce of willpower to not wrap my arms around myself in defense. I would not appear weak in front of a vampire. It was too dangerous.

"She said step back." Phoebe advanced, her agate held high.

David ignored her and tilted his head down until I felt his hot breath on my ear. "You're in danger. The Cryrique sent me to—"

"*Insolate!*" Phoebe's voice drowned out the last of David's words. Light blinded me, making my eyes water. The vampire energy vanished as David fell. Instantly, my wings kicked in, relief flooding me as only a small amount of pain registered in my left wing. *Damn him for bruising my wing.* It would take forever to heal.

"Really, Phoebs, was that necessary?" I asked.

"Uh, yes, and a thank you would be nice." Whipping out her iPhone, she stalked over to where David lay unconscious.

"Who are you calling?"

"The cleanup crew."

"Oh my God. Is he dead?" I landed and crouched down, placing my hand on his cold chest. No burn. No pain. Nothing. It was like I was touching a piece of marble. "You killed him! Shit, Phoebs. He said the Cryrique sent him and he had to warn me about something."

"Calm down. He's not dead. Just knocked out." Phoebe started talking rapidly into her phone. Another howl drifted from the street.

Link. I took flight, descending to the street and landing at his side. "It's okay, bud. I'm fine."

He licked my hand in acceptance, his yellow wolf eyes watching me.

"Come on." He followed me to Phoebe's car and climbed in. He'd be safe from animal control while I spoke with her.

A second later, I rejoined her on the roof. "What will the cleanup crew do with him?" I gestured to David, trying not to look at his stone-pale face. A face of death.

"Take him in for questioning and lock him up if they can." Phoebe peered over the edge of the roof, keeping a lookout for the backup team.

"But he didn't do anything." I sat, exhausted. "It's not his fault vampires affect me the way they do. He doesn't even know what he did to me. How could he?"

"You're telling me he didn't notice the agony he was putting you through?" The expression on her face resembled the one my mom had perfected during my teenage years.

"I don't think he was focused on my well-being, considering you were threatening him with sunlight."

"It doesn't matter. He hurt you."

I wondered if she was referring to the night's activity or the emotional turmoil I'd suffered after the breakup.

Phoebe turned with hardened eyes. "And he's wanted for questioning on another case."

"What case?" I snapped my head up as my mind whirled. "Wait. You knew David had been turned?"

Phoebe nodded, glancing away.

"When?" I breathed.

"I don't know. His profile came up early this week as a vampire of interest." She took my hand and squeezed softly. "Sorry. I was going to tell you. I didn't get a chance."

"Do you think…? I mean, he must have been turned against his will, right?" I couldn't imagine he'd asked for such a thing. He wasn't the type.

"We'll find out." She pulled me to my feet, then handed me the car keys. "Take Link and go on home. I've got it from here."

I fluttered, more than ready to take flight. "You sure?"

Phoebe nodded as sirens filled the air, signaling the arrival of the cleanup crew.

"Okay, but don't forget to get to the bottom of whatever he was trying to tell me, all right?"

"You got it."

Link, back in his Shih Tzu form, bolted through the door of the Greek Revival townhouse Phoebe and I shared. The instant my feet hit the glossy, wide-planked, oak-wood floors, every tense muscle began to relax.

Home. Finally.

I tugged my suitcase up the narrow flight of stairs as Link yelped from the edge of the landing. "I'm coming, I'm coming. Hold on."

He spun in circles, unable to contain himself as I pushed my bedroom door open. The pungent odor of stale old house mixed with the fresh, woody scent from the enchanted oak tree. I took a deep breath, reveling in it. My room took up half the entire second floor, and by the state of things, Phoebe hadn't even cracked a window while I'd been gone.

Too exhausted to care about the dead leaves on the floor, I disappeared into the bathroom. Moments later I reemerged, fluttering up to the bed tucked between the limbs of the old oak. The makeshift elevator designed for Link sprang to life, the old-fashioned pulley system creaking and groaning with his weight. I'd oil it tomorrow, along with the other million things I needed to get caught up on. The bed shifted as Link curled up into a ball next to me. I rested my hand on his soft coat and closed my eyes.

Sleep. I longed for the blissful oblivion. The airplane alone had been enough to take the life out of me. But running into David and then finding out he'd turned vamp was too much.

My eyes filled and hot tears leaked between my closed lids, soaking my pillow. The door I'd slammed shut on our broken relationship had swung wide open, and the pain I hadn't let myself experience after he'd broken things off came out in the form of gut-wrenching sobs as I mourned for what had been and what never would be again.

David was a vampire. Any hope I'd had about reconciliation—no matter how unrealistic—had been shattered. The realization left a gaping hole in the middle of my heart.

Link burrowed closer and placed a sympathetic paw on my forearm. I wrapped an arm around his tiny body and let the tears lull me into a fitful sleep.

Wood splintered, sending me bolting upright from a sound sleep as my door crashed against the wall. Heavy footsteps echoed through the room and Link suddenly shifted, crushing me under one hundred and fifty pounds of wolf weight. He snarled, hackles raised.

"Enough, Link!" Phoebe growled. "And damn it, Willow. Where the fuck is your phone?"

I squinted through the brilliant sunlight, groaning at the ache in my arms and back. Every inch of where David had held me must've been bruised. "Good morning to you, too."

Phoebe snorted, pulling the dead phone out of my purse. "It would have been better if you'd managed to answer one of my phone calls." She jammed the charger in the outlet, connecting the cell to the end of it. "Get up. You've been summoned."

"Why?" I stretched, giggling when the heavy wolf shifted once again into Shih Tzu form and leaped up to lick my face.

Phoebe frowned, her face pinched in worry. "It's about David."

Dread curled in my stomach. "What about him? Is he all right?" I picked up Link, fluttered my wings, and landed softly in front of Phoebe.

She let out a short bark of laughter. "Yeah, he's fine. Better than fine. The bastard cut himself one hell of a deal. Hurry, they're waiting for us." She spun and stalked out.

"What deal?" I cried.

Phoebe yelled back something incoherent, and a second later the front door slammed.

I stared at Link. "This is not how I planned to start my day."

Chapter 3

"For the last time, tell me what kind of deal David made," I demanded.

Phoebe pulled into the narrow garage of the seemingly abandoned brick warehouse and parked. The Arcane kept their headquarters hidden. If anyone went looking for them, they'd never expect the most powerful branch of the government to be housed in the deteriorating structure one block from the Mississippi in the Irish Channel.

"No." Phoebe shook her head. "If Maude finds out I bugged him, the shit's gonna fly. Better it comes from her."

I climbed out of the car. Link yelped, barely escaping without losing a paw as I slammed the door in frustration. He glared at me with accusing eyes.

"Sorry, buddy," I cooed and picked him up, running a hand over his silky fur. He closed his mouth, his bottom teeth protruding. Clearly, I wasn't forgiven.

I kissed the top of his head, set him down, and then fell in step with Phoebe. "How did you get the bug past security?"

She grinned. "I've been experimenting with a few charms while you've been gone."

"You're going to piss off the wrong person one of these days."

"I'm not worried. Just wait until you see what I've worked up."

I snorted. "You're an awfully cocky witch. I wouldn't underestimate Maude if I were you. Our power may be more subtle, but faeries generally rank higher on the magic scale than witches do."

Phoebe's mahogany eyes gleamed. "I know. That's what I'm counting on."

Frowning, I waited while Phoebe passed through security. What kind of crazy plan had she cooked up?

Once Phoebe was cleared, the security scanner flashed green, ready for its next victim. I took a deep breath, tensed, and forced myself into the glass booth, Link by my side. Tension engulfed me, slowly squeezing the air from my lungs. The familiar panic set in, making me struggle to not gasp.

I willed myself to calm down. It's not like I hadn't done this dozens of times before. Everything was going to be fine.

Right, because electrodes stripping away my layers of magic was the perfect way to start the day.

Please don't let this machine short-circuit my brain. I was going to need some form of intelligence, because despite Phoebe's incessant pestering, I had yet to make it to a single defense class. Tomorrow. Definitely tomorrow.

The security scan heightened and sucked away the last dregs of my magic. The sense of loss and vulnerability left me hollow, uncomfortable in my own skin. Why the hell did I put up with this nonsense? I didn't need to work for the Arcane. I ran a successful bakery, a place where my magic could truly shine. I was good at it, damn it. And Maude didn't have any control over me there. Mostly.

The glass doors opened, and I stumbled out. Link followed in a clumsy daze. The security scan had temporarily neutralized his wolf-shifting abilities. The pair of us joined Phoebe, her face white from her own trip through security.

"Let's get this over with." I took off, marching to the director's office. The sooner I got out of there, the better.

The receptionist's desk was unoccupied, and the usually closed door was slightly ajar. I hesitated for a second, then gave one sharp rap before entering.

Maude Jenkins, the director of the Void branch, glanced up, her sharp, angular features set in a scowl. Her mood matched the severe bun coiled tightly on her head and the gloomy gray pantsuit. "Agent Rhoswen, you're late. I do not enjoy being kept waiting."

I stiffened, hiding a scowl of my own. I'd signed on to work for the Arcane under a different director. If I'd known my spiteful aunt was in line to take over, I never would have signed the paperwork. And I sure as shit wouldn't have committed to five years.

Two years, eleven months, and twelve days, I reminded myself. Unless I got lucky and dear old Auntie was promoted again. Or better yet, offed by one of her many enemies.

A pang for my mother rippled through me. Maude hadn't always been a first-class bitch. She and my mom had grown up the best of friends. When Beau and I were young, she'd visited often, winning Beau's affection after she'd brought him a fae chemistry set, complete with beginning water spells. Then, shortly after he'd died, she'd changed. Become obsessed with the Void and turned into someone none of us recognized.

I carefully arranged my expression to match my bored tone. "I wasn't aware I had an appointment."

Maude's inky black wings flared in irritation, a stark contrast to my own pale, ice-blue ones. Her eyes hardened. "Do not act as if you're doing us a favor, agent. You are paid very well for minimal service. If I require your presence, you *will* make yourself available. Your contract sees to that."

I swallowed the snarky reply poised on my tongue. That damned contract. Stupidly, I hadn't realized I'd magically bound myself to the Arcane when I'd signed it. Phoebe's voice rang in my head. *You don't walk away from the Arcane, Willow. Think carefully before you commit.*

One couldn't break a magically bound contract. Not without dying first.

"Of course, Director." I kept my face blank.

"Take care to remember that." She cut her gaze to Phoebe. "Close the door, Agent Kilsen."

Phoebe did as she was told and sat, nodding to me to settle in the adjoining chair. I hesitated, loath to show submission.

The director's eyes seared through me, the force of her will almost pressing me into the chair.

Damned fae! I despised the use of magical persuasion, a gift especially strong in female faeries. I fought the magic just long enough to prove I could. Then, with a pointed stare, I took my seat next to Phoebe. "What can I do for you this morning, Director?"

Maude stretched her wings wider and then slowly retracted them as she eased back into her chair.

I did a mental eye roll at the display of dominance. My aunt already had the advantage. High-ranking Arcane officials weren't subject to magical paralysis in their home offices.

The director leveled her gaze. "Effective immediately, you are suspended from agent Kilsen's service."

"But—"

"Recent events have rendered you a liability. Instead, you will work with a double agent, gathering intel on Cryrique."

My limbs went ice-cold with shock, but I kept my face impassive. I didn't want to give Maude any indication the mob-like vampire corporation terrified me. The company unofficially controlled almost everything in New Orleans... except the Void. Was my aunt insane? I most definitely hadn't been trained for the spy business.

Did Phoebe know about this? Her cool expression implied she did. Would it have been so hard to warn me? Freakin' Phoebe. What was she up to?

I focused on Maude. "A liability? Does this have to do with the cemetery? Because that had everything to do with spending the day in an airplane. You, of all people, should know what being enclosed in metal can do to an earth faery."

"Do not insult me, Rhoswen. While your actions high-lighted your pathetic lack of training, I'd hardly waste energy rearranging your life because of it."

Anger bubbled in my throat. Swallowing, I choked it down. What did I ever do to deserve this disdain? Just because I'd joined the Void without going through the proper channels didn't mean I wasn't good at my job. It was no secret Maude resented shortcuts. Never mind I possessed a skill so rare no one believed it possible.

My record stood for itself. How many agents would've been killed had I not been there to warn them? My talent made the Void safer, kept Phoebe safe, and I'd be damned if I lost someone else I loved when I could do something about it. Spending three years at the academy was out of the question. I hadn't wanted to devote my entire life to the Void. I had a shop I loved, but I couldn't ignore my ability either. We'd struck a deal. I'd go on runs, warn the agents of nearby vamps, and then stay the heck out of the way. No academy training needed.

"What about Phoebe?" I asked. "You can't leave her without backup."

"That is not your concern." Maude didn't bother to hide her disgust. "A *seasoned* agent would be more concerned about her new assignment."

"I imagine I'll be given my new orders before I leave," I said reasonably. "I'm just looking out for my partner."

Maude raised one brow as she smirked. "At least you're loyal. To put you at ease, her new partner will be in place by the end of the week." She passed a packet across her desk. "Here are the details of your new assignment. Be here at sunset to pick up your shadow agent. I expect an update every forty-eight hours until I say otherwise."

Staring at the packet as though it was tainted with flesh-eating bacteria, I kept my hands clenched in my lap.

Maude pressed a button on her intercom. "I'm ready for my next appointment." She didn't even look up when she addressed us again. "You're excused."

What exactly was a shadow agent? The finality of Maude's tone, mixed with her obvious contempt, kept my mouth clamped shut. I'd rather have my wings plucked out than admit my cluelessness. I grabbed the envelope and shoved it in my purse.

Phoebe and I left without another word, Link at my heels.

"What just happened?" I asked Phoebe once we made it back to the lobby. The two guards ignored us, both standing straight with their hands clamped behind their backs.

"You just got into a pissing match with our boss. Our boss who is a spiteful, dangerous faery."

Faeries had a bad reputation for holding grudges. "Please. She doesn't scare me."

Phoebe stopped, turning to face me. "She should. Do you think she became a director by kissing babies or baking cupcakes for a living?"

I bristled. "That was low, Phoebs. Really low."

"You need to take her seriously. I know she's bitchy to you, but damn, Willow. She's good at her job. Making an enemy of her isn't doing you any favors."

The sun peeked out from behind a deteriorating building, making me squint as I studied my friend. A small crease etched her brow and tension filled her face. Under my scrutiny, her expression cleared, erasing any hint of frustration. She was an expert at hiding her emotions when she wanted to.

"Make an enemy of her?" I scowled. "You know our history. You think anything I do now is going to make it *worse*?" Shaking my head, I stalked toward the door. "Whatever. I've got to get to work. Come on, Link."

"Shit," Phoebe muttered behind me. A moment later she caught up to me on the sidewalk. "Let me give you a ride to the shop."

"No need. We'll walk."

"Wil, you know this neighborhood isn't safe. Don't be stubborn."

Phoebe was right. The streets surrounding headquarters housed some of the most notorious human crime lords in the city. The Arcane chose the building for a reason. The more foreboding an area, the less chance of prying eyes. If an agent was too weak to fend off mere humans, no matter how dangerous, they shouldn't be working for the Arcane. Especially the Void branch.

"I have Link. In the unlikely event any thugs are up this early, he'll have no problem taking them out." He'd already be able to shift. The security scan didn't affect him as long as it did the rest of us.

Before she could argue, I strode off, Link running beside me. I stretched my wings, deliberately expanding them wide. If anyone was watching, there would be no mistaking who and what I was. Enemies of the Arcane were usually eliminated. It didn't hurt to let people know which side I was on.

By the time I made it to The Fated Cupcake in Uptown, sweat ran down my back and my tank top clung to my sticky body. Ick. Why hadn't I just accepted the air-conditioned ride? I could give a cold shoulder with the best of them, especially in climate control.

In spite of the sticky morning heat, I took a moment to savor the sight of my shop. The windows gleamed and employees bustled inside. A fair number of patrons scurried in and out of the plate-glass doors. Sure, it wasn't a top-secret government paranormal protection agency, but what I did for a living made people smile. That was important, no matter how insignificant Phoebe made me feel sometimes.

Link gave a small yip as he rounded the corner, heading for the side entrance. I followed, a smile finally breaking through my irritation as I let him into my private office. The chilled air caused goose bumps to form over my thin wings, but the shiver came from the tantalizing smell of chocolate mixed with citrus-tinged magic. Now I was home.

I tossed the new assignment packet on my neatly organized desk and stared at it. Curiosity, tainted with a heavy dose of resentment, formed deep in my gut.

Double agent? I had zero training in that department, and my *loving* Auntie Maude knew it. And what did David—handsome, easygoing, freshly-turned-vampire David—have to do with it? I'd completely forgotten to inquire about his deal. What did the Void want with a vampire anyway?

A shudder crawled up my spine. Having my life drained from me would be worse than final death. As a faery that thrived on life magic, I couldn't imagine anything worse than turning vamp.

The innocent-looking file sat in the middle of my desk, taunting me as my curiosity grew. I'd have to read it sooner or later. Better to give myself some time to process before meeting my new partner. The brass tabs on the flap pinched my fingers as I pried them back.

"Willow!" my assistant squealed as she burst in. "Thank goodness. I heard movement in here, and for a second there, I thought someone broke in to use your phone again."

I'd put a strict ban on cell phones not long after I'd opened the shop. Mostly because the technology interfered with my magic. Not having to deal with constant employee cell-phone abuse was icing on the cake. Since my private line didn't register with the main phone system when in use, some of the employees didn't hesitate to invade my personal space.

"Since when does the morning crew sneak away for private phone calls?" I grinned. Em and Georgie—sisters well into their fifties—were both somewhat phone-phobic. We could barely get them to answer business calls.

Tami laughed, her chin-length, curly black hair bouncing with the motion. "Never. The added pressure must be frying my brain." She ran over, throwing her arms around me. "I'm so glad you're finally back. How's your mom? And Talisen? Did you get a chance to experiment with any new magical herbs?"

"The short answers are: better, hotter than ever, and yes. I can't wait to get back into the lab." While I'd kept Mom's herb shop running, I'd also worked on some new recipes, except for when I was hanging with Tal, staring into his gorgeous green eyes. The ones I tried not to drown in every time I saw him.

"You have that look again," Tami accused.

"What look?"

"The one where your cheeks flush and your eyes go all moony." She winked and pulled on my arm. "Come on, you have to see the progress Georgie made on the mural."

Laughing, I dropped the envelope I'd been holding into the top drawer of my desk and allowed myself to be tugged out of the office, leaving Link snuggled against a blanket on his doggie bed.

Chapter 4

"Someone's been hitting the Molten Muse awfully hard since I've been gone," I declared, eyeing my employee.

"What?" Georgie's face soured in righteous indignation. She scanned her slim, athletic body as if assessing it for the first time. "I beg your pardon. For every Molten Muse I consumed, I spent twenty minutes extra at the gym."

"No wonder you have the body most thirty-year-olds weep for." Amused, I tilted my head toward the wall. "I was referring to your amazing progress on the mural."

On the wall opposite the display cases, Georgie's unfinished whimsical depiction of The Fated Cupcake and two neighboring shops filled the space from floor to ceiling. A pair of college students sat at a sidewalk table, sipping Perk Me Up caramel milkshakes. Nearby a faery and fae fed each other a slice of Light My Fire spice cake.

I ran my fingers along the outline of a musician carrying a box of Molten Muse cupcakes—the store's most popular seller. What else would you expect in a city dominated by creative types? Why wait for inspiration when a Molten Muse would do the trick in five minutes flat?

"Oh, Georgie, it's just gorgeous. I love it." I beamed. "Have as many Molten Muse cupcakes as you can stand, and when it's done, I'll whip you up a truckload of Willpower mints."

"You're going to have to come up with an addiction-buster creation to kick that habit," Em, the fourth member of our day-shift team, quipped from behind us.

Tami hid a giggle as Georgie twisted around, glaring. "Glass houses and all that, little sister."

"I'm not the one obsessed with the scale. So what if I'm a little fluffy? Pete isn't going anywhere." Em replaced an empty tray of Desire Dollops with a full one, winked, and disappeared into the back.

"I swear, she thinks all there is to life is getting and keeping a man," Georgie said.

Tami flashed a wicked smile. "Isn't it?"

Georgie rolled her eyes and turned her attention to a young man entering the shop. "What can I get for you today?"

Tami and I laughed and disappeared into the lab—my sanctuary. Custom-made shelves, integrated with growing lights and a complicated irrigation system, lined the walls along with various plants. I'd magically enhanced as many of them as I could before I'd left for California two months before. After an eight-week absence, the store was bound to be running low on some crucial ingredients. Sure, my exclusive recipes tasted divine, but that wasn't what kept my clients coming back every week. Other shops in town sold tasty, enhanced edibles. But The Fated Cupcake had the best reputation, and I intended to keep it that way.

"Give me the bad news." I grabbed my apron. "I know I have a ton of work ahead of me."

Tami pointed to a long list pinned to the corkboard, her face pinched in sympathy. "It's a good thing you came home when you did. We've been out of a couple of things for a few days now."

"Okay, I'll get right to work on it." I took a deep breath, letting the life of my plants settle around me. The door made a soft click as Tami slipped back into the bakery.

The energy was different here than it was in Eureka, the northern California coastal town I'd grown up in. Mom's shop was comfortable, but this felt like home. My lab radiated with an echo of my creative energy and felt right in a way no other place did. Working here brought me a sense of peace I hadn't known since my brother died four years ago.

An aching loss squeezed my heart.

Remember to breathe.

Deep breath in, deep breath out. I concentrated on the calming motion until my pulse returned to normal. Only a few seconds this time. I was getting better at that.

I glanced at the corkboard, scanned the list, and then pulled a pair of mature wisteria plants onto my infusion island. With one hand on each plant, I closed my eyes, letting the life of the plant flow into my being. The sweet fragrance invaded my senses, making me almost drunk on its perfume. Nothing smelled as heavenly as wisteria. Just before I felt the last bit of energy leave the plants, I reversed the process, forcing my citrus-tinged magic back into the wilted vines. The blooms sprang to life, spreading their delicate flowers. I smiled, pleased with myself.

Carefully, I placed the plants in the augmented section and pulled a large pot of lavender. I hated the scent of lavender, but the herb was one of the best for Kiss Me chocolates. Once chemically altered by the Kiss Me recipe, the ingredient was virtually impossible to identify, thankfully, otherwise I didn't think I could stand to offer the dang things. Which would be unfortunate, since they turned a huge profit.

Gritting my teeth, I wished I could take a Smell Be Gone tablet, but hindering my abilities would defeat the purpose.

Just get it over with.

Taking another deep breath, I placed my hands on the innocent plant and braced myself for the memories I knew would come. They always did.

The vibrant yet delicate energy from the lavender hit me full force, the scent almost buckling my knees as the sweetness turned fetid, tinged with death. Beau's gutted image filled my mind, his unseeing eyes staring past me.

I shuddered, straining to maintain the flowing life force. The painful memories almost overtook me, but I shut them out of my mind and forced my magic into the plant. Slowly, the distinct lavender scent dissipated as my citrus signature masked it.

Shaking, I put the plant next to the wisteria and waited for the pain slicing my heart to fade. I'd never forget the horror of finding Beau butchered in our mother's lavender fields, alone and left for dead. Clutching the counter, my nails pressed against the stainless steel until one of them snapped. I barely even noticed.

Four years later, and the case was still unsolved. I'd promised my mother I'd find the truth, even if the search took the rest of my life.

I probably could've found a suitable substitute for the Kiss Me recipe. My self-inflicted torture wasn't necessary. But reliving Beau's death kept the promise fresh in my mind, right where I intended it to stay.

"Willow?"

"Huh?" I started at the intrusion. No one ever dared bother me when I was augmenting plants. Not since the day I'd been interrupted in the middle of an alteration and lost a whole row of mature plants. My wrath had been enough keep the staff away permanently.

"Sorry! I wouldn't interrupt, but…" Georgie held up a thick ivory envelope scrawled with calligraphy and sealed with wax.

"Mother of demons," I whispered. "What does the Cryrique want?"

Georgie's face paled. Her voice shook. "The guy bought three dozen Orange Influence chocolates before he handed me the envelope."

"What? How the hell—"

"He had a permit!" Georgie yelped, backing up. Tears glistened in her wide eyes. "He did. I checked it, ran the number and everything."

"It's okay," I said, trying for calm. Orange Influence contained a highly controlled substance, very effective in forcing people to do things against their will. Special permits were required for purchases, usually only given out to law enforcement and research labs. But vampires were *never* given permits. Never.

"It's not your fault." I sighed. "We've got to get a line on the messenger. We need to find out who he's working for. If he's got a connection to vampires…" I didn't finish the thought. It was too horrible to even contemplate. I stuffed the message in my back pocket and guided Georgie out of the lab.

"Can you make a sketch of what he looks like?" I asked.

"Yes, but he looked like his picture."

"I'm sure he did, however I'd like the details of a full sketch. With a license we only get a head shot."

"In color?"

"Yes, please." I touched Georgie's arm. "Thank you."

Some of the tension in the older woman's shoulders eased, but the strain didn't leave her face. "You don't have to thank me. I'm happy to help." She shivered as her frown deepened. "Vampires…with Orange Influence."

"I know, Georgie, I know. I'm pulling the order and license and calling this in right away." Anger flowed through my veins at the thought my magic could be used against an innocent. *Please let this all be a mix-up.*

Maybe someone on the street had handed the message to the guy as he walked in, and he wasn't carrying the chocolate wedges off to Frenchman Street and into vampire hands. Gods, I hoped that was true. "Bring the sketch to my office as soon as you're done, but don't rush. Accuracy is more important."

I fingered the thick, weighted envelope, grimacing at the blood-red wax seal. I supposed the old ones felt nostalgia for social etiquette of times past. But seriously? They carried iPhones just like everyone else. What was wrong with a phone call or an email? Of course, modern methods wouldn't have been as dramatic. *Damn vampires.*

I grabbed my antique silver letter opener and carefully broke the seal, trying not to alter it any more than necessary. If there were any lingering energy traces, I might need them later.

One elegant line was scrawled across the textured stationery. *Your honored presence is required at eight o'clock tonight at The Red Door.*

Required, not requested. It wasn't an invitation. It was a summons. And not one I could likely ignore. The Cryrique held political clout in the city. Pissing them off would only put me out of business.

Did this have anything to do with the Influence drug? My stomach turned. I was the only one in the city powerful enough to enhance the plants needed to create the narcotic. If they wanted an inside track, I was the logical choice. And the most obvious.

The phone rang, startling me out of my worried haze, and the note slipped from my fingers, landing on the desk.

Hopefully it was Phoebe with information on the messenger. I'd faxed the details to her a half hour ago.

I picked up the old-fashioned rotary phone. "The Fated Cupcake."

"Ms. Rhoswen, you got my note, I presume," a southern gentleman's voice drawled.

My heart stopped. "Who is this?" I asked through clenched teeth.

He chuckled softly. "I understand you have something of mine."

"I can't imagine what that would be." What the hell was he talking about?

"Not a what, a who, Ms. Rhoswen. Bring Davidson with you this evening. I look forward to our new friendship." The line went dead with the unmistakable clatter of a phone coming to rest in its cradle. No iPhone for this vampire.

Davidson? David?

Why would the Cryrique think I had David? Phoebe said he'd cut a deal. He should've been home by now.

He cut a deal. Oh no…

With everything going on, I'd completely forgotten about my new assignment with the double agent. I yanked the legal envelope open and stared at the name of my new partner.

Davidson Laveaux.

"F'ing Maude!" I shrieked. With a start, Link jumped from a sound sleep, growling, his eyes glowing gold as he scanned for intruders.

"Sorry, boy. It's okay. No one's here but me."

Link paced, responding to the anger in my voice.

I scanned the document, finding the classification. *Sensitive: twenty-four hour detail.* The Void wasn't messing around. Whatever they were after, they meant business.

"Damn it all. How in the world am I going to spend twenty-four hours a day with a vampire?" A vampire who'd seen me naked on several occasions. I slumped in my chair, wishing I could turn the clock back thirty-six hours. Even if it meant being back in my mother's house.

Heaving a sigh, I returned my attention to the file. What did David have to offer as a double agent, and why did Maude put me on the case? My only notable skill was locating vampires.

Then I turned the page and found my answer. *Vampire Laveaux overheard a plot to abduct Agent Rhoswen. Reason unknown.*

Chapter 5

I closed my eyes, fighting for control. So that's what David meant when he'd said I was in danger. Damn Maude for letting me read the news in a freaking assignment report. The rasp of paper crumbling filled the room as I clenched my fingers around the directive.

"Rough day?" Phoebe asked.

I spun to find my roommate leaning against the doorframe. She'd morphed into Reese Witherspoon, *à la Legally Blonde*: long, slightly curled blond hair, a pink business suit, and perfectly manicured nails. I scowled. "You look ridiculous."

"It got the job done. I now have a new informant with close ties to the mayor." When I didn't answer, she strode into the room and lounged in the chair on the other side of my desk. "You're not still mad, are you?"

Her nonchalant attitude made my blood pressure rise. "Did you get my email?" My words came out clipped. Of course I was still mad. My best friend had insulted me and taken Maude's side.

Phoebe nodded, ignoring the tension in the room. "I've got someone working on it. You really think the vamps are after Influence?"

Rolling my shoulders, I stifled a sigh and slumped back into my chair. "I'm not sure, but better safe than sorry at this point. Any chance we can speed up the background check?"

She shrugged. "It isn't considered a priority, but I can call in a favor if you're that worried about it."

I sat up straight. "*Not a priority?* To who? Vampires may be using Influence. Influence I created. It's a pretty damn big priority to me and any potential victims."

Phoebe studied me for a moment, then tapped a message on her phone. "I know you're upset, and I'm still at the top of your shit list, but something else is bothering you. What's going on?"

"Oh, I don't know. Maybe it has something to do with being forced to spend all my days and nights with a vampire for God knows how long." *And being at the top of some vampire's most-wanted list.*

"Not all vampires are criminals, Wil."

"Look at you, being all politically correct. When's the last time you befriended one?"

She shrugged. "I have vampire friends."

I snorted in disbelief. "You have vampire contacts. And you haven't slept with any of them."

"That's true." Her phone beeped. She scanned the message and then typed a short response. "We won't have info on your messenger until tomorrow morning. The tech working the case said the Influence registrar didn't get back to him and now the office is closed for the day."

"Perfect," I said, my voice flat.

"Wil," Phoebe said carefully, softening her voice. "I'm sorry about this morning and for letting Maude blindside you. I was worried you'd go in full steam and rail against her. Which I'm not denying I'd love to see, but today I needed you levelheaded. Or at least as levelheaded as you can be around your aunt."

Her tone, more than the words, got my attention. I exhaled as the pent-up tension faded away. "I'm sorry, too. You were only doing your job. I wasn't even mad anymore by the time Link and I got here. But after I got that phone call and read about my new assignment, the anger came rushing back."

One dark eyebrow rose. "Phone call?"

"F'ing vamps." I hadn't filled Phoebe in on the details. "I got a letter and then a phone call."

After I recounted the day's events, Phoebe sat back, looking thoughtful. "If the messenger does work for the vamps, then picking up the Influence was pretty damn sloppy if they intend to keep buying it from you. Did you check the buyer's history?"

I nodded. "He's been in a couple of times before. Both were months ago. You're right, though. If he's aligned with the vamps, he just fucked up royally. But there's a bigger game being played here, and I have a feeling the Orange Influence is only part of it."

Phoebe nodded. "I agree. Let's form a game plan for your meeting with the Cryrique tonight. There's no way I'm letting you go to the fang den without backup."

"I'll have David."

Phoebe rolled her eyes. "Right, 'cause that's comforting."

"You think they'll let you in uninvited?"

"Hell yes, I'll get in." Her face scrunched up in righteous indignation. She placed a hand over her heart and leaned back. "Your lack of confidence pains me."

The Arcane building cast long shadows as the sun set on the city. I didn't even see David until Phoebe stopped the car and he appeared in front of us. His unnatural vampire energy settled on my skin. Ugh. How long would it take to get used to the heavy sensation always coating my aura? A few days, weeks? Never?

He stared at us, an unlit cigarette dangling from his lips.

"You know you can't smoke that around me," I reminded him, trying but failing to keep the judgment from my tone. He'd never smoked before. Aside from smelling like a rank fire pit, cigarettes had zero consequences now that he was immortal. But they did affect me. My lungs constricted in protest at the mere thought of breathing the foul pollutant.

Rolling the tobacco stick between two fingers, he sent me a self-satisfied smile. "Even unlit, I knew you couldn't resist chastising me."

I bit my tongue to keep from engaging him again. Smug bastard.

"We have places to be. Get in," Phoebe ordered.

He didn't move from his spot against the brick building. "Which one of you is going to contain the wolf?"

"How did he know?" I asked Phoebe. No one outside of the Void was supposed to know about Link's true nature. He'd never shifted in front of David before. There'd been no reason to. David had been mortal. The Shih Tzu snarled silently, pressing his little body against the privacy-tinted window.

"Smell, most likely." Phoebe reached back, grabbed Link, and handed him to me. He flailed, trying to break free.

"Calm down, Link," I soothed, running my hand down his back until he lay in my lap. "Good boy." I sent David a calculating look. "I've got him. Get in and start talking."

David strode around to Phoebe's side and slid in behind her.

Link growled and pressed forward. I barely caught him, my arms weak from David's vampire energy weighing against them. Link lay on the center console, his face sandwiched between the seats, teeth bared.

"He doesn't like you very much," I said.

"He's not the only one," Phoebe said.

I ignored her. "Answers, David. Now, or I'll let Link change."

He shot me an amused look of disbelief. Under any other circumstances his skepticism would be spot on, but today had been a very bad day, and my body was still sore from the night before. It wouldn't take much for me to turn Link loose.

"I mean it, Laveaux. If we're going to be partners, I want to know everything. Who's after me, and when and where did you hear about it?"

"I didn't plan to keep anything from you, Willow." A faint crease of worry touched his brow. If I hadn't been studying him, I might have missed it.

Did he really care what happened to me? *That's stupid. Of course he cares. We dated for over a year. He turned into a vampire, not a monster. But just because he doesn't want to see you dead doesn't mean he wants you.*

The thought brought on a rush of painful memories. I pushed them aside, resolve hardening my heart.

He sighed, the human gesture looking very out of place on his now-chiseled features. Vampires didn't sigh. They didn't even need to breathe. "I don't know who. One of my boss's contacts informed him of a plan to abduct you. I overheard the conversation and wanted to warn you."

I leaned back against the window, my brows furrowed in confusion. "But you were surprised to see me last night. What were you doing there?"

"Looking for Phoebe. I was going to tell her."

"And you just happened to know where I was going to be?" Phoebe asked "Yeah, right. Sounds suspicious, Laveaux."

David's intense gaze bored into mine, and for a moment I wondered if he'd even heard Phoebe. "I didn't know where she would be," he said to me. "I was on my way to your house when I saw her car. Then I saw you sitting against the oak with your suitcase like you were checking into the cemetery. I was going to meet you at your house, but then you went tearing off onto a rooftop. I couldn't leave you there by yourself. Don't you understand?" He paused and leaned forward. "Your life's in danger."

The concern in his voice brought fresh tears to my eyes. I blinked them back. When had I turned into such a blubbering idiot? "I'm an agent of the Void. I can take care of myself."

"Sure, after you let the cemetery drain your energy. And then were almost taken out by a master vampire. Yeah, you looked like you were doing fine."

Smart-ass. Who was he to judge? Suddenly a question I'd been holding back came rushing out. "Why did you volunteer to be a double agent against the Cryrique? That's a good way to get dead…I mean really dead."

"I can handle it."

"The same way you handled not getting turned?" I said it to piss him off, anger bubbling in my chest at the way he dismissed my concerns. He'd left, and now he wanted to protect me—and worse, spend twenty-four hours a day together for however long I was stuck with him. And he couldn't even do me the courtesy of acknowledging the danger he'd put himself in on my behalf.

Sadness clouded his midnight-blue eyes. "It was my choice, Wil. I asked to be turned."

His words silenced me. He'd *asked* to be turned. How? Why? He couldn't have. Not my David. Sweet, gentle, always-there-for-me David. My mouth worked as I tried to form words. Finally I spit out, "When?"

He turned, staring out the window.

"David?" I whispered.

Phoebe glanced at me, her eyes wide with curiosity. I clutched Link and waited. When it became clear he wasn't going to answer, I switched gears. "Do you think someone at Cryrique is after me? Is that why you turned double agent?"

Slowly, he turned toward me and shook his head. "I don't think so. But they're interested in you, otherwise why would they care? Vampires don't usually involve themselves in other races' business. The only way I could make sure you were safe was to get the Void to let me be your partner, and the only way to do that was to turn double agent."

"And to save yourself from a murder rap," Phoebe added.

"What?" I cried.

"I didn't kill anybody, Phoebe, and you know it. The Void would never let me in if they thought I did."

She didn't look convinced. We both knew Maude was known to not only push boundaries, but to erase them altogether to get what she wanted. When I'd accidentally discovered the Influence formula—one I didn't want to pursue—Maude learned of it and forced me into producing the stuff. She'd threatened to take the formula to a competitor, where I'd have no control over who used the dangerous concoction. I hated her for it. All my instincts said this situation had Maude's greed written all over it.

David couldn't be a killer, could he? My stomach rolled. I snuck a glance at him. Impossible. The muscle pulsing in his jaw radiated with righteous indignation like it always did when Phoebe suggested something outrageous. Relief swept through me. Part of my David still remained inside his new persona.

"Have you eaten?" I asked, trying to appear normal. As if asking my ex if he needed blood was any kind of normal.

David flinched.

"What? You have to eat, and we have somewhere to be in an hour. We need to know if we'll have to stop for you to feed."

Phoebe parked the car in front of our house and twisted. "Well, do you?"

"No. I'm fine."

"Good," she said. "We don't have time anyway."

"Where's he going to sleep?" I asked Phoebe as we all filed out of the car.

"Somewhere with no windows." She unlocked the front door and deposited her bag on a distressed side table in the entryway.

"We don't have any rooms without windows. You'll have to charm one of them." I eyed David, who stared warily at Link. He'd started snarling again as soon as the vampire entered the house.

"Link, that's enough! Go." I pointed toward the stairs leading to the second floor.

The Shih Tzu shot me a look of disgust and quit growling, but didn't move. I sighed. It was progress.

"Sure we do," Phoebe called from the hallway.

"Huh?"

"We have a windowless room. It's upstairs."

"No we…Crap! You mean my walk-in closet?"

"That's the one," she quipped.

"Oh, no. David isn't staying in my room. What would I do with all my clothes?"

"Your closet isn't exactly your room," Phoebe reasoned as she walked back into the living room carrying a handful of defense charms.

"But he has to walk through my room to get to it." I folded my arms over my chest. "It isn't practical."

Phoebe opened her mouth to reply, but David interrupted by clearing his throat.

"What?" we said at the same time.

"Since I sleep during the day, it shouldn't be a problem if I occupy your closet. If you don't mind, of course. I would feel much more comfortable there than in a room that has windows...even if they are charmed to block light."

Phoebe grinned. "Don't trust me, huh? Smart vampire."

"Trust isn't the issue. Spells and wards can be broken. I'd prefer to not be caught unaware, especially since I'm now in a volatile situation." He caught my eye and waited.

I threw my hands up. "Fine. But you're going to buy me one of those freestanding closets in the meantime."

David nodded his assent.

Phoebe laughed, then sobered as she checked her watch. "We've got a meeting to plan for."

"This way," David said, leading me past a line of patrons waiting to get inside The Red Door—the most famous vampire jazz club on Frenchmen Street.

I followed, keeping my distance. It was one thing to go to the meeting together; it was entirely another to act friendly about it. He was a vampire, after all.

Vampires. What was I doing here? Unease ran through my limbs, making me fidget with the glass bracelet I wore on my wrist. Through my worry, I barely noticed David's vampire energy. I paused. Why didn't I feel as though I were underwater? David was right in front of me, and the club had to contain at least one other vampire—the one we were meeting. Was David's proximity dulling my senses? God. What else was going to go wrong?

David nodded to the bouncer and we walked in unchecked.

"Huh," I mused, trying to put everything else out of my mind. "The door isn't red, after all."

"You've never been here?"

I shook my head. Vampires never caused trouble on Frenchmen Street. The profits from tourists ensured humans were kept safe. Phoebe and I'd never had a reason to work in the area.

"The club is named for a state of being, not the color of the door."

"Good thing, since it's blue." I wanted to ask what he meant by "a state of being," but the band kicked in, and I didn't want to yell. Instead, David led the way to a secluded table in the back.

"Now what?" I shouted.

"We wait."

I sat, scanning the smoke-filled room for Phoebe, but I didn't see her anywhere. Of course, she had to be disguised. She could be a middle-aged chain-smoker with blue eye shadow downing scotch. Unless I looked carefully, I'd never know.

Besides, I had Phoebe's new magically enhanced bug—a sterling silver brooch in the shape of a beetle—in my pocket. Somehow it transmitted everything it heard to another beetle, and Phoebe assured me whatever happened, she'd know about it. It was the same one she'd planted on David when she'd taken him in for questioning. Since he was knocked out, they hadn't forced him through the security radar. They'd let Phoebe search him. That was how she'd known about his deal.

Please let her be close by. Tension pulsed through my core in time with the bass. I longed for a couple of shots of my magically enhanced spiced rum. The mundane stuff wasn't nearly strong enough to combat the massive waves of anxiety making my wings tremble.

Two songs later, the sax player of Unstrung Blues launched into a slow, sad melody. David stood, holding a hand out. "That's our cue."

Great, a death march.

I rose, walking past his outstretched hand. I'd made the mistake of letting him touch me once. It wouldn't happen again.

He dropped his hand, confusion flickering over his features. We stood uncomfortably for a moment, then he nodded toward a poorly lit hallway. "That way."

I took the lead, peering through the dark, smoky lounge, still fruitlessly searching for Phoebe. As I turned to enter the narrow hallway, a cold, dull ache riveted through the small of my back. I flinched and took several steps, putting plenty of space between me and David.

Son of a…How many times before had he reached out to guide me? Before, when he hadn't been a vampire. When the gesture seemed natural. I forced myself to meet his eyes and immediately regretted it. Something very close to pain flickered through them before they turned cold with that uncaring expression vampires were known for. I swallowed. Why did that upset me so much?

"Sorry. It won't happen again." He clasped his hands behind his back.

"It's not…" What could I say? *It's not you, it's me?* It was him and the fact that he'd turned vampire. I couldn't bear his touch, no matter how gentle. Memories of what used to be filled my mind, making my heart break again.

"Let's go," he said, his tone matching his expressionless features.

"David." I held out a hand, intending to catch his arm, but snatched it back at the last moment.

He stared at my hand, then met my eyes in an unflinching gaze.

"I'm sorry. It's not you. I mean not you, personally. It's…" *Gods, can I ever finish a sentence?*

"Forget it. Follow me." He opened a door I hadn't noticed, revealing a steep set of stairs, and started to climb.

Chapter 6

Guilt made me drag my feet up the wooden steps. My rejection of even a small touch must have made me seem petty. Prejudiced, even. I took a deep breath and focused. He couldn't have thought I'd just accept his new identity. I mean, faeries and vamps don't mix. Ever.

I stared at David's long legs and realized something was off. Well, more off than the fact I was headed into a vamp lair. His energy was back in full force, clinging to me like static, but I still couldn't feel any other vamps. Who exactly was I meeting? A corporate lackey? Now I was irritated. All the drama of a written invitation and an ominous phone call and I didn't even rate a face-to-face with the boss.

David rapped twice on the lacquered oak door. After a few moments it swung open. No one stood on the other side. It had to be magic. How else would the door open on its own? Vampires didn't possess the type of power to produce spells, but that didn't mean they didn't have a witch on staff. I wished there was some way to warn Phoebe.

David stepped aside. "Ladies first."

Every nerve in my body screamed to stay put, my feet as heavy as cement blocks. The last thing I wanted to do was turn my back on a vampire, even David. But I couldn't bear to see his cold, dead stare when he realized I didn't trust him.

I flashed a smile, praying it looked sincere, and forced myself to walk into the room. The vampire energy swirled so strong my lungs seized in protest. My knees buckled. I clutched the back of a velvet settee and steadied myself. Either my gift was way the hell off, or the vamps had found a way to conceal their energy.

Panic coiled in my stomach. What if my power was malfunctioning? And right after I'd caught the attention of the most powerful vamp corporation within five hundred miles.

Worst. Timing. Ever.

No. They had to be using a concealment charm. Their energy weighed me down like a two-ton anchor. But why? Did they know I could sense them? My wings twitched, ready for flight. It took every ounce of self-control to not spread them in a display of weakness.

A teenage male wearing a custom suit rose from behind the mahogany desk and moved to stand in front of the behemoth mass of gleaming wood. He leaned back, oozing confidence and casual grace. The boy…no, not a boy at all. He was a vampire. An old one, judging by the way he commanded the attention of everyone in the room. He held his hand out in greeting. "Ms. Rhoswen. I am delighted you were able to accommodate my late invitation."

Amused. If I had to choose one word to describe his demeanor, it would be amused. As if I'd been summoned for sheer entertainment in a game of predator versus prey.

I'd be damned if I was going to let him intimidate me. Boldly, I reached out and clasped his hand. A mind-blowing, icy numbness snaked up my arm. I ground my teeth together and forced myself not to flinch. Not even when he bent and pressed his cold, hard lips to my fingers.

"What a pleasure it is to meet New Orleans' most-prized faery," he said.

Prized? Since when?

I gently withdrew my hand from his grip. I was desperate to clutch it to my chest but let it fall helplessly to my side. How long until the frostbite wore off? I tilted my head, considering him. "I'm sorry. I don't think we've been properly introduced."

A knowing laugh escaped his wide, angular mouth. "Of course. Pardon my lack of manners." He held out an arm to a gorgeous blonde, who slid easily into his grasp. "This is Pandora, and those two over there are Carter and Tanner." The blonde nodded a hello, her attention barely wavering from her man. The other two vampires continued to stare at me, saying nothing.

"And of course you already know Davidson." His lips twitched. "I understand you two have history."

I raised my eyebrows but said nothing.

He laughed. "Of course, that isn't *my* business." His tone implied it was very much his business. And just like that, the amusement faded, and his true colors shone in full spectrum: domineering, impatient, dangerous.

David stepped forward. "Willow, this is my boss and maker, Eadric Allcot." He gave a slight nod and stepped back.

"You have nothing to fear, Ms. Rhoswen. You're an invited guest. No harm will come to you this night," Allcot drawled.

This night. What the hell am I doing here? "That's good, since I'm not really fit for consumption, as you probably already know."

The room went silent as my words sank in. It wasn't exactly a secret I was the creator of Sunshine, a drink I'd created to discourage vampire bites. The potion made faery blood impossibly bitter and unappetizing. Too bad it didn't work for humans; it might have saved David. Or not, since he'd asked to be turned. Allcot held my gaze. The intensity made my skin crawl and one wing twitched involuntarily.

His laugh started as a chuckle, then blossomed as his companions joined in. "I knew I'd enjoy our meeting."

Tired of the theatrics, I straightened my spine and got right to the point. "Why did you summon me here, Mr. Allcot?"

His smile disappeared as he narrowed his eyes. "Bored of me already?"

Shrugging one shoulder, I dug my nails into the velvet settee. "I could say I'm dying to know what you want from me, but we both know it isn't true. Maybe we should just get down to business."

David cleared his throat, shifting slightly so he ended up almost brushing my arm.

He always was protective.

"Relax, Davidson. Your girlfriend is safe," Allcot said.

David nodded once, but didn't move.

I opened my mouth to deny the association, but caught myself before I blew his cover. *Double agent, remember, Willow?*

Allcot said something into his companion's ear and gave her a slow, sensuous kiss, which she returned with vigor. With one last lick of her bottom lip, he sent her off toward the other two vampires, who'd been watching in rapture. I swallowed the bile rising in my throat. The whole thing made me long for a hot shower.

"Very well." Allcot turned his attention to me. "Since it appears the niceties are over, I won't waste any more of your time. It has come to my attention that my young one here," he said, nodding his head toward David, "is now working with the Void. And you in particular."

My breath vanished, and I had trouble refilling my lungs. What. The. Hell? "What makes you think that?"

"He told me."

Every muscle in my body ached to turn to David. To lash out and maim him. But what if the teenager vampire was bluffing? "Why would he do that?"

"Because he knows where his loyalties lie. Do you?"

"What's that supposed to mean?"

"Not everyone is as they seem. You'd be better served if you employed more caution with those you keep close."

I clenched my fists to keep from slapping the righteous, self-important look from his face. "Are you being cryptic on purpose, or have you completely bought into the master of the universe persona you have going on?"

His eyes turned dark gray and he lowered his voice. "Be careful, faery. You're here at my whim."

"I am well aware of that fact, vampire. What do you want from me?"

Allcot picked up a glass paperweight and tossed it from hand to hand. I couldn't help but wish it would drop and smash his toes. No such luck. He cast me a calculating look and replaced the art on his desk. "Information. It has come to my attention another vampire has turned his focus to you. I am aware Davidson has signed on to help you track him down. I want to be kept informed."

"Why?" I asked, careful to keep any suspicion from my voice. It was highly unusual for vampires to care what happened to faeries. The two races tended to ignore each other.

"To eliminate them, of course."

"Uh, okay, but why would you involve yourself in my affairs?"

"Isn't it obvious? Orange Influence. And Davidson here has a fondness for you. He's under my care. I'd like to keep him happy." Allcot sent David a loving smile, making my stomach churn.

I moved from behind the settee and faced the master vampire. "Does the messenger who delivered the letter today work for you?"

David followed, taking up position beside me.

"No." Eadric's steady response left zero opening to judge if he was bluffing.

"How do I know you're telling the truth?"

David shifted uneasily again. I bet no one ever questioned Allcot. Well, there was a first time for everything.

"You don't. We'll have to learn to trust each other."

"I don't trust—"

"Vampires? What about the lovely Davidson here?" Allcot's eyes gleamed as his gaze shifted back and forth between us.

"I was going to say easily. I don't trust easily."

He stood, his six-foot-two frame towering over me. "That makes two of us, Agent Rhoswen. We'll have to see what we can do to overcome that."

"I don't understand why you're helping me." I studied him, trying to see through his layers of armor. "You know I don't sell Influence to vampires and wouldn't under any circumstances."

"Of course." His expression shifted from arrogant jackass to one of concern. "But if you're captured and tortured, the knowledge of how to reproduce it could be obtained."

I fought the urge to take a step back. Is that what this was all about? A power play to get the Influence recipe? It took more than ingredients to get the drug to work, but in the right hands...

A small shudder ran through me. There was a reason the narcotic was heavily regulated. Was he worried one of his enemies might get hold of it? "Why do you care so much?"

"I have my reasons." He stepped closer, staring me straight in the eye. "Aside from information on what you find out about the rogue vampire, I'm offering my protection for free. It seems a fair trade, does it not?"

I crossed my arms over my chest. "And what if I don't agree?"

"You will." The vampire retreated and relaxed against his desk, the amused expression once again transforming his face back into the young teenager I'd mistaken him for.

Stifling a sneer, I clenched my teeth. Arrogant son of a bitch. "How can you be so sure?"

"You wouldn't want anything to happen to Davidson, would you?" He waved a careless hand in David's direction.

"Are you threatening me?" Would he really hurt one of his own? Sick sociopath.

"A threat?" His eyes narrowed in a flash of anger. "My dear, if I was threatening you, you'd know it."

And I did. The hard, uncaring look on his face told me he was capable of almost anything.

"I protect what's mine. No one but me harms my property. If you don't agree, I can't let Davidson continue working with you. It's your choice."

This was my chance to get rid of David. I could refuse, and he would vanish from my life again. But if I did, would Eadric kill him, torture him, or simply send him away? I had no way of knowing. What I did know is Eadric wasn't messing around. So what if he wanted info on a vampire? What was it to me? Especially if he was correct and the vamp was after Influence.

I still wanted to understand his motivation, but he'd made it clear he wasn't talking.

"Fine, but I want your word you won't harm David and that the messenger today doesn't work for you."

"I've already stated both to be true, but I'll say it again. You have my word."

The vampire pressure had been so heavy that when I finally made it to the landing on the stairs, I stumbled. If it hadn't been for my wings, I'd have crumpled at the bottom.

David led me to the table we'd shared an hour earlier. "Wait here. I need to grab some things before we leave."

"But—"

"It's fine. You're under Eadric's protection now. No one will bother you."

He left before I could protest further. The absence of vampire energy almost made me giggle in relief. Gods, how would I deal with the constant ache? I ordered a green tea and in record time, a steaming cup sat in front of me.

I glanced up and was greeted with a friendly smile from the beautiful waiter. "Mr. Allcot wishes to extend his sincere gratitude."

"Um, thanks?" I scanned the room looking for the teenage lookalike but didn't see him. Of course not, I'd feel him first.

"In addition, he asked that I inform you that all items on the menu are complimentary for as long as you work for him." The waiter bowed and left.

Work *for* him? Is that what he thought? I hadn't agreed to that. High-handed asshole.

Vampire energy brushed my skin, familiar and repressive. I tensed, expecting Eadric. But it was his consort instead. She stopped at the edge of the table, her blue eyes big and round, blond hair flowing down her back in a thick sheet.

"You're his sister, right? The one they killed in the lavender fields?"

My heart stopped beating. A few moments went by before the organ began to pump again. "You knew Beau?"

She shook her head. "I only met him a few times. Someone told me he had a twin. It took me a while, but then it hit me where I knew you from. You share most of the same features. He was such a pretty man."

I nodded. "Everyone always said so."

Pandora transformed her glamorous face into a work of pure sympathy and said, "I just wanted to tell you how sorry I was to hear of his death. I liked him. Too bad the vampire wasn't caught."

I stood up, nearly knocking the table over. "What did you just say?"

Pandora took a startled step back. "Just that I liked him. He was a good guy."

"No, about the vampire not being caught? A vampire killed my brother?"

"You didn't know?"

Chapter 7

"What happened?" Phoebe asked from the porch of our house. Her hair was brown this time, styled in a short, asymmetrical bob. She wore a miniskirt and four-inch platform heels. The tourist barfly ensemble was a staple in her collection of disguises.

I pushed past her through the front door.

"Willow!" Phoebe yelled.

"Give me a minute." I ran up the stairs, leaving her to deal with David. Damn him, the double-crosser. *Double agent, my ass.*

I stopped, scanning my room. Hadn't Phoebe plugged my cell phone in somewhere? There. The white power cord snaked out from under the desk. With trembling wings, I powered it on and hit the speed dial.

Pick up, pick up, pick up. Voice mail. Always the frickin' voice mail. As if I had any room to talk. I hadn't even thought of my phone since I'd landed the night before. Had I only been home twenty-four hours? Double damn.

At the tone, my words rushed out. "Talisen, where are you? It's about Beau. Information and a lead. Get your ass down here."

I ended the call and noticed a missed text message. It was from Talisen. *Glad you made it safe. Call me soon so I can hear that beautiful voice of yours.*

He'd replied moments after my text the night before, just after the battery died.

"Stupid phone." I tossed it back on the desk and headed for the bathroom.

When I reemerged, Phoebe was leaning against the door-frame. "Want to tell me what's going on?"

"I just found—" My breath hitched and I forced a swallow. "—found out a vampire killed Beau."

Phoebe's expression softened. "I know, I heard." She pointed to the magically enhanced silver bug pinned to her formfitting button-down shirt.

"Why Beau?" I choked out, unable to comprehend why a vampire would kill him. Back then, in California, I hadn't even known we'd met any. They didn't exactly frequent the coastal faery lands.

Phoebe reached out and hugged me. "We'll find out. I promise."

I pulled back and straightened. "Damn right we will." This wasn't the time to break down. I had a job to do.

"I'm all in. You know that." The tiny witch stood tall, her shoulders back and fire blazing in her black eyes. Fierce determination lined her face. Beau had always said the feistiest ones came in small packages.

Our eyes met and an unspoken agreement passed between us. We'd find answers to the questions the Arcane hadn't been willing to ask. Coincidence, that's what the officials had said. But dying in the same field and at the same age as your father twenty-three years later wasn't a coincidence; it was a fucking pattern.

If they'd ruled both deaths a murder, maybe someone would have looked harder. Unfortunately, our dad's death was listed as an accident. But after seeing both death reports, I wasn't convinced. Not at all. And now I had a lead.

I flexed my wings as I glided toward the stairs. "Let's go. We have a vampire to interrogate."

Phoebe stood in the middle of the living room with her hand on her hip. She stared at David, who was sitting stiffly in a wingback chair. "Someone want to tell me what the hell happened back there?"

"You know as much as I do." I paced the living room, the sound of my clunky boots echoing off the high ceilings. "You heard what they said."

"No, actually, I didn't." She turned and pointed to the beetle still pinned to her chest. "The bug cut out for about an hour. I was ready to bust in, but then I heard you talking to David again right before the woman showed up to ask you about Beau."

I blinked. "Damn it. The concealment charm. Phoebs, they had the whole room cloaked. I couldn't feel anyone except David until we joined them in Allcot's private room upstairs."

Phoebe stiffened and then rounded on David. "How?"

Confusion flickered over his handsome face. "I don't know what the hell either of you are talking about." His gaze landed on me. "What do you mean you couldn't feel anyone but me? Is the Void tracking vampires now?"

"No." Not technically. Oops.

My ability wasn't exactly public knowledge. *Just perfect.* Maude was going to have a shit-fit when she learned I'd leaked the information. The thought suddenly filled me with a gleeful defiance. I tilted my head to one side. David was my partner now. He would've found out sooner or later. Shrugging, I uttered the words I'd been sworn to keep secret, "I have a vampire spidey sense."

"Excuse me?" David scooted to the edge of the chair. "What's that supposed to mean?"

"You know, spidey sense." I tapped my temple. "I know when vampires are around. I should've felt Eadric and his groupies long before we entered his office. But I didn't. Which only means one thing—a concealment charm." I strode across the room, stopping right in front of him. "And you're going to tell us where it came from and why they're using it."

I glanced at Phoebe. She nodded once and cut her eyes back to the vampire.

David leaned back and said nothing.

What did it take to get a reaction out of the guy? I'd confessed a potentially dangerous talent, and he didn't even dignify it with a response. Asshole. "I'll assume that means you aren't important enough to be in the know."

He glared, a muscle pulsing in his jaw as he clenched his teeth.

"Looks like you hit a nerve, Wil." Phoebe pulled out a cigarette, rolling it between two fingers the way she always did when working out a problem.

"Guess so." I took two steps and crouched, staring David in the eye. "But you can and will tell me how it is Allcot knows about the agreement you made with the Void to be a double agent."

"What?" Phoebe demanded, taking a place beside me. She straightened her spine, making her frame appear much taller than her five-foot-two inches. "Someone better fill me in before our *guest* finds himself with a nasty sunburn."

She held up her agate. I frowned. Right then I'd like nothing better than to fry David myself. Double-crossing, low-life coward who couldn't even break up with me in person. I'd deserved an explanation, dammit. Not a hasty text. Coward.

I filled Phoebe in on the night's events and when I finished we both focused on David. Phoebe pointed to her agate. "You've got five seconds to start talking."

He held her gaze, then quirked an eyebrow, a tiny hint of a smile touching his lips. "This is between Willow and me."

Phoebe snorted out a laugh. "Arrogant bastard. Agent Rhoswen is my partner. Where she goes, I go and all that shit. Now start talking. I'd think you'd know by now I don't issue idle threats."

David's face turned stony. "Unfortunately for you, *Agent* Rhoswen is no longer your partner. She's mine, as of sometime this morning. There's a perfectly reasonable explanation for tonight's events. However, I will speak to her about them in private."

Phoebe's arm rose, her face flushed in anger, light pulsing faintly from the agate. All it would take is one word, and David would be out of commission for days, if not weeks. I clasped Phoebe's wrist, deflecting the growing rays of artificial sun.

"Phoebs," I said, exhausted. "As much as I'd like to see him crispy fried, I do need some answers. Maybe it's better if I fill you in later?" The beetle bug was still in my pocket. Whatever David told me, Phoebe would hear it.

She took a deep breath, pointedly not looking at David. "Fine. I'll be upstairs in the kitchen if you need me."

"Thanks."

David watched Phoebe round the corner to climb the stairs, a trace of smugness flashing on his pale face.

"Knock it off." I crossed the room to grab Link's dog brush and cutting shears. The mats from his two-month-long grooming hiatus weren't going to take care of themselves. I eased onto the couch, sitting cross-legged. Link jumped up and settled onto my lap, ready for his brushing.

"I'm listening," I said without looking up.

Silence, except for the worry of bristles through Link's fur, filled the room. Determined to wait him out, I concentrated on finding and trimming mats. If it hadn't been for his vampireness pressing down on me, I could have almost put him out of my mind. Almost.

The familiarity of the situation set my nerves on edge. How many times had we sat together, sharing a comfortable silence? I swallowed a hollow laugh. At that moment a bikini wax would have been more comfortable.

"I owe you an apology," David said so quietly I barely heard him.

Damn right he did. "Way to state the obvious."

"For the way I left things, I mean."

Oh, that. "I don't want your apologies. I'm over it. I want answers. And I want the truth. Who are you really working for?"

"But I—"

I leveled a glare at him, stopping him mid-sentence.

He shifted, sitting up in the chair, his elbows resting on his knees as he leaned forward. "Fine, we'll discuss it later."

Irritation spread through my limbs. I shifted as my wings spread unconsciously. Why was he acting as if we still had a relationship? I hadn't heard from him in over two months. If he thought he could just pick back up after he'd tossed me aside, he'd either forgotten who I was or he hadn't ever known me at all. And turning vampire wasn't an excuse. People turned vamp all the time and didn't abandon their loved ones. Especially people like David. Loyal, caring, protective David.

I frowned, pushing the thoughts away. It didn't matter.

"Answers," I said.

He leaned back into the chair. "Relax, Wil. There's no rush."

I narrowed my eyes, a torrent of obscenities forming on my lips.

David nodded to Link. "He's going to shift if you don't control your agitation."

Link jumped off the couch, his eyes gold. He was vibrating and moments from shifting. I could let him, but if he decided to attack David, I wasn't sure I could stop him. My agitation fed Link, and he wasn't old enough to control it. I took a deep, cleansing breath, tucked my wings close to my back, and waited. After Link visibly calmed, I turned my attention back to David. "Start talking or next time, I'll let him have you."

He glanced at Link. The dog settled on the carpet, keeping his eyes trained on the vampire. "All right. What do you want to know?"

Why you broke up with me. "Do you know anything about my brother's death?"

He shook his head. "I don't. And if I did, I'd do everything in my power to get you the truth of what happened."

The familiar sincerity in his voice shot pangs of regret through my heart. I forced myself to ignore it. "Fine. Why did you tell Allcot about your deal with the Void?"

David stood and moved in front of me. He kneeled, his blue eyes staring intently into mine. "There's only one reason I agreed to be a double agent." He reached out as if to take my hand but seemed to think better of it and pulled back.

"To save your ass?"

His face transformed, full of worry. "To protect you. And to do that, I need Eadric's help."

"Do you believe him?" Phoebe asked from her spot at the kitchen table.

I grabbed a slice of pizza and shrugged. "I don't know."

"Which part?"

"I don't see how he'd know anything about Beau's murder since he wasn't a vampire then."

"True." Phoebe sipped from her favorite solid-black coffee mug.

"But he works for Cryrique, one of the most powerful vampire corporations in the world. He could've heard something. Or found out something."

"I doubt he has those kinds of connections," she said.

I stared at my plate. Phoebe had a point. Being a newly turned vamp meant he'd have entry-level status. No one tells the new kid secrets. "You're right."

She reached across the table and squeezed my hand. "At least now you have a place to start."

The steel I found in her eyes somehow strengthened my resolve. Phoebe would exhaust every lead, no matter how obscure, until we found Beau's killer. She had a brother she'd lay down her life for. What she didn't know was how soul-wrenching it was to lose one. I prayed she never found out.

"We'll get answers," Phoebe said. "I promise."

I gave her a slight smile. "Damn right. But if the blood-sucker in the other room thinks I believe a word he says, he lost his mind in the change."

Phoebe's eyebrows rose. "The blood-sucker?"

Raising an eyebrow of my own, I tilted my head. "Since when do you stick up for David?"

"I don't. But he was important to you once and vice versa. Don't you think it's at least possible he told Allcot about being a double agent because he's trying to protect you?" She tapped her fingers on the table. "Think about it. If his boss found out he'd been hiding that information, David would be dead and so would you. This way he can claim loyalty to Allcot while controlling the information he passes to him."

"You really believe that?"

"What I believe isn't as important as what you believe. But I do think it's possible."

"So I should give him the benefit of the doubt?" Skeptical didn't even begin to describe my tone. I didn't for a minute believe David had any loyalty to me or any reason at all to worry about my safety. If he cared, where the hell had he been? And to claim he was only protecting me? Right. Going double agent and working two powerful entities against each other was a surefire way to end up shackled to a boulder at the bottom of the Mississippi. Not that it would kill him now that he had changed. But it would hurt. A lot.

"A good agent considers all angles," Phoebe reasoned.

"Whatever. I still can't trust him." I stifled a yawn.

"Go get some rest. I'll clean up."

"Thanks, but I won't be able to sleep with him awake."

Phoebe retreated into the heart of the kitchen, pulled a bag out of the freezer, and then reached for a grinder above the refrigerator. "If you're going to keep vamp hours, you're going to need a little stimulation."

I grinned, spotting the Fated Cupcake logo on the package of Mocha in Motion, a blend of coffee and cocoa beans infused with natural energy magic. Guaranteed to keep me awake for hours, the stuff was better than speed and not at all addictive. It was one of my more brilliant creations.

A few minutes later, with an on-the-go cup in one hand and my phone in the other, I found David in the living room. "Let's go."

He looked up from a battered book. "Where?"

I grabbed my keys. "Work."

Chapter 8

David hovered over my shoulder as I unlocked the door to my bakery. My inner vampire detector squeezed my chest, and it started to throb.

I turned. "Can you give me some space?"

He shot me an irritated look but backed up a few paces.

Despite him moving away, the pain intensified, making me wince. Something was very wrong.

"What is it?" David took a step closer but froze when my knees buckled.

"I can't breathe," I wheezed. "What are you doing different?"

"Nothing, I—"

A blond-haired male figure jumped from the roof, landing inches to my right. I stumbled backward, barely avoiding a collision with David.

Instead, he reached out, catching me by the shoulders, his vampire reflexes steadying me. I barely recognized the sting from David's vampire touch before he shoved me out of the way and leapt in front of me, snarling.

My arms burned and I struggled to inhale, but that didn't stop me from stepping forward to stand next to David.

"What are you doing?" he asked me, his voice low.

"Finding out what this vampire wants." I turned to the stalker. "Want to tell me what the hell you were doing on my roof?"

The vamp reached out, nearly connecting with my arm, but David jumped between us, throwing a punch that sent the intruder scrambling back.

My wings twitched. Holy vampire wars. I backed up, deciding David could take this one. No way was I getting mixed up in some crazy vampire crap.

My stalker straightened, black eyes slanted as he stared David down. "Step aside, young one. That faery is my property."

"Property?" I laughed and started coughing when I couldn't get enough air in my lungs. In vampire language, property meant humans who had been turned or were slated to be turned into vampires. Otherwise known as children. "Faeries can't be turned. It's physically impossible."

"Willow, go inside," David said. He glanced back in my direction for just a moment, but long enough for me to notice the flicker of fear crossing his features.

"Not without you." I took a step closer, unwilling to leave him. It was stupid. I didn't have any physical advantage against either of them. I didn't even have Link. We'd left him at the house.

"Now," David warned.

The tone of his voice had me reaching for the unlocked door, but his vicious growl made me spin in shock.

He leapt, catching the other vampire by his neck. A loud snap crackled through the night, and David sank his teeth into the broken neck of the howling vampire.

Time stood still. I watched in horror as blood seeped into David's mouth. The other vamp, despite his broken neck, grappled for purchase, clawing at David's hands. David gripped tighter. The attacker gurgled, his eyes popping out of his chiseled, white face. His body spasmed and finally went limp.

David took one last gulp and threw the vampire backward. "Don't ever come near her again."

The vamp stumbled, but his quick feet kept him from sprawling out into the deserted street. His head flopped to one side, crooked and unnatural.

Disgusting. I made no attempt to hide the horror that no doubt was written all over my face.

The vamp's eyes stared right into mine. With a slow smile, he brought both hands up and in one quick movement his head was sitting on his shoulders right where it should be. He adjusted it slightly to the left. His smile blossomed to a grin. "You didn't think it was that easy to kill a vampire, did you?"

I gaped. Of course I knew a broken neck didn't kill vampires. I just hadn't known it wouldn't hurt more…or at the very least wound them for longer than a few minutes.

"Leave," David snarled.

"For now."

"I'll kill you next time."

The blond vampire's eyes turned from black to red as he glared at David. "Not likely." He half-bowed in my direction. "Soon, my little faery princess."

Before either of us could respond, he vanished into the night.

"Who was that? And why was he calling me his little faery princess?" My wings fluttered, and I rose a few inches off the ground.

"I think he works for the vampire who targeted you for abduction. That was his way of making sure I knew he was laying a claim."

"But faeries can't turn vampire," I insisted.

David shook his head. "It doesn't matter. They want you. That was their way of staking their territory."

"I'm not anyone's territory." I curled my hands into fists as my wings fluttered faster.

David held the door to my shop open. "I'm not the one you have to convince."

Yawning, I grabbed my phone and checked for new messages. Again. Not one phone call or text since the night before. I tossed it back on the desk and shuffled into the kitchen.

Damn it, Tal. Where the hell are you? Worry inched its way into my chest. He never went anywhere without his phone. And I couldn't imagine him ignoring my message. If anyone was more dedicated to finding the truth of Beau's death than

I was, it was Talisen—the one man I knew I could count on. The familiar ache I'd lived with the last four years blossomed, and I had to fight down sheer panic.

He's fine. Someone would have called if...

I couldn't finish the thought. If anything happened to him, it would be like losing Beau all over again. I shook my head. No sense in being melodramatic; he wasn't the one in danger. He'd call as soon as he could. He'd better.

Rummaging through the fridge, I scoured for something to settle my stomach. The Mocha in Motion had kept me up all night while I worked in the lab at The Fated Cupcake, but it left me queasy. Or was that caused by watching David drink the blood of another vampire?

The blood trickling down David's mouth kept flashing in my mind, and I passed on the waffle Phoebe offered to cook.

Steel-cut oats would do the trick. I hoped. With the microwave set to high, I skipped the Mocha in Motion and settled on a cup of herbal tea—the regular kind, no magic. I needed a clear head to think. While my enhanced goodies didn't necessarily impair brain function, they did sometimes give me a high, accompanying whatever magical ability they were supposed to enhance. Because my magic was used in the ingredients, the high usually came in the form of an adrenaline rush, causing me to overlook important details. Details I needed to focus on before David woke up.

I glanced out the window, noted the late afternoon sun, and opened the case file Maude had given me the day before. I scanned the document, my attention narrowing in on David's statement. *A rumor has been circulating in the vampire community of a plot to abduct Agent Rhoswen. No concrete suspects.* Why would any vampire want to abduct me? I didn't taste good, thanks to my Sunshine drink. Influence? Was that it? My favorite band—Incubus for a Day—started singing from my room, interrupting my thoughts. "It's about time, Tal." I ran for my iPhone and sighed when I read the screen—it was my roommate. "Hey, Phoebs."

"Hey, yourself. I've got the background info on your Influence customer."

"Hold on." I hustled back to the table and picked up a pen. "Okay, shoot."

"Good news or bad news first?"

"Good."

"His Influence permit is valid. He works part time as a research assistant at the college."

A weight I hadn't realized existed lifted off my chest. That *was* good news. "Okay."

"He's also an independent courier. He opened his business sometime last year."

More good news. "That explains why he was delivering a handwritten message. Looks like he was multitasking."

"Maybe," Phoebe said with a heavy dose of suspicion.

"What?"

"He's also a file clerk at Cryrique."

"Wake up!" I demanded, using my toe to nudge the limp vampire.

Link jumped in front of me and growled at David.

I let out a hollow laugh and backed off but didn't close the closet door. "I need answers, Link. I can't afford to sit around and wait for the dead to rise."

My dog stared me down as if processing my words. He didn't understand what I'd said, but he did very well at interpreting moods. He set his paws and shimmered as he shifted into full wolf form. It wasn't a surprise considering the amount of agitation spiraling in my system.

Moving in, I tried to nudge David again, but Link cut me off, blocking me from getting near the vampire.

He was right to be wary. I didn't know when or how David would wake up. The sun was moments from setting. Did dusk act as some vampire internal alarm, or did they wake on their own when they were good and rested? He wouldn't get the chance if I had anything to say about it.

It was eerie how still he was, lying there as if he was…well, dead. Creepy. Why would anyone choose to be turned after seeing that? Especially David. It was a concept I couldn't wrap my head around. He'd never fit the profile of questing for eternal youth. He'd even talked about growing old, sitting on his front porch with grandkids at his feet. What had changed?

Maybe he fell for a vampire.

That's why they all turned in the romance novels. Could a warm-blooded male be expected to resist the eternal beauty? Is that why he broke up with me? The thought made me want to punch him.

Whatever. He'd turned. I needed to get used to it.

"David. Nap time is over."

His eyelids flickered and my internal vampire alarm went off, only this time the sensation brushed against me, light and airy.

That was different. For the first time I noticed I hadn't been aware of him while he slept. I stopped mid-step and studied him. Was that always the case? In the few years since I'd developed my ability, I couldn't remember sensing one during the day. But then I wasn't out patrolling for them, either.

"What's wrong?" he growled, leaping to his feet.

"We're going out and you're coming with us."

According to the file, Lester Daniels, AKA the messenger, had worked for Cryrique for over two years. Even though he was only a lowly file clerk, I didn't believe for one moment Allcot hadn't known Lester worked for him. Vampires like him made a point of knowing everyone they employed, right down to their cleaning crew.

"Is this the one?" I pointed to the dark shotgun house in a rundown block of Lower Carrollton. The overgrown vegetation blocked most of the crumbling path leading to the front door.

David nodded and took the lead. Link followed with his nose to the ground.

I watched them go and took a moment to settle before reaching for my magic. If any other vampires were around, I wanted to know about it. A ball of energy in my core spread out, searching as I focused. David filled my senses. Acknowledging him, I stretched farther. Nothing. My vampire radar remained quiet. Good.

I hadn't expected to find another, but after the night before, I had to check. It wasn't known vampire territory. This area hadn't been touched by Katrina and wasn't anywhere near Frenchmen Street or Midtown, where the vast majority of their kind dwelled.

David and Link had disappeared. I traced their trail toward the distressed front porch. Peeling paint and rotting stairs greeted me. Neglected, just like so many other old houses in the city.

I scanned the overgrown yard, seeing nothing in the shadows. Maybe they were inside already. I raised my hand to knock. Link's wolf howl echoed from inside the house. I froze. Then, without thought, I tore into the house, following the sound. "Link!"

"Back here," David called.

A table crashed to the floor as I ran, dodging tattered furniture and piles of old magazines. A growl sounded from the next room. I skidded to a stop in the tiny kitchen at the back of the house. Link stood in the corner, hackles raised and teeth bared, hovering over a crumpled form on the floor.

I rounded on David. "What did you do?"

He pulled out his cell phone and tapped the screen.

"David!" I stared at his back as he retreated to the other room, his phone pressed to his ear.

"Bastard," I muttered and crouched next to Link, getting a better view of the victim. The shock of red hair and pale face matched Lester's Influence ID perfectly. With a shaking hand, I reached out to check for a pulse.

"Come on." My sweaty fingers slipped off his cold, clammy skin. Panicked, I turned his head and leaned in to check his breathing. Then I saw the bite marks. Angry tears burned my eyes as I stood. David hadn't done this. Lester had been dead for hours.

Link continued to guard the body, pacing back and forth as if to protect the man.

"Cool it, Link. There's nothing we can do for him."

Link whimpered and came to sit by my feet. I searched for my own phone and swore when I came up empty. It was probably among the clutter on my desk. Again.

David reappeared, stepping next to me. "We need to go."

"Give me your phone."

To my surprise, he handed it over without protest. I took a step sideways, giving myself some room, and then scrolled through his contacts, found the number, and hit send.

"Davidson, I didn't expect to hear from you again so soon," the vampire drawled.

David hissed in a breath and grabbed for the phone. Ready for him, I fluttered to the other side of the room, near the ceiling.

"It's Willow."

A pause, then Eadric chuckled. "Ah. To what do I owe this unexpected pleasure?"

"We need to talk."

"Davidson is with you, I presume?"

"Yes." I spared a glance at my partner and nearly winced at the fury vibrating through him. It didn't help that Link had shifted and had him cornered.

"And did he not advise you against calling with such demands?"

"He didn't have a choice."

"I see." A lilt of amusement touched his voice. "How could I pass up such a pleasant offer of your company? I'm at my club. I'll be available for the next hour."

"Fine." I hung up and called the Arcane about the body. They'd want to investigate.

After giving the investigator the address, I slipped David's phone in my pocket and landed beside my wolf. "Link, back off. David isn't going to hurt me."

I hoped.

Link retreated with his hackles still raised. The look on David's face made me question my earlier statement. The scowl and the tension in his arms suggested he'd like nothing better than to rip my wings off at that very moment. Instead, he turned his back to me and stalked out of the house.

Chapter 9

I sped down St. Charles Avenue with David fuming in the passenger seat and Link snarling in the back. Stomping on the gas, I willed the lights to stay green. If the tension got any thicker, one of them would snap. Then what? I couldn't let David hurt my dog, even if he was only protecting himself. I rolled down the window, hoping some air would help.

It didn't.

David's growing agitation sent my internal vampire alarm into overdrive. Adrenaline filled my veins, making me shake. "Cool it, David. You're worse than Link."

David growled. Actually growled.

And that's when Link lunged…in full-on wolf form. His gray and white mass filled the space between the seats as he twisted with his enormous jaws bared. David's pale arm shot out, slamming the wolf into my side. Pain pierced my ribs. I sucked in a sharp breath, struggling to keep control of the wheel.

"Link, no," I cried, but he let out a furious howl and lunged for the vampire again.

Snap! The seat crumpled backward. David scrambled into the back seat, kicking at Link.

I swerved to a stop, barely missing a large oak tree. "Stop it, both of you!" I threw my door open and jumped out to run to David's side of the Jeep.

Neither paid any attention to my demands. David's left hand clutched Link's neck, pressing the wolf against the opposite door. One wrong move, and David's arm would be wolf food.

Horrified, I ran to the other side of the Jeep and yanked the door open.

"Link, David, stop!" I cried, unable to do anything but watch in horror as the pair tried to kill each other.

Link twisted free of his grip, simultaneously slashing with his razor-sharp claws. Bright red blood seeped from David's shoulder. He roared, his vampire fangs seeming to elongate, though I wasn't at all sure that was possible. Link, being a wolf, lunged for the open wound. David countered the move and slammed him against the back window. Link yelped and shrank back before shimmering into puppy form. He fell into a heap, vampire blood dripping from his tiny Shih Tzu paws.

David tore from the Jeep, his image blurring past me. When he finally stopped, he stood half a block away, hidden in shadows.

Heart pounding, I started after him, then stopped and climbed into the car to check on Link. He lifted his head at the sound and whimpered.

"Ah, Link. What were you thinking?" I picked him up, cradling him in my arms. "Poor puppy, you just need time to learn to control your impulses. It isn't your fault."

He licked my hand and snuggled closer.

"You can come back now. He's too weak to shift again," I called.

David didn't respond.

"Seriously, it's safe." I tucked Link back into the Jeep. Blood dripped from the broken passenger's seat. How badly had Link wounded him? I used an old sweatshirt to wipe the blood from his paws and cleaned the seat as best I could before looking up.

I spotted David a few feet away. "Are you all right?"

He glared. "You think I'm scared of your dog?"

"Well…"

"You have a lot to learn, Willow. Your wolf can do some damage, but he'll never survive in a fair fight with a vampire. Learn to control your temper or you're going to get him killed."

I crossed my arms over my chest, meeting his steely gaze. "This is my fault? You're the one who actually growled. You should've known it would set him off. Honestly, growling?"

He lowered his voice. "I'm not human anymore. Remember that next time you deliberately piss me off."

Of course he wasn't human. The evidence was overwhelming. But what the hell was he talking about? Piss him off? "What?"

"Using my phone to call Eadric. Do you have any idea how dangerous this game is you're playing? He does not care for you. If you become a liability, he will have you eliminated. And I'll be powerless to stop it."

"Allcot's not going to harm me. He knows I work for the Void and they're investigating him. If I go missing, there will be hell to pay." Right? Maude would make sure of it. She was a power-hungry, controlling, evil witch of a faery, but she wouldn't stand for anyone offing her Influence-making niece. I was too valuable. That much I knew, but did Allcot?

David closed his eyes for a moment. When he opened them, he leveled me with an intense stare. "So naïve. If Eadric wants you dead, it will happen, and the trail will never lead back to him. I know I've lost your trust, but on this, please, listen to me."

Sadness formed a bubble around my heart as I shook my head. "How can I trust anything? A boy died today. One who worked for Cryrique and bought Influence yesterday. I can't let that go. You know that. If there's a connection, I have to know about it. The Arcane has to know, and my only lead is your boss. Are you going to help me?"

I held my breath and waited. I'd still go if he said no, but for some reason I really wanted him by my side. Why was that?

He frowned. "I committed to a job. I'll see it through."

It wasn't exactly what I'd hoped to hear. Six months ago, David would have been outraged by the day's events. He would have been the first one backing me up on my quest for justice. Instead, I was left with a cool, calculating, almost uncaring David.

Still, having him with me when I confronted Allcot was better than going alone. "Fine, but you're driving. I want to make sure Link doesn't wake up and attack again."

Eadric lounged on the velvet settee with Pandora draped over his lap. Her mid-thigh-length red silk robe gaped open, showing round, ample cleavage usually only obtained by the copious help of a Wonderbra. Were perfect breasts a perk of turning vampire or had Pandora been blessed in life prior to her death? Maybe she'd been augmented. Were there any doctors who performed vampire breast implantation?

"Agent Rhoswen, how kind of you to join us this evening." Eadric slid his hand along his companion's thigh. "Shall we make room for you on the settee?"

Pandora giggled. It sounded ridiculous coming from the flawless-faced goddess.

I cleared my throat. "Uh, no…thank you."

"How unfortunate for us." He caught my eye and bent his head, grazing his teeth along the curve of Pandora's breast. She shivered and pressed closer to him.

Heat crawled up my neck as I tried to focus. The altercation between Link and David had left me frazzled and the seduction scene wasn't helping. I turned to David for support, but he stood frozen, his gaze locked on the couple in front of him.

Great. "I'm sorry for interrupting, but a situation has, uh, arisen that cannot wait."

A low chuckle rumbled from Eadric's throat. "I find myself in the very same predicament." He cast a glance down Pandora's robe before flashing a wicked smile.

More heat burned my face, and I fought for composure. Someone had died. I needed answers, not an introduction to vampire sex games. "You told me Lester Daniels didn't work for you."

Eadric didn't look up from his exploration of Pandora's now-naked upper half. "He doesn't."

I focused on the wall behind the couch, trying desperately to avoid watching the scene in front of me. "Was he working for you when he delivered the message to my shop yesterday?"

Eadric groaned. Involuntarily, my gaze locked on the couple, narrowing in on Pandora's neck where Eadric had bitten her. His tongue darted out, licking a droplet of crimson staining his lips.

Where was the eye bleach? I literally could not tear my gaze from Pandora's throat. Two bright pink puncture wounds stood out against her pale white skin, the bite marks already healed over. Did humans heal that fast when bitten? I doubted it.

"Would you like to find out?" Eadric asked.

"Huh?"

"What it's like to be bitten." His piercing stare burned into me as if I were the only person in the room. "You seem so... interested."

Had he heard my thoughts? That myth wasn't true was it? *No*, I screamed with my mind and waited. When he didn't react, I shook my head. "My blood wouldn't be tasty."

He laughed. "True, but I can't resist a woman in obvious rapture."

I took a step back and crossed my arms. That was enough. "Look, Allcot. A man died and I'm here for some answers. Was Daniels working for you when he delivered your invitation?"

He sat up straighter, a trace of the hardness I'd sensed the night before returning. "Yes."

I hissed in a sharp breath. "Our relationship isn't going to work if you lie to me."

"I didn't lie. He was already dead by then."

Silence hung in the air. When I found my voice it came out low and dangerous. "You had him killed. Why?"

"For you."

"What?" Without thinking, I took two steps forward.

David cut me off. He'd been so quiet I'd almost forgotten about him. "You don't want to do that," he whispered to me.

"I think I do."

"You don't." He reached out and pinned my arm next to him. I stifled a cry of pain as the limb went numb.

Allcot abandoned Pandora and stood. His white button-down shirt had lost its buttons and hung loose over his rumpled black slacks.

"Let go," I said through clenched teeth.

David hesitated and when I sucked in a ragged breath, he released me.

"Don't ever do that again," I warned and then turned to Eadric. "Why would you do such a thing?"

For the first time, we had his undivided attention. His gaze shifted back and forth between me and David. "Isn't that interesting?" he said in an amused tone. Then he met my eyes. "As I said before, you are under my protection. Lester was caught selling Influence to vampires. He was eliminated."

I gaped. "You can't just kill people. We have laws. He could've been charged. Interrogated."

Eadric shrugged one shoulder. "This way was less messy. He's been taken care of. You're welcome."

"Wel…welcome?" I fought to regain control of my speech. "You arrogant son of a demon. How could you—"

"That's enough." David shifted, facing me as if to shield me from interacting with Eadric. "We came for answers, now you have them. It's time to go."

"Your girlfriend seems less than pleased," Eadric drawled and sat down, pulling Pandora back into his lap. "How can we remedy the situation?"

"Don't go killing anyone else, you sick—"

"Willow!" David stepped forward, forcing me back toward the door.

Movement blurred, and a moment later Eadric stood just behind David. The vampire's eyes hardened. He stalked in a slow circle as if tracking his prey. I swallowed the last of the obscenities clogged in my throat.

"Goodnight, Father," David said, his back still to Eadric. "We'll leave you to your activities this evening."

"We are not finished, my son."

"Eadric, I'm bored of this." Pandora stood and let her robe drop, every unflawed inch of her bared. "It's always business all the time. You promised tonight you'd remind me of why I stay faithful to you."

His unflinching stare finally broke, and he turned his attention to the sex goddess across the room. "Of course. My apologies, my love." His voice turned low and dangerous. "Davidson, do not bring her here again without an invitation."

I fumed silently as we wound our way through the blues club. My skin itched and my muscles ached after the constant exposure to vampires for forty-eight hours. Had Maude manipulated the whole situation just to torment me? Not the dead human part. She wouldn't go that far. Would she? No, but she would partner me with David just for spite.

When we'd almost made it to the Jeep, my wings fluttered, and I rounded on David. I placed my hands on my hips, hovering a full foot taller than him. "What the hell is going on?"

David stepped to the side, reaching for the door.

I cut him off. "We're not leaving until we have this out. Why the holy hell did you choose to turn vamp, and for the love of all fae, why did you call Allcot your father?"

He flinched and in a low voice said, "Can we discuss this in private?"

"No. You'll talk now and I will listen."

He crossed his arms. "This is not the place."

We stayed locked in a staring match until I finally threw my hands up and fluttered to the driver's side. "Fine, but before the night is over, you'd better start talking."

We rode in silence back to the lower Garden District. I parked in front of my house, opened the door for Link, and followed him across the street to Coliseum Square Park. I kept a close eye on him, worried the altercation with David had harmed him in some way. Other than keeping his tail between his legs, the Shih Tzu appeared to be fine. "You're okay, buddy. After a night's sleep, you'll be good as new."

Link lifted his head, acknowledging my voice, then lifted his leg and watered the nearby tree. He kept his head low and slinked back to the house.

Just like a man to sulk when things don't go his way.

David waited near the car, no doubt keeping an eye on me in the park. Irritation heated my skin. I hated he was watching me and hated even more to find myself grateful. Link and I spent a lot of time in the park alone, but tonight he wasn't in any shape to protect me. David was.

I stalked past him. I'd reached the top step of my front porch when something moved. Reflexively my wings spread, and I shot up, banging my head on the overhang.

"Ouch!" I clasped my hands over the knot already forming and tried to focus.

A tan hand with long, thin fingers reached out, clasping my arm. Normally instinct would have sent me flying several yards away, but the familiar, easygoing smile transfixed me. I squeezed my eyes tight, trying to dislodge the illusion. He wasn't real. Hallucination was a symptom of a concussion, right?

I opened my eyes to forest-green eyes twinkling with laughter.

"It's about time you showed up. I've been waiting for hours," he said.

I blinked.

"Earth to Willow. Aren't you going to invite me in?"

"Why? Are you a vampire, too?"

Talisen's beautiful face pinched in confusion. "Huh? Are you okay? Did you knock your brains out with that gorgeous display of klutziness I just witnessed?"

"Tal? You're here? Damn, you're here." I threw my arms around him, and he rewarded me with a bone-crushing embrace.

"Of course I'm here," he said, releasing me. "You called. I got on a plane."

"But you never called me back. I even kept my phone on and with me. See?" I dug in the front pockets of my jeans and frowned when I came up empty. Oh, right. It was still on my desk. "Um, I thought I did anyway."

"You'll never change." He laughed, then sobered and nodded over my shoulder. "Who's the bodyguard?"

I glanced back at David and made a face. "No one important."

Chapter 10

Clutching two cups of my special spiced rum, I joined Talisen on my bedroom balcony. "Here."

He wrapped one of his big hands around a mug and eyed the deep purple bruise on my arm. "What happened?"

The concern lining his face touched me deep in my core. My kick-ass-and-ask-questions-later bravado vanished, and I started to shake.

Talisen gently tugged my hand, pulling me down next to him in the cushioned wicker love seat, his arms encircling me into his safe embrace. "Shh, it's okay, Wil. Everything will be all right," he whispered, stroking my hair. "I'm here now and not going anywhere."

Unable to hold it in any longer, I choked out a sob and sank into his strong arms. God, two crying jags in less than two days. What the hell had I come home to? We stayed huddled together, Talisen murmuring soothing words until my eyes finally dried.

"I'm sorry," I mumbled, wiping my face with a tissue. "I didn't mean to do that. I couldn't…"

He smiled. "It's okay. That's what big brothers are for."

Since Beau's death, Talisen had tried to fill the empty hole my twin had left. But no matter how close we got or how much I cared about him, he could never take Beau's place. He knew it. I knew it. Both of us wanted to believe otherwise.

I mustered a weak smile. "Thanks."

A sense of peace started to ease through me as Talisen cupped my cheek. His lips quirked into a lopsided smirk. "Of course, as your brother, I don't think I should have the sort of thoughts I've had about you from time to time."

I laughed and leaned back. "Way to ruin a touching moment."

He shrugged and a lock of sun-kissed, light brown hair fell across one eye. "Anything to see that gorgeous smile."

My heart skipped a half beat, the way it always did when he started flirting, even though I knew he didn't mean anything by it. Tal behaved the same way around all women. He was an equal-opportunity flirt. The moment was so familiar, so comfortable, I slid off his lap and leaned against his shoulder, curling my fingers in his. "How do you do it?"

"What?"

"Make everyone around you trust you completely. Look." I pointed to his feet. "You even have Link snowed."

Talisen glanced at the Shih Tzu and reached down to pick him up with his free hand. Link licked his face once before settling on his lap. "If you recall, I bribed him with copious amounts of raw beef when I was here last spring. As for you and the rest of the females you're no doubt talking about, it's obviously my good looks and irresistible charm. Not to mention the magic-infused eilat stone I plant on anyone I want to exert my powers over."

I started searching my pockets. Talisen was a fae gifted in crystal magic. An eilat stone could hold his power and wield any kind of energy he wanted to infuse it with. When I came up empty, I narrowed my eyes at his amused expression. "What? It's not like you haven't done it before."

He shook his head, his lips twisted once again into a smirk. "When we were twelve."

"Yeah, well, I haven't forgotten." One summer day, I'd followed Beau and Talisen the two blocks to the beach. At first I'd kept my distance, spying on them, convinced they were there to practice water magic, which we were all strictly forbidden to do without supervision. But after watching them throw a baseball for half an hour, I finally emerged and demanded they let me play.

They refused. When I wouldn't leave them alone, Talisen suggested I cool off in the ocean…naked. An odd, complacent sensation had washed through me, and I'd instantly started unbuttoning my dress. Thank goodness Beau had stepped in, demanding Talisen revise his command. The last thing Beau wanted to see was his sister naked. I still ended up in the fifty-degree ocean, freezing my wings off. And my dress had been ruined.

"You deserved it," he said.

I snorted. "Probably, but if you two hadn't ditched me all the time, I wouldn't have been nearly as annoying."

"Again, we were twelve."

"Yeah." I sighed. If I could have Beau back, I'd gladly relive the times when he and Talisen had tormented me relentlessly as only a brother and his best friend could.

"I miss him, too," Talisen said quietly, stroking Link.

"I know."

We were silent for a moment. Then Tal lifted Link off his lap and set him on the ground. Shifting to catch my eye, he caressed my fingers, still clasped in his. "Now tell me, what has you so depleted?"

"Huh?" It took me a second to register he meant my energy level. Tal had a healing gift. He'd probably known as soon as we'd hugged I wasn't one hundred percent. "Oh, I'm just tired. It's been two very long days."

He raised a skeptical eyebrow and passed me my cup of spiced rum. "Start at the beginning."

I took a long sip. What could I say? My work at the Arcane was classified. Leaking information to an outsider wouldn't get me fired; it would get me locked up. But only if Maude found out about it. I tilted my head, gazing at the man I trusted most in the world. The only one besides Beau I'd ever truly given my heart to. I didn't give a damn about Maude or the Arcane. With the information I'd learned, I needed to tell him for my own sanity. Needed him to know about my secret life, especially after learning a vampire had killed Beau. I could never live with myself if I kept him in the dark and that's all it really came down to.

I took a deep breath. "I can sense vampires."

Once I started, I didn't give Talisen a chance to speak. The words poured out, starting with the unexpected discovery of my new talent, my induction to the Arcane, Maude swooping in right after I signed my contract, the threat to my well-being, being partnered with David, and on to the discovery of Daniels's death.

"See." I stared at my clenched hands with anger and helplessness consuming me. "If I hadn't discovered the Influence, that kid would still be alive. Damn Maude! This is exactly why I didn't want to produce it."

Talisen lifted my chin up with two fingers, forcing me to look at him. "Because you were afraid a dumb kid would get messed up with vampires over it?"

"Yes."

He frowned, his lips forming a thin line.

"Okay, not exactly. I never wanted to produce it because it's dangerous. Forcing people to do things against their will is evil. You know how I feel about that."

"You think someone forced this kid to get involved with vampires?"

"No, that's not what I meant." I stood and paced the balcony. "Something I created resulted in the death of someone just starting his life. Allcot even said he killed the kid to help me." Though Eadric must've had his own reasons for ending Daniels's life. He was entirely too self-serving for me to believe otherwise.

Talisen leaned back in the loveseat, casually draping his arm across the back. "Wil, how is this different from drug dealers using cold medicine to make meth?"

I opened my mouth, but he cut me off.

"It isn't. Influence is important to law enforcement. Think of all the criminals they've caught by using it and all the innocent suspects who've been exonerated due to your drug."

He was right, and I knew it. Influence was used in criminal trials and by court order. It wasn't a truth serum *per se*, but when used, if the witness was ordered to tell the truth, they did. A lot of falsely convicted criminals had been released after it went to market.

Talisen continued. "And what about its uses for hospitals? It's used to help calm patients, get them to follow doctor's orders. Your drug has been a miracle breakthrough in natural weight loss."

Also true. One prescription of Influence, followed by an order to follow a strict diet, and people didn't have to have invasive surgery to lose weight. They did it on their own and in the meantime established healthy habits.

"That's different. All those people choose to take Influence under careful supervision so they aren't taken advantage of." I stopped pacing and crossed my arms. "You aren't talking me down from this one. I'll still blame myself, no matter how you spin it."

He sighed. "You can't be held responsible for the mistakes other people make. You don't think this kid knew he was playing with fire when he went to work for vampires?"

"Not all vampires are evil." I winced, realizing Phoebe had made the same argument just yesterday.

"No. But I'm sure he knew dealing Influence wasn't the safest career move."

I hated when he was right. Everything he said was true. But I couldn't help feeling responsible. What if Daniels had been forced into it? Threatened, or just desperate enough for some reason or another. I didn't want any part of it. The world survived before Influence, it could survive without it.

"You can beat yourself up all you want," Talisen said. "But the truth is, Influence exists. It isn't going to go away. Other faeries and witches are already trying to duplicate it. Hell, the university is working on something similar. If you bow out, you'll have no say in how it's controlled."

Maude had made that all too clear when she'd forced my hand into producing the drug. My lovely aunt had even copied the formula and had come up with her own recipe. A deadly version, if the administrator wasn't careful. That alone had been enough to convince me.

"I know. But it doesn't make it any easier." My voice cracked with emotion.

Talisen rose and pulled me into another hug. This time his left arm found the deep bruise gracing my right side. "Ouch."

"I'm sorry." He pulled away, his forehead creasing as he frowned. "You're really hurt."

I wrapped my arms around myself. "It's nothing."

"Nothing? Is that what you call this?" he asked, gently pushing the sleeve over my elbow.

"It was…David," I stammered and squeezed my eyes shut. When I opened them again I met Talisen's blazing eyes. I rushed to explain. "But it's not his fault. I mean, he didn't mean to do it."

Talisen stared at me in horror. Suddenly he yanked the door open and stalked across my room toward the stairs. He'd almost made it to the first step before I caught him. "Wait!"

"Are you kidding me?" His voice rose with each word. "When did you turn into the whimpering victim? I *cannot* believe this. It's not his fault? He didn't mean to?" He spat the words out.

I grabbed his arm. "Let me speak before you go all crazy macho fae on him."

He gritted his teeth and pulled away.

"Please, Tal. Give me a minute, and then if you aren't satisfied, I promise you can stake his ass to the wall if you see fit."

That got his attention. He turned back, arms folded. "One minute."

A jagged breath escaped my lips. "It really isn't his fault. He doesn't know he hurt me."

His face turned to granite.

"Holy hell. I'm doing a terrible job at explaining. Look, I told you I can sense vampires, right? Well, there's something else. If they touch me, even just brush up against my skin, it hurts like I've been beaten with an iron wrench."

"An iron wrench?" he asked in disbelief. His eyes narrowed as if he was trying to determine if I'd lost my mind.

I nodded and crossed my arms over my chest. A wrench on its own was bad enough, but an iron one? Yeah, iron sucked the life energy right out of me. Double whammy. "I got this bruise tonight," I said, pointing to my arm, "while David was trying to protect me from doing something stupid at Allcot's place. He held my arm down so I wouldn't touch something. He didn't intend to hurt me." I raised my arm for inspection.

Talisen leaned closer. "Jesus, Wil. He doesn't know his touch does this to you?"

"No. I didn't want the word to get out to any other vamps."

He nodded and tugged me toward my bed. "Good. Lie down. I have something with me that can heal this."

"Healing crystals?" At his nod, I laughed. "Didn't I already tell you crystals are for amateurs?"

"And once again, I'm going to make you eat those words, Rhoswen. Now let me get to work."

I fluttered to my queen-sized bed in the enchanted oak and waited while Talisen scaled the trunk. Fae spent a lot of time in the woods. Climbing for him was as natural as flying was for me.

"Show-off," I muttered, lowering myself onto my stomach.

"Can't let you think I'm going soft." He produced a canvas bag and rummaged through it until he found his crystal of choice. Amethyst.

I smirked. "I should've known. The cure-all."

He leveled me with a glare. "Do I question what materials you use to concoct your edibles?"

"All the time. Wasn't that you who bugged me nonstop in my mother's lab the whole time—?"

"Okay. You've made your point." He shifted, catching his foot in the comforter and losing his balance. His hand made contact with my back as he stabilized himself.

I hissed in a sharp breath, pain seizing my already battered spine.

"Sorry, did I hurt you?"

With my eyes squeezed shut, I shook my head.

Talisen said nothing and shifted again. I opened my eyes to find his shut tight and his arms stretched out above me, his beautiful hands clutching two dark purple crystals. Watching him draw on his magic was fascinating. Power seemed to glow beneath his skin, giving him an ethereal tan, his muscles tightening as he focused.

The graceful strength of his body heightened his natural beauty, and I couldn't help but wonder if I'd ever looked even half as good as he did when he worked his magic mojo. I always envisioned myself resembling a day laborer in the fields while I tended my plants. Judging by the amounts of soil I washed from my hands, face, and garden apron, I knew my suspicions were close.

His hands came down, lightly caressing my back. "What happened?" he asked again.

"Huh?"

His fingers glided back and forth underneath my wings, barely touching the tender area. "Willow." Impatience laced his tone.

Crap. "Another vampire incident."

"David again?" He barely concealed his anger.

"Yes, but I already told you it wasn't his fault."

"You either need to tell him about this new…ability or stay the fuck away from him. Your whole left side is beat to hell." His fingers slid under my shirt, leaving traces of tingling magic on my skin.

I shivered as goose bumps rippled down my arms.

"Sorry," he whispered and increased the pressure of his touch. "Didn't mean to tickle you."

"It's okay." Telling him I wasn't ticklish didn't seem like the best idea under the current circumstances. Talisen had healed my injuries more times than I could count, but being with him, alone and on my bed, evoked fantasies I hadn't entertained since we were teenagers.

Stop it. Talisen is like a brother. Sort of.

Not really, but he'd been Beau's best friend, and that meant we'd never explored the harmless flirtation we'd shared for the last nine years. I knew if anything ever went south between the two of us, Beau would've taken my side. It's what twins did. It wouldn't have been fair to risk their relationship when Tal was never serious about anyone for longer than a month.

I figured he'd never made a move for the same reason. Now that Beau was gone, a romantic relationship was still out of the question. I never wanted to mess up the closest connection I had to my brother.

I just needed to remind my traitorous body of that fact. And soon. Talisen's healing touch sent shivers of desire through my sexually deprived body, and I swallowed the moans rising from the center of my being. Forget the bruises. I wanted to feel his hands everywhere.

In my lust haze, I became aware of his fading magic as he moved on to a full back massage. My breath quickened and my wings tingled. His fingers kneaded steadily down my spine. Unable to hold back, my wings flickered in pleasure.

He chuckled, low and satisfied, moving his fingers from my back to glide delicately over the tips of my wings. I arched my back and flexed, pressing the sensitive tips into his touch.

"Excuse me," a strangled voice interrupted.

Link bounded in from the balcony, growling and pacing in front of my door.

"Crap," I mumbled and sat up, adjusting my shirt back in place. I'd been so engrossed with Talisen, I hadn't even noticed David approach. In fact, I barely felt him now. Had Talisen's magic dulled my senses? No, the tension between us moments ago had been anything but dull. I was just worn out. A good night's sleep in my oak would cure me. "What?"

"Phoebe called. She needs us to meet her in Midtown ASAP."

"She called *you*?" I jumped down and strode to the door.

He nodded toward the desk. "Check your phone. She says she tried you first." He glared over my shoulder. "Looks like you had other things on your mind. I'll meet you downstairs after you compose yourself." David stalked back out of the room, his boots echoing on the stairs.

I glanced down and winced. A button had come loose, exposing more than a little bit of cleavage. The see-through lace bra I'd chosen that morning wasn't helping matters. "Damn it."

Talisen laughed.

"What's so funny?"

"You. You're cute when you're flustered."

"Stop. Just stop. This is your fault." I stomped toward my closet. Then I remembered David had emptied it and changed course toward the freestanding canvas wardrobe in the corner. Talisen watched as I picked out fresh jeans and a tank top, my standard autumn uniform for hunting vampires. "Stop staring."

"Can you blame me?"

I rolled my eyes but smiled as I locked myself in the bathroom. Goddess help me. Having David and Tal in the same house wasn't a good idea. Not a good idea at all.

Chapter 11

The last thing I wanted to do was share a car ride with David and Talisen. But what was I supposed to do, leave Tal at home? Not a chance.

"Come on." I tugged Talisen down the stairs.

David started to protest, but I cut him off as I climbed in the Jeep. "Link's coming and Talisen keeps him calm. With your current mood, I think it's necessary. No one wants another incident."

It wasn't a lie. Talisen really was the only other person besides me that put Link at ease. God, I hoped no one else realized all it took was a few slabs of raw meat. But controlling Link's mood wasn't the only reason I'd insisted on including Talisen. I dreaded being alone with David after what he'd witnessed, even if it was mostly innocent.

Innocent. Right. Who knows what would've happened if David hadn't barged in? Why did I even care what David thought? Hell, he'd dumped me.

He'd. Left. Me.

I had nothing to feel guilty about. My stomach clenched, tying itself in knots. Yeah, no guilt here. David settled in the hastily repaired passenger's seat, Link and Talisen in the back. "Did you fix that?" I asked David, eyeing the seat.

"Yes. While you were busy with your...friend."

I gritted my teeth and put the Jeep in gear, trying to ignore the mounting tension.

"Make a right," David said.

I slowed. "Can't. That's a one-way street."

"Oh. Right. Go left."

Apparently I wasn't the only one preoccupied. After I navigated the turn, I glanced in the rearview mirror. Link lay curled up in Talisen's lap. I smiled at the image of my two favorite men. Link had never taken to David like that. It should've been a warning. What could I say? My dog was a better judge of character than I was.

Several blocks later, David pointed to the opposite side of the street. "It's the next house on the left."

I pulled to a stop but didn't kill the engine as I eyed the two-story Victorian. Shutters covered the floor-to-ceiling windows on both levels. "This is the middle of vampire territory."

"I know." David climbed out of the car and took off toward the house. Talisen followed him with Link in tow. I killed the ignition and scrambled to catch up.

"Tell your *friend* he isn't welcome here." A muscle pulsed in David's jaw.

"Says who?" I stopped in the middle of the walkway, hands on my hips.

"I do." David produced a key and unlocked the solid oak door. In typical New Orleans flair, a scrolling fleur-de-lis was carved right in the center. "You and your wolf can come in, but he stays outside."

"What?" I raised my voice to a decidedly unladylike level. "Who put you in charge, and where's Phoebe?"

"Here," she said, appearing in the doorway wearing a leather micromini, a silk halter top, and thigh-high stiletto boots. She completed the look with platinum board-straight hair that covered her naked back. What was with the hoochie outfit?

She waved at Talisen. He gave her an appreciative nod as he admired all her exposed skin.

"Sorry, Tal. Official business and all that crap." Phoebe threw him her keys. "Take my car and meet us back at the house."

I frowned. "But—"

"It's okay." Tal draped an arm around my shoulders and squeezed. "Now that I know Phoebs is here, I can rest easy you'll be safe. See you back at your abode." He brushed his lips against my temple and then strode off.

David narrowed his eyes, a scowl firmly in place. Yeah, he'd loved that little PDA. Not.

Link watched Tal speed off, a forlorn look on his doggie face.

"What's going on?" I snapped my fingers, and Link instantly jumped to my side.

David stood on the porch in stony silence, studying me as if he was peeling back the layers of my emotional armor. The violation made me want to wrap my arms around myself for protection. But I forced myself to relax and turned to Phoebe.

She threw me a dirty look. "Damn you and your phone. Don't make me call David again." She lowered her voice as if to spare David's feelings, but there was no way he couldn't hear her. Not with his vampire powers. "You know I can't stand that guy."

He didn't even flinch.

"Right." I cleared my throat. "Sorry, it won't happen again."

Phoebe didn't even have the decency to hide her rolling eyes.

I threw my hands up in defeat. "I said I was sorry. Will you please tell me what in holy hell is going on? Whose house is this?"

"It's mine," David snapped and strode inside. "If you two are done insulting me, we have a vampire to question."

"I wasn't…never mind." Nothing I said would change his mood after the night's events. "What vampire?" I asked, following the pair into the house. Neither acknowledged my question.

A scream started to bubble in my throat. I gritted my teeth together, holding it back. If they weren't going to talk to me, why did they bother making me tag along? *Damn David and this stupid assignment.*

I glanced around, taking in the tastefully decorated living room. Period antique tables and an ornate hutch from the eighteen hundreds were intermixed with newer, modern-day settees and armchairs, giving the room an elegant but useful feel. When had he acquired this house?

Five months ago, David had lived in a one-bedroom bachelor-pad apartment, complete with garage-sale furniture. Someone else must have decorated this place.

The walls showcased contemporary paintings, rich with New Orleans history and architecture. The place begged to be featured in *Southern Living* magazine. Only the white metal casings from the motorized blackout window coverings screamed vampire lair. When closed, nothing penetrated the patented metal sheet.

I followed Phoebe into a large library. The walls, packed floor to ceiling, housed everything from rich leather-bound books to contemporary science fiction. Not a romance novel in sight. Somehow that knowledge lightened my heart…until the soft, feminine voice filled the silence.

"David," a sleek redhead purred. "It was thoughtful of you to bring entertainment. You know how I like variety." She sipped from a pewter cup, the contents leaving a tinge of red on her lips.

Disgusting.

The female vampire held the cup toward David, but he ignored it and fixed her with a glare. "Clea. Why are you in my house? Uninvited."

Her perfect porcelain brow wrinkled as she tilted her head to one side. "Ah, don't be like that," she cooed. "You'll ruin all the fun. Besides, you don't want to disappoint your playmate." She cast Phoebe a sidelong look, leering at my friend.

"Don't fuck around," he snapped at her. "You won't like the result."

"Such language, young one." The vampire vixen waved one finger in a shame-on-you motion. "You don't want me to tell Eadric you're being ungracious to a guest, now do you?"

David let out a hollow laugh. "You seem to be under the impression you have the upper hand here."

She rose from the chair, her face transforming from fake innocence to outraged hatred. "How dare you—"

"I'd sit down if I were you," David warned.

"Or?" She crossed her arms and glared.

"I'll let the witch fry you."

Phoebe held up her sun agate and smiled sweetly. "Sorry, Clea. I don't take nicely to those who try to Influence me."

"What?" My whole body went rigid with shock. She'd tried to Influence a witch?

Phoebe shook her head and whispered, "I'll fill you in later."

A flicker of understanding, followed by rage, crossed Clea's face as she realized Phoebe had set her up. The moment passed and she assumed a bored expression. "Please. You were begging for a taste."

"Where'd you get it?" David asked Clea, ignoring my outraged glances.

She shrugged.

David stepped toward the bookshelves closest to him and rested his hand on a thin leather spine. "Perhaps you'd prefer different accommodations."

Clea leaned forward, rested her chin in her hands, and fixed him with a sneer. "Don't tell me you have a secret vampire dungeon?"

"Something like that."

Her smile faltered as they locked eyes.

"How do you feel about sunrooms?" David asked.

She visibly relaxed and leaned back in the chair. "I have yet to see one I can't muscle my way out of."

"There's a first time for everything." He pulled the thin book forward. I glanced around, looking for a secret passage or doorway. Nothing moved or revealed itself.

Clea laughed and stood. She stalked slowly toward David. "What's Eadric going to say when I tell him about this pathetic attempt at intimidation?"

"Nothing, since you'll be nursing a full-body, third-degree burn…if you survive." He launched himself, meeting her halfway in the middle of the massive room. I fell back, flattening myself into the bookcase behind me. Link hovered at my feet, already shifted and growling.

They spun, moving so fast I couldn't tell who had the upper hand until Clea smashed against the wall and David pinned her there with his hands around her neck.

"Last chance," he said. "Where'd you get the Influence?"

Clea spit in his face. "Fucking faery lover. You think I don't know who she is? We all thought since you'd turned, you'd finally come to your senses. Guess we were wrong. Now get the fuck off me before I tear her to shreds."

"Such confidence for someone in a position to get her neck broken."

"Breaking my neck won't stop me."

David let out a low, sinister laugh. "I know, but it will hurt. A lot."

"Sadistic bastard. Too bad you're such a waste. We could've had a lot of fun exploring that tendency." She turned her head and licked his hand. "Would have been nice to know last week when I had you in my bed."

I had to fight off a gagging reflex. David had been with *her*?

"Shut up," he hissed.

"Oh, don't want the little girlfriend to know all about who you've been doing while she pined away for her lover? What difference does it make, David? You know she won't have you now that you've turned vamp, and you didn't even have the decency to tell her before Eadric ordered you to—"

In one swift motion, David snapped her head back with a sickening crunch. Her head flopped to the side at an unnatural angle.

I pressed my back against the bookcase, trying to get as far away from the scene as possible, and ignored the stabs of pain shooting through my pinned wings. My knees buckled, refusing to support me. I struggled to stay upright. This was the second time I'd witnessed such violence from David. When we'd been together, he'd been sweet, gentle, loving. Now he was a monster.

David didn't say a word as he dragged a struggling Clea to the opposite side of the room.

I caught his tight expression in a full-length mirror just before he pushed the antique frame. The whole thing swung open, revealing a glassed-in sunroom. He hadn't been bluffing. One of Clea's red, patent-leather heels flew across the sunroom as he tossed her inside and slammed the mirror shut.

"Security glass?" Phoebe asked.

David nodded, running his fingers along the top of the mirror. The reflective surface evaporated, revealing Clea writhing in pain from her broken neck.

"How long will it take for her to recover?" Phoebe peered through the clear glass.

"Not long, since it looks like she fed recently." He glanced at the pewter cup. "Unless you drugged her."

She shook her head. "Not for a lack of trying though. Damn vampire had a grip on her drink tighter than this leather skirt."

David's gaze traveled the length of her body. "Nice disguise."

Phoebe preened. Actually preened.

"Stop it!" I shouted. "Just stop. Since when do you two work together? And what in the name of Lilith is going on? I swear, if someone doesn't start talking soon, I'm going to sic Link on both of you."

Phoebe stared past me with her eyebrows raised high.

I glanced over my shoulder to find Link back in Shih Tzu form, curled up on a throw rug. "Damn it!"

Phoebe put an arm around my shoulders and pulled me from the room. "If you'd had your phone turned on, I would've already told you."

A low growl rumbled from my chest.

She laughed. "I'm just sayin'. Come on. Let's get something to drink, and I'll fill you in. David, holler if that vamp so much as twitches."

He mumbled his agreement.

Phoebe led me to a pristine, high-end kitchen, outfitted with restaurant-quality appliances and solid black marble counters, a pleasant contrast to the slate-gray painted cabinets. The décor

would have been cold if not for the pop of red shelving behind
a section of glass doors. Not a thing was out of place.

Of course it wasn't. Vampires rarely ate solid food. They
could, they just didn't need to.

Phoebe pulled out a chair from the breakfast table and
nudged me toward it. I sat, focusing on the napkin holder
and the half-full salt and pepper shakers while she headed for
the refrigerator. I imagined David sitting with his morning
coffee and laptop as the sun highlighted auburn streaks in his
dark hair. The image unsettled me almost as much as seeing
Clea's snapped neck. That person was gone. Our days of lazy
Sunday mornings were over. I had to get out of here. Standing, I knocked the chair back in my haste. The resulting crash
reverberated through the house, and before I turned around,
I sensed David behind me.

"Go away," I demanded.

Silence ensued. If it hadn't been for my vampire senses, I'd
have thought he'd actually left.

Taking a deep breath, I righted the chair and sat to wait for
Phoebe. Two could play the ignore game.

"Are you all right?" David finally asked in a low voice.

"No, David. I'm not." I didn't turn to look at him. "You
just broke a woman's neck so the rest of us wouldn't hear about
your intimate affairs and whatever orders you have from Eadric.
Turning vampire doesn't change someone's nature that much.
So, no. I am not all right. Not at all. I just found out a man I
thought I loved is a raving, murdering lunatic!"

"Willow!" Phoebe exclaimed from across the kitchen. "Clea's
a vampire. She can't die from a broken neck."

"Let it go," David said, steel in his voice. "She's entitled
to her opinion." He retreated, and a moment later a door
slammed, making me jump in my chair.

"Wil," Phoebe said with a sigh.

"I can't believe you're taking his side," I accused.

"I'm not, but—"

My glare silenced her. She took slow deliberate steps in my direction as if waiting for me to cool down. Finally she handed me a bottle of juice and sat in the chair to my left.

Suspicion rose as I studied the bottle. Pomegranate juice. My preferred nonmagical drink. The one David had once claimed tasted like rotten grapes. "Did you bring these?"

Phoebe shook her head. "It was the only beverage in the fridge."

Odd. Had David stocked his kitchen specifically for me? I shook the bottle and then nodded to Phoebe. "Spill it."

She leaned back and stretched her legs. The miniskirt rose, revealing a splash of hot-pink silk. She caught my pointed look, grimaced, and wrapped a sweater over her bare thighs. "Work hazard."

"Why are you dressed like a high-priced call girl?"

"I'm in disguise."

"Obviously."

"Hunting a vampire."

I held my hand up in a stop motion. "Can we drop the buildup for once and just get to the details?"

"But that's my favorite part." She pursed her lips into a pout, then grimaced at my exasperation. "Fine. I was investigating your case and David told me Clea had been asking questions about you. I'm pretty sure she targeted him for information. Anyway, any vamp interested in a faery is unusual, so I started with her. Then she tried to Influence me and here we are."

My heart started to race. "Do you think she's the one threatening me?" I couldn't imagine why—I'd never even seen her before.

Phoebe shook her head. "I doubt it. She seems more the type to deal Influence. I called you, but we all know what a useless waste of time that is, so I tried David. He said he'd pass you the message but also offered his place for questioning if I tagged her."

Any vampire caught with Influence was breaking the law. As an agent of the Void, Phoebe was required to arrest her. I narrowed my eyes. "Why?"

"I figured it was as good a place as any. Turns out it's better than I imagined. Did you see that sunroom? Talk about a handy vamp death chamber."

"Yeah. Why do you think he had it installed?" Everything about him seemed so dark and violent now.

"No idea. It sure is convenient, though. This bitchy vamp has somehow got a hold of unsanctioned Influence. We need to find out how before Maude does, otherwise we'll both be kept out of the loop. He offered a place and I took it. End of story." She grabbed one of the bottles off the table and stalked out, heading toward the library.

I slumped. Phoebe was damn good at her job. I knew it better than anyone. But I couldn't shake the feeling something other than goodwill was driving David's cooperation. He'd disappeared for months. Now suddenly he cared?

I left my unopened juice on the table and followed Phoebe. Sulking in the kitchen while they interrogated Clea was unacceptable.

Just before I reached the library, an anguished moan followed by a frantic gasping sounded from the open door.

"Phoebe?" David's concerned voice followed.

"Phoebs?" I ran.

The witch lay writhing on the floor, her hands clawing at her neck. Her wide, dark eyes bulged from her maroon-shaded face.

"What did you do?" I fell to my knees, covered Phoebe protectively, and verbally lashed out at David. "Did you bite her?"

"No! Jesus, Willow. I didn't do anything. She took a drink of that juice and then fell."

"The juice?" The bottle lay on its side in a puddle at Phoebe's feet. I reached for it. The faint whiff of distilled cherries permeated my senses. I snatched my hand back. "Cherry Bomb," I whispered before bolting across the room to my purse, which was lying next to Link.

Frantic, I dumped everything out in a heap on the floor and rummaged, tossing keys, receipts, and other clutter aside. Where was my pillbox? "It's here somewhere. It has to be." I cursed, checking each pocket and compartment. With everything emptied, I dug through the mess again and spotted my baggage-claim receipt from my trip home. "No. No. No. This is not happening."

David had stayed at Phoebe's side, trying to keep her from hurting herself further as she convulsed on the floor. "What are you looking for?"

"The antidote. It's in my pillbox, but I couldn't fly with it. It's sitting on my dresser." I ran to Phoebe's side, scanning the room. "Did she have a purse?"

He didn't answer.

"David! Did she bring a purse?"

"I don't know. Check the desk." He smoothed Phoebe's hair back, trying to soothe her.

I jumped up, swallowing a frustrated scream. "Damn it! Where is Phoebe's emergency kit?"

Please let her be as prepared as she usually is. If not, I'd have to risk my own life to save her. The search of the desk came up empty.

There was only one other option. I'd have to extract the Cherry Bomb from her manually. Then I'd be the one burning from the inside out. My heart sped up and a thin sheen of sweat covered my entire body. I had a slight chance of surviving the poison. Phoebe didn't.

"As soon as I reverse the effects, get me home," I ordered David.

"You can't—"

"Just do it, David!" Between my tree and Talisen, I was almost positive I'd be okay. I kneeled beside Phoebe.

Link barked. Right next to him was a thin black jacket. Phoebe's.

I snatched it up, searching the inside pockets first. Right away my fingers brushed against a cool metal box. "Thank you, God!" I cried, ripping the pocket as I yanked the box out. I jimmied it open. Right there in the middle sat the deep purple pill I'd been looking for.

"Move." I shoved David over as I collapsed at Phoebe's side. Tilting her head toward me, I spoke clearly. "Phoebe, I have the pill. You just need to open your mouth, and I'll take care of the rest."

Tears streamed down her face. Oh, Goddess help us. Phoebe did not cry. Ever. Not from physical pain and certainly not from emotional pain. But some things are too awful to bear. Being eaten from the inside by the magic-enhanced drug, Cherry Bomb, was one of them.

Phoebe managed to open her mouth just enough for me to tuck the pill under her tongue. There was no hope of being able to swallow it. The intense burning caused by the poison would make that impossible. I'd formulated the pill to melt rapidly under the victim's tongue. It also made it easier to administer in advanced cases when the victim had already passed out. Phoebe wasn't far from that point.

"How long does it take to work?" David asked, looking skeptical.

"A few minutes. It's already started."

"She'll live?"

I turned hard eyes on David. "Of course. Why? Were you hoping for something different? Is that why you laced the drinks in your fridge with flesh-eating drugs?"

He sat back, his expression horrified. "You think I did this?"

"You offered your house to Phoebe. The drinks were in your refrigerator. How else did they get there?"

"You're being ridiculous. I haven't even been here for over a week." He leaned over to inspect the bottle. "Pomegranate juice? Does that look like something I would buy and keep around on the off chance I could lure a mortal here?"

I wasn't convinced. "You were quick to offer us your house. Quick to take Maude's deal. You know we both drink it. You didn't offer it to us, but maybe you were waiting until later. After we'd interrogated your girlfriend, you could've tried to off Phoebe. Or both of us." I unconsciously scooted over to Link.

The wounded look on David's face made him look as if he'd been shot. "I cannot believe you'd think those things of me. You *know* me, Wil. Does any of that sound like something I would do?"

No, it didn't. My confidence faltered. But nothing I'd learned about him since I'd gotten home made sense either. "I thought I did. Know you. But the David I knew wouldn't have turned vampire, and he sure as hell wouldn't have kept it from me."

"I told you I'd explain when the time is right."

He held my gaze, but I turned away and whispered, "I don't trust you anymore."

Phoebe stirred and a few moments later she sat up. "Ouch." She looked around. "What happened?"

"The juice was laced with Cherry Bomb," I said.

"Fuck me. No wonder I feel like my insides have been charbroiled." She pulled at her skirt, which had inched up, and winced.

"It'll hurt for about a week, but you should be okay. Or did you want to go see a Healer?" I grabbed her hand and squeezed lightly.

"No. No Healer."

I smiled. Phoebe would have to be dying to consent to a Healer. Then I sobered. She *had* almost died. "I could call Talisen."

She shook her head and climbed to her feet, wobbling with the effort. Taking a few careful steps, she moved to sit in a chair. "Thanks, but not now. I'll have him check me out when we get home. Right now we have a vampire to deal with."

I rolled my eyes. Phoebe never let anything get in the way of the job.

"I could use something to drink, though." She bit her lip, still pale. "I don't suppose you know if there's anything to drink here that's safe?" she asked David.

He shrugged helplessly. "I haven't been here."

"Wait just a second," I demanded. "You aren't even the least bit suspicious David planted the Cherry Bomb?"

Phoebe's eyes widened in surprise. "No. Why should I be?"

"It's his house. He's a vampire. He...he doesn't like you."

"And I don't care much for him." She glanced at David. "Sorry. Nothing personal."

He shrugged.

My fingernails bit into my palms. "Since when did you decide to take his side?"

She frowned. "I'm not taking sides. But we need David to sort out this mess. If he wanted me dead, he's had a few days to make a move. Spiking pomegranate juice on the slim chance I'd pick one up is lame. David's smarter than that."

I fumed, irritated they'd used the same argument. "Someone tried to kill someone. If it wasn't for us, then who?"

Neither of them said anything.

I rounded on David. "Who else do you bring here?"

He shook his head slowly. "No one. At least not anyone mortal."

Phoebe shrugged, a bit of color returning to her cheeks. That juice had to be meant for one of us. Most likely me. It was my favorite drink. David was my ex-boyfriend. I was the one with a death threat. Someone really did want to kill me. Or at the very least scare the shit out of me.

"We'll make a list of possible suspects when we get home," Phoebe said. "After we question the vamp."

I blinked, unable to process her lack of urgency. "Whatever. I'll take Link and go get you something to drink."

Phoebe smiled. "I'd appreciate it."

"Let's go, Link." Not bothering to conceal my frustration, I wasn't surprised to see him change to wolf form. It was just as well. We were in vampire territory.

"And get me a pick-me-up bar if you can," Phoebe called.

"Fine."

Twenty minutes later, Link and I returned to find David and Phoebe sitting close on a leather couch, their heads bent in conference. With David's enhanced hearing and Phoebe's tracking skills they must have heard me enter. I set the snacks on the desk and waited. Animated and engaged in their conversation, Phoebe appeared perfectly normal. No one would've guessed she'd almost died thirty minutes ago. Tired of being ignored, I bit back a snide remark and cleared my throat. "Would you like me to play good cop or bad cop?"

Phoebe grabbed a bottled water and nodded thanks. "Neither. We've got this."

"I suppose I'm just a liability then. Maybe I should wait in the car."

"You can if you want," Phoebe said.

I clenched my teeth and stalked to the mirror, studying the female vamp on the other side as she tentatively tried turning her newly healed neck. "Forget it. I'm not going anywhere."

Phoebe mumbled something I didn't catch.

"I'm going in," I said.

Before I could locate the lever on the window frame, David appeared and clutched both of my wrists. "You can't. She'll kill you."

The agony made my vision blur as pain seized my muscles. I twisted free as I stepped back. "A simple 'wait a second' would have done the trick," I spat. "Fireballs. That hurt!"

"I barely touched you."

"You obviously haven't gained control of your strength yet," I lied, rubbing my wrists.

David frowned as he gazed at the fresh bruises already blooming on my flesh. "Jesus. Sorry." He reached out, no doubt intending to inspect his handiwork, but I skirted sideways toward the glass.

"Fine. I won't go in unescorted, but don't think for a second you're leaving me out of this party." I pointed to the lever. "Open it. I want to know who that vampire got the Influence from."

Chapter 12

"Hold on a minute." David smiled and flicked a switch on the wall. "No need to let her out just yet."

Clea's head snapped up. She sprang to her feet and flew at the door, her fists pounding on the reinforced glass. "David, you son of a fucking washed-up vampire lord! Who the fuck do you think you're messing with? Let me out of here. Or I'll slice up that pretty faery of yours and stuff the remaining parts down your throat."

I shot David a look of disgust. "She's lovely. I can see what you saw in her."

Clea kicked the glass, making it vibrate, and turned to me. "Shut up, bitch."

"Witty, too." The switch David hit must have turned on an intercom.

He ignored me and spoke into a tiny speaker camouflaged in a miniature painting. "What makes you think I'm letting you out? I apologize if I left you with the impression I'm less than competent. Or did you think since we shared blood I would be bound to you?"

I gaped.

What? They'd shared blood? Only mated vamps did that, and it created a powerful bond. Mates shared a passion unimaginable to any other beings. Or so I'd been told. With that passion came overwhelming, all-encompassing lust, love, and pain. But never betrayal. David could torture her all he wanted, but if they were mated, he'd never kill her.

David met my eyes and shook his head ever so slightly. What did that mean?

Clea moved closer to the glass, her chin lifted and hip jutting out in defiance. "You're bound to me, you fucking prick. I can feel it right now."

Phoebe moved, situating herself next to David. "Sorry, honey. You lose. It's a spell."

Clea's face turned a pale shade of gray. "It isn't. We're mated."

"No," David said softly. "If you hadn't been so high last week, you would've realized I never drank from you. I told you that vamp dust would kill you someday. Looks like your time just arrived."

"You did!" she screeched. "I feel your presence in a way I didn't before."

Phoebe turned to David. "Damn, she's slow. Didn't I just tell her it was a spell?"

David nodded. "I think she's having trouble processing."

Our prisoner wasn't the only one confused. Why had Phoebe worked a bonding spell? And when? I'd left them when I went to the store, but as far as I could tell, they hadn't let Clea out of the sunroom. What were they up to?

Clea's eyebrows pinched together as she considered him. After a moment, her expression cleared. "You're lying. You wouldn't go through the trouble of creating a bonding spell if you're planning to kill me. Seems I'd be more likely to cooperate if I thought I was going to die."

David shrugged. "I had hoped for better cooperation. If you really thought we were mated, you wouldn't be as keen on killing me."

Phoebe leaned in. "I cast it right before he arrived. Tricky, huh? You remember the sex-appeal spell you asked for? Well, I didn't quite give you what you asked for."

Her lips moved in a silent expletive.

"Now you're seeing reason." David smiled. "Let's make a deal, shall we? You answer our questions, and I'll consider letting you see another moon."

Clea glared at David, her eyes blood-red with fury. "You're crazy if you think I'm going to cooperate with you, junior. I don't give a fuck who your sire is. Eadric will not stand for this traitorous bullshit. You kill me, and you'll be dead by sundown tomorrow. Although, it'd be worth it to see your ugly ass in hell."

"Who do you think sent me?" His predatory smile made me take an involuntary step sideways. Who was this new David? Cold. Calculating. Frightening. "Eadric is just as interested in your extracurricular activities as my companions are," David continued. "If you don't start cooperating, he might be inclined to come down here and torture it out of you himself."

Clea didn't break eye contact. Only the slight sag of her shoulders indicated she was starting to believe.

David's smile turned indulgent. "Why were you asking me about Ms. Rhoswen?"

She laughed. "That's what you want to know? You're an idiot." The vamp eyed me. "Sorry, honey. I was trying to figure out how to get him into bed. I wanted to know if we'd need to work out a threesome."

I suppressed a gag. She was truly atrocious. It was a good thing she was behind glass. David looked like he'd stake her if he had half a chance.

"Okay, that was TMI," I said. "Now, where did you get the Influence?"

Clea stared at her bare feet in silence. One of her red Jimmy Choos lay abandoned near the door. The heel had broken, presumably when David had thrown her in. Poor innocent shoe.

"It's simple, really," I said. "All we want to know is where you got the drug."

"I can't say." Her voice wobbled. "They'll kill me."

"Newsflash, sweetheart. You're dead anyway," Phoebe said.

Clea clamped her mouth shut. Finally, David spoke. "I have no problem leaving you there until the first rays of daylight start to burn your retinas. I'm sure that will get you talking, but I might be too pissed off by then to worry about what happens to you."

Clea pulled back, shoulders stiff with anger, and then she spat at the glass. The blood-tinged saliva splattered and one mucus-like string dripped down.

"Classy." Phoebe wrinkled her nose.

David glanced once at the gob of spit before raising his indifferent gaze back to Clea.

Her lip curled and she kicked the glass once more.

"I've got a call to make." David turned and closed the door with a soft click.

The vamp inside the sunroom hung her head.

"He's gone," Phoebe said, tapping the glass to get Clea's attention. "I don't blame you for not talking to David. Between us girls, I agree with you. He's a low-class, sick piece of shit. I'm ready to dust him myself, but if I do, it'll cost me my job. So, I'm just biding time."

"The fucker broke my shoe," Clea said as she pouted and glanced at her feet.

"Reason enough to end his sorry existence."

I settled into a black leather armchair beside Link and wondered how long David planned to let Phoebe try her good-cop routine. Clearly, they'd worked out a plan while I'd been gone at the store. It wasn't in Phoebe's nature to be soft on a vamp.

Clea's face turned dreamy. "I'd like to truss him up with a hook through his heart and watch his blood run dry."

Phoebe chuckled. "That has appeal, but how about nailing his feet to the floor while using a wench to stretch his arms until the bones separate? That sounds much more painful to me."

"While stabbing him with a red-hot poker."

I blanched as the pair continued to one-up each other in the gruesome department.

Phoebe turned somber. "Too bad we won't get a chance to implement any of those ideas. Well, not on David anyway. I'm going to write down the one involving wasps though. I had no idea vampires were allergic to them. Of course, wasps aren't night creatures, so how could I have known?"

Clea's head snapped up. "Don't be ridiculous. Just let me out and the two of us can take David tonight."

"I can't. I'm under orders to keep him alive. For now." A long blond lock from Phoebe's wig fell into her eyes as she shook her head, expression pained. She slowly ran one hand along the silver frame of the door. "Besides, this entry is tuned to David's energy. He's the only one who can open it. But if you tell us who you got the Influence from, he'll let you out. He has no other reason to see you dead."

"I'll kill him for this. One way or another."

Phoebe's lips quirked. "You need to work on your poker face. If you give him reason to believe you'll kill him, he'll never let you out."

The library door swung open and David strode in, tall and dark, brimming with power. Link jumped to his feet and growled. I didn't even bother trying to soothe him.

David ignored him and came to a stop beside Phoebe. "Any progress?"

She shrugged and took a seat in the leather chair next to me. "Some, but I'm pretty sure she was waiting for you to appear before spilling the dirt."

Clea hissed.

"Or not."

"Fine." David moved to the other side of the room and sat behind a massive banker's desk. "I have some paperwork to finish. If she isn't in a talkative mood when I'm done, we'll lock up and send a cleaning crew in the morning."

"You bastard," Clea spat.

When he didn't respond, she ran through a litany of colorful expletives.

"Impressive," I whispered to Phoebe. She nodded in agreement and picked up a travel magazine from the mahogany end table.

David traveled?

After a while, Clea calmed and mumbled something.

"Excuse me?" Tired of being an observer, I stood and moved to the glass door.

"Fuck." She ran a nervous hand through her mussed hair. "I got the Influence from Daniels. Lester Daniels."

"When?" I asked, holding my breath.

"Early this morning, about an hour before daybreak."

I caught David's eye before asking, "Was that before or after you murdered him?"

"What?" she demanded with what appeared to be genuine surprise. "Why would I murder my supplier?"

"No idea, but he's been dead for a good twelve hours. So you either saw him right before his death, you murdered him, or you're lying and you didn't get the goods from him. Which is it?"

She blinked, moisture gathering in her eyes. "Those bastards. I told him to watch his back."

Whoa. Since when did the vamp bitch have feelings? My lips formed into a shocked O. The vampire actually cared about a human? It wasn't totally unheard of, but I wouldn't have pegged Clea as the sensitive type.

I stepped closer and leaned against the glass, my tone gentle. "Who did it?"

She shook her head and a pale stream of pink tears slid down her cheek. "It had to be someone from the inside."

I waited while the vampire collected herself. Then our eyes met, my blue ones imploring her red-tinged green ones.

"It's your fault, you fucking sellout." She pointed a long, elegant finger in my direction. Her deep plum nail scraped against the glass. "You and everyone else associated with the fucked-up corruption of the Arcane. I told Lester to not trust any of you. Now look where it got him. Dead. Fucking dead."

"Are you implying Daniels had associations with the Arcane?" Phoebe asked, moving to stand beside me.

"How do you think he got his Influence license?" Clea sniffed.

"He worked for the university," I said. "The research department."

"That's what they want you to think. You of all people should know how they cover their tracks."

I glanced at Phoebe and an unspoken acknowledgment passed between us. The vampire could very well be telling the truth. The Void branch of the Arcane moved without boundaries. We couldn't rule out the possibility someone we knew and worked with was trafficking Influence. But why would they? Agents of the Void could get a license easily if they had just cause.

Clea stepped back and sank into a white wicker chair, the pink tears flowing faster.

"Crying won't help you," David said, ice in his tone.

The vampire sobbed and mumbled something incoherent.

"What did she say?" I whispered.

Phoebe tilted her head. "I think she apologized to Daniels."

"Why?"

Phoebe shrugged, unfazed by the sobbing mess in the sunroom. "Maybe she's holding something back. David, how long until sunrise?"

He stood and joined us. "A few hours."

"Good. After she's done with the hysterics, we can get to those torture techniques we discussed earlier." Phoebe turned to study Clea. "Maybe then she'll remember what she isn't telling us."

"Whoa!" I stepped between them and held up my hands. "I can't allow torture."

"She's a vampire."

"So is David."

Phoebe pursed her lips. "I'm not above torturing him if he gets out of line."

David growled.

A snarling wolf leapt in front of me, teeth bared as he forced David to take a few steps back.

David's eyes flashed red, a sure sign he'd lost all patience. "Call him off before I end this permanently."

"Good luck with that. Link wouldn't be an easy opponent even if a witch and a faery weren't here to help him." Phoebe turned to me. "How long do you think it would take the three of us to disable your boyfriend?"

"Damn it, Phoebe. No one's fighting anyone." I took a step forward and snapped, "Down, Link."

David's lips curved in satisfaction.

It took every ounce of willpower I could muster to not rescind my command and let Link do his worst. "If you ever threaten my wolf again, that pretty vampire face of yours is going to need reconstructive surgery."

David stared at me, then his eyes crinkled slightly.

"I'm not joking, David. Consider yourself warned."

His face cleared, and I knew he didn't believe me. Why would he? Vampires had super-healing abilities. He had no reason to feel threatened.

I turned my attention back to Clea. In the time we'd taken to have our petty argument, no one had been paying attention to the prisoner. Now she stood with a small knife aimed directly at her heart. *Where the hell did that come from?*

"What are you doing?" I asked, my voice steady.

"I know there's no way you'll let me live, and I refuse to spend the last moments of my life in service to any of you." She inched the knife slowly and deliberately into her chest.

"No!" I cried, grasping the frame of the door, searching for the secret opening. My finger caught and the enchanted glass shimmered. Before either Phoebe or David could stop me, I leapt through.

Clea watched me through already deadened eyes, the knife a quarter of the way in her chest. Once it passed through the heart, she'd be gator food. "I knew the witch lied. You could've let me out at any time."

"Did you expect us to?"

"No, but I had to try."

High-heeled boots clattered on the tiled floor, and I knew Phoebe had moved to stand right behind me. "How about we make a deal? You tell me everything you know about the Arcane and the Influence, and I'll make sure you live and neither of them hurts you."

Clea studied me, her expression lined with skepticism. "You're full of shit. Without your enhanced edibles, you're useless. You must think I'm an idiot. If they decide to kill me, there's no way you're strong enough to stop either of them."

"You underestimate the power of this particular faery," Phoebe said, her voice hard. "If she wants you to live, you will."

It wasn't a total blatant lie. My power went beyond infusing plants and baking. I could manipulate just about any living thing, which meant I could exert some control over Phoebe if I wanted to. David was another story. Technically, he was dead. My life magic wouldn't do anything but be sucked into the ether. Complete waste of time.

The air seemed to move behind me and I spun, coming face to shoulder with David.

Clea hissed and something silver clattered on the floor. The knife. She must have dropped it after yanking it out of her own chest. Clea tackled me, and I slammed into David, my entire torso erupting into a burning inferno from the vampire energy. David grabbed me, trying to shove me away, but Clea's rock-hard limbs trapped me between them. They each grabbled, trying to choke the other one. My ears rang in time with a loud, piercing scream, and only when I gasped for air did I realize the sound had come from me.

I jerked in agony, vaguely aware of Phoebe chanting in the background as the vamp fire intensified. Pain overrode my brain, my world spinning as lightbulbs exploded behind my eyes, and though I knew I was in the crossfire of a death match, everything went weirdly silent.

My world slowed to a dreamlike state and my life force left me. Was this really how I would die? Trapped between two vampires intent on killing each other? Of all the stupid—

A brilliant flash of white light flared. The two vamps froze and fell away from me. I crumpled, landing sprawled on the hard tile floor, its coolness easing the fire from my limbs. Blinking, I stared blindly into the dark twilight of predawn.

A shadow hovered over me. "Wil?"

I opened my dry mouth and tried to swallow.

"Wil," Phoebe said again.

"Yeah," I croaked.

"Thank the gods. Can you get up? We need to get back inside."

"Hmm." I didn't move.

"I think the door is going to seal. You have to get up." Phoebe tugged on my arms.

A tingling of comprehension worked its way into my consciousness. I lifted my head, clamping my hands over my temples as dizziness threatened to claim me.

"Crawl," Phoebe demanded.

I obeyed, placing one knee after the other as if I'd been force-fed Influence. When I breached the door into the library, I flopped back down, my head landing on something solid. Pain lanced through my cheek and I flinched. My eyes swam, fighting for focus.

"Lie back," Phoebe said.

I turned my attention toward her soft voice and my eyes cleared. "What happened?"

"I dusted them."

"Good." I closed my eyes, allowing Phoebe to place a pillow under my head. "Where's David?"

"Shhh. Just relax. I'll get you some water."

The floor creaked as Phoebe left the room. I lay motionless, waiting. A few moments later my eyes popped open. Wait, what did Phoebe say? *I dusted them.* Them? As in both of them?

"David!" I shouted, sitting straight up, my eyes locking on the limp male form crumpled on the floor.

Chapter 13

I half-crawled, half-dragged myself to David's side, tears blurring my vision. Peering down at him, I wiped them away. His slack face grossly contrasted with the wide, shock-filled eyes staring past me at the ceiling.

"No!" I threw my hands down on his rock-solid chest, pounding furiously as if I could pump life back into his still heart. "You can't die," I sobbed. "I forbid it."

Resting one trembling hand on his cold cheek, I gently tilted his head back with the other, determined to force air between his tight lips. I locked my mouth over his and my lungs constricted, straining with pressure. But my effort was met with a solid wall of resistance. I just didn't have enough strength to fill the concrete lungs of a vampire.

Vampire. Vampires don't breathe. Nor do they have beating hearts. As the realization crossed my panic-stricken mind, I slumped, laid my head on his statuesque body, and whispered, "We weren't finished."

All of the anger and resentment I'd harbored since David stepped back into my life fled. Why had I been so mean, so judgmental, about his life choice? Now he'd never know I hadn't stopped loving him.

None of that mattered. He was dead. My heart thundered in my chest and blinding fury took over my senses.

I wouldn't let him go. Not like this.

I sat up and rested my hands lightly on his chest. He really was gone—the contact no longer pained me—but I had to try.

No matter how futile the effort. I closed my eyes and imagined David as I knew him before, muscular and tanned from his oil-rig job with softer, less-chiseled features and an easy smile. I bent down to place a soft kiss on his closed lips, catching a trace of his familiar, faint woodsy scent still clinging to his silk shirt.

A single tear spilled as my breath caught and my heart seized. If my magic failed, I'd never again hear his deep laugh or peer into his midnight-blue eyes. Unacceptable. I'd find a way, even if it killed me.

Trembling, I forced in a steadying breath and let my senses take over. The granite shell beneath my hands radiated with emptiness, barren of any tendrils of life. I pushed my will deeper, searching, until finally a whisper of something familiar washed over me.

"David," I said softly, barely daring to believe a tiny piece of him still existed. It wasn't life energy, but something remembered, a recollection or shadow. I didn't care. It was something.

The sensation slipped through my magical grasp. I dug deeper, struggling to force my magic through David. A part of him was in there. I'd just touched a piece of his energy.

"Come on," I pleaded. Sweat rolled, stinging my already-damp eyes. I shut them tight and pulled my magic back, wrapping it around my heart, the place most concentrated with faery magic. Then I poured every ounce of love, fear, disappointment, and even the anger I carried for the vampire back into him on a wave of desperation.

My head swam with emotion as I registered the slowing of my heartbeat, but I held tight and forced the magic into him. The stream of power resisted, and I pushed harder, only managing to straddle the magic between my heart and David's soul.

It wasn't going to work. His soul was gone.

Beau's face flashed in my mind. "No!" I wouldn't survive another loss of someone I loved.

I barely noticed Link press his Shih Tzu body against my thigh as I wrapped my arms around David, pressing my chest to where his heart would be. A pale green cloud of magic swirled, engulfing us both. I didn't have the strength to keep forcing my will into him. Unwilling to let him go without a fight, I built a mental barrier in my mind, one solid glass block at a time. Once the last piece was in place, if I severed my magical link, the power would have no choice but to latch onto the one it was created for. In theory, anyway.

It worked with animals. At least that's what I'd learned in all the reference books. But I'd never tried it before, and David was a vampire. Ruled by death, not life. With my wall one block short of being mentally constructed, I severed my magic and finished the barrier. My strength waned, weakening my mental wall as my magic strained to return to me. "No! Go to David," I huffed out.

Blackness crept into the edges of my vision. My hands started to numb, and I knew I'd soon pass out, or worse. The plan wasn't working.

"Willow! What the hell are you doing?" Phoebe demanded, reentering the room. The door slammed with enough force to rattle the bookcase.

Startled, I let my wall crumble and the magic slammed back into me, overwhelming my senses with all the emotion I'd poured into it. My heart swelled with love while simultaneously shooting out darts of pain. Tears welled in my eyes and adrenaline made me tremble.

"Saving him," I shot back. Stubbornly, I leaned down and placed both hands on David's cheeks and whispered, "Take what I give you, for it is all I have." I pressed my lips against his and forgot everything as I forced my magic-filled love into his being.

The sensation crashed like a wave flowing in and out, siphoning small amounts at a time from me into the vampire. The resistance vanished like a dam had broken, and everything I had rushed into him in a startling whoosh.

I froze and opened my eyes to David staring at me, confusion and wonder lighting up his face.

"What happened?" he rasped.

"You died," I said and the room faded to white.

I sensed the familiar weight of Link's body on my feet and pried one eye open.

"Good morning."

Turning my head, Talisen came into sight. He sat against the wall, dark circles rimming his usually bright green eyes. It was then I noticed the lush leaf canopy overhead and realized we were in my room, on my bed.

"It's morning?" I asked, peering through the dim light.

"Afternoon, actually."

"Oh." Someone had closed my blinds, blocking the sun. I turned my attention to Link, who had moved to my chest. "Keeping an eye on me?"

"He's not the only one." Talisen gestured toward the door and Phoebe, standing inside the frame.

"Hey," I said in a small voice. Her narrowed eyes and thin, tight lips didn't bode well for the looming conversation.

She nodded and left without saying a word.

"Shit."

"She'll get over it." Talisen scooted closer, his kind eyes reassuring me I hadn't totally fucked up. "Can you sit up?"

"Not with Link on my chest." I tried to smile, but it felt more like a grimace.

"Down, Link," he commanded.

To my astonishment, Link scrambled to his elevator. When it was a few feet from the floor, he jumped down and sat obediently at the foot of my oak tree. Wow. He didn't even do that when I told him to get off the bed. It was the one place he thought he was truly the alpha in this partnership of ours.

"How'd you do that?" I sat up, then clutched my pounding head with both hands. "Ugh."

"Nearly draining your life energy will do that to you."

"I...Where's David? He's alive, right? I mean, I saw him alive. Did it work? Did I save him?"

Talisen gazed at me, his eyebrows pinched. After a moment he nodded. "He's alive, as much as a vampire *can* be alive, I guess."

I sighed in relief and slumped down.

"Wil?" His quiet, serious tone radiated with concern.

Uh oh. I cut my gaze away, avoiding eye contact, and stared at his big hands resting on my bed. A smooth black stone protruded from his fist. A worry stone.

Alarm bells went off. I sat straight up. "What's wrong? He's okay, right? I mean, I'm fine, or will be as soon as I get my strength back. Phoebe's okay. Is it Clea? Did she get away?"

"Clea? Who's that?"

"Oh. They didn't tell you about her." Of course not. It was Void business. "No one. Just a vampire Phoebe dusted."

He nodded an acknowledgment, his fingers working against the stone. "I see. And did David get caught in the crossfire, or did Phoebe mean to dust him, too?"

I frowned. So Phoebe had filled him in on at least that part. Had she meant to kill David? Was that why she was so mad? No, he worked for the Void. She wouldn't dust an operative, even if he was a vampire. "I'm not sure. I was standing between David and Clea when they started fighting. I'm pretty sure I would've died if she hadn't stepped in."

Talisen stilled his fidgeting fingers and reached out, gliding his hand down the side of my face. Time stood still as he peered into my eyes, intense and soulful. I opened my mouth to speak, but nothing came out.

"Damn it, Wil. Don't...ever risk yourself like that again." He leaned forward and wrapped me in both arms. "You're okay?" he whispered.

My breath caught, and I choked down a belated sob. "Yeah. I'm okay." My hands trembled and a shiver ran over my wings. It hadn't occurred to me until I'd heard the catch in his voice that I'd been in serious trouble.

Talisen's arms tightened. "Don't worry. I've got you."

I pressed closer, warm and safe in his strong embrace. A pit formed in my stomach. What had I done? Nearly killed myself to save a vampire. I started to shake in horror and clutched Tal, my fingers digging into his shoulders, holding on as tight as I could. I shouldn't have risked myself. Not even for David, but I knew deep down I'd do it again.

Once I found the strength to pull back, he relaxed his grip and pressed his lips to the top of my head. "Want to tell me about it?"

"I don't think I can," I said into his chest, guilt clutching my heart. What would Tal do if anything happened to me? How would he survive losing me, after what had happened to Beau?

"You can tell me anything."

Was that pain I heard in his voice? "No. I mean it was Void business. I don't think I'm allowed to disclose the details."

His body relaxed, and I almost smiled. "How about the magic and what happened with David, or is that too much as well?"

"I don't know. But I have to talk it out with someone, because I don't understand what happened. Phoebe has magical skills, but they aren't like faes'. Her knowledge won't help."

Talisen searched my eyes, his gaze serious and intense. What was he looking for? "You can trust me with anything. You know that, right?"

Ah. He'd been searching for the link. Our common thread of trust. "Of course I do." I took his hand and squeezed. "Sometimes I think you're the only one."

He raised an eyebrow. "Not Phoebs?"

"Oh sure. But it's harder. She has strong opinions on everything."

He laughed, and the sound helped ease some of my tension.

I smiled and flung the covers back, preparing to head to the bathroom. The shock of cool air-conditioning on my bare legs startled me, and I gasped, realizing I was wearing nothing but my tank top and black lace underwear. I scrambled to cover up as my face grew hot.

Talisen pretended mock innocence with wide eyes. "I didn't see anything."

I squinted. "Right. So you kept your eyes closed while you were healing my bruises?" After the scene at David's house, I should've been black and blue. The only way I could be blemish-free was due to Talisen's skills.

"Something like that." He hopped off the bed and headed toward the door. "I'll be in the kitchen making dinner when you're ready."

I nodded. Just as he was closing my door, I called, "Tal?"

"Yeah."

"Thanks."

"Anytime."

Link squeezed out the door just before Talisen shut it softly, leaving me alone.

Or so I thought. Twenty minutes later, I emerged fresh from the shower to find David sitting at my desk, dressed in black pants and a gray silk shirt. Not a hair was out of place. Impeccable as always.

"What the…?" I faltered and spun to the window. Sunlight seeped around the edges of my closed blinds. "How…I mean…" I shook my head and stared at him in confusion. Even though my room was dark, the sun was still up. He should've been dead to the world.

He shrugged. "I don't know. Usually it takes centuries to acclimate to daytime hours."

I eyed my closet. "Did you just wake up?"

He turned his head to follow my gaze and hesitated before speaking. "I haven't slept yet."

My wings started to spread, lifting me off the floor as comprehension dawned. I hovered and then forced myself to land with a soft thump. I sank to the floor and gazed up at him. "No vampire your age can stay awake during midday."

David nodded in a slow agreement.

"Then how…?"

He got up from the chair and settled on the floor in front of me. "You tell me."

I straightened my spine. "You think I did this?"

"Didn't you?"

"No!" It was impossible. Wasn't it? My magic couldn't change the basic makeup of a vampire. I couldn't breathe life into death. *Isn't that exactly what you did?* I mentally asked myself.

Tiny hairs rose on the tips of my wings, which fluttered involuntarily.

"Wil," David said. Nervous energy shot through my veins at the familiarity of my nickname on his lips. "What happened?"

Tears burned the back of my eyes again, and before I could blink them back, one silent tear fell. The words caught in my throat, and I mouthed, "You died."

"That's what Phoebe said, but how is that possible? I'm right here." He lifted one hand and studied it as if to make sure he really did exist.

I opened my mouth to speak, but a sharp knock at my door cut me off, followed by Phoebe barging in. "The director wants to see us."

"When?" David asked.

"Now."

"Okay," I fluttered my wings and rose gracefully off the floor. "David, we'll…uh, continue this when I get back."

"David's been summoned as well."

My head snapped up. "Wait, how's he going to go outside with the sun still up? And how does she know he's awake?"

Phoebe eyed David. "You haven't told her yet?"

"We didn't get that far."

I settled my wings, standing rigidly as a foreboding settled over me. "Tell me what?"

David's eyes crinkled, and he visibly tried to dampen a smile threatening to break through.

"What? Tell me what?" I demanded again.

Phoebe glanced at David and frowned. "Sunlight doesn't affect him at all anymore."

Chapter 14

"And Maude knows!" I cried. My heart stopped. Actually stopped. Now Maude knew I could alter a vampire. Maude, the one who'd found a way to manipulate me into producing Influence.

Not to mention all the other harmful pieces of unusual magic she'd somehow discovered and managed to get approved by the Void. How else could Cherry Bombs be allowed as sanctioned weapons? Anything that could melt a mortal from the inside should have been buried the moment it was discovered. Thank the gods I'd stumbled on an antidote. It had taken recreating the awful stuff and studying it for months, but I'd finally done it.

My blood pressure rose, kick-starting the frozen organ in my chest. I clutched Phoebe's arm. "Who told her?"

She shook her head. "Not either of us. At least not at first. She knew when she called to summon us."

"She must have a spy or surveillance on the house," David reasoned. "I was outside for quite a while after we realized what happened. She demanded to talk to me, and I had no choice but to relay the details."

"Do you have any idea what this means?" I asked Phoebe in a tight voice, my fingernails digging into my thigh.

She clutched my hand, eyes full of pity. "Yes, and I'm sorry."

The muddy tang of the Mississippi River wafting in the open window lingered in my nostrils as I fumed.

"Wait a second," Phoebe said. "You can't hold them against their will."

Maude leaned back, studying the three of us. Her casual pose smacked of victory. "I can. As you might recall, they both signed contracts. They belong to me."

"No one *belongs* to you, you selfish, power-hungry, two-bit excuse for a faery," I seethed.

"My dear niece, that is no way to talk to your auntie. What would your mother say?" Glee lit Maude's eyes and her black wings twitched in anticipation.

I took two steps and leaned over the desk. "My mother will be horrified when she learns what you've turned into."

Maude pursed her lips. "Then we'd best keep you here until you see reason."

David, who'd been silent ever since Maude had announced the Arcane's intention to sequester the pair of us until they'd exhausted a comprehensive set of tests, stood. "I cannot be party to testing from the Arcane. Eadric will not be pleased. You'll have to excuse me. He's expecting me."

David opened the office door to a pair of guards, each pointing silver spikes at his chest. He turned a steely gaze on Maude. "Call them off."

She shifted and crossed one ankle over the other. "We aren't finished here."

David eyed the guards, seemed to make a decision, and then closed the door and retreated to stand next to me. "How long will these tests take?"

She shrugged. "Until our scientists can replicate what Willow has achieved."

I balled my hands into fists and placed them on my hips. "No. I will not consent to these tests. What happened was a freak accident that I have no intention of repeating."

"Why do you need me?" David asked, ignoring me. "Seems you'd be better off using any other vampire."

Maude nodded her agreement. "True, and that is on the

agenda. But you must see testing your new abilities is in both of our interests."

David sat, crossing one leg over his knee. To anyone else he would have appeared casual, unconcerned. They wouldn't notice the tiny squint of his right eye. His one and only tell that he was seconds from losing his patience. Last time I saw that look was right before he'd fired one of the contractors who'd worked on his company's oil rig. The guy had made one too many inappropriate remarks about tasting my faery bits. Yeah, those bits. The ones reserved for my boyfriend.

"I understand the Arcane's interest in my situation, but I'm under no obligation to consent." David nodded toward the door. "And you must know your guards can't stop me if I decide to leave."

"But you won't."

He smiled with mocking amusement. "What makes you think so?"

Maude jerked her head in my direction. "You won't leave your girlfriend here unattended."

David didn't even spare me a glance. "You overestimate my affection, Director. Besides, Agent Rhoswen can take care of herself."

The heavy weight of betrayal made bile rise in my throat. What the devil was David up to? He really wasn't planning on leaving me here, was he?

Maude opened her mouth, shut it, then said, "You're under contract. You know the consequences if you breach the agreement."

"My *contract* specifically states my only duty is to protect Agent Rhoswen from any hostile vampires and to gather intel on my sire. Nowhere does it stipulate I would be used in your lab. However, I can't think of a better place for Willow to be protected from my kind. You are in the business of bringing down rogue vampires, are you not?"

I gaped at David as he stood and strode to the door. He really did plan to leave me here, and after I'd saved his life. The bastard.

"I'll be in touch." He pulled the door open once again. "Step aside, please," he said to the guards. "The director and I have reached an understanding."

Maude's face tightened, unable to conceal her growing anger. She gave a curt nod, and the guards retreated.

David stepped into the hallway, paused, and turned to meet Maude's furious gaze. "Oh, and don't damage my *girlfriend*. I wouldn't like it."

My aunt straightened, her wings spread wide. "Do not threaten me, blood-sucker. You have no idea the connections I have. One phone call and you'll be just as dead as that vampire whore you were associated with."

David gave her a wry smile but said nothing as he strode off. I sat, stunned, staring at the now-empty hallway.

"What are you waiting for? Follow him." Maude's tight voice came out terse with fury.

I jumped to Phoebe's side and we both headed for the door.

"Not you, Agent Rhoswen. You're needed here," she demanded.

Determined to give David a piece of my mind, I ignored her, but Phoebe paused. She turned. "Willow's my partner. I'll need backup if I'm to investigate a daywalking vampire."

"And I told you last week she wasn't your partner anymore. Her replacement is waiting for you in the conference room. Get going."

I stopped in the doorway. Phoebe, halfway between me and Maude, turned and met my intense stare. Keeping eye contact with me, Phoebe said, "I'm sorry, Director, but that is unacceptable. I cannot in good conscience leave a fellow agent here to be studied against her will."

"Do not push me, witch."

My muscles tensed at Maude's tone. I'd only witnessed her rage once before, and right then she was dangerously close to her breaking point.

Phoebe moved to stand in front of me, blocking me from Maude's view. "I am well aware of the Void's policies on studying abnormal gifts. Forcing someone to submit is illegal. Maybe if you take some time to formulate the studies you wish to conduct, Willow can look them over and make an informed decision. I'm sure she's as eager to understand what happened last night as you are."

"Phoebe," I began.

"Right, Willow?" she said loudly.

"Yes, but—"

"She isn't going anywhere," Maude bellowed. "Guards!"

Out of nowhere, half a dozen Void security guards rushed in. Where had the other four come from? Surely a vampire warranted more muscle than a defenseless witch and faery. The magic neutralizers in the lobby had seen to that.

"Apprehend them both." Maude pointed at Link. "And bind the wolf."

One of the guards did a double take and started laughing. "That ankle biter is a wolf?"

"Link, run," I shouted as I rammed my elbow into the side of one of the guards. He let out a surprised grunt and doubled over in pain. Link, unable to shift, growled a sad little dog growl but grabbed hold of the laughing guard's leg and didn't let go.

"Fuckin' dog." He spat and kicked him with his other foot.

Link yelped as he flew across the room but scrambled back up and launched himself at the back of his attacker. His jaws clamped down and the man roared.

I started to laugh at the Shih Tzu hanging from the guard's backside, but another guard grabbed my shoulders and slammed me against the wall. My cheek met the brick, scraping along the rough surface. "Ouch!" I yelped. "That wasn't necessary."

A linen sack came down over my head, muffling my cries. Tiny pinpricks of light penetrated the tight weave, saving me from total blackness. I only heard one last yelp from Link and an agonizing groan I thought for sure came from Phoebe before someone picked me up and carried me off.

"Let go!" I screamed, writhing in my captor's grip. "I'm an agent. I work for the Void. You can't do this."

The arms tightened around me, crushing my ribs. A voice I didn't recognize spoke in my ear. "Sorry, Rhoswen. Director's orders."

"Get your hands off me!" I kicked, ramming my foot into something solid. Pain darted through my ankle and I groaned as it went limp.

"I don't want to hurt you. This will be easier for both of us if you calm down."

No way was I going to make this easy for anyone. Not everyone in the Arcane was corrupted by power. Someone would step in. They had to. The agents of the Arcane were the good guys. Of course, I had a bag over my head and my wings were crushed against the guard. How could the good guys rescue me if they didn't know who I was?

Anyone who heard my screams would likely assume I'd been taken into custody for some wrongdoing. Not for unauthorized scientific testing.

That's when a lightbulb went off. "My name is Willow Rhoswen, Agent Rhoswen from the Void branch, and my rights are being violated. The director wants to use me for experimental testing. Someone help!"

"Sorry, Rhoswen. No one's here but you and me." A door slammed shut and the guard plopped me down on a hard surface. A chair of some sort.

Pain seared up my tailbone. "Argh!"

Before I could get my feet under me, cool, smooth metal glided over my right wrist, followed by a quiet snick of a lock sliding into place. I jerked both arms up. My right wrist bounced back, shackled to the chair, but the left collided painfully with a mass in front of me.

"Oomph."

I felt more than heard the guard tumble at my feet. Reflexively, I grabbed the linen sack and yanked. My eyes watered as the glaring bright lights blinded me. "My retinas! What's with the lights?"

"It's an interrogation room," the dark-skinned fae mumbled as he got to his feet. "You didn't have to hit me."

"You handcuffed me."

"Only because they could walk in at any minute and it would look suspicious if I didn't."

Hope blossomed and I stilled. Was it possible this guard could be on my side? I took in his solid, confident stance and met his kind, hazel eyes. "I don't belong here."

He frowned. "I know."

"Can you help me?"

With a pained expression, he shook his head. "I'm sorry," he croaked and moved toward the door.

"You can't leave me here." I tried to scoot the chair in his direction, but the front legs caught and it tilted forward. I slid to my knees. "They plan to use me as a lab rat."

He stared down at me, eyes conflicted, and then took a deep breath. "I truly am sorry, but I have kids to take care of. If I help you, they'll kill me." The metal door closed behind him before I could respond.

I slammed my fist on the concrete ground, barely noticing the reverberating pain shooting up my arm. Damn it all to hell and back. I'd just lost my best shot of getting out unscathed. No doubt Phoebe would be locked up soon. And Link...oh, gods, Link. Would anyone think to check if he was okay? And if he wasn't, would they get him help? Fear rushed through my veins. If those bastards hurt my Link, I'd kill them. Or at least spike their food with nettle sticks. The resulting month-long rash would teach them not to kick dogs...wolves, whatever.

For the next two hours I sat alone, staring at the ticking clock on the wall, waiting for my fate to be revealed. No one materialized to so much as even check on me.

After five hours passed, I started visualizing new and inventive ways to torture David. The asshole had sold me out. What on Goddess's green earth had he been thinking when he'd told Maude about what had happened? Then he'd just left me to fend for myself. The rancid, no-good, two-bit, fanged loser.

Less than twenty-four hours earlier, I'd saved his sorry ass. If I had to do it over again, I'd dust him myself. Now I'd have to hang him by his ankles and feed him his toenails for dinner. If he was lucky, he could lap up the resulting blood running down his legs.

Just as I envisioned dousing him in honey and unleashing a horde of fire ants on him, the metal door swung open.

Maude appeared in a white lab coat, carrying a clipboard. "Did you have enough time to clear your head?"

I stared at the door, refusing to engage.

Maude moved into my line of vision and pursed her lips. "No? Do you need more encouragement?"

Silence.

"I see. Maybe you've been too comfortable. That's fine. I could use a few more hours to formulate our experiments." She pushed an intercom button I hadn't noticed and said, "Brockman, bring the straps."

I jerked back and my eyes narrowed.

Maude chuckled, her cold eyes crinkling in amusement. "That got your attention. Would you like to start over?"

Through gritted teeth, I said, "You'll have to kill me first."

"Oh no, not me. Though the vampire might if you don't behave."

Chapter 15

Blood rushed to my head. My wings flared, stiff with anxiety. If a vampire wanted to kill me, I'd be dead. With my magical ability neutralized, I was vamp food for sure. I didn't even have any backup. Link and Phoebe were probably locked up somewhere. "You're willing to let me die if I don't cooperate?"

Maude opened the door, letting in a stocky agent holding leather straps. The white pentagram symbol on his badge identified him as a Void witch.

Oh crap.

He moved through the stark room, his face blank. In one swift movement he grabbed my right arm and secured it with another cuff.

"Hey!" I cried, kicking out. He sidestepped what would have been a painful blow to his treasured jewels and grabbed both my legs. Holding them tight with one large, unnaturally strong hand, he wrapped them with a leather strap, yanking hard until the edges cut into my ankles. No doubt his strength was magically enhanced. Powerless to stop him, I glared at Maude. "You're a pathetic excuse for an aunt."

She tugged at the straps. Forcing myself not to wince, I aimed a two-footed blow at her chest. With a disgusted snarl, she launched herself backward into a roll and landed on her feet. "Do that again, and I'll have those legs chained to the floor."

I clamped my mouth shut, pressing my lips together in a tight line. In my current state, I couldn't walk due to the restraints holding my legs together. But at least I could stretch them out or maneuver into another position if need be. Risking further bindings wasn't worth it just then.

"Considering your insubordination, it's within my rights to have you killed, but I don't think your cooperation will be a problem."

My ankles throbbed, and I swore silently. "You're awfully sure of yourself."

A cat-that-ate-the-canary smile transformed Maude's face. "I have information on your brother's death."

It took a moment for the meaning of the words to sink in. I struggled against the restraints as my wings fluttered in anger. I rose only a few inches before the wall chains jerked me back into my hard wooden chair.

"I see I've struck a nerve." The metal door creaked as Maude opened it. "If you behave, I'll consider filling you in."

"Murderer!" I screamed as the door clicked shut. I didn't know how or why, but suddenly I was convinced Maude was responsible for what had happened to Beau. If she hadn't done it herself, she'd had a direct hand in it.

A variety of toxic plants flashed in my brain. For the first time in my life, I seriously considered magically concocting an edible poison. One I would force-feed to Maude with my own hands.

After hours of lying on the cold floor under bright fluorescent lighting, I had a plan. As gratifying as it was to fantasize about a Maude-free world, murder wasn't in my chemical makeup.

But I could develop a neutralizing potion.

Something to render her harmless. Like shock therapy. And with a little help from my Truth potion and Influence, I'd have the ability to force Maude to incriminate herself. A vision of her in an orange prison jumpsuit sent a chill down my spine.

Maude's life in lockdown would be worse than death. All the concrete coupled with the total absence of nature would drain her until she was a shell of her former self. She'd exist in a perpetual zombie state, withered wings and all.

I suppressed a shudder. Death would be kinder.

Time to focus, Willow. One way or another, Maude needed to be neutralized. But first, I had to get out of there.

If I had any chance of being released from my chains, I'd have to appear to cooperate. Fighting back would only get me more restraints, or worse—drugged. I made up my mind to be the model prisoner. The only thing left to do was wait for someone to appear.

I didn't know how much time had elapsed, but when the door finally opened again, my dry throat ached and my eyes blurred from lack of sleep.

"Here." A large man in a pale blue uniform squatted and held out a cup with a straw. "Drink."

"What is it?" I croaked.

"Water. Go on."

I shook my head, not trusting it to be drug-free.

"Please, Agent Rhoswen. You've been left here alone for hours. You must be thirsty."

I turned and met hazel eyes. "Can't. Could be drugged."

"I promise you it isn't. Please, take the water. I couldn't help you before, but I can with this."

Taking in his lean build and dark skin, I finally recognized the guard. "You brought me here."

"Not out of choice. Now take the straw." He moved it closer to my lips.

A faint scent of hand soap filled my nose as I sniffed, trying to catch a whiff of any potions or drugs. I shouldn't trust him. He had, after all, told me he couldn't defy the Arcane. But I couldn't resist. With my throat screaming, I took the straw and drained every last ounce of the liquid and asked for more.

He nodded in approval. "I'll be back."

I tucked my bound legs up and pulled myself into a sitting position, ignoring the aches in my shoulders. Gods, what I wouldn't give for a hot bath.

The door opened again. Maude walked in, holding a clipboard. "Good evening."

It was evening? Did that mean I'd been there for over twenty-four hours? I squinted at the clock with blurred vision—a sign of dehydration. No luck. "Where's Link?" I asked before I could stop myself. If he was chained in a kennel…forget about cooperating. Maude could go to Hell.

She tapped a pencil on her chart. "Didn't anyone tell you? No, they wouldn't have since I ordered you sequestered. Time usually does wonderful things for unsavory attitudes."

I bit my tongue, unwilling to be baited.

"That's good. I knew given enough time you'd settle down." She barely concealed a smug smile. "Your shifter was released into Agent Kilsen's care shortly after you were detained last night."

Imprisoned was more accurate. "You mean Phoebe wasn't *detained* also?"

"Why would she be? You're the only one who refused to cooperate."

What exactly happened the night before? Hadn't Phoebe taken on a few guards while I'd fought my captors? I replayed the scene of Link leaping to my defense, but unless I was addled due to lack of food and sleep, I couldn't recall Phoebe getting into the mix. Why hadn't she fought for me?

Phoebe had to have a plan. And Link was with her. The black cloud hovering over my heart lifted. Help was coming. I had to be out of the restraints when the cavalry arrived.

"I see," I said, trying to keep my expression neutral and failing as a cramp claimed my left shoulder. I cried out, unable to even cradle it for support.

"Not very comfortable, I see," Maude said. "If you've decided to consent to the testing, I can have you released."

"Okay," I huffed.

"Excellent. Your guard will be in with dinner momentarily. He'll release you then." She didn't bother to hide the self-satisfied smile.

You've won this round, Auntie, but the battle is far from over.

Moments later, my sympathetic but useless guard arrived. Once my hands were released, I spent a great deal of time rubbing life back into my muscles.

"Here." He pushed a plate of fruit and a bran muffin in my direction. The fruit was on the verge of rotten and the muffin was stale, but I ate it all anyway. I needed whatever energy I could get.

"Do you have any protein bars?" I asked when he picked up the plate.

He frowned. "I don't think you're allowed special requests."

"Oh, come on. It's just a protein bar. I've barely eaten, and I'm starving. There are usually some in the conference room." I widened my eyes and pushed my lips into a pout. "Please?"

He glanced around the room as if checking for witnesses, then nodded. "Fine. I'll look, but I'm not promising anything."

I smiled. "Oh, thank you…um…I'm sorry, I don't know your name."

He smiled back. "Billings. Henry Billings."

The name fit his apologetic, meek persona. How in the world had he become an Arcane Guard? He was more suited for the accounting department. "Thanks, Henry. I owe you one."

He grinned and hurried out.

It took a few minutes to get my legs untied, and by then the overwhelming urge to use the restroom had taken over. I scanned my empty, one-room cell and grimaced. The place was worse than jail.

A few minutes later, the metal door creaked and Maude stepped in with two new guards. "We're ready for you. Behave and we won't use the restraints."

So much for my energy bar. "Restroom?"

"In a minute."

I nearly wet myself right there.

Gods save me from this. I promise to be a better person.

Guards flanked me on each side, offering me no choice but to walk with them through the halls of the Arcane. Most of the labs had wide windows with sinister metal instruments surrounding examining tables. I imagined vampires, were-wolves, and all walks of demons being dissected and studied on those tables. The Arcane was big on understanding anyone or anything who might be an adversary.

Was I the first faery to undergo such treatment? It was likely, unless Maude had uncovered another fae in town with unusual abilities. New Orleans just wasn't home to many of us.

Maude stopped and motioned to a door marked Women. "You have two minutes. After that, the guards will come after you."

I didn't hesitate. After I finished my business, I frantically searched the tiny room for any opening. No windows or easily removable ceiling tiles or vents in sight. I suppressed the urge to slam a fist into the wall. Instead, I took my time washing my face and finger combing my hair. When the door popped open, I raised my hands in surrender and continued with my escorts.

At the end of the hall, Maude produced a key and turned to me. "Your testing will be done here. I'll be monitoring from another room and the guards will stay positioned right outside, so don't get any ideas."

Maude pulled the door open and pushed me inside. I stumbled, barely keeping my balance with outrage clouding my brain. How dare she? I righted myself and then froze. The hair on my arms stood up as the overwhelming sensation of vampire hit my awareness. In reflex, I turned to flee, but the door shut tight with an ominous click. I knew without checking it was locked.

Sensing vampire movement, I dropped and rolled, only to hear chuckling from across the room. I stood and brushed invisible dirt from my jeans. His medium-length black hair covered his profile as he shook with mirth.

"What are you laughing at? It's not like you aren't locked in here with me."

He leapt. In one swift movement, he closed the gap between us. His close proximity forced me against the wall, his fangs dangerously close to the vein in my neck.

I gasped. "I'm the inventor of the Sunshine potion. This won't go well if you bite me."

Careful to not touch me, he placed a hand on either side of my body. He leaned in, his sharp teeth raking against my skin, leaving trails of pain. I pressed into the wall, barely breathing.

Ouch. Even their teeth made me hurt. He had to know I'd taste horrible, but that didn't mean he couldn't or wouldn't attack if he was hungry enough. How long had this one been locked up?

There was no way I was strong enough to fight him off. I had to try, though. I shifted, spreading my legs for a better stance.

His chest rumbled with laughter again while his mouth worked its way close to my ear. "It'll be better for you if you follow my lead," he whispered.

"That's the last thing I intend to do."

He pulled his head back and grinned. "Feisty. I can see why David keeps you all to himself."

I moved. One fist shot out, catching him in the gut. Before he could recover from the surprise, I brought my knee up, aiming for his man bits. Vampires might appear to be made of stone, but even they had sensitive areas. Anticipating my move, he shifted and caught my leg before I could connect. He twisted and a moment later I lay face down on the cold concrete floor, my back blazing from his contact.

"Get off!"

"Oh, I am, sweetheart. I am."

"Freakin' perv. Let me up." I struggled to keep the whimper from my voice. With his body covering mine, I feared I'd pass out soon.

Through the agony I barely noticed the hot breath in my ear until he whispered, "Chill out, Rhoswen. David sent me."

"What?" I threw my head back, clocking him.

He swore and gripped me tighter. "Attack me one more time, and I'll have no choice other than to hurt you," he said, his voice still barely audible. "They're listening and watching." When I didn't move, he rolled off me and raised his voice. "There we go, that's a tame kitten. We'll get along just fine after I've fed."

My mind whirled. David sent him? Was that good or bad? David had just strolled out, leaving me, as if he didn't give a damn. He hadn't even tried to bargain for my right to leave. Was he trying to help? I grimaced. If so, it was way too late. Even if what the vampire said was true, what could he do? He was imprisoned, too. And now he was going to feed off me.

I clamped my eyes shut. Maybe I should let him do it and get it over with. He would anyway, eventually. A weight settled in my stomach. Had I really just considered letting a vamp bite me?

The thought of fangs in my skin made me queasy.

I sat up and eyed the vamp. "What's your name?"

His lips curved into a half smile. "Getting friendly now? I like that."

I gritted my teeth and sent him my she-devil glare.

His smile turned into a full grin. "Damn. I like a girl...uh, faery with attitude."

"The name is Willow. And yours would be...?"

He shook his head, still grinning. "Nathan. Nathan Fuller."

I gaped and then closed my mouth, remembering I was being watched. I'd heard about Nathan. David had talked about him. Hell, I'd even spoken to him on the phone once when I'd answered David's phone. My eyes met his, and he gave me the tiniest of nods.

Maybe David did have a plan. Although for the life of me, I had no idea what it could be. He'd now gotten his girlfriend—or ex-girlfriend—and his supposed best friend locked up in the Void division. Escape would be impossible. Or at least highly improbable.

"So the easy way or the hard way?" he asked.

"Excuse me?"

"They want me to feed from you, and it appears we won't be leaving this room until I do."

I crossed my arms over my chest. "What makes you think they're ever letting us out?"

"I was told to feed, then they'd run tests. I don't see any equipment here, so it seems logical we'll get moved."

"Who told you that?"

"Some faery in a white coat with black wings."

"That's Maude." I sought out a camera in the corner and glared at the lens, knowing she could hear me. "She lies."

He nodded. "They all do, but I have to eat anyway. I haven't had a drop in five days."

I scooted back in reflex. He must be really old, or he'd have lost control and taken me already. Five days was way too long to go without eating for most vamps.

He moved closer, slow and deliberate. "I don't need much. It'll be over before you know it."

Fear kept me rooted to my spot. "But the Sunshine potion."

"I know, little Willow. Don't worry. I've tasted it before. It isn't as bad as everyone makes it out to be."

Crap, crap, crap.

His words pushed my fear into full on terror. He'd tasted Sunshine-tainted blood before. He didn't mind? It wasn't that bad? Had David really been best friends with a vampire for all those years? Is that why he'd turned?

One hand came to rest on my shoulder. Through my fear, I didn't even register the pain it caused. His eyes stayed trained on mine, and when he gently guided me into a prone position, I didn't resist. My mind had gone blank.

His head came down, the strands of his black hair creating a curtain, shielding our faces from prying eyes. He mouthed, "Don't worry. I won't hurt you."

A faint *no* tried to work its way out of my mouth but died on my lips.

He'd already pressed his teeth to my neck. Oh, God. I could feel my vein pulsing against him. Thump, thump, thump. I squeezed my eyes closed and waited, knowing with one puncture my whole neck would be on fire.

Chapter 16

I wasn't wrong. It hurt. A lot.

Nathan's fangs pierced my skin in one smooth motion. Liquid acid exploded, charring my insides instantly. His arm circled around me, forcing me closer.

Molten lava flowed through my neck, my chest, my back. I clenched my fists, frantically pounding against his shoulders in protest. My head swam and a vision of Phoebe's sun agate entered my mind. One flash and the horror would end.

Screaming, I bucked.

Nathan dropped his hold and scrambled to the opposite wall.

I curled into a ball, whimpering as I rocked.

Slowly, the pain succumbed to a dull ache, leaving me battered and bruised. After a while I sat up, wincing with each tortured movement.

Nathan still sat against the wall, watching me.

"What?" I asked.

"What happened?"

My vision blurred as I glared. "You bit me and took enough blood that I probably need a transfusion. Or some orange juice at the very least."

He frowned, studying me. After a moment his frown deepened.

"What?" I asked again.

"First of all, I barely took any blood from you. Way less than I normally would because, let's face it, you don't taste that good."

"It's the Sunshine potion."

"Obviously. Second, you have a purple bruise right where I bit you."

Fingering my neck, I carefully explored the puncture marks. Curiously, they didn't hurt at all. How was that even possible? The rest of my body still suffered from his assault. I met his eyes and clamped my hand over the area.

"I don't leave bruises," he said.

"I bruise easily."

"I can see that." His gaze traveled over me from head to toe, lingering on sections of my exposed skin.

I glanced down at the black-and-blue marks visible in every spot he'd touched me and scowled. Perfect. Talisen had his work cut out for him. Again.

"Do you have some sort of disorder?"

Yes. A vampire one. I focused on the wall just above his shoulder.

A key rattling in the door drew his attention, and I was saved from further questioning as two guards walked in. I jumped to my feet, ignoring the screaming in my back.

The shorter one reached for my arm, stopped, and took a moment to study my appearance. "Whoa, looks like the vamp roughed you up. Shoulda played nice, I guess."

I jerked back, bumping into the other guard.

"I'll take her," said the tall, lanky one.

"Whatever. I don't need a hassle tonight, anyway. You, vamp. You're with me. Don't try anything stupid, or I'll have to tag you." Shorty crossed the room and pulled out a small gun designed to hold vampire tranquilizers.

"Don't accidentally shoot yourself with that thing again," Lanky said to his partner. "I have better things to do than take care of your sorry ass."

Shorty glared and aimed the gun toward my guard.

Lanky snickered, gripping my arm.

"Hey!" I protested.

"Move it, sister." He pushed me through the threshold and practically dragged me down the hallway.

"Where are we going?" I demanded.

"The director ordered tests."

"I know that. Are we going to another lab?"

He ignored my question and turned left at the end of the hall. I knew this wing. There weren't any labs here. But there was a stairway to the dank basement. It was rumored to be magically enhanced to stay dry despite the New Orleans high water table. I flared my wings as if they could somehow slow us down. The basement door came into view, and a familiar panic rose in my chest. They wouldn't do scientific testing down there, would they?

They would if it wasn't sanctioned.

I dragged my feet and stumbled.

"Keep up," he barked. "I thought you fae were supposed to be graceful."

"Not when we're locked up for hours and then fed to vampires."

He laughed. A bemused, casual laugh. It didn't fit the don't-mess-with-me attitude he had going on. "I guess that could make anyone feel off-kilter."

"Off-kilter. That's one way of putting it."

His steps quickened as we neared the door. I scanned my surroundings, desperate for any means of escape. If I stayed, at best I'd have weeks of painful testing ahead of me. At worst, Maude would find a way to capitalize on whatever I'd done to turn David into a daywalker. It was the kind of power my aunt couldn't resist. Maude would kill for it if she had to.

There had to be a way out.

Lanky stopped and positioned me between him and the basement door.

Now or never.

The guard fumbled with his massive key ring. Why the hell hadn't I paid more attention when Phoebe tried to force me into those self-defense classes? What would she do? I mentally scoffed. Knowing her, she'd verbally bait him and then kick the shit out of his sorry ass.

I had no such skill.

Instead, I used the only strength I had. I stomped my foot down hard on his instep. He jerked his head up, eyes wide with surprise. I seized the opportunity to tackle him to the floor. My knees connected with the tile, and I swallowed the cry of agony caught in my throat. Flailing forward, I elbowed him in the back. Then, with a surge of determination, I thrust my burning wings and flew down the hall. My heart thundered, adrenaline fueling my flight.

"You bitch! Get back here or those wings will end up in a paper shredder."

Yeah, right. Like that was going to convince me to turn around. I pumped my wings faster than I'd ever even attempted before and soared down another dark and empty hallway. Where was everyone? It must have been after-hours or the place would be teeming with Arcane staff.

Excited voices drifted from an open door. I cut to the left, ending up in a dim, narrow hallway I didn't recognize. Trying to get my bearings, I slowed. All I needed was a way out. Every room offered nothing but abandoned stainless steel tables and old lab equipment. Not a window in sight.

Couldn't a girl catch a break?

I whirled, intending to go back, but the loud clatter of heavy boots on the tile stopped me mid-flight. Heart hammering, I landed silently, darted into the nearest room, and tucked down beside the door, waiting.

The steady footsteps grew louder. I held my breath, trying to keep every muscle in my body completely still. As the footsteps moved on, I stifled a relieved sigh.

Then silence filled the hallway. One second. Two. Three. The clattering of the heavy boots resumed, moving in my direction. Oh, no. This was *not* happening. I hadn't even breathed, let alone made a sound.

The noise stopped just outside my door. My heart pounded in my ears. Now what? I squinted through the darkness, searching for better cover. That was when I saw it. A stainless steel cupboard illuminated with a tiny streak of ambient light and a partial reflection of my shadow right in the middle of it.

Shit.

I rolled just as my tracker lunged into the room. My shoulder hit the floor, and I kicked out as a hand clamped over my ankle.

"Ouch," my assailant huffed. "Willow, for God's sake. Stop it."

I froze and studied the guard in front of me. She wore the standard uniform of polyester pants and a crisp, white button-down shirt. Combined with the mousy brown hair and nondescript wire-rim glasses, I never would have recognized her had she not spoken. "Phoebe?"

"Yes, damn it. Hurry up before they find us."

I scrambled to my feet and waited as Phoebe scanned the hall. "Why were you stalking me?" I asked her in a hushed tone.

"I had to be sure it was you. Now shush and follow my lead. We can't afford to have you mess this up again."

"Mess up? Again?"

"Shhh." She grabbed my arm and marched me back down the hallway toward the basement door. When she spoke, her voice was deeper and tinged with maniacal glee. "One more stunt like that, and we'll be forced to use the manacles."

She grinned at me and kept up the illusion of dragging me along as we passed another guard, one I didn't recognize.

"Looks like you could use some help." He fell in step with us.

Phoebe glared. "Are you insinuating I can't do my job? Just because Phelps is an idiot and lost her doesn't mean I need someone breathing down my neck. Get back to your post. This one isn't going anywhere." Phoebe yanked my other arm, closing them behind my back as she propelled me forward.

"Watch it!" I complained loudly.

"Shut up. You're lucky I'm letting you walk under your own power." Phoebe yanked me back, and pain shot through my shoulder. If I hadn't known better, I'd swear she was enjoying the act.

A trickle of doubt ran through my mind. Was Phoebe really on my side? She hadn't said a word or tried to stop the guards from dragging me from Maude's office.

Stop it! Of course she's on my side. Why else is she disguised as a guard?

Phoebe was the one person I could trust besides Talisen. Whatever had happened earlier, she had obviously thought it was the best plan.

"Calm down," the other guard said. "I'm not insinuating anything. Just thought you might want some backup."

"I've got plenty of backup right here." She tapped a tranquilizer gun on her hip. "Now get lost before I use it on you."

"What the hell? Are you threatening me?"

"Damn straight. I don't know you..." She peered at his name tag. "Fitz. All our asses are on the line with this one. High priority with the director, and I'm not taking any chances. So either you back off, or I'll put you out. Your choice."

"Fine." Fitz held his hands up in surrender. As he retreated, he mumbled, "That witch needs professional help."

I stifled a bubble of laughter, not daring to look at Phoebe. A moment later, Fitz disappeared around the corner.

"Come on." Phoebe broke into a run, forcing me to use my wings to keep up.

"Where are we going?"

"Out." Phoebe took a sharp turn and stopped in front of an emergency exit. She held me back, keeping me from bursting through. "I need to silence the alarm first. We stand no chance if it goes off."

At least one of us knew what to do.

Phoebe produced a small bag from her pocket and pulled out a pinch of gray powder. Sprinkling it over a sensor, she chanted an incantation, waited a few seconds, then blew the dust away. A faint sizzle ran down the wire and ended with a pop.

"How did you do that without your magic?" It should be neutralized.

"Guards aren't stripped of their magic."

Right. They would need it.

"Now go!" she said and pushed me out first.

A blast of thick humidity hit me in the face, the stark contrast to the stale air-conditioning making it hard to breathe. I sucked the air down, trying to acclimate as I scanned the parking garage.

Phoebe bolted through the door right behind me. "What are you doing? Move it."

"I don't know where the car is," I snapped, running to catch up.

"No car. They're watching me. Someone is waiting a few blocks over." A few feet from the exit, Phoebe pulled up short, holding her hand out in a stop motion.

I froze mid-step and almost knocked her down. "What is it?"

"Look at what we have here, boys," Fitz said. "Nice try, Kilsen. You almost had me going there for a minute."

The guard Phoebe had threatened was flanked by four other guards.

Phoebe stepped forward. "You think you and your wannabe agents can take me?"

He laughed. "It's five to one unless you count the faery, but she's useless and you know it."

"Hey!" I cried, insulted, and peered around as my skin started to tingle. Someone else was coming.

"That just goes to show how stupid you are. I suggest you and your cronies step aside and forget you ever saw me, or you'll regret it," Phoebe said.

Fitz signaled and the guard clones spread out, blocking our path.

Phoebe pulled out her tranquilizer gun. "Last warning."

Fitz's eyes narrowed. "It's not loaded. Besides, you can't hit all of us at once."

"I don't have to." Phoebe nodded past them. The one on the far right turned and gasped. No less than a dozen vampires stood behind them with David and Eadric at the center. All five guards brandished their sun agates, aiming them at the vampire gang.

"Oh, good. You've made it," another voice called from behind us.

I whipped around and stared at Maude dressed all in black, emerging from a shadow.

What? She'd been expecting them. This couldn't be happening.

"Tell your goons to back off," Eadric said.

Maude quirked an eyebrow but waved a dismissive hand toward the guards. "Stand down."

One by one, they each moved to stand behind my aunt. Eadric sent her an indulgent smile. "Thank you. We've got it from here."

"Don't rough her up too much, Eadric," she warned. "We still need to finish our testing. But as a consolation, Kilsen is all yours. She was just a tool and of no consequence."

Phoebe turned, her face pinched in anger. "You set me up?"

Maude laughed. "Don't be a fool. Did you really think it would be so easy to penetrate my security? When it comes to my niece, you've never been trustworthy. Now I have my proof." She waved to Eadric. "Get rid of her."

"I don't think that will be necessary," Eadric said. "Ms. Rhoswen, will you join me?"

I took a step back, met Phoebe's eyes, then David's, and finally turned to Eadric. "Why would I do that?"

"I'm asking you to accept my protection."

Dread snaked its way through my limbs. I'd already accepted his protection, but now he was forcing me to acknowledge it publicly. Everyone would know he considered me one of his own.

My worst nightmares stood both in front of and behind me. I gulped. "From what?"

"Not what, but whom." He gestured to Maude.

"What do you think you're doing, vampire?" In an instant, Maude hovered right behind me, her powerful black wings working up a wind. "I demand you live up to our agreement and apprehend these traitors."

Eadric barely glanced at her. "Change of plans, Maude. You lose this round."

"You were working with the director?" Phoebe shouted and rounded on David. "Goddamn you. I knew I couldn't trust a blood-sucker. You were going to give us up? Fuck!"

He gave a small shake of his head as he kept his eyes trained on me.

"They've been playing both sides the whole time." I met David's gaze. "Haven't you?"

He ran a nervous hand through his hair. "You don't understand."

"He's only done what he thought best. Do not blame him." Eadric moved toward me, his hand stretched out.

Maude hissed and grabbed my arms, dragging me back. "She's mine. Of my own blood. You will not take her from me."

I grunted and tried to twist from her grasp. She clutched tighter, digging her fingers into my flesh. "Let go, you evil bitch!" I cried, jamming my elbow into her gut.

She only grasped me tighter. Damn it if I wasn't tired of being manhandled.

Eadric took a step. "You don't want to test me, Director."

A warm trickle of power brushed my skin as my aunt started to spin a spell. I struggled, trying to escape her grip. "No!"

Maude levitated, pulling me above the crowd with her. Something cold and dark prickled as Maude's power intensified. I gasped, a chill turning my limbs numb. Whatever spell she was spinning, was bad. Probably life-ending bad.

The vampires swarmed and then scattered as flashes of light illuminated from the guard's sun agates. Only Phoebe and David remained.

Maude chanted something in Latin. Panic took over. If someone didn't do something soon, Maude would kill them all. "Phoebe!"

Her eyes narrowed as determination settled on her features.

My muscles started to seize as the chant grew louder. Phoebe's mouth was working, but I couldn't hear her. Unwilling to go without a fight, I did the only thing I knew to do. I opened myself up and took in Maude's spell.

My entire body convulsed, fighting the curse. I briefly wondered if my plants suffered as much when I stole their life before I rejuvenated them.

The thought triggered an idea. I tensed as I reversed the energy and forced Maude's magic back into her.

She jerked her hands away, sending me falling to the ground. If I hadn't been focused on releasing something dark and painful, I might have remembered to flex my wings. Instead, I landed on one of the guards, arms and legs flailing. Rolling off, I huddled near a car, trying to make sense of the scene in front of me.

The vampire gang reappeared, quickly neutralizing the remaining guards. My aunt swayed above me, struggling to keep airborne. Her body dipped and, her face tight with concentration, she flexed her wings, stabilizing herself. She glanced down at me, hatred in her black eyes. "This is far from over."

Before I could respond, she sailed out of the garage and disappeared around the corner. Phoebe took off at a dead run after her.

"Willow?" David said.

"Huh?"

He wrapped me in his arms and pulled me into a hug, resting his chin on my head. "Are you okay?"

I stiffened and looked up. "Your touch doesn't hurt anymore."

Chapter 17

The aged water oak's limbs created a cocoon around me and an illusion of safety from the vampires within the large Victorian mansion. My wrecked body soaked in the tree's cool life force, slowly healing itself.

I'd been too drained to worry about where David was taking me after we'd left the Arcane parking lot. To his credit, he bypassed the house and led me straight to the majestic oak in the gardens. He hovered awkwardly until I shooed him away, then he disappeared. I hadn't seen anyone since. Not even Phoebe, though I knew she had to be here somewhere.

They were probably all inside, discussing some new plan they had no intention of sharing. For days they'd been keeping me out of the loop. Phoebe had started investigating my case without telling me and even gone so far as to work with David to get information out of Clea. Hell, together they'd worked a spell on her. And who knew what David was up to? This was my life on the line. I'd been the one threatened. Not them. The least they could do was tell me what in God's name was going on.

Forget them. All I wanted was Link, Talisen, and a hot bath. And maybe a little Chimney Bark. If there ever was a situation for a little indulgence, this was it.

Anything to stop the confusion swirling in my mind. David's touch didn't hurt anymore. A warm sensation, something eerily close to hope, blossomed in my chest.

Stop it. You're not in high school. And I was mad at him right?

I squashed the traitorous desire. David was not mine. Not anymore, and he never could be. Fae did not get involved with vampires. Ever. I didn't even know if this new development would last. Maybe Nathan's bite had left me with a short-term immunity. Was that possible? No one could answer that question. I was the only faery I knew affected with the insane vampire curse.

A door slammed shut, and a moment later Phoebe appeared across the garden. Her wig was gone, revealing her spiky, black, one hundred percent Phoebe hairdo.

"Hey." She sat on the grass next to me, tucking her jean-clad legs under her.

I picked at a blade of grass, staring up into the oak.

"Link's at home with Talisen."

I'd figured as much, but that was good to know.

"Maude got away," she added.

I nodded. Of course she did. "Are we fugitives now?"

"Likely. If I'd caught her we could've brought charges. But there aren't any witnesses except you, me, and Eadric's vamps. Maude will have already built a cover story. To go to the Arcane now is suicide."

I turned hard eyes on Phoebe. "What the hell is going on?"

"We should wait for David. I have questions, too."

Barely restrained rage propelled me to my feet. "No! I want to know whatever it is you know. You've obviously been working with David. From the scene with Clea to the vampire Nathan to whatever is going on here." I gestured toward the house. "The very fact you've been invited here after all the vampires you've apprehended over the years is ludicrous. Spill it."

Phoebe's brows lifted and her mouth dropped open in a sheer display of shock. Outbursts and temper tantrums weren't usually my MO. "I've been trying to protect you."

"Don't you think things would've gone easier if I'd been in on the plan?" I straightened my shoulders and raised my chin in offense. How dare they treat me like I was just another human, too weak to fend for myself?

Phoebe rose, locking her gaze on mine. "I promise you, nothing I've done has been intentionally behind your back."

I stared her down for a few beats, then sighed, too tired to argue. "Fine, but start from the beginning."

"I already told you what happened with Clea. But speaking of her, I took the pomegranate juice bottles to the lab for testing a few days ago while Talisen was watching over you. The results are in: your fingerprints, mine, and a trace of carpet fibers."

"Any idea where it came from?"

She nodded. "I sent David to check out Clea's apartment. Perfect match."

My eyes went wide. "We were her target?"

"Maybe. I'm not sure. I tagged her, remember?" She flopped down on her back and fiddled with a fallen leaf. "But I'm certain the poisoned juice came from her."

And David knew her. Like *knew* her, even though he obviously hadn't cared for her. What was I missing? "David has to know more than he's letting on. They'd spent time together. Remember Clea said…" I didn't want think about the two of them in bed together, much less say it out loud.

Phoebe studied me and her eyes narrowed. "You mean they had a relationship."

Heat crawled up my neck and burned my cheeks. "No."

"Yes."

I swallowed and avoided her gaze.

She sat up, her eyes pinning me to the tree.

"Fine, yes." I backed up against the tree for support. "But something else is going on, and I intend to figure it out."

"Okay, but I still say he was just investigating the Influence."

Maybe she was right. He could've been looking out for me. But that didn't explain why he suddenly turned vampire sometime in the last three months, or why he didn't even tell me about it, or why he disappeared from my life. In order to turn, he had to have some sort of relationship with Eadric. Powerful vampires like him didn't turn just anyone. David had never told me about his long-term ties to the vampire world.

He'd lied by omission. I had no reason to believe he'd told the truth about anything.

I stood, staring down at Phoebe. "Tell me what happened after Maude had me locked up."

Phoebe closed her eyes, and I swear she was asking the Goddess for strength, or maybe patience. When she opened them, she put on her no-nonsense face. "If we'd fought, all three of us would've been locked up. Once I saw what Maude wanted, I knew she'd never let you leave. You knew it too."

I didn't respond.

"David, and I agree with him, walked out so he could formulate a plan to get you out safely. I followed his lead. The first thing he did was call Nathan, who apparently has spent time in the past investigating the Arcane. One of the ways he gets in is by volunteering for testing. I don't know how he did it so fast, but next thing I knew, David said Nathan got himself recruited for Maude's latest experiments, and based on Nathan's intel, we formed a plan."

"To bust me out?" And ruin our lives and careers?

"What else were we supposed to do? Neither of us was going to let you go through that." Her eyes flashed with anger.

"Sorry." I slumped. Her career was in greater danger than mine. I had the store; she only had the Arcane. "I should be thanking you, not biting your head off."

"It's okay."

"Not really." I gave her a small smile. "Thanks for busting my butt out of there."

She laughed. "Any time."

"All right, what did I miss?"

She pulled out her silver beetle bugging device. "I have it all right here, but there's something you need to know first."

Now what? The concern in her voice shot a dart of panic through my otherwise numb heart. "What is it?"

She took a deep breath. "Eadric is David's adoptive father."

I frowned. "I know. Eadric turned him."

"No, Wil. I don't mean vampire father. Eadric adopted David when he was ten. David has been a part of Eadric's family for twenty years."

An hour later, I stormed into Allcot's house. Unfamiliar vampires lay draped over the ornate antique furnishings. No one moved, but every pair of eyes tracked me. I stopped in the middle of a sitting room, my hands balled into fits on my hips. "Where is he?"

A flawless teenaged immortal tilted her head. "Who are you lookin' for, sugar?"

"Eadric."

"He's with his inner circle. You don't want to disturb him." She flipped her luxurious, Pantene-commercial brown locks over one shoulder and snuggled up to a Greek goddess who appeared twice her age but was just as striking.

"The hell I don't." I focused on the heavy vampire energy weighing on me and marched up the grand staircase, following the strongest concentration.

"Wait!" the teen vampire called.

"Let her go, Felice," her companion said, stroking her arm. "David will take care of her."

I clenched my teeth at the mention of David but was grateful the older vamp had other things on her mind. In my rage, I'd likely get myself bitten again if they tried to stop me.

At the landing I followed my spidey sense down the hall. Gooseflesh covered my bare arms as the energy pulsed around me. Just as it had during both meetings with the leader of Cryrique.

Eadric was close. Right on the other side of the closed double doors. I'd bet my store on it. Without knocking, I barged in and skidded to a stop.

Inside, the walls were draped in black silk, offset by snow-white carpet. At the center stood a luxurious canopy bed, trimmed with sheers that barely concealed the naked flesh of three vampires.

I stumbled back, my body knocking the double doors closed with a loud click.

A voluptuous redhead moaned under Eadric's touch while another I recognized as Eadric's consort, Pandora, peeked between the panels. "Ah, the faery. Eadric, you didn't mention you'd invited such a lovely morsel."

"I didn't." He lifted his head from Pandora's neck to gaze in my direction. "But she's welcome all the same. Willow," he called, sounding amused. "Care to join us?"

"No...ah, no thank you." I yanked the doors open. They slammed behind me. I leaned against the door and waited for my heart to start beating again.

"Willow?" David strode toward me from the opposite end of the hall, shirtless, his hair damp. "What the hell are you doing?"

His faint cypress scent reached me before he did. I held up a hand, keeping my distance. He looked too damned sexy, and my traitorous body was responding in a way my head did not approve of. I was mad at him, not to mention he was a vampire. "I intended to have a conversation with your maker—oh, I'm sorry, I mean your *father*." I averted my eyes, feigning interest in the gleaming wood floor. "But he's a little busy at the moment."

"Uh, yeah. I imagine he is." The irritation in his voice vanished, replaced by something close to embarrassment.

"Forget it. Eadric's bedroom activities are of no consequence to me." I stepped forward, shaking a finger at him. "But you have some serious explaining to do. What the fuck is going on, and why have you been lying to me?"

His shoulders stiffened as he took a deep breath. "Phoebe told you."

I crossed my arms and glared.

"I..." He grabbed my hand and pulled me down the hall. "Let's talk in private."

His fingers squeezed mine gently, and despite my instinct to pull away, I couldn't. There was no pain, only comfort and familiarity. Back at the Arcane, when I'd blurted his touch didn't hurt, he'd only stared at me in confusion. Of course he had. He didn't have any idea what I'd been talking about.

When we reached the opposite end of the hall, David paused to glance at our joined hands and gave me a curious look.

"What?" Butterflies danced in my stomach.

"You're letting me hold your hand."

The question in his tone made me try to pull away, but his fingers gripped mine.

He stepped closer, invading my personal space. "What did you mean earlier when you said my touch didn't hurt anymore?"

"I…nothing." Crap. No one was supposed to know about my intolerance to vampires.

Lifting my hand, he pressed it against the door and trailed his fingers over my palm. "Does this hurt?"

I shook my head, not trusting myself to speak. A ripple of unwanted pleasure ran down my arm, and I tried to pull back.

He held tighter and clasped my other hand. "But it did before, right? That's why you kept pulling away?"

It wasn't the only reason, but it was the main one. I nodded.

Dropping my hands, he stepped back, hurt showing in his deep blue eyes. "Why didn't you tell me?"

Shoot. Now I'd gone and wounded a vamp. I sighed. "I don't tell anyone. It's not just you, it's all vampires. Well, not you anymore for some reason. If word got out…"

He stared at me for a moment. Then he took a deep breath. "I see."

I shrugged. What more was there to say on the subject?

David produced a key and unlocked the door. The modest sitting room was furnished with a leather couch and matching armchairs. I scanned the walls, noting the black-and-white land-scape photography, and nodded. "This is your space, isn't it?"

He glanced back in surprise. "Yes. My room is through there." He gestured toward a connecting door. "How did you know?"

I felt my brows pinch as I stared at him with my you've-got-to-be-joking look. "I dated you for a year."

His lips eased into a sexy half smile. The same one that made me say yes the first time he asked me out.

All my earlier anger returned, and I fought back the impulse to sucker punch him. "A full year, David. In all that time did you not once think it was appropriate to inform me you'd been adopted by a vampire?"

His smile disappeared and he took a step back. "I couldn't. Just like you couldn't tell me about your intolerance to vampires."

I narrowed my eyes. "That's not at all the same. My disability puts me in danger."

"It is the same. We live in different worlds. Live by different rules. Revealing information has consequences."

"Like what? Did you think I'd leave you? Judge you? Or think less of you? It's not like you had a choice."

"You don't understand."

I took two steps, stopping inches from him. "That's the problem. You never gave me a chance."

He stared down at me, his eyes intense, and sighed. "I did have a choice. How could I tell you I chose to live with Eadric? That I was forever bound to him?"

I shrugged. "So what? You were a kid. You can't be held accountable. If the courts weren't so corrupted, a vampire could never adopt a child."

"Listen to me, Willow. It's not like that." David kicked a table leg, and a glass lamp shattered on the floor. "This is why I didn't say anything. You're so prejudiced when it comes to vampires. And then I was turned. What would you have said? I spent two months trying to figure it out, then I thought…Well, I figured it would be better to just let you think I didn't care."

I shuffled back, putting more distance between us. My chest constricted. "You didn't…you were scared about what I would *say*?"

He turned away and nodded. "Yeah. I guess so."

A knot eased in my stomach, and even though my head demanded I should be angry at everything he'd omitted, my heart said something else. He hadn't stopped caring. If anything, he'd cared too much.

David stood there in only his jeans, looking sexy as hell, but his expression was lost. Almost dejected. The pain of whatever he'd gone through by straddling two worlds was clearly taking its toll.

I hesitated, wanting to wrap my arms around him, but still wary. A lot had happened. I'd been so angry at him for leaving me, for keeping me in the dark, for not being honest. At the same time, I understood—at least partially—why he'd kept me at arm's length.

He turned to face me, hands stuffed in his pockets, shoulders hunched. I couldn't help but still care about him. I took careful steps and slid my arms around his waist, resting my head against his shoulder. "I don't know what I would've said if you'd told me, but right now I'm okay with it."

His arms circled around me and after a moment, he bent and gently brushed his lips against mine.

The pain and stress of the last week took over, and I couldn't stop myself from sinking into the kiss. The chill of his tongue on my heated mouth stirred an unexpected response deep in my center. Everything fled my mind except the feel of him. My David, familiar and yet new at the same time. I was tired of being scared. Tired of being hurt. Tired of letting everyone else control my destiny. All I wanted was to feel something good. To feel his body against mine. I moaned and pressed closer.

"Willow," he whispered.

"Hmm?"

"This is probably not a good idea," he said as his hands worked their way into my hair.

"You're thinking too much." I clamped my teeth over his lower lip and nibbled.

His breath caught short, and a second later he lifted me in his arms, carrying me toward his bedroom door. I gave him a wry smile and buried my head in his neck as he crossed the threshold.

The door slammed as David pressed me against the nearest wall. His lips were on me, sucking and teasing as they moved to nuzzle my neck.

"Careful. You don't want to get bit," a soft voice said.

David froze.

I twisted and spotted Allcot. All the anger I'd possessed earlier in the garden came roaring back. "You bastard!" I spat at Eadric, struggling to untangle myself from David's arms. "Let me down."

David kept an iron grip, not appearing to be bothered by my attempt. "Did you need something, Father?"

Eadric leaned back against the doorframe and shrugged. "Not at the moment, but your girlfriend appeared to want an audience with me. I can see she found a suitable way to occupy her time."

"David," I warned. He loosened his hold, and I slid to my feet. I stepped in front of him, glaring at Eadric. "Using your son to get to me, Allcot? How do you live with yourself?"

"Wil." David rested his hand on my shoulder.

"Oh, right. You're not alive." I crossed my arms over my chest.

A slow smile spread across Allcot's stony face. "She's perfect, Davidson."

Chapter 18

I spun to stare at David, then shuffled to the side until both vampires were in my view. "Perfect for what?" My words came out clipped, my tone dangerous.

David closed his eyes. When he opened them, he glared at Allcot. "Agent Rhoswen is an upstanding member of the Arcane. She deserves to be spoken to with respect."

The unexpected display of support helped ease a bit of the tension strumming through my muscles. It was the first time David had displayed even a hint of defiance toward his father. Though I had a feeling Eadric spoke to everyone any damned way he pleased. He was that powerful.

Allcot chuckled, rolling up the sleeves of his black silk shirt. Dressed in wool pants and shiny black loafers, he was completely unruffled. No one would've guessed he'd just risen from a *ménage à trois* moments ago. "I doubt after today's events, the Arcane agrees with your upstanding-member analysis."

The muscle in David's neck flexed. "You know what I meant."

My gaze traveled back and forth from father to son. Allcot, still standing against the frame, kept his cocky, devilish smile in place. Only the clenching of his right fist indicated he was annoyed at David's reprimand. I had no doubt if any other vampire spoke to Allcot in that tone, they'd be snail food.

David kept his head high, his eyes trained on his father. He wasn't backing down. If Allcot challenged him, I'd be in the middle of a vampire smackdown. Again.

Allcot straightened and stalked toward David, his electric power making my skin itch. Although David's broad shoulders and height gave him the advantage, his father's very essence dripped with danger.

"Hey, now." I jumped between them, holding my arms out as if I could stop either of them from ripping the other apart. Look what happened last time I got between two snarling vamps. "There's no need for this. I'm certain we're all capable of a calm, rational discussion."

Neither spoke, but Allcot stopped his progression toward us, raising one curious eyebrow. "Your loyalty to Davidson bodes well for your survival."

"Father," David warned again.

I did a mental eye roll. The testosterone in the room was enough to complete a sex change. "Can we go in the other room to talk?" I pointed toward the door. "I'm sure we'll all be more relaxed." I would be.

Allcot took a step back, bowed slightly, and swept his arm in invitation. "Ladies first."

Vampire balls. Now I had to walk right past him. Gritting my teeth, I held my head high and strode through the door, praying he couldn't sense the fear threatening to take over. The first rule of dealing with vamps: Never turn your back on them. Especially this one.

Allcot fell into step right behind me, close enough his cool breath chilled my ear. I shivered and kept walking.

Back in David's bedroom, I heard the rustle of a wardrobe opening and prayed that meant he was putting a shirt on. As gorgeous as his chiseled chest was, now was not the time for distractions.

I headed straight for one of the armchairs. Settling into the soft, rich leather, I crossed my ankles and eyed Allcot. He lounged back on the couch, his foot propped over his left knee.

David emerged, dressed casually in jeans and a long-sleeved navy thermal shirt. The way he used to dress before he turned vamp. I bit the side of my cheek to keep from commenting.

Memory lane was closed. He glanced between us and took the chair next to me.

I gripped the arms of the chair, waiting. "What am I doing here?"

Allcot glanced at David, his lips twitching.

"Did your brain freeze in a prepubescent state when you turned?" I huffed out a frustrated breath. "God, Allcot, you act like a twelve-year-old. Not everyone is totally consumed by sex every second of the day."

David caught my eye, and I swear he had to hide a smile. Did he think I was being funny?

Eadric leaned forward, elbows on his knees, his cold blue eyes piercing me with his gaze. "I assure you, if I wanted you in my bed, you'd be there...willingly."

Every muscle in David's body stiffened.

I gave Allcot a blank stare. "What is it you want from me then, since clearly I'm not begging to join the harem in your bedroom?"

Allcot glanced at David and gave him the tiniest of nods. David unclenched his fists, visibly relaxing. Was that some sort of acknowledgment on Allcot's part that I wasn't destined to be one of his groupies? As if I'd ever be part of one of his undead lovefests. No way was I going anywhere near his freak show.

"Well?" I prompted, tired of the power play.

Allcot shifted forward until he was perched on the couch, staring me in the eye. "I have a proposition for you."

I raised a skeptical eyebrow.

His lips turned up in that cold smile of his. "Considering your current predicament, you'll probably want to consider our offer."

Our current predicament, indeed. Phoebe and I *were* in a quandary. We couldn't go home or to work. Maude would find us there. Then I'd be a test faery again. I had two options: listen to what Allcot had to say or run. New Orleans was my home, where my store was, and the only place I'd felt comfortable since Beau died.

I didn't want to run. "I'm listening."

The smile vanished. "We suspect one of Maude's spies has infiltrated Cryrique. This is unacceptable. Cryrique is a privately held company with confidential research in many areas, including, but not limited to, vampire medications, creationism, and mind enhancers. Multi-million-dollar investments. You can see why we'd be concerned."

The medication and creationism wasn't a surprise. Vampires had long been studying the effect of their powers on humans. From healing to mind control to the turning. Certain vampires were reborn more powerful than others. If Cryrique could determine why, bottling their healing properties could be a big business.

But mind enhancers? Yeah, he was talking about drugs. The vampire community brushed that label aside, instead insisting their research was closer to the edibles I made. But the rumors implied something much more potent.

"Okay. Say Maude does have a spy. I don't see how I can be useful," I said.

Allcot brushed invisible lint from his trousers. "I'd like you to be our inside source at the Arcane."

"What?" I stood, suddenly angry. "Did you miss the part where Phoebe and I are now fugitives? I can't even go home, much less back to work."

David rose and put a hand on my arm. "Hear him out, Wil."

I cut my gaze to his hand resting above my elbow. "Let go."

He hesitated, a flicker of frustration flashing through his eyes, then shoved his hands in his pockets. "Sorry."

"This is why you're the perfect person," Allcot said, mildly.

I scrunched my face up in frustration. "What the hell are you talking about? I'm aligned with you now. Everyone will assume I'm working for you and your corporation."

Allcot rose, shaking his head. "As it turns out, thanks to your partner, Ms. Kilsen, we have evidence of Maude's illegal behavior concerning you and her attempt to contract us to do her dirty work. I suspect she'd be most eager to keep that information under wraps." He swept his hand out, inviting me to sit once more.

I did so, begrudgingly, hating that he towered over me.

"You, my lovely faery, are perfect because your obvious disdain for us shines through, even when you're trying to hide your emotions. No one will suspect you're working for me. And you'll have reason to meet with us since you've been assigned to work with Davidson." He sank back into the soft leather and once again rested a foot over his knee.

I took a moment to consider his words. Working for him was suicide. If the Arcane found out, I'd be locked up for sure. If I pissed off the wrong vamp, I'd be dinner. A no-win situation. "If Phoebe captured the evidence, why should I submit to you? She's more than capable of a little blackmail."

"She could try. But are you willing to risk your friend's life? How far do you think Maude will go to cover her tracks?"

Goddamn him. Maude wouldn't hesitate to take Phoebe out. She'd make it look like an accident, too. I gritted my teeth. He'd used the trump card. "So in exchange for me working undercover for you, you'll blackmail Maude to drop whatever bogus charges she'll bring against me and Phoebe?"

"Yes. That is what I'm offering."

I shook my head. "Not good enough. You'll need to sweeten the pot. Working for you goes against everything in my nature. And it's open-ended."

Allcot's lips transformed into something that resembled a satisfied smile. "Name your terms."

I straightened, setting my shoulders back. "One, you'll dedicate someone to investigate my brother's death. And two, no one will ever ask about, study, or use me in testing regarding the effect I had on David. In other words, no one is to know the cause of his new sunwalking ability."

Allcot stood again. "Done." With a nod, he strode out.

I gaped. That was too easy. What had I missed? I twisted toward David. "What just happened?"

He smiled. "You negotiated a pretty good deal with the boss."

"But why did he give in so easily? He has to be dying to try to exploit the sunwalking thing."

David's smile vanished. "Yes, I think he is. But I already requested he leave it alone. We don't know if it's permanent or if you can even replicate it." He picked up a pen from the end table, fingering it absently. "We both almost died. Father knows that. He's not willing to risk any of his people unless we have definite information."

"Really?" My voice pitched high with disbelief.

"Yes, really. It probably helps that I asked him to drop it. As his only son, I still hold some clout."

A sick wave of nausea washed over me. No matter what David believed, Allcot stood to make a lot of money if he could create sunwalking in a bottle. Every instinct screamed he'd exploit me, given half a chance. A vision of my body suspended in a vise, being juiced of all its magic, flashed through my mind.

Argh! I shook the image off. No one was going to lock me up again. Never.

Our make-out session aside, I still didn't entirely trust David. Too many things had happened. I still had too many questions. Ones I should've asked before I stuck my tongue down his throat. I stood and paced the room. "Tell me what you were doing with Clea."

David flinched as if I'd slapped him. "What do you mean?"

"Oh, come on." I rolled my eyes. "You'd spent time with her before Phoebe tagged her. Why?"

He leaned forward but didn't try to touch me. "She came to me, asking questions about you, all under the guise of trying to help me mend my broken heart." He grimaced. "She wanted to know about Influence, who your friends were, what you did in your spare time, what I saw in you. Her behavior was suspicious to say the least. I had to investigate her. Especially considering the abduction threat."

"You had to take her on a date to *investigate* her? Make her think you were *mated*?" I heard the jealousy in my tone and cringed on the inside. Why couldn't I be cooler?

To David's credit, he pretended not to notice, but I saw his lips twitch ever so slightly in satisfaction right before he spoke. "I needed to search Clea's place, so I asked Phoebe for an illusion spell, took her on a date, and then hit her with the charm once I got into her apartment. While I was there, I found traces of Influence, but nothing else. That's when I tipped off Phoebe. She hunts down vampires that break the law, doesn't she?"

"Of course." I ran a hand through my tangled hair. "Wait, you got an illusion spell from Phoebe?" Back at his house, when David said the blood-sharing had been a spell, he'd meant the night they'd had their supposed date. I'd misunderstood, thinking Phoebe had spelled her while I'd been out. That meant Phoebe had known for at least a week about David turning vamp. Damn her. She'd deliberately not told me.

"Yes. Is that a problem?" David's forehead wrinkled in confusion.

"No." Not really, except I was once again the last to know. "So where does that leave your investigation? Do you really think someone wants to abduct me?"

"Honestly, I have no idea, but I'm not taking any chances."

"And what about this spy business Allcot wants me to investigate? Is that tied to the threat too?"

"That, I really don't know." David shrugged. "Maybe."

I plucked at a seam on the armrest of the chair. David's explanation seemed reasonable enough, but we still had to get something straight. I raised my gaze and stared him straight in the eye. "No more secrets. No more leaving me out of the loop. Got it? This is my life on the line. Ignorance will only get me killed faster."

He hesitated, but only for a second. Then he gave me a curt nod. "No more secrets."

"Thank you." My words hung in the air, and I wondered if either of us could hold up the bargain. Too tired to care about anything else, I asked, "When can I go home?"

"Tomorrow, most likely. Father needs time to put the deal in place."

I could survive until the next day. An overwhelming yawn took over, making my eyes water. Maybe not. "Fine. Until then, where am I sleeping?"

David walked to the door leading into his private bedroom. "You'll share with me."

Um, *what?* "No…I mean…That's not a good idea. Don't you have a guest room around here or something?"

"There's nothing to be afraid of, Wil. We've been sharing a room at your house for a few days already."

"Yeah, but you've been sleeping in my closet. We weren't sharing a bed. That's just…well, inappropriate."

He laughed. "Not as inappropriate as what happened here right before Father interrupted us."

I mentally groaned. "That was a momentary lapse in judgment. I'll find another room. Or sleep in the garden."

David moved so fast I hardly even saw him twitch a muscle. He appeared right in front of me, his eyes deadly serious. "No. It's not safe outside. I know you prefer an oak to recharge, but this is vampire territory. If word gets out about the sunwalking, which you know it could if Maude decides to leak it, I won't be able to protect you. Even on Father's property, another master could decide to take you for himself."

"I was outside not even an hour ago and no one batted an eye," I said stubbornly.

He shook his head. "You're not hearing me. I left you there because I knew you needed the tree. But with each passing minute, the likelihood of vampires hunting you increases. I'm not willing to compromise your safety because you're a little uncomfortable."

I bit my tongue to keep from screaming. This partnership was going to be hell. "I'll find another room."

He pursed his lips and shrugged. "You can do that, but you might end up witness to a scene like what you saw in Father's room. The guests here are very…open."

"I'll share with Phoebe. She'll work a charm or something to keep the sex fiends out."

Holding his phone out, David tapped a key. The screen lit up, revealing a message from the witch in question. *Gone for supplies. Tell Willow not to worry. I'll be back before sunup.* Damn it! Phoebe wasn't even here.

My palms started to sweat. Where was Link when I needed him? With him along, I was guaranteed at least a small level of protection. He'd keep any sleazy vamps from making a move on me. He'd also likely stay in wolf form for his whole visit, which meant I'd be too nervous to sleep. I sighed. "Fine. I'll share your room."

Light brightened in his dark blue eyes. "After you."

Chapter 19

Place one foot in front of the other. That was all I needed to do. No big deal, right? Except David stood between me and the doorway, and my traitorous hormones were screaming for his attention.

Goddess help me. He was a vampire. This could not happen again.

The feel of his cool lips claiming mine came rushing back the moment he opened the door, inviting me back into his sanctuary. A thin sheen of sweat blossomed on my brow. I clutched my hands together to keep from wiping my face. David could probably already sense my nervousness, but the last thing I wanted to do was call attention to my unfortunate reaction.

"Willow?" A look of concern pinched his face.

"Yeah?" I averted my gaze, too chicken to meet his eyes.

"I'm not going to hurt you."

"Of course not." *Jeez, Willow, get your shit together.* "Why would you say that?" Without waiting for his reply, I strode past him. My wing brushed his shoulder, and a shiver rushed up my spine. I sucked in a breath. Damn, that felt good. A low chuckle rumbled from his chest, followed by a fake cough.

Stupid hyperaware vampires. This was bad. I had to get a grip on my emotions.

I came up short in the middle of David's massive bedroom. The four-poster bed, covered with a stark white down comforter, sat centered on a windowless wall. Three layers of white and chocolate-brown pillows sat against the smooth walnut headboard.

Very masculine. Undeniably inviting.

Oh, hell no. I had to get out of there. I turned and came face-to-face with David.

He placed his hands lightly on my bare arms. "Going somewhere?"

"N...no," I stammered and bit my tongue. Shaking my head, I cleared my throat. "I could use some clean clothes." I hadn't changed in over twenty-four hours. "And a shower."

David nodded and disappeared into what appeared to be his closet, though from the quick peek I managed, I judged it to be slightly larger than my own bedroom back at home. He reemerged with a set of cotton pajamas.

"Here." He handed them to me.

"Thanks." I stood still, clutching the garments, not sure what to do. He'd seen me naked plenty of times before, but no way was I revisiting that scenario. Even though my body seemed more than willing, my common sense had kicked in after the meeting with Allcot. David hadn't meant to, but he'd hurt me. Not to mention that pesky vampire-faery thing. What would Talisen say? Oh lord. And what about Talisen? We weren't together, but if I was honest with myself, there was something going on between us. I just didn't know what.

I opened my mouth to ask David to leave but he cut me off.

"The bathroom is through there." He pointed behind me to an almost seamless door. "Take your time. I'll hunt up some food from the kitchen."

As I watched him walk away, a pang of guilt gnawed at my stomach. Here I'd been worried about my modesty, and David was worrying about my needs. The way he had when we'd been together. I sighed and disappeared into his oversized, sleek marble bathroom.

Twenty minutes later, warm and clean from the shower, I slipped into David's soft PJs. I rolled my shoulders, ignoring the irritation of my wings straining against the cotton. Vampire clothing didn't have slits for faery wings. But anything was better than my dirty T-shirt. Gathering my courage, I poked my head around the doorframe. My breath came out in a whoosh of relief. David wasn't back yet.

Thank God. I strode across the room to the bed, tossed half the pillows on the floor, and climbed in. I lay there for a while, staring at the stark white ceiling. How long had it been since I'd been able to relax? Days, it seemed. Turning on my side, I closed my eyes and breathed in the faint scent of cypress. David's scent. Sadness washed over me.

Everything had changed. My work at the Arcane, my relationship with the city's vampires…David. He was so different, and yet still the same in so many ways. What used to be soothing now filled me with apprehension. What was I doing in his bed? I put it all out of my mind and imagined I was back in my own soothing oak bed. Sleep didn't come easily, but eventually I fell into a restless oblivion.

I woke with a start to the sound of voices. Bolting upright, my head exploded as I collided with something solid. "Son of a…" I clutched my head as my eyes watered.

"Are you all right?" David's voice broke through the ringing in my ears.

"Uh huh," I mumbled, squinting. David stood beside the bed, leaning over me. "Was that your head?"

"Yeah. Sorry, I didn't mean to startle you."

I waved a hand, indicating it wasn't his fault. "Who's here?"

"No one." He gently placed one of the discarded pillows under my head. "Lie back."

"I heard someone," I insisted, scanning the room.

"That was Nathan. He came to check on you, but left when I told him you were sleeping."

"Oh." I relaxed into the pillows. "Sorry. I didn't mean to clock you."

He shook his head, a small smile tugging at his lips. "I'll survive."

"Right." Vampire strength. He probably had barely felt my blow.

The bed shifted as David sat next to me. "Are you hungry?"

Before I could respond, my stomach rumbled.

He laughed. "I guess so." The bed shifted once more when he stood. "Sit up. I've brought fixings for a bedroom picnic."

I shifted, eyeing a silver cart next to the bed. "What type of picnic?" I asked with a heavy air of skepticism. The last time we'd shared a meal in the bedroom, I'd been slipped at least one magical edible. One of my own, no less.

He held up his hands. "It's all untainted. Promise." When I didn't respond, he lifted the cover off a large platter. "Check for yourself."

My lips twitched and broke into a smile. The entire tray was covered with food from my favorite grocery store, Organic Market. Goat cheese, hummus, flat bread, mixed berries, and baby carrots were all still sealed in their prepackaged containers. Definitely not tainted.

David pulled an unopened bottle of wine from the bottom of the cart and held it out to me for inspection.

A ten-year-old Cabernet from the Napa Valley. Another one of my favorites. I gazed at him, one eyebrow raised. "Are you trying to seduce me?"

His eyes crinkled with humor as he dislodged the cork. "No, but if helping you relax turns into something more, I won't complain."

My neck warmed, and the heat crawled upward, no doubt setting my face aflame. I forced a laugh and sat up, cross-legged. "Forget it, buddy. All I'm planning to do here is sleep. Now pass the hummus. I'm starving."

David placed a tablecloth on top of the pristine comforter, filled it with his offerings, and then sat across from me. He handed me a half-full wine glass and tipped his goblet in my direction for a toast. "To starting over."

I hesitated. What did that mean? Our working relationship? A friendship? Or something more?

"Relax." His eyes clouded with a slight air of frustration. "Wherever we go from here, we'll figure it out. Together." He lifted his glass higher and nodded toward it.

I wasn't sure our situation deserved a toast, but there was no denying that whatever happened from here on out, we were in it together. The fact that I'd saved him from death and changed his chemical makeup in the process had sealed the deal. The smooth crystal weighed heavy in my hand. I raised my wine, letting him close the distance with a soft clink. "To the future," I said.

"An amazing one," he promised.

His words, low and soft, were a vow, touching me deep in my heart. A flutter rippled through me and turned into a painful ache. I was dangerously close to crossing a forbidden line. An action I didn't think I'd recover from.

Our eyes met, holding each other's gaze as we sipped the rich Cabernet. Heat that had nothing to do with the alcohol coiled in my stomach. I glanced away, concentrating on the picnic spread out in front of me. Only I wasn't the least bit hungry anymore.

David shifted. The sound of a drawer opening reclaimed my attention. He rustled around in the bedside nightstand and came up with a pair of scissors. I furrowed my brows in confusion and tensed when he moved to stand behind me.

"What are you doing?" I asked.

"Hold still." He swept my hair aside, his fingers gently brushing against my neck, until it hung in an auburn sheet over the front of my left shoulder.

I sucked in a breath, clutching my wine glass so hard I feared I'd break it. His touch was almost too much to take. Light and familiar. Sensual. Everything about him set me off.

David stepped closer, running a gentle hand along my spine. "Why didn't you modify this for your wings? You can't be comfortable."

I shrugged, ignoring the fireworks going off in my nerve endings. "These are borrowed. I didn't want to ruin your PJs."

David paused, and I wondered if he was waiting to see what I would do.

This was it. The moment of truth. Did I trust him or not? Other than not telling me about Eadric, I didn't have any reason not to. And at least I could understand why he kept that secret. Who tells a prejudiced faery his adoptive father is a vampire? I took a deep breath and held still.

Finally, he chuckled. "Haven't you figured it out by now?"

I twisted to stare him in the eye.

Shaking his head, he gave me a wry smile and leaned closer. "I'd do just about anything for you. A sacrificed piece of clothing means nothing." He brought his hand up, caressing my jawline with his gentle fingers.

My breath caught, and I turned my back to him, afraid of what I might do if I kept staring at his gorgeous midnight-blue eyes.

Two careful snips later, David set the scissors aside. My wings twitched, straining to be free of the fabric. He adjusted my top to one side and then the other, easing my wings out of their restraints. "Better?"

"Much." I stretched, reveling in the sheer pleasure of my newfound freedom. David didn't move, and I knew he was watching me. My wings had always fascinated him. Deceptively delicate with their almost sheer appearance, my wings' resilience always amazed other species. I leaned back, wanting him to place his hand on my neck the way he used to.

He didn't disappoint. His firm hand cupped the base of my neck, his fingers lightly caressing my exposed skin. I closed my eyes and tilted my head, giving him easier access. After the last twenty-four hours, I no longer cared what was right or wrong. I only wanted to be comforted. And at that moment, David's touch was filling the bill.

His cool breath brushed over my ear. "Is this okay?"

I shivered but wasn't cold. Nodding, I clamped my mouth shut, afraid of what I'd say if I spoke. All my objections seemed to fly out of my head. All that mattered was his touch.

Hands roving down my spine, he pressed his lips to my

neck, brushing soft kisses over the area I knew was bruised from Nathan's bite.

"No one will ever bite you again," David said, steel in his quiet voice.

"Okay," I breathed, flexing my wings as his fingers traced the sensitive edges.

"That's a promise."

My wings started to tingle and heat shot to my center. I'd believe anything he said right then. And he knew it. He'd long ago discovered my weakness for being caressed.

"I've missed you," David mumbled into my neck and wrapped his arms around my waist. He rested his cheek on the top of my head and hugged me to him, like a long-lost lover he'd never wanted to let go.

My heart squeezed. I'd missed him too, but couldn't bring myself to say the words. I was too overwhelmed. Too comfortable in his arms. Too unsure of anything. I covered his hands with mine and squeezed gently. It was enough for now.

A frantic scraping at the door startled me out of my thoughts. David's head jerked up just as the door burst open. Link, in wolf form, took two large leaps and landed directly in the middle of the bed, snarling at the vampire behind me. Hummus splattered across the bed and berries went flying. The once-pristine comforter was a goner. David straightened but kept one protective hand on my shoulder.

"Link!" I cried. "Stop it. You're making a mess."

"He's doing what he was trained to do," a familiar male voice said from across the room.

My whole body went cold. *Shit! Shit! Shit!* Slowly I raised my gaze, grimacing as I spotted the other man in my life. "Tal? I didn't know you were coming."

His angry green eyes narrowed as he glared at David from the doorway. "Obviously."

Scrambling to my knees, I shook David's hand off and clutched Link. "Calm down, boy. David isn't going to hurt anyone."

"Get your hands off her, you sadistic bastard." Talisen took two steps into the room. "If she has even one tiny scratch, one pinprick of a bruise, I'll kill you."

"Tal," I warned. "Stop. He's not hurting me. I promise."

David backed off and headed toward the door. "I'll give you three some privacy."

"Wait," I called after him. Jesus, what was I doing? If Tal took a swing at him, David would crush him. A fae was no match for a vampire.

He paused and glanced back.

"This is your room. You don't have to go." I jumped off the bed, wincing when I remembered what I was wearing.

He shook his head and sent me a resigned smile. "Better you have this conversation here where the rest of the house can't hear you. I'll be downstairs if you need me."

"David…"

He didn't turn back but paused as he reached Talisen standing in the path of the doorway. The pair glared at each other, tension mounting with each passing second.

Talisen's fists clenched.

David eyed Tal and in a measured tone said, "Step aside, fae. I'm only granting you this courtesy because of Willow. Challenge me, and I'll have no choice but to defend my territory."

Territory? Was he talking about me or his room? It had damn well better be the latter.

"Tal," I pleaded.

The outrage in Tal's expression told me he was thinking the same thing. He cast David a look of disgust and sidestepped just enough for David to pass.

When the door closed with a soft click, I sat back on the bed, my back to Talisen.

With the vampire gone, Link shifted and crept up beside me. His wet nose nuzzled my hand until I scratched his ears. He licked my wrist, pressed against my thigh, and rolled over, sticking his paws in the air. Despite the tension in the room, I laughed and rubbed his belly. "You goober. For such a vicious animal, you sure do shift gears fast."

"So does someone else I know," Talisen said from the end of the bed.

I snapped my head in his direction. "What's that supposed to mean?"

He leveled a flat, dry stare in my direction. "Come on. Look at you. You're in his clothes, on his bed, letting him touch you the way—" He clamped his mouth shut and a touch of pink colored his cheeks.

The way what? The way a lover would? The way he, Talisen, would? Or the way he wanted to? I swallowed, my throat suddenly dry.

Tal moved closer, eyeing me. "Did he hurt you?"

I shook my head. "No. I'm sorry. So much has been going on, I haven't had a chance to tell you. After I…changed David, something odd happened."

He raised an eyebrow. "More odd than turning him into a daywalker?"

Grimacing, I forced the words out. "His touch doesn't hurt me anymore." Before he could respond, I did my best to change the subject. "Where's Phoebe? I thought she went out for supplies."

His lips formed into a hard line. "She did, but now she's downstairs."

"Well, where are they?" I glanced behind him toward the door and plucked at my cotton pants. They'd been fine before, but with Talisen in the room, I couldn't stand to see him look at me with those accusing eyes. Like I'd let him down.

"We're what she was really after." He gestured to himself and Link. "But I guess you didn't need us after all. I mean, now that his touch doesn't leave you black and blue, your *vampire* can take care of you."

That did it. I jumped off the bed and whirled on him. "Are you kidding me right now? Stop it with your judgmental bullshit. You weren't there. You weren't the one locked away in the Arcane wondering if you'd ever get out alive. You weren't—"

Talisen grabbed my arms and pulled me toward him, his hands digging into my flesh. "You let him bite you, Wil. Bite you! What the hell were you thinking?"

"Let go," I spat and twisted, dislodging myself from his grip.

He stepped up, his face a mix of anger and pain. "What would Beau say?"

Stunned, I took a tiny step back. Then anger took over. Uncontrollable rage rolled through my limbs, and before I knew what I was doing, I raised my hand and slapped him. Hard. So hard my hand stung.

His hand flew up to cup his assaulted cheek. He stepped back and took a deep breath, visibly trying to calm himself. "I can't believe you did that."

"And I can't believe you'd think I'd ever willingly let a vampire bite me." Fuming, I stalked toward the door with Link at my side. When I reached the threshold, I glanced over my shoulder. Talisen's face had gone stark white except for the red handprint on his left cheek. "Just to be clear, even if you'd walked in on me and David naked and writhing with pleasure, you have no business judging anything I do. You've made it clear for years you're not a one-woman man. So don't start acting like you have some sort of claim over me, because we both know you'd never survive a committed relationship."

He opened his mouth but no words came out.

I shook my head. "Exactly what I thought you'd say."

Chapter 20

Once back on the main floor, the sticky vampire cloud returned, making my already upset stomach roll. How dare Talisen bring up Beau? The asshole. He knew bringing up my brother would leave the deepest wound. He'd done it on purpose, hurting me in a way only those who knew me best could.

And I'd snapped. Shame washed over me. My guilt for letting David inside my heart had pushed me over the edge. No matter what Talisen had said, my behavior was inexcusable. Especially since I *knew* my actions hurt him. Even though he'd never admit it.

Damn him.

I stopped in the foyer at the bottom of the stairs, forcing myself to not bolt through the front door. Until Allcot made his deal with Maude, I was stuck in the twisted vampire orgy house. I turned, intending to head into the sitting room, when a small ball of fur bounded down the adjoining hallway.

"Link!" I cried and took off after him. "Stop!"

He barreled through a slightly open door at the end of the hall. I groaned. What was I going to walk in on now?

"Get off!" Phoebe's voice carried into the hallway. "Bad dog!"

I scooted into the room to find Link sitting in the middle of a pile of clothes on the bed. Various outfits from jeans to cocktail dresses were lined up side by side. I snapped my fingers. Link raised his head and glanced at me. I leveled a glare. "Now, Link."

With his head hung low he jumped off the bed and slinked to my side.

"Going somewhere?" I focused on Phoebe, taking in the Tulane hoody and rolled-up jeans that hit just above her ankles. The black plastic-frame glasses and book bag marked her as just another nondescript college student.

She yanked on the ponytail of her artificial honey-blond hair and threw the wig into the suitcase. "I was until Allcot's lackeys stopped me. Something about Maude's spies watching the house. You should've seen the antics they used to smuggle me out of here when I left to get Link and Talisen. And even then they wouldn't let me go home. I had to have them meet me on vamp row." She pulled a silver credit card from her back pocket. "Allcot gave me this. I did a little shopping while I was there."

I took one more look at the bed and finally noticed the tags hanging off each piece of clothing. "Looks expensive," I said.

She snorted. "Yeah. I think he was expecting me to buy fresh undergarments and clothes for tomorrow. Not an entire undercover wardrobe."

"He should get to know you better." I smirked. Phoebe never went anywhere without at least four changes of clothes, three wigs, and about ten pounds of cosmetics. She hated to be unprepared.

"Check this out." She held up a purple sheath dress. "I overheard some of Allcot's people talking about a Cryrique fundraiser tomorrow night. I'm going to crash and see what dirt I can dig up. One of them might know something about the threat against you."

"Gorgeous. Be careful, okay."

"Aren't I always?"

I rolled my eyes. "Mostly. Anything for me over there?"

She scanned me from head to toe. "Looks like you've made do."

I grimaced and strode to the bed. It didn't take long to realize not one piece of clothing was larger than a size four. "Thanks a lot, Phoebs."

She rolled her eyes and leaned down at the end of the bed. She came up with another shopping bag. "Here."

Inside I found a few T-shirts and a light sweater, all made for faeries. There were also some undergarments, yoga pants, and jeans. Size ten. I sent her a grateful smile and headed for the bathroom. As comfortable as David's pajamas were, I couldn't wait to get out of them. I didn't need any more reminders of what had happened in his bedroom.

Five minutes later, I sat cross-legged on the bed in yoga pants and a soft blue T-shirt, rifling through Phoebe's stash of disguises. I held up a bright pink satin top that dipped in a V low enough to reveal her navel. "Where were you headed?"

She snatched it out of my hands and gestured to what she was already wearing. "This was for the college library. And this," she said, waving the halter top, "was for the college bar afterward."

"And you were going there because…?"

She tossed the shirt into one of her shopping bags. "Daniels's sister works at both."

I pursed my lips. "You think she'd be there today? He just died."

"Of course not. But people she knows would be and they'll be talking. You'd be amazed at what people say after someone dies." She kicked the shopping bag. "And I'm going to miss it, being holed up here like one of the house slaves."

I sighed and leaned back against the headboard. "I know it sucks, but I really do think he's trying to protect us."

"More like control us."

The vampire sensation hit me right before he spoke. "Don't tempt me, Agent Kilsen." Allcot strode into the room, and Talisen stumbled in after him.

Tal glared and clenched his fists as he stared back out into the hall.

"I believe this fae belongs to you." Allcot waved an impatient hand toward Talisen. "If you don't want him to get his neck ripped open, take care to keep him away from my people." He turned to Phoebe. "You can go at nine in the morning. The deal will be finalized by then." His deep blue-gray eyes found mine.

"It's best you pretend nothing ever happened with Maude for the time being. Treat her just as you always have."

"You mean with little respect and plenty of disdain?" Phoebe let out a hollow laugh.

"If that is the norm, then yes. We don't want anyone who may be watching to think anything's changed. Don't pretend she didn't hold Willow in lockdown. Too many people know about it already. Brush it off as necessary testing and resume the job you've been contracted to do. Got it?"

I nodded but Phoebe narrowed her eyes. She placed one hand on her hip and raised her chin. "What about Maude? Will she resume as normal? Or will Willow find herself locked up in some remote place out in the swamps? What's to stop Maude from going off the reservation?"

Allcot's expression hardened, turning his appearance marble-like. "I've got that covered." He nodded to me and was gone in one blink.

Talisen stood against the wall, staring at me.

Heat rose to my face. My outburst had left a gaping crater between us. The truth was, I had no idea what he saw when he looked at me. A sister? A close friend? A backup girlfriend if he ran through the world's female population? I shifted so I wouldn't have to meet his eyes and ran a hand over Link's soft fur.

"What trouble have you been getting into?" Phoebe asked him, gathering up the last of her clothes.

He grunted.

Phoebe tilted her head and eyed him. "Why did Allcot march you in here?"

"Oh." He cleared his throat. "One of the female vamps tried to lure me into her den and when I said no, words were exchanged."

Words. Yeah, I bet. After the coal-raking I'd gotten over the bite on my neck, he'd probably invited her to fang herself. Prejudiced jerk. A small voice whispered in my mind, *hypocrite*. I shook my head and crawled into bed. I rolled over and faced the wall, trying to forget I was now sharing a room with Talisen. Morning couldn't come soon enough.

The burning in my neck woke me. I shot straight up in bed, my fists connecting with the person hovering over me. "Get off!" I shoved with both hands and rolled out of the bed.

"Willow, calm down. I was only healing your neck." Talisen, who I'd knocked to the floor, hopped to his feet and took a step toward me. "I didn't mean to startle you."

My heart pounded as I took deep breaths, trying to get myself under control. I clamped my hand over my pulsing bite marks. Talisen's healing had never felt like that before. "It hurts," I ground out through clenched teeth.

His eyebrows burrowed in confusion. "What do you mean?" Gently, he pulled my hand back and inspected my wounds. "They're red and angry."

When he traced a light finger over the punctures, I winced. "Stop. That burns."

He yanked his hand back and frowned at the amethyst clutched in his other hand.

"Maybe there's too much vampire energy here. We can try again when we get back to my house." I flicked the light on and rubbed my gritty eyes.

Talisen cleared his throat and his voice came out low and husky. "Am I still allowed at your house?"

I peered at him, trying to focus. "Of course you are." I stepped closer and grabbed his hand. "About what happened last night…"

"Forget it. Like you said, I have no right to judge you. I was worried and in my overprotectiveness, I didn't stop to consider the circumstances." He squeezed my fingers and let go.

Circumstances? What did that mean? My war with Maude or the fact that I was forced to work with my vampire ex? Or the not-so-subtle insinuation that I just might be interested in Tal if he wasn't such a commitment-phobe? I put the entire question out of my mind. I didn't want to talk about Maude, and I definitely didn't want to argue about David or my relationship with Talisen.

I glanced at the clock. Seven a.m. "Where's Phoebe?"

She'd shared the other half of the bed with me, but now it was empty.

Talisen shrugged. "She was already gone when I woke up."

I strode into the empty bathroom and then returned to the foot of the bed. All the shopping bags were gone except for the one filled with my clothes. "Shit. She took off." I glanced at Link. "You couldn't have woken me when she left?" Who knew what time she'd fled? Link put his head on his paws and glanced away.

"Be ready in five minutes," I told Talisen as I grabbed my clothes and headed to the bathroom.

David caught up to us as we headed down the front walk. With the sun burning bright, he was the only vampire who could stop us. I braced myself for an argument. Allcot had said we could leave at nine, but I wasn't waiting another minute to find out what Phoebe was up to.

"The car's this way." David pointed to a long driveway.

I stopped. "You're not going to try to make us stay?"

Talisen moved a half step closer, and I held back a frustrated sigh. I hated this new display of dominance he had going on. We were just friends and always had been, despite how he made me feel sometimes. This new Talisen confused me.

David cut a glance to Talisen but ignored the subtle challenge and told me, "The deal is done. No need to hang around here any longer." He started walking up the driveway. "You can wait here. I'll bring the car."

Talisen and I stared after him. "Something's brewing," I said.

He draped a light arm over my shoulders. "Do you think he knows where Phoebe went?"

He'd wrapped his arm around me in the same fashion hundreds of times before, but it felt different this time. Like he was claiming me. I bent down under the guise of tying my shoe. "I doubt it. She doesn't check in with anyone when she's on a mission." When I stood, I stepped aside, putting distance between us.

"Then why do you think something's off with him?"

"He's not mad I didn't tell him I was leaving. This is too easy." David seemed as if he'd expected me to try to ditch him. Had he been watching for us?

Talisen chuckled. "Maybe he's started to pay attention."

"What does that mean?"

His lips twitched as he squeezed my shoulder. "You've never been one to ask permission from anyone. And you sure as hell don't wait around for a man to do anything. It's not a surprise you'd disregard any plan put in place by anyone other than yourself or Phoebe."

Momentarily stunned at his assessment, I gazed up at him, my head tilted. Finally, I asked, "Was that a compliment?"

He snorted a laugh. "Your call."

A silver Mercedes zipped down the driveway and stopped beside me. David lowered the window. "Ready?"

I raised my eyebrows. "New car?" I'd only ever seen him drive a Ford truck.

He nodded and his expression turned blank. "A gift from Father."

The hollow ache in my stomach returned. Another turning gift, just like the house. Of course he got a fancy new car. Eadric couldn't have a new vampire driving anything less. There was an image to uphold.

Talisen held his tongue as he climbed in the back with Link. I really wanted to join them but forced myself to take the front seat. I slammed the door and stared out the window, unable to even look at David. After what happened the night before and having Talisen in the car, the whole situation was just too awkward.

"Where to?" David asked, peeling out of the driveway.

"Home. If Phoebe stopped by there, she may have left me a note."

"Okay." The inflection in his tone made it clear he thought the idea highly unlikely. I concentrated on the traffic, never once glancing in his direction during the fifteen-minute ride.

The second the car came to a full stop behind Phoebe's, I jumped out and ran to the house.

Before I could get the door unlocked, David placed a firm grip on my arm. "Let me check to be sure no one's waiting inside."

"Like who? Every other vamp is hidden behind blackout shades." I pressed forward, but his iron grip held me in place. "Let go."

Talisen strolled up the walk, an amused smile lighting his face.

"Stop it." I glowered at him and then back at David.

"Maude could have people waiting."

"Allcot said he cut a deal. Maude's not supposed to be a threat anymore." I yanked my arm back, trying to get away from him.

David let go, probably realizing his caveman act wasn't helping his appeal. "Right. But it doesn't hurt to be cautious. At least let me go in first."

"Fine." I threw my hands up and stepped aside. "But hurry up."

David brushed past me through the unlocked door. He froze mid-step in the threshold, his body filling the space.

"What is it?" I pressed forward, trying to peek around him, but couldn't see past his solid shoulders.

"Phoebe," he said carefully. "What's going on?"

Phoebe? My internal panic button went off full steam, and I barreled into David's solid form. "Ouch!" I cried, holding my shoulder. Damn him and his chiseled vampire physique.

He glanced down at me once, then stepped aside, giving me room.

I stumbled inside, gasped, and backpedaled right into David. His cool hands gripped my arms, keeping me steady on my feet. Every inch of the place had been ransacked. End tables lay on their sides with broken legs, stuffing from the couch cushions covered the wood floor, and papers from Phoebe's desk had been scattered everywhere.

In the middle of the room sat a dark-haired, wide-eyed, college-aged girl tied to a chair with duct tape covering her mouth. And right in front of her stood Phoebe, in her low-cut satin top and four-inch heels, a small chocolate-orange wedge in one hand.

"It's about time you got here," my roommate said. "We were just about to find out who put a hit on Willow."

Chapter 21

"Phoebe, no!" I lurched forward and knocked the Orange Influence from her hand. "Where the hell did you get that?" Was she out of her mind? Not only was she breaking the law, she was going against everything I stood for.

She reached down, fumbling for the magically enhanced chocolate. "Where do you think?"

I kicked the Influence across the room.

"Willow. Stop it." Phoebe moved, but I grabbed her arm.

"No, Phoebs. Absolutely not. What you're about to do is illegal. I won't be party to it." I kept a death grip on her arm, praying she wouldn't spell me before this argument was over. Not that I had any reason to believe she would, but then again, I never would have thought she'd resort to using Orange Influence. She knew how I felt about it.

The girl in the chair whimpered. I dropped Phoebe's arm and took a step toward her.

"Willow!" Phoebe yanked me back. "Goddamn it! I tied her up for a reason."

I stumbled back and buried my desire to lash out at Phoebe. It's not as if I was going to set the girl free. "Let go," I said, my voice tight with anger.

She tightened her hold and I twisted, trying to break my arms from her death grip. My patience gone, I snapped, "Link, help!" But he ignored me, already shimmering gold. His limbs elongated and his bones shifted as he leapt in front of the girl. He landed in full wolf form, growling.

He hunched forward, jaws snapping. The girl was just sitting there. What was setting him off? I stilled and gazed at the prisoner. "Is she a witch?"

Phoebe relaxed her grip and when I didn't fight her, she let out a frustrated huff. "Yes. A powerful one."

Why was a witch ransacking our house? I turned to face my friend, truly bewildered. There were better ways to elicit information. "Why are you trying to Influence her? Don't we have any Truth Clusters around?" I started up the stairs toward the kitchen.

"I already gave her some. They didn't work."

Phoebe's words stopped me mid-step. Slowly, I retreated back down the stairs.

Talisen raised his eyebrows and met me at the bottom of the steps. "Is there some sort of vaccine that can keep people from being affected?"

I shook my head, clutching the banister. "No, not that I know of." I turned to Phoebe. "Could she have spelled herself to be resistant to it?" Was that possible? I'd never heard of such a thing, but then my edibles had always worked before.

Phoebe stalked over to the fallen chocolate, scooped it up, and waved the Influence at me. "If she's already under the Influence, your Truth Clusters won't work, right?"

Dumbstruck at my own stupidity, I stared at the Orange Influence bobbing in the air as Phoebe continued to wave it at me. "Shit. You're right."

"And if we force-feed this to her, we can break the original spell and get the information we need." Phoebe didn't wait for me to respond. She kicked her way through the debris as she strode across the room.

"Wait!" I ran after her. Influence was a powerful drug. Whoever administered it had complete and sole control over the subject, including forcing them to tell the truth. Used without a person's consent, it was the worst kind of violation.

David, who'd been oddly silent through the whole ordeal, did that thing vamps do and suddenly materialized in front of our prisoner, his arms folded. He glowered at Phoebe. "I believe Willow has something she'd like to say about using the Influence."

I sent him a grateful smile and skidded to a stop in front of Phoebe. "I know using the Influence seems like the logical action here, but I can't allow it. Controlling someone against their will is wrong."

"Willow," Phoebe said, her tone measured. "Look at what she did to our house." She walked over to the ransacked bookcase and picked up a shredded notebook. "Look at what she did to your reference journals."

"Is that…?" I stalked to Phoebe's side, my hand outstretched. The leather journal was missing at least half its pages. Hot blood rushed to my head, burning my ears. "My recipe records," I said through clenched teeth. That freaking witch had destroyed the notes I'd meticulously logged with years of recipe experiments.

"Now can I use the Influence on her?" Phoebe gave me a pointed look.

I inhaled a deep, ragged breath and slowly let it out, willing myself to calm down. Talisen followed Phoebe's path through the mess and stopped beside me. His cool hand cupped my neck. A tingle soothed its way through me.

"Better?" he asked, holding up a blue stone.

Blue lace agate. The calming stone. I nodded. "Thank you."

"What the fuck, Tal?" Phoebe sneered. "That anger was helping her get a backbone."

"Phoebs." I held a hand up, ignoring the insult. Another witch had invaded her space. It wasn't a surprise she was lashing out. Witches don't play nice when other witches encroach on their territory. And I was stopping her from using a surefire weapon. "We're not using the Influence. Give me ten minutes. I can whip up the antidote."

Phoebe's nostrils flared, but she clamped her mouth shut.

I brushed past David and whispered, "Don't let her do anything stupid."

He raised his eyebrows and glanced over my head at her. "You sure about that?"

"Tal can't stop her. Someone has to." I took the stairs two at a time. Light footsteps sounded behind me, and I knew without glancing back it was Talisen. Perfect. I wondered how long Phoebe and David would last before one of them attacked the other. The current score was two to zero in Phoebe's favor.

"I could use a calming force down there," I said, striding through my kitchen door.

"The only one I have any effect on besides you is Link. And right now he's doing exactly what he's supposed to. No one else is open enough to accept the magic from the agate. Calming stones are very different from healing stones. It won't work without trust." Talisen leaned against the counter, his hands stuffed in his pockets.

"Still. If Link loses it, you can keep him in check." The last thing I needed was for Link to eat the intruder. Then where would we be? Knee-deep in witch guts. I slammed the cabinet door shut and placed a handful of dried herbs on the counter.

"Willow," Tal said with no small amount of impatience in his voice.

I spun to face him. "What?"

He took my hands and gently squeezed. "Why are you being so stubborn about this? If you use the Influence on her, you'll be able to order her to tell the truth."

"Not you, too." I threw my hands up and grabbed a copper bowl from the rack hanging above. "It's not right!"

"The world isn't black and white. Your life is on the line here. Now isn't the time to be so worried about your morals." He shifted to stand behind me, his breath warm in my ear. "I'm not going to lose you. I can't. Not now, not ever. Remember that when I cross some imaginary line." He pressed his lips to my cheek, kissing me ever so gently, then turned and took off back down the stairs.

I threw the herb container across the kitchen, satisfied when the glass container shattered on the floor. My shoulders slumped and I pressed my forehead to the cabinet in front of me. None of them understood. Not even Talisen. I'd expected him of all people to stand by me on this. Our whole lives we'd been taught our magic was a privilege. Something to be used to help people. It was not to be used as a weapon.

Power was too much like a drug. People lost control once they started abusing their abilities. Just like Maude. She'd lost every ounce of decency she'd ever had. Power was above all else for her. Even family.

No. That wouldn't be me. I wouldn't compromise my inner strength just to take the easier route. Mixing the antidote to the Influence wouldn't take that long. Then we could interrogate the intruder like normal agents.

I glanced at the broken herb bottle on the floor, sighed and searched the cabinet for a fresh jar.

Exactly seven minutes later, I descended the stairs with a powerful herb tea that should neutralize the Influence immediately.

Phoebe held open a small blue wallet. "Stacy? Seriously?" She took out an ID card and peered at it. With a snort, she threw it to the ground. "Fake. Of course."

The witch held still in her restraints but kept her gaze locked on Link. He'd crept forward, now only inches from her legs. One false move and he'd rip apart a limb. Talisen stood against the wall close to Link, and David lounged on the couch, one foot crossed over his leg.

"What's going on?" I stopped next to Phoebe and glanced at the wallet.

"Fake credentials. Fake eyelashes. And fake hair." Phoebe yanked off the witch's short black wig. The woman cringed as hairpins tangled in her wispy blond hair. "No idea who she is yet."

"This should help." I ripped the tape off her mouth in one ruthless motion. She gasped and grimaced through the certain pain. I brought the cup to her lips.

She clamped her mouth shut and glared.

"No need to be difficult. All this will do is break the Influence hold." I tilted the cup once more.

The glare vanished, and the witch's expression turned skeptical as she eyed the cup.

"Oh, get over yourself." Phoebe rolled her eyes. "You heard our argument. You don't think we put that on just for your pathetic ass, do you?"

The witch turned hard narrow eyes on Phoebe. Her lips formed silent words.

"Son of a witch's crow." She was casting some sort of spell aimed at Phoebe. Before she could mouth the last of it, I grabbed her neck and poured half the contents of the tea into her open mouth.

She sputtered and spit most of the concoction right in my face.

Phoebe sprang forward, wrapping her arm around the witch's neck in a headlock. Her other hand came up, covering the intruders nose. "Now, Wil."

I didn't hesitate. "Please just drink it. You'll be yourself in a few minutes." The tea hit her mouth and the witch started to spew. Phoebe shifted and clamped a hand over the girl's mouth. She squirmed, struggling against her restraints.

I wiped my face with the bottom of my T-shirt and glanced back at David. He sat perched on the edge of the couch, ready to join the fray if I needed him. I gave him a small smile. "We've got this covered."

He nodded. "I can see that."

Link spun and snarled at David.

"Link! Chill out," I ordered. He glanced at me and slinked off to sit at Talisen's feet.

"Traitor," I mumbled and turned back to Phoebe. The witch had gone slack in her chair. "What happened?"

Phoebe shrugged. "I think she passed out."

I stared down at the unconscious woman in horror. "From your strong-arming her or my tea?"

She shrugged again.

"Ugh!" I knelt and tugged at the duct tape binding her to the chair.

"Stop it." Phoebe pulled me backward. "We don't know if it worked."

"Phoebs, she passed out. We have to help her."

Talisen strode over, his amethyst clutched in his right hand. "I got this."

Reluctantly I shuffled back, giving him room.

Phoebe sidestepped and leaned closer to me. "I'm sorry. I know you don't agree with my tactics, but you weren't here when I stumbled into this mess. She's powerful. Possibly more powerful than I am. We can't risk letting her loose until we know for sure she isn't a danger."

I cut a sideways glance at my friend. "Looks like you handled yourself okay."

"Humph. Barely." Phoebe rubbed a hand over her eyes, and I noticed for the first time how stressed and tired she looked. Her cocky, kickass attitude hid a lot if one wasn't paying attention. Clearly, I hadn't been.

I placed a hand on her forearm. "You okay?"

She stretched her neck. "I'm fine. Nothing a good night's sleep," she said and flashed me a cocky grin, "or a roll in the sack wouldn't cure."

This time her quick change in demeanor didn't fool me for an instant. She was exhausted. Nothing I could say would get her to back down though, so I let it go.

Talisen's amethyst turned faintly pink against the unconscious witch's skin. He ran the stone along her neck and brought it up to her left temple. Leaning in, he whispered, "Heal thyself." He rocked back on his heels and waited.

Her eyelids fluttered open. Frowning, she wrinkled her brow in confusion as she tried to focus on Talisen. "Who are you?" she asked in a raspy voice.

He ran his amethyst over her forehead, but this time it didn't glow. "No one important." His gaze met mine, and my heart squeezed at the trace of sadness in his eyes. He blinked and the emotion vanished. Pocketing the healing stone, he turned back to the witch. "The more interesting question is who are you?"

She shook her head as if to clear cobwebs from her brain, then spotted Phoebe. "You!" she spat. "Let me out of this chair."

"Ha!" Phoebe laughed. "And let you try to bind me again? I don't think so, sister. Why don't you start by telling us who fed you Influence and why exactly you trashed our house?"

The witch clamped her mouth shut again. At least she wasn't forming spells this time.

I pressed my palm to Phoebe's back and guided her across the room. "I think we might have more luck with a soft touch."

Phoebe crossed her arms and glowered. "Fine. But if she so much as moves her tongue in the wrong direction, I'm neutralizing her again."

"So it *was* you," I accused. "What did you do, press on her wind pipe until she passed out?"

Phoebe glanced up at the ceiling and said nothing.

"Jesus, Phoebs. Get a grip."

David shifted forward, peering at the captive witch.

"What is it?" I asked him.

He got up and slowly walked toward her.

"David?" I asked again.

"I've been trying to place her all this time." Pacing around the chair, he didn't take his eyes off her. Once he made a full circle, he stopped and faced her head-on. "Do you remember me?"

What the...he *knew* her?

She stared up at him with wide eyes.

David crouched down to meet her at eye level. "Who gave you the Influence?"

I held my breath, afraid of what she might say. Was she affiliated with the Cryrique? I'd just formed an alliance with Allcot. If he was involved, my situation was a thousand times worse than I'd thought.

The witch blinked and a single tear slid down her cheek.

"Nicola," David said softly. "It's all right. No one here will hurt you." He wrapped his arms around her and, with one swift tear, freed her hands from the duct-tape bindings.

"Hey!" Phoebe cried from behind me.

"She's not going anywhere. David's right there." She could try to spell him, but it would be suicide. Vampire reflexes could stop just about any incantation. Especially one complex enough to take down a vamp.

David reached up and brushed back Nicola's rumpled hair. "Who did this to you?"

She clutched David's hands and shook her head violently. Was she too traumatized to speak? She'd seemed like a pretty badass witch five minutes ago. Influence didn't usually affect personalities so drastically.

Worried, I kneeled beside David. "Are you hurt? Talisen can help."

I gestured for him to join us, but he shook his head. "There isn't anything wrong with her physically. The amethyst would've picked up on it."

"Nic," David soothed. "Everything's going to be fine. Tell us who did this to you so we can stop them."

A choked sob escaped her thin lips. She sent David a scared, pleading look and blurted, "Eadric gave it to me."

Chapter 22

David pulled back, his posture rigid. "Excuse me?"

My whole body went cold as I got to my feet. I knew Allcot's deal had been too easy. Was he giving me tasks to keep me out of the way? I rounded on David, ready to tell him exactly what I thought of his father, but froze at the trace of color rising in his face. There was only one reason blood rushed to a vampire's face. Blood lust.

"David?" I asked tentatively.

His hardened eyes focused on me, and that was when I noticed the red tinge around his irises.

"Willow!" Phoebe said sharply. "Back up. Now."

I'd thought blood lust referred to young, hungry vampires. Not angry ones. Yes, David was newly turned, but he'd been so controlled, so sure of himself, I'd forgotten all about the struggle most vamps went through in the first months after they turned.

On shaky legs I stumbled back, grateful when Talisen's hands clutched my arms. Link brushed up against my leg. Thank the Goddess he hadn't shifted. I couldn't handle another wolf-vamp fight.

Talisen was murmuring, but through my anger and fear, I couldn't make out the words. *Link?* Is that what he said? I tried to focus. Yes, he was keeping Link calm with a mystical fae chant. Too bad it wouldn't work on a vampire.

"Eadric forced the Influence on you?" David retreated and clutched the back of the sofa. The wood frame creaked under his grip.

Nicola closed her big brown eyes, tears escaping from under her lids, and nodded.

"Fuck." The muscles in David's arms tensed, and the sofa frame splintered with a deafening crack. "Why?"

"Damn you, Laveaux." Phoebe glared at David.

Nicola wrapped her hands around herself and shook her head.

I steeled my resolve and forced myself forward to stand next to her. "She's been through a lot today. Maybe we should let her rest while we figure out what to do from here."

David's red gaze raked over me. Another chill caused gooseflesh to ripple over my limbs. I straightened my spine. Enough was enough. This witch couldn't be held responsible for actions she was forced to do. David wouldn't really hurt any of us, would he?

He glanced back at Nicola, his jaw clenched. "Don't move." And just like that a streak of black zoomed up the stairs, making the breath catch in my throat. He was gone.

A loud, wood-splintering crash came from my bedroom. I winced, praying it wasn't my bed, or worse, part of my tree. If he messed with my oak, he was vamp dust. I turned to Nicola and kneeled in front of her. "Are you all right? Can we get you anything?"

She licked her swollen red lips and croaked, "Water?"

"Phoebs?" I glanced up to find her glaring at us. "What's wrong?"

She stood with her hands on her hips, feet apart. Her narrowed eyes focused on Nicola. "Were you Influenced to try to kill me as well, or was that your idea?"

"Phoebs," I warned. Accusations weren't going to get us anywhere.

"It's okay," Nicola said, her voice stronger, but still wary. "I'd be pissed as hell, too." She shifted to get a better look at my roommate. "My instructions were to do or say anything to get the information I needed without getting caught or betraying my master. You were overpowering me. That spell was the last tool I had."

Phoebe's eyes went wide with disbelief. Her entire five-foot-two frame vibrated with barely contained rage. "You expect me to buy that horseshit? That little spell packed more punch than my granddaddy's one-hundred-eighty-proof moonshine. You tried to steal my magic and, by extension, my lifeline. That spell is no one's last resort. It takes far too much energy."

"Whoa." I took a step back. Who was this chick?

Nicola closed her eyes again as if struggling to form thoughts. Shaking her head, she held up a thin hand. She wore a silver ring with a ruby the size of an almond on her middle finger. With her other hand she caressed the stone. A second later it popped open, and barely a whisper of magic escaped.

Phoebe pounced, tackling me to the floor. "Ouch," I cried as pain shot through my elbow. We landed in a tangle of limbs, her body covering me as if a bomb had gone off.

After a moment, Phoebe jumped to her feet. "What the fuck are you doing?" She stalked to the other witch and clasped a hand around her wrist. Nicola cried out as Phoebe tore the ring from her delicate finger.

Talisen helped me to my feet and, with an amused smile, flicked away a piece of garbage stuck to my shoulder. A half-eaten dog bone flopped to the ground. Gross.

"Thanks." I turned. His fingers got caught in my mass of hair, and the whole tangled mess shifted, revealing my neck. He scowled, his eyes clouding with anger. Damn it all. My vamp marks were showing. Couldn't they heal already?

He cut his gaze away and held his hand out for the ring Phoebe was inspecting. "It contains a spell, right?"

Nicola gave him a tentative nod.

Another crash rumbled upstairs. We all glanced at the ceiling. Jesus. Good thing David came from money, because anything he broke, he was replacing. With an upgrade.

"Where'd you get this?" Phoebe demanded, ignoring Talisen's request. She clutched the ring in her hand as if she could keep any residual magic contained.

"The spell is spent. It can't hurt anyone now." Nicola slumped in the chair, squirming for a more comfortable position.

David had freed her hands, but her feet were still strapped to the legs of the chair. My conscience screamed for me to cut the tape away. But something held me back. Phoebe's unease, maybe? She didn't scare easy, and this witch had gotten under her skin.

"I can test it," Talisen offered.

Phoebe shook her head and forced the ring into a tiny, invisible pocket in her skirt. "I'll do my own testing."

Footsteps beat against the stairs. David took them two at a time, landing with a heavy thunk in the living room. Before I could stop him, he freed Nicola from her remaining restraints. "Let's go."

"Where?" Nicola cried, backing up and stumbling on a broken lamp littering the floor.

"Cryrique." David moved to the door. "Eadric is waiting for us."

She gasped.

"What!" I jumped in front of Nicola. Had he lost his ever-loving mind? "You can't take her to him. He abused her."

David's cold hard stare was back. "We have no idea if she's telling the truth."

Phoebe shrugged. "I don't trust her."

I kicked papers and broken glass out of my way as I marched over to David. "We need to work through a few things."

His jaw muscle pulsed again. "We don't have time for this."

"We'll take all the time we need." I brought a finger up and stabbed him in the chest. "You're not putting her in danger again. If Eadric has anything at all to do with this, he'll kill her for telling us the truth."

David's brow creased with impatience. "No. He won't."

"I know he's your father, David. But, he's dangerous. No matter what you say. Don't you think your opinion of him is a little biased? Just because he won't hurt you doesn't mean he won't make an example out of someone else."

"He won't," David said again. "She's Pandora's sister."

"Allcot's sex kitten?" Phoebe sneered in disbelief. "This one is related to her?"

I shot Phoebe an irritated glance, then turned my attention to Nicola. She didn't resemble Pandora at all. Was it the vampire change that made Pandora so beautiful? No. She must have been curvy and voluptuous while living to have turned out the way she did. A vampire's physical build is accentuated after they turn. They aren't magically transformed. Nicola was small without a curve in sight and had thin, straight blond hair. Her only noticeable feature was her big brown eyes that were almost too large for her face. "I thought Pandora was older, closer to Eadric's age."

David nodded. "She is older, but not as old as Father. Nicola is her half sister, born twenty-two years ago to her aging father and his much younger mistress."

"And Pandora would be upset if the interloper was hurt?" Phoebe looked Nicola up and down, her expression conveying nothing but contempt.

Nicola turned on Phoebe, a spark of life transforming her from a broken witch to one who'd snapped. "Look, bitch. I'm the only family my sister has besides Allcot." Her voice got stronger with each word. "I'm not a goddamned interloper. She came looking for me ten years ago. Got it? I didn't ask for any of this. And I'm not staying one more second."

She got all the way to the door before I blocked her. "You're not leaving until we get to the bottom of this."

"The hell I'm not." Her back was straight, her head held high. She'd gone from scared whimpering victim to she-bitch in a nanosecond. I guess Phoebe hit a nerve. "Get out of the way."

"Sorry," I said. "I don't think you're going anywhere on your own just yet." I snapped my fingers. Link jumped to attention and trotted to my side. Talisen and Phoebe backed me up, flanking me on either side. I nodded to David. "Let me talk to her."

"No." Certain finality resonated in his tone.

I straightened my spine and my wings fluttered with irritation. "What did you say?"

"No. We don't have time for this."

Talisen let out a very faint whistle. "Not a good answer, dude. Not cool at all."

I jammed an elbow into his gut. "Not now, Tal," I snapped and shot David a look of disgust. "We have no idea what's going on, other than a vampire somewhere wants to abduct me, and Maude wants to study me for my abilities. We don't know where Allcot stands—" David opened his mouth to interrupt. I held my hand up and kept going. "And I'm not about to blindly trust anyone. Especially not your father."

I glanced around at the trashed living room. "Can we all go upstairs to the kitchen and sit?"

Everyone stared at David. With the commotion he'd wrought earlier in his vampire craze, who knew what we'd find up there?

He gave a tiny shake of his head, like he couldn't believe he was caving to my request. "The kitchen is safe."

"Good." I swept an arm out. "After you."

If Nicola hadn't been surrounded, I'm certain she would've bolted for the door. It didn't take a genius to figure out a witch, a vampire, and two faeries outnumbered her. That didn't mean she was happy about it. The way she dragged her feet, one would've thought she was a teenager who'd just been told to clean her room.

At the top of the stairs, my bedroom door hung askew on one hinge. I paused for just a second and nearly stopped breathing. An antique chair lay crushed under my massive chest of drawers. My bed was leaning over, barely hanging on to its position in my oak, and everything, and I do mean everything, from my temporary closet was strewn across the floor. Shoes of every style and color. Blouses, skirts, dress pants. And my little black dress I'd only worn once lay ripped with a large oil-slick stain. Fucking bitch.

That part had to be Nicola. David wouldn't take the time to ransack my closet. She'd ruined all my dress-up clothes. For what purpose? I rarely wore any of them. My daily uniform consisted of jeans and T-shirts. And what in the blazes was that stain? Blood? No. There next to it was a blue metal can. Candle oil. Was she going to burn my shit? Oh, hell no!

"Sorry," David said into my ear.

I jumped, my heart thumping in my throat. "Don't do that."

"Sorry," he muttered again. "I'll make more noise next time."

"And next time you have a tantrum, take it out on someone else's stuff. Like your own," I snapped.

His eyebrows rose and he peered down at me. "You think I did that?"

"Not all of it. I doubt you'd ransack my closet, but the door, my bed, my chest of drawers…"

"The door, Willow. Only the door." He nodded at the wrecked room. "The rest was already trashed."

"We heard—"

"The crashing was me trying to consolidate the broken-down furniture so you could actually get back in here." He gave a tiny shrug. "I wasn't exactly gentle about it."

I rubbed my temples and marched into the kitchen. Slamming my hand down on the pinewood table, I leaned in close to Nicola. "Did you trash Phoebe's room, too?"

She bit her lip and barely shook her head no.

"Why mine? Why my little black dress? And my shoes? Why would a vampire, one who dresses in clothes that cost more than my rent, want you to destroy the only decent clothes I have?"

Silence.

I pounded my fist on the table, aware my clothes were my most insignificant worry at this point. But damn her. A girl's shoes were her identity. It was too freaking personal.

"Nicola?" Phoebe prompted, her tone sickeningly sweet. "Do you want to answer Willow now, or wait until I force you?"

"I was ordered to," Nicola said quietly.

"By?" I ground my teeth, growing more impatient by the minute.

"The one in charge." Her words came out slow and strangled.

I glanced at David. He was studying her again as if trying to piece together a puzzle.

"The one in charge," I repeated. "You mean Allcot ordered you to burn my clothes?"

Her hands clenched, and her pale face flushed in what I could've sworn was frustration. Something was seriously off. If Allcot ordered her to trash the house and she'd told us about it, why wouldn't she just come clean about my clothes? "Allcot's not in charge, is he?"

"No," she forced out before her eyes rolled into the back of her head and she passed out.

Chapter 23

"She's been spelled." Phoebe tucked a thin blanket over Nicola's lifeless form. Talisen took up position on the other side of the bed, healing stone in hand. We'd moved her down to Phoebe's bedroom, the only place besides the kitchen that wasn't a disaster.

"What does that mean?" I asked. "What kind of spell?"

"A truth blocker, I think." Phoebe pressed her lips together in thought. "She isn't Influenced anymore. You broke that, but I think something's forcing her to lie, and she passed out because she was trying to overpower the spell."

That made a certain amount of sense. It certainly explained her struggle while trying to answer questions. "Faery or witch?" I stood leaning against the doorframe, more than a little jealous. All of Phoebe's shoes were neatly tucked into the elaborate shoe organizer hanging on the far wall. She had a pair for every occasion.

"Ninety-five percent positive a witch did this. Fae magic feels different. Lighter or something," Phoebe said.

"Tal?" I cut a glance to Nicola. "Can you check?"

He ran a light hand over her forehead, stopped right before he reached her temple, and shuddered. "Witch for sure."

"Thanks." I pulled Phoebe aside. "We can't sit around here waiting for whoever did this to her to strike again. We have to do something."

She nodded. "I'm way ahead of you." With our heads huddled together, Phoebe filled me in on her plan.

A few minutes later, I turned and walked back into the living room where David was pacing a small circle around a sea of papers littering the floor. "What other witches are on Allcot's payroll?"

He paused, fished his iPhone out of his pocket, and touched a button. "Besides Nicola?"

"Yeah," I said with very little patience.

"No one in the US. There's one in France and one in Australia, and last I heard he had a contact in Rio." David touched the screen of his phone once again and then shook his head. "Vampires and witches don't exactly get along. Or hadn't you noticed?"

I sent him a flat stare.

"I guess you have."

Phoebe appeared, dressed to the nines. "Here." She handed me a small tote bag. "Everything you need should be in there."

"Going somewhere?" David broke the circle he'd formed and shifted so he was between me and the door.

"Yes. And so are you. Phoebe's going to Cryrique's fundraiser to scope out any possible suspects. Everyone who's anyone is on the guest list. There's an excellent chance whoever did this to Nicola will be there. Only someone with a lot of power would dare to mess with one of Allcot's employees." I pulled my long hair back into a low ponytail and adjusted the tote on my shoulder. "And you're coming with me on our own fact-finding mission."

"Jesus, Willow. Your neck." Phoebe grimaced. "You can't go out like that. I'll get Talisen."

I clamped my hand over the vampire marks still marring my skin. "No. Wait. He already tried. It didn't work."

"Really?" She kicked a toppled magazine rack to the side and reached out to pull me closer. "I thought that amethyst of his could heal anything."

I frowned. "It usually does. But not this time." Just thinking about the burn from the morning made me break out in a sweat. It had hurt. A lot. Just like when Nathan bit me.

Phoebe pulled her keys out of a tiny silver clutch. It offset her plum sheath dress, giving the illusion she ran with the upper echelon of New Orleans. "You'll have to cover it up. Maybe you should change to a turtleneck or wear a scarf."

"In September?" Was she out of her mind? Because neither of those things would be suspicious in ninety-two-degree weather.

"Makeup?" She held her hands out, palms up. "I have the professional stuff if you want."

I fingered the two puncture marks and struggled not to wince. They hadn't hurt before Tal tried to heal me, but now they ached under any sort of pressure. Using thick makeup would be a bitch. I took a deep breath and nodded. What else could I do? No way could I go out flashing my vamp bites. Talk about calling attention to myself. Faeries never let vampires bite them. Never. "Okay," I said.

"I'll be right back." She disappeared into her bedroom again.

David appeared by my side in another flash of vampire speed.

I dropped my hand from my irritated neck. The pain was making me lose focus. "I'd prefer if you acted like a normal person. This super speed thing is giving me whiplash."

"Sorry. I'll slow it down." Shifting half a step closer, he brought his hand up and gently caressed the area around Nathan's bite marks. "I can heal those if you'd like."

I swallowed. "Talisen already tried. It didn't work. They must be infected or…"

"I can heal them," David said again. "Trust me."

The way he said it and the sincere look on his face had me nodding before I thought through what I'd just agreed to. It wasn't until David leaned in that I panicked. "No." I pushed at his shoulders, struggling against his rock-solid form. I couldn't have his lips on me. Not again.

He caught my hands in his and brought one up to kiss the palm. A tingle rippled from the touch of his lips all the way up my shoulder. "I'm not going to bite you. Not now, not ever. Okay?"

I stared at the tiny scar above his left eye, not saying a word. So much for staying away from his lips.

He bent his knees, lowering himself until our eyes were level. I had two choices: deliberately look away like a seven-year-old or meet his calm, steady gaze like the supposed adult I was. Reluctantly, I chose to be an adult.

"Okay?" he asked again.

"Yeah," I breathed. It wasn't his teeth I was worried about.

"I promise it won't hurt." David stood inches from me. His familiar cypress scent filled my senses. And his touch was so gentle that when he leaned in this time, I didn't try to stop him.

Suddenly, his cool lips were brushing against my skin, forming a circle around the wounds. A bit of the burn eased and my muscles began to relax. I hadn't realized how much I was actually hurting before he started to contain the pain.

Another circle. This time he pressed deliberate kisses, sealing the trail. I tilted my head to the side, giving him better access. No need to make him get a crick in his neck just to help me out. His lips spread into a smile against my skin. I wanted to smack him. Nothing about this should've been amusing. Not my pain and definitely not my desire. Which even if he wasn't a vamp, he would have sensed. Lord help me, my body was tingling all over.

"Ready?" he asked, his cool breath numbing the puncture wounds.

Afraid I'd chicken out, I nodded once and braced myself for the worst. I mean, how could he know what was going to happen? Vampires rarely bit faeries. He couldn't have bitten and healed one in his short vampire life. Could he?

David wrapped one arm around my waist, pulling me toward him.

A fear that hadn't been there before materialized out of nowhere and trepidation froze me in place. Not that I could've moved if I wanted to. I forced myself to breathe. *Snap out of it. He's not biting you,* I scolded myself. *He's not Nathan. He's healing you.*

"Relax," he whispered, and his magical lips pressed against my wounds, instantly soothing the last of the dull burn. He flicked his tongue over the raised marks, slow and deliberate.

I clutched the front of his shirt as the mess around us faded into nothing. Nicola and my friends in the other room disappeared. Maude, Eadric, Cryrique, and the Arcane ceased to exist. My whole world was David, our legs tangled together, his touch healing more than the marks marring my skin.

I'd missed him. Missed his body pressed against mine. Missed the tenderness I knew lurked beneath his hardened exterior shell. My David, who I'd always believed would follow me into Hell, was holding me in his arms. And at that moment, I never wanted him to let go.

Everything heated except where his tongue caressed my neck. A soft moan escaped from the back of my throat, the sensation tender and unbearably erotic. I wrapped my free arm around him, pressing my fingers against the base of his neck.

David pulled back, and traced his thumb over my neck. "Better?"

"Uh huh." I met his blazing eyes, breathing heavily. I nodded, thunderstruck by the wonderful sensations still consuming my neck.

David was the first to break eye contact. His whole body tensed as his face hardened.

"David?" I asked.

He let one arm drop but kept one hand on my hip. Then he gave the tiniest nod over my shoulder.

I followed his gaze, and my heart plummeted. Standing near the staircase, his face white with what could only be shock, was my oldest friend. My stomach fell to the floor, and I stepped away from David. "Tal?" Oh good God. How long had he been there? What had he seen? David kissing my neck? Please, no. Why did that bother me so much? He was only healing me. Right. I could lie to myself all I wanted, it wasn't going to change what happened.

He glared at David. "She'll never be yours."

David didn't betray any reaction to Tal's statement. He stood still, waiting.

"You're not good enough for her," Talisen said.

"Tal!" I cried, but he ignored me.

"And you are?" David asked dryly. "You've known her for how many years? Ten? Fifteen? And you're just now interested? Seems you've had plenty of time to make a move. Looks like you need to work on your technique."

"David!" I scolded. Damn them both. I wasn't a piece of meat to be fighting over.

No one even acknowledged me. It was as though I were an invisible toy.

Talisen took two steps closer, leaving me trapped between them. "You can make this out to be about me all you want. But we both know she'll never end up with a vampire. Her very nature demands she should be surrounded by life magic. You bring death. Eventually she'll have to leave you, if only for self-preservation."

A tiny flicker of something close to concern flashed through David's eyes as he glanced at me. But then it vanished. He turned his attention back to Talisen. "I think whoever Willow decides to spend her time with is her decision."

Talisen finally turned to me, anger clear in his deep green eyes. "Yeah. It's her decision. But make no mistake, I'm not going to stand by while you break her heart again. Or get her killed."

His last word hung in the air like poison, slowly filtering its way into my system. Whether Talisen had romantic feelings for me or not, he was my family and his concerns were more than merited. I looked at each of the men I loved and suddenly didn't know if I wanted to scream or cry.

"Noted," David said.

Talisen stared him down, then abruptly turned and went back into Phoebe's bedroom.

"Well." I let out a frustrated breath. "That was tons of fun."

David held his hand out to me. "He's only filling the role your brother was meant to take."

I closed my eyes. *Beau.* He would have hated my involvement with David. Still, I'd like to think he would've trusted me to take care of myself. Or at least tried to see things from my perspective. My relationship with Talisen was a lot messier. I opened my eyes and took David's outstretched hand.

He pulled me close to his side. "Now, what's the plan?"

Plan? Oh, right. We had work to do. "You and I are going to the Arcane building. It's time for answers."

Chapter 24

"I'll drive." David guided me toward the door. "We need to stop and see Eadric first."

I planted my feet. "No. Phoebe's going to do some recon and then track him down."

"Willow," David warned. "I need to talk to him about Nicola."

"Fine. Call him from the car. But I'm going to the Arcane."

"Why?"

"Because even though we think Nicola's been hit by a truth blocker, we can't know for sure. Allcot *could* have force-fed her Influence. I think it's unlikely, but her information is suspect at best. And no matter what your father says, I'm not going to be able to trust his word. I need evidence."

"You think you're going to find it at the office?" He raised a skeptical eyebrow.

"Maybe. Look, Eadric wants information about who's working with Maude. And the Arcane is the first place to look for it. If we find out why she's investigating him, the information might lead us to answers. Or at least lead us to the right questions."

He jammed his hands in his jeans pockets. "Father's going to want to see me in person."

"Tell him we'll meet him later tonight, after the benefit." I brushed past him toward Phoebe's bedroom to let her know we were leaving. While staying at Allcot's mansion, Phoebe had managed to snag a copy of his schedule. Goddess only knows where she lifted it from. But, like the highly trained Void agent she was, she didn't take anyone's word at face value. And having an agreement with Allcot meant keeping careful tabs on him.

Once back in the living room, I noticed my destroyed recipe journal peeking out from under a throw pillow. I kicked the pillow aside and grabbed the book. To the right, the Orange Influence wedge lay exposed, ready for anyone to use. I grabbed it and shoved the chocolate in my front pocket. It wasn't an ideal spot. The chocolate would probably melt, but I couldn't just leave it lying around. The last time I did that, Phoebe'd almost used it.

"Phoebs," I called from her open door.

"In here," came a muffled voice from her closet.

Talisen sat on a chair near the bed. I gave him a halfhearted wave but avoided looking him in the eye. Phoebe was knee-deep in a pile of clothes, searching through pockets. "What are you looking for?"

She held up a silver beetle. "The other bug. I want to be able to hear what's going on. Especially if, for some reason, you can't get out again."

"It won't work once I go through security." What was she thinking? She knew as well as I did all her charms would be neutralized by the disarming machine.

"Ahh, that's what I never got around to telling you." She grabbed a faded pair of jeans, and as she pulled them toward her, something landed with a thud at her feet. "There you are!" She snatched up the other beetle, turned it over, and flicked a tiny switch. Its mate gave off a faint buzz. "Perfect." She handed me the one that wasn't buzzing and made an adjustment to stop the noise on the other one. She pinned the beetle to her dress and flashed me a satisfied smile. "There."

I glanced at the bug in my hand. "And the thing you forgot to tell me is…?"

"Oh. Right. You know how the neutralizer doesn't affect Link as much as it does us?"

"Yeah." I eyed her suspiciously.

"Well, while you were in California, I did a lot of experimenting. One of the things I worked on was smuggling magic into the Arcane building, just to see if I could. You know, testing limits." A satisfied smile lit her face.

"And Link is the secret?" Please tell me she wasn't going to make him eat something. I was not going to fish the bug out of his waste. Not in a million years.

"One of them. If he carries it in his body, the magic is so insignificant compared to his wolf abilities, the machine doesn't pick up on it. Voilà. Problem solved."

"Ugh, Phoebe! That's disgusting." I glanced down at Link. He tilted his head to the side in a quizzical glance. "Not on your life, buddy. No way. I'm never doing that." I grimaced at Phoebe. "Besides, I don't plan on being there that long."

She jumped over the pile of clothes and landed back in the bedroom. "What are you talking about? All he has to do is put it in his mouth and when you get somewhere private, he drops it. Get a grip, Wil." She pulled a white cloth out of her chest of drawers. "Wrap it in this if you're so slobber adverse."

"In his mouth? That's all?" I clutched the handkerchief.

"Yeah. What did you think I meant?"

A low chuckle came from Talisen across the room. "She thought you wanted Link to swallow it. Then wait for it to work its way through his system."

I shot Talisen a dirty look.

"Gross." Phoebe wrinkled her nose. "God, no. Can you see me digging—"

I held my hand up. "Stop. Just stop. I got it now. Link will carry the bug in his mouth. Great. Then what?"

She tapped her beetle. "I'll be able to listen in. If there's any trouble, I'll form a plan. We can't have you locked up in there again. Breaking you out a second time will be virtually impossible. Maude will leave nothing to chance."

"David will be with me," I countered. "Even if they lose their minds and decide to incarcerate Eadric's son, he'll be hard to overpower."

"He's not your savior," Talisen said, contempt clear in his tone.

Phoebe cast him a sidelong glance.

I clamped my mouth shut, refusing to get into it with him. We needed to have a serious conversation, but now wasn't the time.

"I think she means her chances are better with an important vampire around," Phoebe reasoned, then narrowed her eyes. "Willow doesn't wait around for anyone to 'save' her."

Thank you, I mouthed. Talisen's shitty attitude was really starting to piss me off. He could be mad at me all he wanted, but he didn't have to be an ass.

Phoebe grabbed her silver bag and shrugged as if to say her support was no big deal. "I'm off to the fundraiser. Remember to turn on your bug as soon as you get to the Arcane."

"Okay. Be careful."

"Aren't I always?" She cast me a wicked smile. There was no doubt Phoebe had phenomenal undercover skills, but this was different. She was headed to a high-end fundraiser attended by the right hands of all the important supernaturals in New Orleans. It would be a fantastic place to pick up hints of the truth about whatever was going down with the upper class. The only problem was no matter what Phoebe looked like or how convincing she was, she was still an outsider. They'd regard her with suspicion no matter what. And that meant she needed to be a hundred times more careful. Blending in wasn't easy in that tight-knit crowd.

I sighed. "Just don't get locked in a vampire's dungeon, all right?"

"No dungeons. Got it." She saluted me with two fingers and walked out.

I turned to find Talisen watching me. "You'll stay with her?" I nodded to Nicola.

He leaned back against the headboard. "Where else would I go? Fae aren't welcome at Phoebe's function and you have Link and the vampire."

The vampire. Damn him. When this was all over, we were going to have words. I swallowed a snarky reply and glanced at the unconscious witch next to him. Phoebe was convinced she'd been spelled into silence when she'd given us information we weren't supposed to have. Her vitals were stable though, so instead of rushing her off to a hospital and bringing unwanted attention, Talisen was keeping a careful eye on her. "Can you text if there's any change in her condition?"

His eyebrows rose as he looked me up and down. "Do you have your phone?" His tone implied he doubted it.

"It's right here." I pulled the iPhone from my back pocket and waved it at him. "Look, fully charged."

He shook his head. "A lot of firsts happening around here today."

Anger shot straight to my fingertips, and I squeezed the phone until my hand hurt. Smug son of a bitch. Was this really about keeping me safe or his pride? He could choke on his righteous indignation for all I cared.

I didn't respond as I stalked to the door.

"Wil?" he said.

I stopped in the threshold but didn't look back. "Yeah."

"Take care of yourself." His tone was soft, all accusations and resentment gone.

Some tension drained from my shoulders. Grateful for the temporary truce, I glanced back. "You, too. If Nicola wakes up, don't let her spell you into becoming some sort of witch's slave."

His lips curled into the first smile I'd seen all day. "Not against my will, anyway."

That was the Talisen I knew and loved. My heart eased a tiny bit. "Keep it clean, Tal. Keep it clean."

"Not if I have anything to say about it."

David, Link, and I stood on the street in front of the Arcane. The afternoon sun beat down, burning my exposed arms. Link panted, and I lifted the hair off my neck, fanning myself. David stood to the side, his pristine, button-down shirt wrinkle free and not a bead of sweat anywhere. That was one perk to being a vamp. Their internal temperature never rose.

I crouched down, petting Link. "Ready, boy?"

He snuggled close to my leg, and when I scratched his chin, he licked my hand, slyly taking the beetle into his mouth.

"Don't swallow," I whispered as I leaned down to kiss the top of his head.

He gave me another puzzled look.

"He thinks you're crazy." David rolled a cigarette between his fingers. He'd lit it, but had taken only the initial puff, letting the rest burn to ash. If anyone was watching, they'd assume we were waiting for David to finish before we went in.

"No, he doesn't. He thinks Phoebe's crazy." I glanced at the cigarette. "Put that out. I'm too hot to stand here any longer." Besides, if I had to inhale one more lungful of rancid smoke, I was going to vomit on his pristine Italian leather shoes.

His phone buzzed, and he glanced at the screen. "Pandora's on her way to your house as soon as the sun goes down."

"That's good." I took out my own phone and sent the message to Talisen. On the way to the Arcane, David had called Eadric, but he'd been unavailable. Instead, he'd spoken with Pandora. Judging by the hysterical cries coming out of his phone, she hadn't taken the news well. David soothed her as best he could, but she'd hung up before they could discuss a plan of action. "Hopefully Nicola will be awake by then."

David pressed his lips together in a thin line. "If not, we're going to have a homicidal vampire on our hands."

"I think that ship has already sunk." I snapped my fingers, and Link trotted to my side. "Let's go."

David followed me through the parking garage to the side entrance. Surprise flickered over the face of the usual guard. After last night, I guess he wasn't expecting to see me so soon.

"Records," I said as I tossed my phone into my purse and placed it on the conveyor belt to be screened. The guard nodded and waved me through. Link pressed against my leg as we stood in the neutralizer chamber.

The green lights flashed, and I gritted my teeth. Tiny electrodes stole the magic simmering beneath my skin. Link growled. Moments later we stumbled out into the hallway. I flexed my wings and rose a few inches in the air. At least I had one defense.

David took his turn in the chamber. He stood there appearing unfazed, waiting for the green lights to go off. The machine couldn't affect him—vampirism wasn't a magical ability. It was a chemical change. No, the guards were making sure he wasn't carrying any magical objects. Like the one still hidden in Link's mouth.

The lights went out, and David was waved forward.

"ID and purpose?" the guard asked him.

"Records." David pulled out his Arcane badge. "I'm her partner."

The guard checked his list, scowled, and made a note on his computer screen. "Nowhere in here does it say you're a vampire." He peered out the window and then eyed David. "It's still light out."

I shrugged. "We parked in the garage." No doubt this guard hadn't ever seen a vamp during the day before. Last time we'd come during business hours, Maude's assistant had taken us through security. Apparently she hadn't been ready for the rest of the building to know about David's situation. "Trust me. He's vamp. Maude appointed him herself."

"Damn this place. How do they expect me to do my job if they don't do theirs?" The guard glanced at me, skepticism broadcasting loud and clear on his lined face. "With the sloppy reporting around here, I doubt you'll find anything useful, but good luck."

I gave him a nod, picked up Link, and strode off down the hall. As soon as we rounded the corner, he spit the beetle into my hand. Dog slobber and everything. Gross. Better than the alternative. I stuffed it into my back pocket and wiped my wet hand on my jeans.

"Here." David handed me the handkerchief I thought I'd left back at the house.

"Thanks." I put Link down and wiped the remaining dog spit from my hand. Then we took off. Our boots and Link's nails clicked on the tile floors.

Arcane agents and workers cast us curious glances but no one stopped us. When we rounded the next corner, anxiety flooded my brain, and my wings started to tremble. The basement door loomed in front of me. The place they'd tried to hold me before Phoebe had stopped them last time. What was down there? Cages? Electrodes? Influence? Oh Goddess. *Don't think about it.*

I kept moving until we reached the room we needed. With one swipe of my ID card, the door swooshed open. "This is it." I waved Link and David in, then hit the button from the inside. The room fell into darkness as the door shut. "Lights," I said.

A soft glow flickered to life around the vast file cabinets.

"Neat trick," David said.

"All I did was say the word. The spell is an old one designed to keep electricity costs down. Or so I'm told. Let's get started." I moved to the two large file cabinets that housed current Arcane employees' records. "I'll take this row." I pointed to the section on my right. "You start on the left."

"Sure. What exactly are we looking for?" David pulled the top drawer open and ran a hand over the manila folders.

"Any name that looks familiar to you. My goal is to find out who's working for Maude to spy on Cryrique." I opened my purse and pulled out a list of New Orleans Cryrique employees I'd asked Allcot's secretary to fax over an hour earlier.

After searching four drawers, I threw the latest file back into the cabinet and flopped down on the floor. "Ouch!" Something sharp poked into my left butt cheek. Rolling to the side, I fished out the bent silver beetle. "Oh shit. Phoebs is going to kill me."

David glanced at me. "Does it still work?"

I shrugged, inspecting it. "No idea. It's only supposed to transmit information to her." I turned it over and flicked the tiny switch a few times. "Testing. Phoebe, can you hear me?" I pressed it to my ear. "No sound. I think it's dead."

"It doesn't make sound anyway, does it?" David shoved a stack of files back into the drawer and pulled out another handful.

"When Phoebe flipped the switch it did." I pressed the button again. Nothing.

"It doesn't matter. No one seems to care we're here anyway." The papers rustled as he opened a file.

I stared at the bug for a minute, then shoved it in my purse. David was right. No one had bothered us. Link nudged my leg with his nose and sneezed. I patted his belly. "Nothing at all?" I asked David.

He flipped another page and peered at a photo ID. "Nobody looks familiar."

This was useless. I stretched my legs out in front of me, and glanced at the clock. A quarter to six. She might be gone for the day. It wouldn't hurt to check.

"David? I think we need to go to the source."

He raised an eyebrow. "Maude? And do what, just ask her who's on her payroll?"

"No. We'll go through her private files." I gestured to Link, and he followed me to the door.

"Are you sure that's a good idea?" David joined us and placed a hand on the doorknob, preventing me from leaving.

"Sure. She's usually gone by five thirty. It won't take long. There's only one file cabinet in her office."

He didn't budge.

"Five minutes, tops. I promise. Come on, David. We need to find a clue of some sort. I feel like I'm flying blind here."

He studied me as if he were contemplating my request. Reluctantly, he nodded. "Let me take the lead."

Fine with me. We left the records room and took the stairs to the second floor. David opened the stairwell door, scanned the hallway, and waved me and Link to follow. All the other offices appeared to be empty. Only two hall lights lit the area.

Maude's door was shut and locked for the evening. "Good. That means she's gone."

"The guards will probably be making their rounds on the hour. That gives us ten minutes." David jiggled the door handle and pulled out two thin metal files.

"Lockpicks?" I whispered. They looked exactly like the ones Phoebe carried.

He brought his finger to his lips and quickly popped the lock on the door.

Handy. I brushed past him, heading straight for the file cabinet behind her desk, Link on my heels. Locked. Of course. David closed the door behind him and strode over, a smile in place as he once again put his tools to good use.

"Thank you," I said as he slid the drawer open. Inside was a thick file labeled Rhoswen and five smaller ones: Thompson, Daniels, Allcot, Laveaux, Kilsen. My fingers itched to snag my file, but the clock was ticking. It was two minutes to six. We didn't have time. I grabbed Thompson and Daniels and flipped them both open on Maude's desk. They each had a signed contract and a picture. My mouth dropped. Thompson was Clea Thompson, the vampire, and Daniels was her college-student boyfriend. They'd both signed on a month ago to work undercover for Maude.

"Shit." David slammed a fist down on the desk. "That's why she sought me out. She was spying on me."

"The Cherry Bomb," I said tightly. "Maude contracted her to kill me and Phoebe." My chest tightened. The low-down, double-crossing bitch. We had to get out of here. Hastily, I stuffed the files back in the drawer and turned to flee.

The doorknob squeaked, and I froze. Link stayed by my side, his hackles raised. There was nowhere to hide. David jumped in front of me, knocking my purse to the ground. My phone and the little silver beetle spilled out. Shit.

I peered over David's shoulder and found Maude standing with her arms crossed. Two guards flanked her on either side. She pressed her lips together in an angry sneer. "Agent Rhoswen."

I tensed, ready for a fight. "Director."

"Care to explain your actions?"

"We were looking for you," I lied.

"In my locked office?" Her skepticism rang through loud and clear.

I shrugged. "It was unlocked. We assumed you'd be back."

"Director," David said pleasantly. "We spent the last hour in the records department going through employee files. It was our hope we might spot any suspicious employees that might be leaking information about Willow and her abilities. We were hoping to find a lead. But so far, no luck. If you can think of anyone, please let us know."

"You think someone's feeding information from the inside?" Maude asked.

I wasn't sure if the contempt in her voice was for anyone who would betray the Arcane or the fact we thought anyone she'd hired would go off the reservation. Considering Maude crossed lines all the time, I had to assume the latter.

She gave each of us a hard look. "You'll need to be debriefed. Come with me." She stalked toward the door, obviously expecting us to follow.

"I don't think so," David said. "We have someplace else to be. But we can make an appointment for later."

She froze and slowly turned back to face us, her mouth open. She shut it and raised one menacing eyebrow. "You will make time. Now."

David grabbed my hand and pushed past her. "We'll be in touch."

Maude started to say something again, but a loud buzzing started from behind her desk, cutting her off. Then it stopped and clear as day, Phoebe's voice sounded from the darkened corner. "Can't you make a tiny exception? I won't cause any trouble. Promise." Her tone was sugar sweet, almost nausea inducing. "There's someone I'm supposed to meet here."

"Sorry, Kilsen," a man replied. "The boss warned me you might show up. I can't let you in."

"I know all about David's arrangement with the Arcane and how he's really working for Allcot. What do you think Maude will do once she finds out? Just let me sneak on in, and I'll make sure that stays under wraps. Hmm?"

Oh shit! The beetle. It was transmitting Phoebe's conversation with the doorman at the fundraiser. I met David's eyes for a split second, then we both took off running down the hall.

"Seize them!" Maude yelled, and to my horror, a dozen guards rounded the corner, heading straight for us.

Chapter 25

I snatched Link and fluttered high in the corridor, speeding after David. He tossed one guard after another out of the way, clearing our path. I stuck close to him, acutely aware I was a major liability. As was Link, who wouldn't be able to shift until we got outside. Neither of us could hold our own in a fight against the guards.

"Hold it!" Maude yelled from behind me.

Yeah, right. Not after she'd just heard my best friend confirm David was working for Allcot. It's not that Maude wouldn't have already put two and two together, considering last night's breakout, but now she had confirmation and witnesses. She could lock us both up with the full weight of the Arcane behind her. Deal or no deal with Eadric.

David barreled through the last of the guards and down the stairs we went. Once back on the main floor, we turned right, the emergency-exit sign glowing ahead. If we could get outside, they'd never catch both of us. David was too fast, and I could wing my way into obscurity.

Just as we reached the emergency exit, someone grabbed my foot and twisted. Sharp agony shot straight to my hip as the guard yanked me down. Oh shit, that hurt.

Yelping, Link slipped from my grip, and I grappled to keep him in my arms. But it was no use. He tumbled to the floor with a loud thud.

"Link!" I cried, using the force of my wings to try to jerk away from my captor.

His little body quivered as he lurched forward, favoring his front left paw.

"Let go!" I twisted and cried out, my knee screaming in protest. I tilted forward, barely able to keep myself from face-planting on the gleaming white tile.

Link snarled at the guard, his hackles raised. Poor kid thought he was bigger than he really was.

In one blink, David appeared, neutralizing the guard clutching my leg with one lightning-fast punch to the head. Instantly, he crumpled to the floor.

"Let's go." David grabbed my hand and pulled me down the hall, my wings fluttering hard to compensate for my throbbing knee and hip. Rage fueled me as I watched Link do his best to catch up on his three good legs. They'd hurt my dog. The bastards.

Another white-clad guard dove and caught Link by the tail. Link whipped his head around and sank his teeth into the guard's hand. *Good dog.*

"Son of a bitch!" the guard yelled but didn't let go.

David cursed and sped back to Link as I held the exit door open. And then everything slowed. David reaching down for Link. Link squirming away from the guard. And Maude, feet apart, holding an oversized tranquilizer gun pointed right at David's chest.

"No!" I launched myself forward, but a double blast reverberated through the corridor and instinctively I hit the floor. I glanced up as David sank to the ground, two large yellow darts stuck in his chest. His wide, unseeing eyes stared past me.

"David!" I crawled to his side and yanked the darts out, but I knew it wouldn't help. Arcane-grade tranq darts put vampires out for hours.

I swallowed the emotion rising in my throat. There was no time to fall apart. As Maude closed in on me, I grabbed Link and thrust my wings out. I had to get out of there. Commotion filled the hallway as I focused on the exit only a couple of feet in front of me. Just a few more seconds, and I'd see daylight.

"Grab her!" Maude demanded.

My left hand hit the lever for the exit, and the door burst open. I could smell the muddy stench of the Mississippi wafting over the bank. Freedom.

"Gotcha." Someone grabbed a chunk of my hair, and my head jerked back. Crying out with pain, I clutched Link tight to my chest. A rough male voice rasped in my ear, "Get used to it, faery. I'm going to really enjoy our time together."

Bile rose in my throat. This was it. How could I have thought we'd survive a trip to the Arcane? How long would it be before I was strapped to an evil scientist's table while they shot me full of drugs and forced me to cooperate?

"Put her down," Maude ordered from behind us. The guard spun me around and planted me on my feet. Link, still in my arms, growled. I almost wanted to mimic him.

"Step back," Maude commanded the guard, waving him away. He made a disgusted sound deep in his throat and shoved me toward my aunt. She towered over me, her eyes the same color as her black wings. Her pupils dilated so far not even the rim of her blue irises showed. She leveled the gun right at my heart.

Glaring at her, I stood with my shoulders back. "Vampire-grade tranq darts can kill faeries. You're not going to pull the trigger."

She let out a mocking laugh, and her lips turned up in a grim smile. "Don't tempt me."

Then she pulled out a crumpled piece of paper from her pocket. Holding it up, she asked, "Look familiar?"

I stared at Clea's picture. The contract must've fallen out of the file. I closed my eyes, wondering if the situation could get any worse. There was literally nothing I could do. My only skills lay with modifying plants. David and Link were my weapons. But Link was totally harmless in his current state. My bug was broken and lost in Maude's office. No one was coming. So when two higher-ranking guards—I could tell by the insignias pinned to their uniforms—grabbed my arms, I walked with them, praying David woke up soon. Or Phoebe had somehow heard the mess we were in. Deep down I knew neither was going to help, but the thoughts kept me sane. Until we rounded the corner and they stopped in front of the basement door.

My lungs constricted and my heart sped up. Oh God, oh God, oh God. My wings stretched as if they could somehow hold me back. I twisted to find Maude directly behind me. "Why here?"

Her steely, evil gaze told me everything I needed to know. I was being punished in the worst possible way. Underground, with no hope of escape.

A guard, with hands larger than my head, clutched Link as he squirmed and howled his protest. Ice froze my heart. I couldn't help him. Just like I couldn't help David. Or myself. *David.* Was he still lying sprawled on the floor where they'd left him? What would they do to him? Where would they keep him?

Fear crawled up my spine, quickly transforming to utter panic as the guard behind me pushed me onto the tiny stairway. No railings. No light. Just walls on either side. My eyes refused to adjust to the pitch-blackness. All I could do was keep putting one foot in front of the other or risk being pushed into the abyss.

"Put her in the one to the left," Maude ordered. A small click sounded from behind us. A bulb in the middle of the room came to life, barely illuminating the dank space with pale green light. A wall of diamond shapes floated in front of me in the darkness. I squinted, trying to identify the odd images.

"Move," Maude ordered. The barrel of the tranq gun stabbed me in the back, scraping one of my wings.

"I'm going," I snapped. "Get a grip. It's not like I can see anything down here in your horror-movie dungeon."

The tip dug deeper into my shoulder blade. I stumbled forward and landed face-first against cold metal wire. The links crisscrossed over my face and that's when I realized what the odd diamonds were. A cage. A faery-sized cage. They weren't just going to leave me down there. They were going to lock me up.

"You can't do this!" I brought my hands up, clutching the front of the cage, my fingers digging into the metal. "I'm an agent of the Void. I deserve—oomph," I cried as something hard swept against my legs, knocking me to one knee.

"Shut up or I'll break your ankle." It was Maude. She hovered over me, swinging her gun as if it were a billy club. She yanked the cage door open, the rattle of metal on metal echoing through the room. "Get in. Now."

Fear paralyzed me. Nothing could make me voluntarily climb in a metal cage. *Metal* for Goddess's sake. Underground, surrounded by metal. She was trying to kill me.

"Do it," Maude ordered, her voice lower and harsher than before.

I didn't move.

Boots clicked against the cement, and then someone grabbed me around the waist, tearing the metal from my death grip, and threw me. Hard. I slammed against the back wall. A sickening crunch registered in my brain before I realized anything was wrong. But as I fell to my knees, a sharp, piercing pain enveloped the entire right side of my back. My wings flexed in protest. A sharp lightning bolt of agony pierced my chest. No air expanded my lungs. I couldn't breathe. Something was terribly wrong.

"You know, at first when I found out Clea tried to kill you and Kilsen, I wasn't pleased. That wasn't in the contract. She was only supposed to bring me information from the Cryrique. I guess she blamed you for the death of her idiot lover. Such a stupid mistake, pairing Cryrique business with his Influence purchase." She shook her head. "But now I'm thinking a little dose of Cherry Bomb might be exactly what you need."

I moaned, realizing Clea had played us. She'd known all along Daniels was dead.

Maude let out a demented laugh. "Let's see you try to fly out of here now."

The door to the cage slammed shut. A second later, a lock snicked closed with cold finality.

Fading laughter and the sound of retreating footsteps drifted down the stairs as I curled into a ball, trying to control the pain blazing along my right side.

I don't know how long I lay there, trying not to move. All I could think about was Maude's final words. *Let's see you fly out of here now.*

The blow to the wall had crushed my right wing. I couldn't move it one little bit without my stomach trying to turn itself inside out. Hot, angry tears pricked my eyelids. The bitch had taken out David, grabbed my dog, and mutilated my wing. If I didn't get medical attention soon, I knew I could be crippled. Wings were durable in that they could withstand a lot, but if they were crushed, they needed specialized attention, or they'd never heal right. What good was a faery without two working wings?

A dose of good old-fashioned self-pity washed over me and I whimpered. What else was there to do but feel sorry for myself? A faint scraping sounded from outside my cage. Panic sent adrenaline through my veins. Had someone stayed behind? I held my breath, listening.

Scrape, scrape. Scrape, scrape.

"Link?" I said, my voice trembling.

The scraping grew louder, more urgent.

"Link!" My voice rose a few octaves, bringing fresh fire to my upper back. I stifled a gasp as I tensed and battled the pain. Where was he? Did they take him? Oh God, was he locked up too? And what had they left behind?

Gritting my teeth against the fire running from my wing tip to my shoulder blade, I grabbed the cage door and hauled myself into a sitting position. White spots swam in my vision as my back seized up again. Holy shitballs, that hurt. I blinked away the flares clouding my vision and peered through the diamond-shaped openings.

It took a moment for me to make out what was just ahead. A much smaller cage than mine, and Link trapped inside. My heart lightened. They hadn't taken him. "Hey, buddy," I called.

His attention was focused on the door. *Scrape, scrape. Scrape, scrape.* He was using his one good paw to dig as fast as he could, but it was no use. We were sitting on a concrete floor.

"Link," I commanded. "Stop."

This time his head popped up, and he tilted an ear toward me.

"I'm right here. Digging won't help. See?" I reached down to pat the floor. My hand settled over a thick layer of grime. "Ugh!" I wiped the moist dirt on my jeans. No wonder he was trying to dig his way out. I summoned as much strength as I could and forced the words out. "It's no use, little dude. We're trapped."

He gave a few more halfhearted scrapes, then settled with a heavy sigh on the ground, staring in my general direction.

"I know exactly how you feel."

Link touched his nose to the door of his cage, sniffing the air.

"Is something else here?" I forced myself to stand on shaky legs. I could barely see more than a few feet in front of me. Nothing but the eerie green light and darkness. Feeling my way along the edge of the cage, I peered at our surroundings. Through the gloom, I spotted two more cages. Empty.

Better that than a whole host of prisoners. Right? A sinking feeling of helplessness took over, followed closely by rage. How could Maude do this? Whatever happened to justice? I could stand trial. I deserved a lawyer. This was still America, after all.

But Maude wasn't working under the law. She was the director of the Void. That meant she did whatever she pleased. And right now, she wanted me locked away.

The power-hungry bitch. But why? What good was I down here? I could make Influence. And apparently change the chemical makeup of vampires. Was that it? Was she afraid I'd turn all vamps into sunbathers?

Damn it! I would not just sit there in a cage and wait to be given orders. Tucking my injured wing close to my body, I ran my hands along each section of the cage. If there was a weak point, I'd find it. I spent agonizing minutes fingering every single connection on the gate, every joint, even the bottom where it hit the floor. Not one area showed a sign of weakness. In total frustration, I grabbed the side of the cage and yanked as hard as I could. Agony brought me to my knees. I gritted my teeth and waited for the worst of the pain to subside.

Idiot. My tantrum had been useless. Not one single sign of movement.

Beyond annoyed, I leaned my head against the cage door, too exhausted to form a plan. My head started to spin, and I vaguely wondered if it was from exhaustion or my broken wing. It throbbed with each breath I took. In a hazy, pain-filled stupor, I slumped down and curled up on my left shoulder.

Exhausted, I faded in and out of consciousness, waking each time Link sighed or moved. After what seemed like hours, I fell into a deep slumber. And dreamed I was sinking in quicksand.

I woke to a sharp pain in my wing and cried out, rolling to my stomach in agony. Gasping for breath, I pushed myself up on my knees, remembering the dream and the panic of trying to fly to safety. Great. I couldn't even sleep without hurting myself. I blinked, trying to focus as I processed once again where I was. Arcane. Basement. Cage.

How long had we been down here? I had no way to tell. The room was still cast in horror-movie green and darkness.

Across from me, Link growled.

My body tensed. Was someone coming? Nervous energy ran from head to toe. I cut my eyes to Link. He stood rigid, attention focused on the stairs.

Someone *was* coming.

At the top of the stairs the door creaked. Bright fluorescent light spilled down the stairwell for a moment, followed by soft footsteps. I pressed deeper into the shadows of my cage, but Link lunged forward, snarling and biting at the crisscrossed wire. Then he started to vibrate.

"Link, no!" How was this happening? He shouldn't be able to shift. This was bad. Very bad. His cage simply wasn't big enough.

A fraction of a second later, he shifted into full-on wolf mode. He howled as his large body smashed against the sides of the cage. Panicked and trapped, he began to shake, frantically trying to dislodge himself. I couldn't do anything but stare as my poor wolf toppled the cage over. Lying on his side, he scrabbled at the walls, rolled again, and ended up on his back.

Goddess, help him.

The footsteps grew slow and hesitant. Then, with a burst of energy, Link flipped again, causing the cage to land at a forty-five-degree angle right where the two sides were seamed together. Something snapped. Link went crazy, bucking, kicking, and biting. In wolf form, the cage didn't stand a chance.

Before our visitor could get all the way to the bottom of the stairs, Link was free, head down, hackles raised, and teeth bared. My wolf was ready for a fight.

Chapter 26

The guard's white uniform glowed in the dim light of the basement. He stopped at the base of the stairwell and squinted.

The wolf watched him through gold eyes, his shoulders lowered, legs bent, ready to pounce. I sucked in a breath. Watching him wait for the exact moment made the hair stand up on the back of my neck.

The guard spotted Link and his eyes went wide with recognition. "What the hell? How—"

Link lunged, his entire wolf body engulfing the short, pudgy guard in one swift motion. A high-pitched scream of terror filled the room, making me wince. Some guard he was. He sounded like a girl. Link swiped a heavy paw across the man's face, silencing the earsplitting noise. The guard collapsed. Knocked out or dead, I didn't know. Nor did I care. Blood pooled a few feet from my cage. Link snarled and nudged the unmoving body with his long nose.

"Good job, Link." I rose, arching my back, favoring my right wing as I tried not to hurl from the pain. That was one man down. But Link couldn't get them all. And he wouldn't leave me. I stared at his massive form. How *had* he shifted? We were still in the Arcane. As long as we were in the building, he shouldn't have been able to. Was it because we were underground? Maybe the magic keeping the place dry interfered with the neutralizing ward.

Had my magic come back? I clutched the door of my cage and glanced around at all the cement and metal around me.

Useless. Even if I did have a spark somewhere, I didn't have anything to siphon life from. And I wouldn't weaken Link. Unless…"Link!"

He snapped to attention and turned his giant head toward me. "Pull the guard over here."

His eyebrows twitched as if he was contemplating my request.

"Just grab him and pull him to me." I pointed. *Come on.* Who knew when the next visitor would be down or when they'd miss the guard?

Link circled the man with his lip raised and then sniffed his black work boots. He jumped back as if the scent offended him. What could be so bad that even a dog wasn't interested? I wrinkled my nose in sympathy. I wouldn't want to put my mouth on the ruddy man, either.

Gingerly, Link wrapped his muzzle around the man's ankle and dragged him inch by inch until he lay along the edge of my cage. The wolf spat out the man's limb and hacked, a full-on, hairball-raising hack.

"Yikes." What could possibly make Link gag? I knelt down to inspect the guard. Halfway to the ground, a sudden assault of formaldehyde hit my senses. "Oh, yuck. I'm so sorry, buddy."

The wolf lowered himself to the floor and covered his nose with one paw.

"Yeah, no kidding. What is this dude, a zombie?" He reeked of chemicals and death. I placed a hand over his chest and let out a relieved sigh when it rose on an intake of breath. At least he wasn't dead. If he was, he'd be useless to me.

Moment of truth. I needed a life source. If I'd regained any sort of magical strength, I'd know as soon as I touched him. But where? I'd need an exposed section of skin. His hands or face. Because no way was I stripping down the stinky super geek. His hands were caked with blood from defending himself against Link and so was the right side of his face. Jesus. My dog was lethal. I'd known it intellectually, but he'd never had to take on a human before. Only vampires, and their wounds stitched themselves closed within seconds of splitting open.

I grimaced as I rested two fingers on the man's left temple. Then I snatched them back. I couldn't take life energy from his brain. It would make me sick. Faeries could share energy. Faeries and humans, not so much. But I could take a little just to see if my magic was back.

Get it over with, Willow. Closing my eyes, I touched his blood-soaked hand and searched deep inside myself for a spark of magic.

Nothing.

The little tingle that usually sprang to life at the tips of my fingers stayed dormant. I let out a frustrated sigh. Maybe my body still needed time to adjust. Link always did regain his magic before I did after a trip to the Arcane.

I pressed my fingers against the guard one more time, but no matter how far I searched within myself, no magic came to the surface.

Well, crap. Now what? I needed a weapon. Or better yet, a key. A key! The concrete and metal must be zapping my brainpower. Why hadn't I thought of that first?

"Link, help me search." Trying not to breathe in the sickening stench of the man, I dug into his coat pockets. "He might have a key to this cage."

Link sniffed along the opposite side of the guard's body while I frantically moved to his pants pocket. The only thing I found was a wallet. Henry Mincer. Lived in Kentwood. No other identifying information except a credit card and a health ID card. "Come on, Henry. You've got to have something useful."

I found a ballpoint pen in his shirt pocket. Great. A makeshift weapon. I set it aside and tried to reach forward to get to his other pockets, but my wing and back froze in protest. I hissed and sat back, holding my wing tight to my body.

Link gazed at me with worried eyes.

"I'll be okay once we get out of here." I hoped.

He nudged the jacket pocket I hadn't been able to reach with his nose.

"Did you find something?" I sat up on my knees, pressed against the door, and peered over his body. Tentatively, I stretched my arm through the diamond-shaped wire but snatched it back when the lightning bolts shot through my back. No way was I going to be able to reach it without passing out. I clenched my fists and tried to stabilize my breathing.

Across from me, Link shimmered and returned to his Shih Tzu form. He eyed me, wagged his tail, and went to work on the guard's pocket. His much smaller Shih Tzu paw slipped right in and a loud *tink* sounded on the concrete. He fished whatever it was away from the body with his paws and then grabbed the shiny metal cluster in his teeth.

"The keys!" I cried. "Link, bud. You really are a girl's best friend."

He trotted up to me, his hurt paw healed by the shift, and dropped the key ring near my hand. Then he sat there, his tongue hanging out in happy satisfaction.

I gave him a pet behind the ears and scratched his chin. "You're such a good boy."

With shaky hands, I grabbed the keys, trying each one. By the time I got down to the last three, I could barely jam the key into the lock. They all fit. Every single one. But none of them would pop the lock.

"Please, please, please," I whispered, nearly dropping the key ring. I'd just got the final key stuffed in the lock when another short burst of fluorescent light rushed in from the top of the stairs. A door slammed, followed by the sounds of multiple footsteps descending into the basement.

Shit! How many were coming? Two? Three? I clutched the pen, knowing in my heart I'd never beat them all. I wasn't trained in combat. It would be a miracle if I could take out one. I steeled myself and tightened my grip on my pitiful weapon. No way was I going down without a fight.

Link jumped up and, to my complete surprise, shimmered slightly and shifted. He was getting stronger. Or maybe it was my fear that boosted his stamina. Either way, I had to stifle a gasp of relief.

I cranked the key in the lock, but it didn't turn. My last damn key didn't work. A hopeless dread crawled into my gut. Would I ever find a way out? Still unable to see our visitors, I eased back, not wanting to appear suspicious, and jammed my hands in my pockets. My right fingers hit something warm and mushy.

Gross. I pulled my hand out, eyed the brown, waxy coating, and sniffed in the cocoa-orange scent. Influence. My heart sped up. Another weapon. My lonely pen had a partner in crime. And I was just desperate enough to use it.

Clunk. Clunk. Clunk. Heavy footsteps pounded down the lower stairs.

Link hovered near the wall, out of sight from the stairwell opening.

"Fuck," came the sound of a deep male voice. "Can't anyone put a brighter bulb in down here? I can barely see anything."

"Stop bitching." Maude's voice was flat, barely audible. "Just find out what Mincer's doing and get back up here."

"Fucking Mincer," the male voice muttered, then raised his voice. "What the hell is going on down here? Got a hard-on for the faery?"

His steps slowed. "Mincer?"

Link crept closer to the stairwell opening.

"What the fuck is that smell? Jesus, if you took out the faery, the director's going to eat you for breakfast." The tall, lanky guard came into view as he stepped out of the stairwell and into the basement. His eyes flickered over me, caught sight of Link's broken cage, and then landed on Mincer's unconscious body. "Oh, fuck."

Link leapt. In less than a second, he had the new guard pinned to the concrete. The guard howled with pain as Link held him down, mauling his face. The guard's limbs flailed around the wolf, but Link was too strong.

I turned away, not at all comfortable with watching my dog attack the guy.

"What's going on down there?" Maude's voice floated from the top of the stairs. "Bass, Mincer, get your asses up here now."

Bass brought up one arm and clocked Link right below his pointed ear. Link shook his head as if to ward off a fly and sank his teeth into his victim's shoulder. Bass shrieked.

"Link!" I cried, clutching the side of my cage. "Look out!"

Maude flew down the stairwell, tranq gun aimed at the wolf.

"No!" I shook the cage, terrified for Link. My wing jostled against the metal bars, sending pain shooting through my shoulder and down my arm, but I shoved the burning aside. If that was a vampire dart, Link would be dead.

Maude fired.

My world narrowed to include only Link, half of his body illuminated by the green bulb, the rest in shadows. Link's head turned toward the noise as his body crouched in defense. The dart sailed deadly silent through the air and landed with a piercing thunk in Link's right paw.

His body slumped, landing on Bass in a heap. Those glassy, unfocused eyes darted around the room before they settled on me. I rattled my cage, unbridled fury filling every inch of my being. "You killed him!" Kicking out, I yanked as hard as I could on the metal. I was so angry I didn't even feel the pain anymore. "You evil bitch. You killed my dog."

Maude stepped into the basement and kicked Bass's shoulder. A whimper escaped his bloody lips.

"Your *dog* deserves to die for what he did to my assistants." Maude flashed me an impatient grimace.

"Deserves?" I ground out. "All he did was try to protect me from your illegal imprisonment." Hot tears welled in my eyes. I forced them back. No way was I breaking down. Lowering my voice, my tone came out hard and flat. "You're a monster."

"Drop the act, Rhoswen. We both know you're at the mercy of my goodwill." She fluttered slightly off the ground, her black wings shimmering in the faint glow. She landed beside Mincer and nudged his face with a high-heeled Mary Jane sandal. He didn't move. Her gaze ran the length of the cage as if checking to be sure I really was locked in. Then she spotted the keys hanging from the lock. She laughed. "At least you aren't weak-willed. That's good. Very good."

I longed to spit on her. She deserved worse. Much worse. But pissing her off wasn't going to get her to open the door faster. I cut my gaze to Link, lying limp on the floor. My heart pounded against my ribcage. There was nothing I wanted more at that moment than to be by his side.

Maude tilted her head and eyed him. "First your vampire and now your dog. Next it will be Agent Kilsen...or maybe your fae friend."

Every muscle tensed with rage. I had bottled up all the anger, all the hatred, and every ounce of strength I had left. She would not hurt one more person I loved. Not one.

Staring at her with an expression as blank as I could muster, I slipped my hands into the front pockets of my jeans and took a small step back.

A wide, triumphant smile broke out on her face. "That's right. Now you're seeing reason. Give me your word you'll behave and I'll take you upstairs for your assessment."

Assessment. Right. She was going to run experiments on me until they understood two things: my ability to sense vampires and how I had turned David into a daywalker. Hell, they'd probably also keep me locked up and force me to pump out Influence while they were at it.

I said nothing, avoiding her gaze, too afraid she'd see the calm resolve hidden behind my false obedience.

Maude pulled a phone from her pocket, hit the screen, and a second later barked, "Get to the basement." She stuffed the phone back in the pocket of her blazer and pulled out a key. "You honestly didn't think I'd give this to anyone else, did you?"

I stared at it, willing her to insert the key into the lock.

She held it up, turning it over in her hand. "Are you ready to cooperate?"

Grinding my teeth together, I forced a short nod.

"That's what I thought." Her slender hands gracefully slid the key into the lock, and with one twist the heavy metal came apart. "If you don't cause any trouble, there might be food and water for you."

I licked my dry lips. Water. I took two steps forward.

Maude opened the gate, then instantly slammed it shut again. She pressed close to the door, her face almost touching the metal. "But if you so much as even breathe wrong, I'll break your other wing and throw you back in this cell. Got it?"

Numb from sheer hatred, I forced myself to give her another tiny nod.

"Say you'll behave."

She'd lost her mind. How had a faery, a relative of mine, turned out to be so…evil?

"Say it," she demanded.

Faint footsteps started at the top of the stairs again. In panic, I blurted out the words, "I'll behave."

"Good." Maude nodded in approval. "Very good."

The sound on the stairs grew louder with each second. Time to move.

Maude held the door to my cage open and waved an arm, inviting me out. I forced one steady step in front of the other, keeping my hands stuffed in my pockets, hunching as if I were defeated. I stepped over Mincer, still lying on the floor, and strode past Maude.

"Wait." She stuffed the key back in her coat and stalked around me. "That wing is really bad."

I nodded, wincing when she touched the sensitive tip. It trembled under the pressure.

"A shame really," she said with a glint in her eye. "If you come up lame, you'll have to quit your field job and work in the lab."

Oh. Hell. No. She'd already formed a plan for transferring me. If she had her way, she'd do more damage to my wing just to make sure no one decided I should help track vamps again.

"Follow me," she said. "And keep up."

Her massive wings fluttered, and she rose a few inches off the ground, flying beside me.

I snapped. One second my right hand was stuffed into my front pocket with the melted Influence and the next, I cocked my elbow, twisted, and struck a blow.

My fist bounced off her cheekbone.

Maude fell from flight and stumbled, appearing more surprised than hurt. "You little—"

Despite the pain trying to claim my senses, I struck again. Only this time, I jammed my fingers in her open mouth. The ones that were laced with Influence. I stuffed them as far as they would go, only withdrawing when she started to gag.

"Swallow," I demanded.

Her eyes went round with shock and panic. "No, no, no," she mumbled and started wiping her tongue, as if that would do any good.

The person on the stairs finally appeared. A medium-built, dark-haired man, wearing dress pants and a button-down shirt, stared at us. "What's going on here? Maude? Are you all right?"

He almost appeared normal. As if he cared about her. But the handcuffs and the gun in his holster gave him away. I'd bet my other wing he was an undercover agent, just like Phoebe. He had a serious, thoughtful quality about him.

Maude stopped dabbing at her tongue and slowly stood up straight. She glanced around, her eyes taking in the moaning bodies on the floor, the agent, Link, and then finally landed on me. "You're hurt."

I nodded, cautious in case she was putting on an act.

"You need help." She fished around in her pockets until she came up with her phone again.

"Maude?" the agent asked.

She glanced at him as she hit a button.

"No!" I rushed forward, grabbing the phone from her. "No help. I'll take care of it."

Her eyes narrowed in concern. True concern. Not something I'd ever seen her express in the last three years.

The agent moved forward. "Maude, I really think you should—"

"Do as I say," I blurted.

She straightened, her thin body appearing two feet taller than normal. Then she shuddered and her face went slack for a moment.

The agent moved closer to her, his hand outstretched. "Do you need to see someone? You look…off."

But she didn't look off at all. Not to me. Her shoulders relaxed, a hint of a smile on her angular face, and when she turned to me she said, "What are you doing down here? You hate being underground."

Fat tears of relief sprang to my eyes. She wasn't the director I'd come to loathe in the last few years. She was my aunt. The one who used to visit when Beau and I were kids. The sweet, loving, caring aunt I'd long since forgotten. I clamped down on the joy blossoming in my chest.

You can't trust her, Wil.

Her act could be a very clever ruse.

"Take me home, Maude," I whispered the order, casting a sideways glance at the agent.

"Of course. Sure." She snapped her fingers. "Agent, arrange for my niece to get home as soon as possible."

He glanced between the two of us, clearly suspicious. Maude was not following the plan. Oh no. Maude needed to get her she-bitch back in gear, stat. Or else he was going to be a problem.

"Now, Agent!" she demanded. "Can't you see she's hurt? And get someone to carry her dog out to the car."

"Yes, ma'am." The agent cast me a cold hard stare and then ran up the stairs two at a time.

He wasn't buying Maude's sudden change of heart. We had to get out of there. Fast. Before the cavalry came. I turned to Maude. "Listen."

She smiled and nodded.

"Whatever happens, your first priority is to get me and Link out of the building. You are to follow my orders and no one else's. Are you clear?"

"Clear," she parroted.

"Good," I said more to myself than her as I eyed Link. No way was I leaving him, but we couldn't carry him either. I crouched down beside him, and let out an enormous sigh of relief when his chest rose. He was indeed alive. Thank the powers that be.

I ran my hand over his fur, reached down, and yanked out the yellow dart still stuck in his leg. The shimmering glow encircled him and a second later he was Shih Tzu again. The dart. That's what had kept him wolf while he'd been out. And his wolf form had saved his life.

Whooping for joy, I grabbed him and hugged him to my chest. I glanced back at Maude. "Let's go."

"You're the boss," she said cheerily and swept past me up the stairs. When she got halfway up, she glanced back. "You know, I don't think the director is going to like this."

I stopped my laborious climb and braced myself against the wall with my free hand. "The director? *You're* the director."

She laughed, a deep throaty sound. "No. That's what he wants you to think. He likes moving the players around the board. But now…Well, things just got really interesting."

She was amused. Completely and utterly thrilled to be under my control. And I hadn't compelled her to think or feel any particular way. A horrible realization washed over me. "Maude?"

"Yes?"

"How long have you been under the Influence?"

"Combined time?"

I nodded.

"Three years. Right after you invented it."

Chapter 27

"Oh, Jesus," I whispered, barely able to breathe. "Three years. All because of my creation."

Maude's face turned grim. "We'll talk about it later. Right now, we need to get out of here."

I nodded. But who was the director? Since the guard could be back any minute, the information had to wait. Once up the narrow stairs, we crept into the brightly lit, deserted hall.

At the end of the corridor we came to the first connection. White gleamed in every direction, only broken by nondescript gray doors. Maude grabbed my arm, clutching it so tightly my knees almost buckled.

I jerked, my back throbbing with a dull ache as I whirled on her. "What are you doing?" She should be under my Influence. Had it all been an act? If so, she was vying for an Oscar.

She smiled. "Relax. I'm doing what I have to in order to get you and your dog out of here."

"Oh." I forced the suspicion out of my mind. All kinds of flags would be raised if anyone saw her letting me waltz out of the building.

She pulled me close to her body once more and pushed me down the hallway.

"What about David?" I whispered. I'd forced myself to not think about him while I'd been underground. There wasn't anything I could do from there anyway. But now...I couldn't just leave him.

She shook her head. "He's being monitored. There's no way you're getting to him now. But Allcot will probably work a trade." Her hand tightened on my bicep when a clean-cut scientist with black-framed glasses strode toward us, a crooked sneer pasted on his face.

"Director." He bowed his head in a patronizing nod. "I'll take the subject from here."

From the corner of my eye, I saw her raise her chin. Her tone shifted back to evil-bitch mode. "You'll have your chance, Felton. My plans won't take long."

Felton's lips formed two thin, straight lines. His eyes narrowed and his pupils constricted. "Director." He dragged the word out in barely controlled anger. "I think maybe you misunderstood. We have an experiment ready. I must *insist* you bring Rhoswen in now." The tension drained from his posture, and his tone turned neutral, almost uninterested. "We'll be quick. And I'll personally bring her to your office when we're done."

Link twitched and opened his eyes, staring up at me in confusion. I clutched him to me, ready to run. Felton wasn't negotiating. He was ordering her. This man was the true director. He had to be the one Influencing Maude.

Maude smiled tightly, exactly as her Influenced personality would have, and then gave him an impatient nod. "Make it fast."

Then she sprang into action, propelling me forward with enough force that I slammed into the slimy little bastard. My shoulder jammed into his chest, and I took him down in a heap. A fireball of frustration blazed a path through my sanity as I fought to extract myself from a tangle of limbs.

Link rolled and came up snarling. Felton didn't hesitate. Knocking Link aside, he lashed out one arm and clutched me around my neck. Before I could even attempt to throw him off, his grip tightened, abruptly cutting off my air.

"Let go," I tried to choke out, but the words wouldn't form. My face grew hot with effort as I clawed at his forearm and kicked with zero result. Panic gripped my mind. *Do something, Willow. Anything.* But I couldn't move and all too soon my vision started to blur. Phoebe's face flashed through my mind, along with the memory of her insistence I take a self-defense class. Everything started to fade. The light. The agony seizing my battered body. A faint sound of voices.

Peace settled over me. A faded memory of Beau and Talisen, arm in arm on the beach, lulled me into a soothing fog of tranquility. The world went dark. Was this it? Was I dying here on the cold floor of the Arcane? Maybe Beau was waiting...

The harsh slap of fluorescent lighting blinded me. Sound rushed in with the air filling my lungs. Vicious growling blocked everything else. I tried to lift my head but my muscles wouldn't cooperate. Shifting my head to the left, I caught Link, still in Shih Tzu form, doing his best to rip Felton's arm off. Needless to say, without his wolf teeth he wasn't getting very far.

Felton scrambled to his feet, desperately trying to shake the twenty-pound Shih Tzu clinging to his shirt sleeve. Link dangled in the air, his little paws desperately trying to find purchase. I stared in horror as Felton picked up the tranq gun and swung it butt first like a baseball bat.

"Link," I rasped through bruised vocal cords.

Maude appeared from nowhere, jumped on Felton's back and slammed her hand down hard on the crook of his elbow. The man's arm deadened with the impact, and the gun clattered to the floor, barely missing Link.

"I'm not taking orders from you anymore, you sick, power-hungry vamp killer." She kicked, spiking the back of his knee with her Mary Jane heels. He crumpled a few feet from the gun.

Lucky for me and Link, it seemed Maude had taken self-defense lessons.

Link scrambled to my side and nudged my cheek with his nose.

"I'm okay." I pressed my face against his fur, enjoying the warmth of his body. "Thanks to you."

"Get up!" Maude demanded, grabbing Felton by his coat. With one hand, she managed to slap handcuffs on him and then tossed him into the nearest room, kicking him in the ass before she slammed the door shut. She eyed me. "Can you walk?"

I rolled onto my knees. "I'll have to." I squeezed my eyes shut and hauled myself to my feet.

"David?" I asked again. How could I live with myself if we left him there?

"Not now," she snapped and grabbed the fallen tranq gun. "More guards will be here any second. Just move."

I stared at my feet, focusing on keeping one foot in front of the other, ignoring the screams of protest in my aching muscles.

Maude stopped in front of me, forcing me to glance up. "Take this." She held the gun out. "If we run into trouble, shoot first and ask questions later."

I took the gun and nodded. "Got it."

She hit a hidden button, revealing a door with a glowing green keypad. She hastily punched in a code and the door slid open. I followed her inside. Stainless steel tables lined the perimeter of the room filled with sparkling clean, scientific-looking cooking apparatuses. A research lab.

No. Not just a lab. *The* lab. The one where they messed with Influence and anything else they wanted to alter for their own benefit. I paused in front of a glass case, staring at the pounds of familiar chocolate goodies. "Is it all Influence?"

"Not now, Willow." She strode to another hidden door. "We have to go."

A piercing alarm slammed through the silence. Link howled, scrambling alongside me to the door.

"Move," Maude ordered, then swore when the door wouldn't budge. The alarm must have locked it down. She scrambled to one of the tables, grabbed a sharp-edged knife, and returned to the door. Just to the right, she used the blade to whittle away at something on the concrete wall. I inched closer, realizing there was white metal sheeting she was trying to pry off.

The knife slipped and clattered to the floor. "Damn Void and their overzealous protective measures!" She grabbed the knife and went to work once more.

I stood behind her, tapping my foot to the tempo of the panic rising in my chest. They were coming. Something pounded on the door across the room, making the hinges vibrate. "Hurry," I whispered.

Maude grunted in frustration.

The door from the hallway banged open, and Felton filled the threshold. "Maude Jenkins. Stand down. That's an order."

"Fuck off, Felton." She gave the knife one more thrust and the metal plate popped off. A red light flashed in unison with the alarm on the small keypad. "Your hold on me is broken."

I inched as close to the exit door as possible while Felton led the guards into the room. All of them wore nondescript white lab coats over the weapons strapped to their utility belts.

Maude punched in a code. The light stopped flashing.

I rushed toward the door, expecting it to open of its own accord. But the light flickered to life again.

Felton weaved closer.

I raised the tranq gun and aimed at his heart, my hands steady. Dogs weren't the only ones in danger of dying from a tranq dart.

He slowed his steps, attention focused on me. "If you pull that trigger, my men will tear you apart."

"Only if they can get to me."

Maude punched in another code. The alarm didn't stop blaring.

"You won't get far." His low, commanding voice made me acutely aware of just how suited he was to be a puppet master. He had to be fae. If he were a witch, he would have spelled us already. And he certainly wasn't a vampire. That meant he could have almost any sort of power. There was no way to know what it was until he showed his cards.

"Farther than you," I said.

Maude's face broke out in a relieved grin, and even though the alarm didn't fade, the blinking light went out. And stayed out.

The door opened with a pressurized whoosh. I backed up, keeping the gun trained on Felton.

"Go," Maude ordered.

"You first." I wouldn't leave her with the possibility she'd get captured after all the years she'd suffered because of my creation. She was my aunt again. The one I remembered from my childhood. The one my mom mourned for.

"Rhoswen!" Maude jumped in front of me as a yellow dart sailed toward us from somewhere behind Felton.

I fired. But Maude had knocked the gun to the side and the dart bolted into the table leg two feet in front of me.

Maude wasn't so lucky. The other dart stabbed her in the left shoulder. She crumpled at my feet.

"No!" I cried, and threw the gun at Felton, wishing it would bash his head in. He shuffled back, avoiding the blow. With angry tears and blind rage, I grabbed Maude by the shoulders, took two steps, and hauled her out the opened door.

"She won't get far." Felton's faint voice barely registered over the rushing in my ears.

Link bolted as soon as we hit the humid September night air. *Vampires.* They were close. My skin itched with the sensation. A few blurred past me, one of them undeniably familiar. Nathan, David's best friend. Good. He'd get him out.

"Shit!" I heard Phoebe's voice from somewhere far off. Footsteps pounded on the pavement. Tears blurred my vision as adrenaline pulsed through me, fueling the last bits of my energy.

I hadn't had anything to eat or drink in hours. My magic was neutralized, and my wing had to be broken. Not to mention, I'd been beaten to hell.

I stumbled off the sidewalk, bringing Maude with me, and landed on my back, crushing my fragile wing with Maude's dead weight on top of me. The all-encompassing pain took over my senses and nausea hit me. I threw Maude off and rolled, just in time to vomit in the street.

"I've got you," a soft male voice soothed. "You're okay now." A cool, numbing sensation spread like heaven through my tattered body. I glanced up, knowing without a shadow of a doubt who it was.

Tal's forest-green eyes shone above me.

Emotion closed my throat. "Tal…"

"Shh." His soothing charm intensified, causing my vision to fade. He was putting me under. Cutting off all the pain.

Shouts echoed and guns fired around us, but my focus narrowed to his intense worried eyes. "Maude. Influenced."

"Don't worry about that now," he said, caressing my cheek.

"No!" Frantic now, I clutched at his shirt. "She was Influenced. Help her."

Talisen said something else, but I couldn't focus enough to understand. "Save them," I mumbled. "Maude and David."

Chaos swirled around me in a frenzy of lights and sounds. Nothing made sense. "Save him," I said again and the world went dark.

Chapter 28

I floated in the hazy, dreamlike state between sleep and consciousness, content in my world of oblivion. I felt nothing but the gentle caress of soothing magic.

Peace settled over me until liquid-fire pinpricks snapped me out of my heavenly state, stabbing my battered back muscles. My eyes flew open as I sucked in a sharp breath. I groaned and pressed my stomach flat against the soft surface I lay on.

"It'll be over in a minute," Talisen's soft voice penetrated my fog.

Warmth started to tingle from the depths of my gut. Tal was here. I wasn't locked up being tortured somewhere. He'd taken care of me. His tender fingers trailed over my skin, bringing a blessed numbness with his touch.

"Hold still," he said softly.

"I'm not moving," I mumbled into the pillow.

Despite the magical anesthesia, I felt an increased pressure at the base of my wings.

"You'll want to in a second," Talisen said.

A shot of paralyzing cold ice spread through my wings. "Stop!" I gasped and then bit the pillow to keep from whimpering.

"Shh." In one fast motion, Tal flattened my right wing against my back, readjusting the dislocated connection. The loud pop was muffled by my scream as my muscles convulsed from the torture. Tears soaked the pillow as I trembled. My muscles were numb, but the sensitive nerve endings in my wings were not.

"I'm so sorry, Wil." He placed a gentle hand on my cheek and bent over, his breath warming my ear. "I don't think there's any permanent damage. One bone was crushed, but I healed that. The base of your right wing will be sore for several days, if not weeks. There's no way to fix a dislocation other than popping it back in."

I nodded, knowing he'd done his best. Link repositioned himself beside me, cuddling into a small ball, breathing deeply. The dog was out cold. Thank the Goddess he'd made it home safe. But was he okay? "Link?"

"He's fine. Just needs a day or two to sleep off the lingering effects of that tranq they hit him with." He held up a cup with a straw. "Here."

Water. Thank goodness. My mouth was dryer than Death Valley. I sucked down the entire contents of the flavorless liquid. The trembling stopped instantly. No, not water. I pressed up on one elbow. "What was that?"

He smiled. "Something new I've been working on."

Impressed by the instant effect, I stared at him, my eyebrows raised in anticipation.

His smile widened. "It restores strength and numbs the senses at the same time. It's sort of like Chimney Bark, only it doesn't affect your cognition."

"Plant-based?" I asked, eyeing the cup. No color. Not likely.

He shook his head. "Stone-based. I've been working on it for months now."

"Months?" This new drug could be a game changer. Why hadn't he said anything? I tried to keep the frown off my face, but Tal knew me too well. Holding back this kind of discovery was like not telling me he'd gotten married or something.

He helped me to sit up and wrapped an arm around my shoulders, careful to not bump my wing. "Sorry." He grimaced. "I didn't tell anyone. I honestly didn't know if I could pull it off or what the ramifications would be."

"No one?" My voice rose with my disbelief.

He shifted and jumped off the bed, running a hand through his hair. "Look at what happened with your Influence. I couldn't take the chance of anyone trying to manipulate this. It's too dangerous."

His concerns weren't lost on me. A potion that boosts strength and numbs the senses is wrought with dangerous potential. Mortals would be a lot harder to bring down. In the hands of criminals, such a drug would be a nightmare. Still, of all people, I'd think I was the one Talisen could talk to about this. "So dangerous you couldn't trust even me?"

Talisen met my eyes and then came to stand right in front of me. "I didn't tell anyone."

I climbed out of bed, marveling at the steadiness in my legs. Minutes ago I'd thought I'd never get up again. His numbing juice was a work of genius. "Yeah, but we spent all summer together. You never once even hinted at this." I waved a frustrated hand at the cup. "I tell you everything."

He leveled a hard stare at me, one eyebrow slightly raised. "Not everything."

"What are you talking about? Of course I do." I started to pace, antsy from the argument and his potion.

"Really? You never told me how serious it was with David. You said you'd casually dated someone, but it was over. Yeah, I spent all summer with you. And only you. You never once told me how you felt. But then again, it hardly matters now since you're clearly not over the vampire."

I stopped and placed both hands on my hips. "What the *hell* are you talking about?"

"This." He took two steps, grabbed my upper arms, and yanked me to him. His lips met mine in a hard, demanding frenzy, his hot tongue claiming mine with each expert stroke.

My hands came up, curling in his shirt as I met him with passion, all the years of pent-up, barely hidden desire pouring out of me.

Tal's arms came around me, cradling me close against his lean frame. His teeth scraped my bottom lip, holding on for just a moment before he murmured, "Dammit, Willow. I've been waiting ten years to do that."

A short, startled laugh bubbled up from deep in my throat as I choked back emotion. "Don't wait so long next time."

He smiled against my lips and pulled me tight, kissing me softly. Slower this time. A sweet, savoring kiss. I melted into him. How many times had I imagined this? Dreamed of being wrapped in his arms? Wished he'd finally get around to choosing me?

Then Beau had died.

Fresh, raw pain blossomed deep in my chest. There were reasons why we'd never pursued a relationship. Really good reasons. I took a deep breath and pulled away, clasping my hands over his wrists and holding him at arm's length. "We can't do this."

He took a small step forward, his cocky I'm-too-cute-for-words grin in place. "Who says?"

"Tal." I sighed, blinking away the tears burning my eyes. "I say. You know why."

His eyes narrowed as he pressed his lips together. "Your vampire? You know that will never work, right? It's doomed from the beginning." A trace of uncertainty flashed over his features. "Are you seriously telling me you'd rather be with him than me? Your best friend?"

David. God! What a horrible person I was. I hadn't even asked about him. Or thought about him at all. And where was Maude? Panic took over. "Where is he? Did they get him out? Is he still locked up at the Void building?" I spun, heading for the door.

Talisen didn't move. "So that's it, then? You're in love with a vampire." His voice was hard and flat. Cold.

"No! I..." *Shit!* I forced myself to walk back to Talisen, even though every cell screamed to go find answers. I took his hand, clamping both of mine around his, my heart breaking into a million pieces. "No. I'm not in love with him." At least I didn't think so. I cared for him. And if I was honest, I was still wildly attracted to him. Vampire and all. But love? "My reason for not pursuing a relationship with you has everything to do with Beau. Not David. Or anyone else."

"So you're turning me down? You think Beau didn't think I was good enough for you?" The hurt was plain on his face.

A lump formed in my throat. Why did we have to do this right now? "No." I bit my lip and stared at my feet. "Beau loved you like a brother," I choked out. "I'm sure if he was here, he'd give his full blessing." I forced myself to meet his tortured eyes. "But he isn't here. And you…" I swallowed. "I can't risk losing you. If this didn't work out…"

His stormy eyes darkened with raw emotion. "You'll never lose me. We're family. No matter what happens between us. You have to know that."

I shook my head, standing taller. "I've seen firsthand what happens after one of your relationships ends. Have you spoken to any of your exes? Ever? I'm sorry, Tal, as much as I think I want this, I can't risk it. Not with you. After Beau, I wouldn't survive the loss." And if I did open my heart to him, I'd die if I had to watch him with another faery. A wave of nausea rolled through my stomach at the mere thought.

Talisen jerked back as if I'd slapped him. "You think this is some passing infatuation or that I haven't thought this through? Jesus, Willow. Why do you think those other relationships never worked out?"

What could I say? That he had a wandering eye? He didn't take his relationships seriously? That he wasn't ready? None of those statements would help. I said nothing and studied Link, still curled up, sleeping on my bed.

He let out a frustrated huff. "None of those other women were *you*."

A strange ache in my chest made it hard to breathe.

Using two fingers, he tilted my head up. "These last few days, seeing your strength and your willingness to fight for what you believe in, no matter who's on the other side, has only made me want you more. As if that was possible." He closed his eyes for a moment. When he reopened them, pain reflected back at me. "And the agony of seeing you hurt. Willow, I've never been more scared in my life. I want to fight with you. To be by your side through it all."

I stepped back, surprised. Did he really just say he wanted me? Joy burst from my heart, followed by blinding fear. The two emotions fought for dominance as I imagined us hand in hand, kissing and laughing at nothing. And then the pair of us fighting, stalking away from each other, our relationship damaged beyond repair. My thoughts jumbled, too overloaded with what might come to pass in our future. "I can't do this right now," I stammered, backing up toward my door. "There's too much going on. I can't process."

All the vulnerability disappeared from his expression, leaving a blank mask.

"I'm sorry, Tal. We'll talk later." I whirled and ran out the door, ignoring the all-encompassing urge to throw myself into his arms. Let him hold me. Feel his strong, safe arms around me again. Bask in the love I'd always thought might be there, but was too afraid to act on.

I shook my head, dislodging the thoughts. The last week had been a roller coaster of emotions. What if he woke up in another week and changed his mind? I couldn't risk it. I loved him too much to lose him. I took the stairs two at a time, anxious to put distance between my thundering heart and the man I'd always wanted more than anyone else. Even David.

"Phoebe," I cried, running into the almost-tidy living room. There was still a pile of debris in one corner, but most of the broken furniture and trash had been removed. I kept running, following a low murmur of voices coming from Phoebe's office. "Phoebs?" I called again.

"In here." Her voice was low, hushed, as if she was in a library.

She looked it, too. All her books and some of mine were stacked up against the walls, waiting to be put away. I paused in the doorway.

Pressing a tiny speaker to her ear, she used her other hand to frantically scribble notes on a legal pad.

When she didn't look up, I cleared my throat.

That got her attention. She finished writing and then threw me her keys as she grabbed her notepad, pen, and the silver beetle attached to the tiny earphone. Grabbing my arm, she pulled me to the front door. "Hurry. We're running out of time."

"David?" Fear stopped me in my tracks. "Does the Void still have him?"

"No. Allcot's lackeys stormed the building right after you busted out and tackled Maude." She ran down the walk and yanked the passenger-side door open. "David's back at Allcot's club. Hurry. You don't want to miss the action."

I glanced up the stairs, finding Talisen and Link watching me. "I have to go," I told him.

He gave me a resigned nod and turned around, slamming my bedroom door behind him.

I sighed. "Keep an eye on him, Link."

The Shih Tzu yelped once and went to the door. A second later, Talisen reappeared and my sidekick slipped in, the door closing this time with a soft click.

"Willow!" Phoebe called.

I ran down the front walk and jumped in the driver's side of her Camry. I gripped the steering wheel and threw the car in gear. The tires squealed as we shot down the street.

Phoebe eyed me with suspicion. "Are you okay?"

I gripped the steering wheel tighter. "I'm fine. Don't I look fine?"

"Sure. I mean, Tal said you were. I had no reason to not believe him, especially since you're upright and walking under your own steam." She leaned back and studied me. "There's something else though."

I tsked. "Of course there is. I need to talk to Maude. Where is she?"

"Allcot has her."

I turned to her, horrified. Maude needed healing and rest after everything she'd been through. Not an interrogation. And a vampire that powerful wouldn't give up until he was satisfied there was nothing else to get. "What's she doing there? She should be back at the house with Talisen healing her."

"Uh, Wil? What's going on? Why are you worried about Maude? She deserves everything she gets."

I slammed the accelerator to the floor. "No, Phoebe. She doesn't." The car skidded around a corner, barely missing a parked van.

"Whoa. Watch it. I'm all for some speed racing, but I'd rather not end up wrapped around a tree."

"You don't understand." I pressed on, barely making it through an intersection before the light turned red.

She clutched the dashboard. "Enlighten me, then."

I glanced at her once, that pain in my chest returning. "She's been Influenced for three years! It's not her fault."

Phoebe let out a low gasp of surprise. "Oh, shit."

"Yeah."

She turned slowly in her seat and I could feel the tension streaming off her. "Faster, Willow."

Another tire squeal. "I'm going as fast as I can."

The car bounced, and the underside scraped on the asphalt as we hit a pothole while going sixty through the city streets.

"Goddamn it." She banged a fist on the dashboard.

"What?"

"We didn't know. Talisen said you mumbled something about helping her, but we didn't know what that meant."

"Phoebs?" I warned. "Spit it out."

"Your aunt...shit! David's torturing her right now."

Chapter 29

I slid the car catawampus into a tight space about a block from Eadric's club, The Red Door. The key was barely out of the ignition before I jumped out onto the sidewalk. In my haste, I fluttered my wings to fly, but the instant pain kept my feet on the ground. *Ouch!* Talisen had done what he could to help speed the healing, but I wouldn't be flying for quite a while. I broke into a run, ignoring the throb in my shoulder blade.

The crowd waiting to get in cast me aggravated glances as I pushed past them.

"What's the hurry, honey?" The bouncer looked me up and down and motioned to the back of the line. "You'll have to wait your turn."

I lifted my chin and cocked a hip. "Tell Davidson Laveaux Willow's here."

The bouncer blinked.

Raising my eyebrows, I took a step closer. "You heard me, right?"

A dark shadow crossed over his features as his eyes narrowed.

Phoebe finally caught up, breathing heavily. "Jesus, Willow, you could've parked so the ass of the car wasn't blocking half the street. I had to do a spell to set a caution flare." She glanced between me and the brooding bouncer. "What's going on?"

I fought to keep from barreling past the asshole. Getting clocked by the doorman wouldn't get me inside any faster. "Mr. Power Trip won't let me in. Nor will he take half a second to call David."

Phoebe pulled her phone out of her pocket. I frowned, wondering when I'd last seen mine. Cripes. It was still in my purse on the floor in Maude's office. She held a finger over the screen. "You have two seconds before I press call."

The man straightened his back, towering over us. "You'll need to leave the premises now. Mr. Allcot has specifically asked for his family to not be disturbed."

Phoebe sighed. "Don't say I didn't warn you."

I glared at the jackass bouncer in front of me. Clenching my fists, I dug my nails into my palms. What I wouldn't give to take a swing right then. Phoebe spoke low into her phone. I couldn't hear her over the growing buzz of the crowd.

A girl behind me whined. "Jeez. What makes you so special? Just because you have wings doesn't make you better than the rest of us. Go to the back of the line or get the hell out of the way."

I spun, anger streaming off me in waves. "Fuck off."

The girl huffed out a laugh and glanced at the two men beside her. "Hear that, boys. The faery wants a piece of this." She ran her hands over her chest, cupping her breasts, and blew me a suggestive kiss. "But I'm not into skinny, entitled bitches."

I took a step forward, all the stress of the last few days churning inside me, straining to explode. The fury on my face must have been a warning because the smirk disappeared from the curvaceous blonde, and she took a few steps back.

"That's enough." The bouncer grabbed my arm.

"Let go!" I tried to shake him, but his iron grip held me firmly in place.

"You're causing a scene," the bouncer said quietly. He leaned down, his breath rancid with onions. His harsh tone sent an angry shiver down my spine. "Either leave under your own power, or I'll force you to."

The thick sensation of vampire energy coated my skin. I stilled.

"Lucas," a silky female voice said from behind us. "What are you doing?"

The bouncer straightened and glanced back. "Ms. Pandora.

My apologies. This *faery*"—he said faery as if we fae were toxic waste—"was just leaving."

Pandora's elegant face flashed from breathtakingly gorgeous to vicious terror. Her fangs popped out and her eyes turned red. "Let go of Ms. Rhoswen."

The bouncer froze, his eyes going wide with fear.

"Now," she growled.

In slow motion, he let go and stepped back. The blood pulsed through my bruised arm. Phoebe pushed me forward into the club while Pandora waited for us to pass.

"Next time," the vampire hissed, "you'll not only let her in, but you'll alert the residence we have a guest. Or else Eadric will void your contract for eternal life. Understood?"

I peered over her shoulder. Good Goddess, he was on the list to be turned? He'd be terrifying as a vampire. I swallowed the ball of unease rising in my throat. There was absolutely no time to be worrying about future vampires when a present one was torturing my aunt.

Without waiting for Pandora, I took off, Phoebe close at my heels. We headed straight for the back stairs. It wasn't long before I felt Pandora catch up to us. I increased my pace, taking two stairs at a time.

The big double doors loomed in front of me. I came to an abrupt halt. Maude. What had David done to her? No time to be a chickenshit. Maude needed me.

I flung the doors open. A blast of vamp energy hit me full force. I let out a muffled groan and pushed my way through the thick, invisible mass.

Allcot leaned back in his chair and nodded in Pandora's direction. "Davidson's expecting you."

Pandora nodded once and disappeared.

I glanced around the empty room and then stalked to his desk. "Where is she?"

He raised his eyebrows in exaggerated calm. "Nicola is recuperating. On behalf of Pandora and myself, we extend our appreciation for the role you played in her recovery."

I planted my palms on the desk and leaned in. "Not Nicola. My aunt, Maude. Where. Is. She?"

He brought his hands together, holding his index fingers and thumbs in a triangle. "Davidson is handling her interview. As soon as he's satisfied, you'll have a chance to speak with her before she's terminated."

Horrified rage exploded from deep in my gut. "Terminated!" I shrieked and ran to the nearest door, trying but failing to yank it open. It was locked.

"Willow," Phoebe demanded in her don't-fuck-with-me voice. "Stop. You'll never leave this room unless Allcot decides he wants you to." She huffed in disgust and turned to glare at the vampire. "Isn't that right?"

"I'd say that's accurate," he agreed.

"That's what I thought." She jerked her head, indicating I should join her. "Agent Rhoswen has reason to believe Maude was under the Influence, and now she isn't. Your *tactics* are highly inappropriate."

"Where is she?" I asked again, this time my voice low and barely controlled.

He ignored me and studied Phoebe with interest. "My *tactics?*"

She held up the tiny silver beetle and flicked a switch. David's voice boomed, filling the room. "Your lies are only prolonging our time together." He paused and there was a moment of silence before a low, tortured moan turned my heart to stone.

Phoebe flicked the switch and tossed it on Allcot's desk. "David has an identical one. I've heard his demands. Her pleas. Every scream, every protest, and every fucked up vamp-biting moment." She pulled out her sun agate and aimed it at him.

I stifled a gasp. Though I was all for her using it if it meant we could get to Maude faster.

He stood, deliberately slow. I knew there was no chance of Phoebe having enough time to activate the agate should he decide to move. A vampire his age could only be caught off guard. All it would take is one flinch, and he'd disappear before our eyes.

"Do not threaten me, Agent Kilsen. The result will not benefit you."

Phoebe didn't move, but she didn't back down, either. "Take us to Maude and there will be no need to threaten you."

Allcot crossed his arms over his chest. "I'm not pleased you planted a bug on one of my people."

It was my turn to huff. "She didn't bug him, you arrogant fool. David offered to take one so she could trace him if need be. How do you think she knew where David and I were?" I spit the lie out before I could stop myself. Phoebe had given me one, but I'd crushed it. She must have planted another one on David just in case.

Phoebe lifted her chin, agreeing with my statement.

Allcot loomed over us. No emotion passed over his unreadable face. Just when I was ready to scratch his clear blue eyes out, he snapped his fingers and one door slid open, vanishing inside the wall. "This is your one pass. Test me again, and you'll be the ones in chains." He turned and disappeared into thin air.

"Huh," Phoebe said, sounding surprised. "That went surprisingly well."

"Really?" I choked out, not believing I'd verbally challenged Allcot. I'd bet not many mortals survived such altercations. "Threatened to be chained up isn't my idea of going well."

She waved a dismissive hand. "He had to say something to maintain his almighty persona."

We took slow, deliberate steps into the adjoining room. I paused, letting my eyes adjust to the darkness. "They couldn't turn a light on?"

"Why? Vampires have super sight." She swept past me, giving my arm a slight reassuring squeeze. "David, get your skinny ass out here."

"Phoebs," I scolded in a loud whisper.

She ignored me and moved deeper into the room. I could barely make out her form in the darkness. "Where are you, you useless, cold-blooded—?"

"That's enough." The warning in David's quiet tone came through loud and clear.

"Lights would be good here," Phoebe said, totally unfazed.

I cleared my throat. "David?"

A flash of air made me shiver, and I jumped when David appeared beside me. His chiseled arms came around me, pulling me in close for a hug. "You're okay?" he asked into my hair.

My pulse raced, but not from excitement. Irritation. I pushed him back. "Where's Maude?"

He stared down at me with puzzled eyes. "You don't want to know what happened after we were separated?"

I squinted, studying him in his unwrinkled gray silk shirt, black jeans, and perfectly groomed hair. Not a scratch on him. He didn't look like he'd suffered a great deal. "Later. Right now, I want you to take me to Maude."

He shook his head. "Pandora's with her now. When she gets what she needs, we'll go in."

"Now!" I demanded.

He crossed his arms, his expression going carefully blank, the way it always did when he hid his thoughts. "No."

Phoebe laughed. "Dude, get your head out of your ass and take us to Maude. Otherwise you're likely to never see this one again." She pointed at me. "And we both know you don't want that."

I mimicked his stance, arms crossed and a careful emotionless expression. At least I hoped so. I was so pissed my eyes should've been crossing. "David, Maude was manipulated. Under the Influence. Whatever you've done to her is unacceptable. Stop whatever's happening to her or I swear to God, I'll make it my mission to bring you all down."

He glanced between the two of us, wariness flashing in his eyes. "She told us that, too. But it isn't true." He turned. "I'll show you."

Another door across the room swooshed open.

I ran, barreling into the room, ready to pry Pandora off Maude with my bare hands. But what I saw made me skid to a stop. Nicola was curled up in a ball on a velvet settee, tears streaming down her face. Where the hell was Maude? And what happened to Pandora's sister?

I turned abruptly, coming face-to-face with David. "What did you do to her?"

That muscle in his jaw pulsed again. "Not long after Pandora brought her home, she woke up like this. I was going to *ask* you the same thing."

"Nothing. I…" The poor girl was shaking with what seemed to be fear. Was she terrified Allcot would punish her for first accusing him, or even getting caught in the spell in the first place? My stomach churned. Had my potion caused this? An internal battle raged as I tried to decide what to do next. Maude needed me, but so did Nicola. I couldn't leave the poor girl now. I moved forward and placed a gentle hand on her forehead. "Nicola, what is it?"

She shook her head slightly, but her big brown eyes pleaded with me. For what, I didn't know.

"Are you sick? Was it the potion I gave you?"

She squeezed her eyes shut and then popped them open, keeping her intense gaze locked on mine. Shaking her head, the trembling intensified.

"Talisen's healing spell?"

She shrank back, trying to curl into herself.

"That's it." I got to my feet, turning to tell Phoebe to call Tal, but Nicola grabbed my arm and pulled me back down.

The effort left her winded as she huffed out, "The witch." Her eyes rolled and she passed out again. But this time she woke almost instantly, gasping for breath.

I glanced once at Phoebe and David, then crouched back down. "Nicola, I need to ask you a few things. The last thing I want to do is hurt you further, so just hold up a finger if you can't answer. Is that all right?"

She clutched the side of the settee and bobbed her head.

She couldn't mean Phoebe; she hadn't done anything to her other than fight physically. It had to be the one who gave her Influence. Hadn't I broken that spell? "I'm going to ask some things that might not make sense. I'd appreciate it if you could answer as honestly as possible. If you can't, it's okay."

She didn't respond, only kept staring with her giant brown eyes. I took that as consent.

"Did David force you to eat Influence?"

He shifted behind me as if he'd taken a step forward in protest. I chose to ignore him.

"No," she said, her voice feeble. Her eyes stayed big and round, unchanged.

"Did Phoebe?"

My partner gave a small huff, and I held back a smile. I knew damn well she hadn't done any such thing.

"No."

"Pandora?"

"No!" Nicola's voice was stronger.

Good, that's what I was hoping for.

"Allcot?"

Her mouth worked and her pupils dilated, but no words came out.

"Yes or no?" I said gently.

"N...yes." The light brown line of her irises disappeared for a fraction of a second as her pupils took over. She blinked and her regular color returned. If I hadn't been watching for it, I never would've seen it.

"One more. Did someone spell you to keep their secrets, even if the Influence wore off?"

She stopped rocking and stared at me, her eyes filling with tears. She seemed frozen, unable to move or speak.

"It's all right, Nicola. I've already figured it out. You don't need to answer."

One fat tear spilled down her temple. "Hurts…"

I nodded and wiped it away. "I know. We're going to fix that right now." I kept a hold of her hand. "Phoebs?"

"Yeah?"

"You got a spell-breaking curse handy?"

David stepped between us. "You can't use anything like that here."

I shoved him with one hand. "Go tell Pandora we need her. And tell everyone to keep their hands off Maude until we work out what's going on with Nicola."

He cast me a dark look and did his vampire disappearing act. It was obvious they wouldn't believe anything I said until I broke the hold over Nicola. One of their own had been hurt, and the only suspect they had was my aunt.

"Wil," Phoebe whispered into my ear. "I don't have anything like that. They didn't let me bring my spell case."

"Shit!" I stood and glanced around the plush room. The door swung open and Pandora rushed in. "What's going on? Is she worse?" Pandora dropped gracefully beside Nicola, cradling her hand. "We'll fix this, I promise."

David came back into the room, and the first thing I noticed was blood on his shirt. I poked a finger into his hard chest. "Where did this come from? Maude? Or a feeder? Huh?"

He stood, stoic and unmoving.

I scrutinized Pandora for bloodstains. There weren't any. "Where's my aunt?" I demanded again. I knew how to fix Nicola's aliment, but I didn't have the tools.

"Take her to the director," Pandora ordered, her voice thick with emotion. "Do it, David. Maude's been useless for the last six hours anyway."

Pandora's long sheet of blond hair covered her and her sister's faces, giving them an illusion of privacy.

David huffed out a long-suffering sigh. "This way. Try to remember the measures we take are necessary."

Heat burned my skin from the inside out. Necessary measures my ass. Another door whooshed open, but this time bright fluorescent lights filled the stark white chamber.

I stepped through the opening and shielded my eyes. Then I spotted her. Maude sat slumped over, her black wings crumpled and pinned to the wall. Blood trailed from her neck to her thighs, bite marks everywhere. Nathan stood to the side, blood dripping from his fangs.

My heart stopped. It took a moment to start breathing again, but when I did, I turned cold, hard eyes on David.

"Wil," he said, reaching for me.

I stepped back, my muscles trembling with the effort to stay in control. Every fiber of my being screamed to stake him. If only I had one and the strength to execute such an act.

The only weapon I had was some small piece of his heart. "Don't ever touch me again. I'm not your Wil, and never will be. Got it?"

He stared at me for a long time, then took a step back.

I ran to Maude's side. Her head listed to the left. "Aunt Maude," I soothed. "I'm here. Everything's going to be okay now. Hear me?"

A soft moan came from the back of her throat.

I glanced up, finding Allcot standing beside his son.

"Unchain her." I wrapped an arm around my aunt, pressing her head to my shoulder. She winced with the effort. "She risked herself to save me. She isn't the mastermind behind this…" I waved a hand in the air. "…crazy situation."

Allcot studied us curiously, almost amused.

Sick bastard.

"Come up with a solution to cure Nicola of her condition and I'll free her."

I started to argue but Maude lifted her heavy head, and her eyes focused. "Willow's Influence. It'll break the hold." She collapsed back on my shoulder, her body limp.

"Maude?" I cried, shaking her a little. "Damn it, Maude, wake up!"

"It's the pain killers," Allcot said and took out his phone. A second later he commanded, "Bring it up."

I stood. "You gave her painkillers?"

"Yes, young Willow. It became clear a while ago either she was telling the truth or she was too delirious to tell the difference. There was no need to keep her suffering. Pandora administered the drug ten minutes ago."

I gaped. He was a total enigma.

The door swung open and a cart was wheeled in. Did every vampire move at warp speed? It was enough to give a girl vertigo. He thanked his servant and waved a hand. "A fresh dose of your Influence. Administer it to my sister-in-law."

"Oh shit," Phoebe mumbled and took a step closer. "This cannot end well."

Chapter 30

I held up an impatient hand to silence Phoebe, my insides churning with betrayal and frustration. Never ever trust a vampire for anything. "Where did this come from?"

"Daniels," Allcot said, appearing unaffected by my disrespectful tone. "We found it in his office and confiscated it."

"And you didn't *think* to hand it over to me?" Of course he didn't. Despite his platinum cufflinks and overpriced wardrobe, he was no better than a street thug.

He gave me an indulgent smile. "Do you honestly think any vampire would give up such a valuable resource?"

I stared at David. "An honorable one would."

David averted his gaze and focused on something over my shoulder.

The look confirmed my suspicion. He'd known about it. What else was he keeping from me? I turned to Allcot and bit back the threat to turn him in for harboring illegal enhancements. My complaint would fall on deaf ears. The board enforcement practically worked for him.

"Let's do this, Willow," Phoebe said moving toward the cart.

"No!" I cried and jumped in front of her. "Don't touch anything." If this breach was somehow reported, I didn't want her prints anywhere near it. It would be a lot easier to explain mine. The truth was we did need the Influence. There wasn't any at my shop since I'd been too busy trying to stay alive to make any. The one piece I'd had at home, I'd used on Maude. "I'll do it."

I grabbed a chocolate wedge, and as I moved past Phoebe, I whispered, "Get Talisen here. Maude's going to need him." I knew I should call him myself after the way I'd run out on him. Especially since I wasn't asking for a small favor. This would put him on Allcot's radar. Who knew what consequences that would bring? But I couldn't risk the possibility of him turning me down. If he was really pissed, he might do just that. He wouldn't dare say no to Phoebe, though. If he did, she'd find some way to force his hand.

Please don't let me have messed up so badly he ignores the request. We'd never be able to move Maude without his healing powers.

Leaving Eadric and David behind, Phoebe and I slipped back into the other room. I kneeled beside Nicola and heard Phoebe talking to Talisen, but she was too far away and I couldn't make out the words. Judging by her tone, it wasn't going well. *Come on, Tal. Don't let me down now.*

Pandora stood behind the settee, smoothing back her sister's light hair. I took a deep breath, forcing myself to settle down. The last thing I wanted was a vampire's sister under my control. Hell, I didn't want anyone under my control. Now I'd have two people.

Just get it over with.

"Nicola," I said softly.

The witch looked up at me through dazed eyes.

"I need you to eat some of this." I held a small chunk up to her lips.

She twisted in protest and strained to sit up. Her legs kicked out and one foot landed right in the middle of my chest.

"Oomph," I cried and fell back on my ass, jarring my still-sore wing.

Pandora placed a firm hand on Nicola's shoulder. "You have to do this, Nikki. It'll help."

Nicola started to mouth words, and I leaned closer, trying to hear.

But Phoebe jumped in front of me, her hands held in front of her, casting a protective circle. Whatever spell Nicola had conjured crashed into Phoebe's barrier, shattering it. Both spells dissipated into the ether.

Phoebe fumed, her fists clenched in tight little balls.

Pandora clamped a hand around Nicola's mouth and nodded to one of the other vampire lackeys to restrain Nicola's hands.

I touched Phoebe's arm. "It's the spell she's under. I don't think she can control herself."

My roommate narrowed her eyes, glaring at the other witch. "If she tries to cast that death spell one more time, I'm going to put her in a coma."

"Death spell?" I whispered. Vampire balls. She'd tried to kill me. I glanced down at the ruby ring on her right hand. "I thought her ring was empty?"

Phoebe nodded. "It was. Maybe she has another spelled piece of jewelry."

Pandora ripped the ring off Nicola's hand and handed it to Phoebe.

"It's empty," Phoebe said. "Totally useless." She handed it back to Pandora and eyed Nicola. "I don't see any other jewelry, but that doesn't mean she doesn't have another spell hidden."

That was it. All my reservations about using the Influence vanished. "Forget it. Once she's Influenced, it won't matter anyway." I took a place next to Pandora, gritting my teeth against the burning sensation when her shoulder rubbed mine. "We're going to have to force-feed her."

Pandora nodded once, her big round eyes conflicted with emotion. She shifted her hand from Nicola's mouth to cover her nose. The second Nicola opened her mouth, I stuffed the Influence in. She began to spit, but Pandora clamped an iron hand over her mouth and waited for her to swallow.

We all stood there staring, not certain the Influence had worked.

"Say something," Phoebe said to me.

"Right." Crap. I was the inventor of the stuff. You'd think I'd remember I had to give her directions. "Let her go," I said to Pandora. I wanted to see how she reacted before I gave instructions.

Pandora nodded to her lackey, and they both released her. Nicola slumped on the settee, sighing as the tension seemed to roll off her. She stared at her wrists, inspecting the fresh bruises.

Poor thing. Though that's what happens when you go throwing death spells around.

"Nicola." I waited for her to meet my eyes. "The only thing I want you to do is tell the truth. Other than that, you are under no one's control."

She nodded slowly, then reached out and grabbed my hand. "It wasn't Eadric. He had nothing to do with what happened to me."

I smiled reassuringly. "That's what I thought. Can you tell us what did happen?"

She shuddered. "The director came to speak to me at home."

"Maude?" I asked, my heart pounding.

"Yes." She gulped. Then her voice hardened. "And she brought that traitor vampire."

Pandora moved to sit next to her. She held out her hand and Nicola took it. "Who?"

Nicola shook her head. "I don't know. She called him Beals, but I'd never heard of him before. He's old, but I don't think as old as Eadric. Old enough to block my defensive spells."

I glanced at my roommate. I thought she'd said Nicola was powerful. Even more powerful than Phoebe.

She seemed to understand what I was asking and shook her head. "She doesn't have Arcane knowledge."

Ah, advanced spell knowledge. No matter how strong she was, Nicola's spells wouldn't be as powerful as a Void agent's. Arcane spells were highly classified and in a league of their own. "What happened when they came to your house?"

Nicola glanced at Pandora, who nodded. I hadn't commanded her to answer my questions, only to tell the truth. She'd already been through hell.

She closed her eyes. "He bit me. And drank enough blood I passed out." Her eyes flew open and she stared hard at Phoebe.

"He was too fast for me to defend myself. Your spells are so much stronger than mine. I want you to teach me."

"Whoa," Phoebe said. "One step at a time."

"All I had with me were a few paid-for death spells." She reached into her pocket and pulled out another ring. Dropping it on the table, she shuddered. "I was spelled to use those. I won't be vulnerable again. Please. I'm a fast learner."

Phoebe tilted her head, taking in the slight-framed woman. "If I can get it sanctioned, I'll do what I can."

"What does that mean, exactly?" Pandora wrapped an arm around her sister. "Sanctioned?"

"Arcane spells are confidential. But if I can get someone to sign off on training Nicola, I will." Phoebe tucked a lock of black hair—her own this time—behind her ear. "Considering the Arcane has violated her rights, I should be able to negotiate the knowledge as payment."

Pandora met Phoebe's gaze. "Good. If not, they'll have me to answer to."

Phoebe shrugged. "That's their problem."

I cleared my throat and faced Nicola. "Can you tell us what happened after you woke up?"

Nicola huffed out a humorless laugh. "Yeah. They'd compelled me. I had to do everything they said. Spy on Eadric. Break into your house. Look for information I could never seem to find. And every few days, that vampire showed up in the middle of the night to give me a new assignment and force-feed me that awful chocolate with the acid aftertaste. By then, I wasn't a threat. Every time I tried to protest or tell someone, my brain stalled and my mouth said something else. It was like I was programmed and I had no choice in the matter."

"And Maude was the leader?" Pandora asked, her fingernails ripping a hole in the velvet settee.

I leaned back, afraid of what Nicola might say. If she confirmed Maude was in charge, Pandora would never believe my theory.

But Nicola shook her head. "I don't think so. The first time she came over, she took direction over the phone. She's working for someone."

"Not for," I said. "She was compelled, just like you were. But the real question is what were they looking for?"

"Information." Nicola stared at me, her eyes full of pity. "They wanted to know more about your vampire abilities. They seemed to think you're not being one hundred percent truthful."

Pandora tensed, panic ringing in her voice. "What did you say? Do they know?"

"Know what?" I asked.

Nicola shook her head quickly and spoke to Pandora. "No. Nothing. They never asked the right questions."

With a heavy sigh, Pandora sank back against the cushions. "Thank the Goddess."

"What aren't you telling me?" My pulse quickened as unease settled in my chest. I knew the Void wanted to study me, but I hadn't realized they thought I was hiding anything. What were they looking for?

Nicola glanced at Pandora, silently asking a question.

Pandora held up a hand and pressed a button on her phone. A second later she said, "It's time."

I stood, and took a step back. "What's going on?"

Pandora tossed her phone on a side table. "You're about to get a piece of your puzzle."

The double doors opened with a loud creak. I turned, expecting Eadric or even David, but it was Talisen, his face pinched in anger.

"Tal," I breathed and ran to his side. "Thank you for coming."

He gazed down at me, a hint of concern in his conflicted expression, but then he gave me an impatient nod and stalked to Phoebe. "Where is she?"

Phoebe, ignoring his surly demeanor, tucked her arm through his and led him toward the room where they'd kept Maude chained. "I'll be right back."

My blood rushed to my head just thinking about my aunt's condition.

The doors swung open again, and this time Eadric glided in. He'd changed into faded jeans and a red silk shirt. Ugh, was he sharing a wardrobe with David or something? He didn't acknowledge me as he made his way to Nicola's side. He gently touched her cheek. "Better, love?"

She nodded. "I didn't want to betray you." Angry tears sprung to her eyes. "I'd never do such a thing."

He held on to her gaze. "I believe you." Pandora moved to his side, placing a reassuring hand on his shoulder. The three of them looked very much the devoted family.

I felt like an intruder of the worst kind. I'd never given much thought to vampires having a family. But they clearly were. They weren't just what they seemed on the surface: Lustful, greedy, self-serving. These two loved each other and Nicola. It was the first time I'd really seen the evidence.

Allcot stood and faced me. "Why didn't your Influence neutralizer work?"

I frowned. It had. Sort of. But she'd been spelled as well. Or had she? What did she say? They'd forced her to eat chocolate with an acid aftertaste. My Influence didn't have any unappealing flavor. I'd never sell something that wasn't heaven on the taste buds. "I think I know the answer, but let me confirm first. I'll be right back."

I ran to the other room where Talisen was hovering over Maude. Her eyes were half-open as she murmured something to him.

The lights had been dimmed in the white room, but it was still entirely too harsh on my eyes. I shielded them and moved to stand on the other side of the reclining chair Maude now lay in.

"Not now, Willow," Talisen said, running his healing stone over Maude's raw wrists.

"I'm sorry," I said to him, hoping he realized I was apologizing for more than just interrupting him. "Really sorry."

He gave his head a tiny shake and went back to work.

"Maude?" I clasped her other hand gently.

Her eyelids fluttered and she focused on me. "Willow? Is that poor girl okay?"

"I think so. Listen, do you know what the vampire was feeding her? It doesn't sound like the Influence I make."

She gave me a tiny nod. "The lab-modified Influence." Her breathing became heavy as she struggled to get the words out. "More powerful than yours. Harder to undo."

"And that's why you suggested my Influence. It cancels out the lab-modified version in a way my neutralizer can't?"

"Yes. Sort of." Her eyes closed and she gave a muffled groan.

"Willow." Talisen's harsh tone made me step back.

"What?" I asked.

"Go away. I need to concentrate." He turned his back, rummaging through his healer bag.

"Sorry," I said again, my voice so low I wasn't sure he heard me. I left and Phoebe followed.

"He just needs time," she said as we moved back into Eadric's sitting room.

I hoped she was right. He'd come, hadn't he? It was a start. I sat in a chair opposite Nicola. "They fed her modified Influence. The Arcane has had scientists working on duplicating it. None are sanctioned for use because they're too dangerous. Though it's not hard to see why someone in a position to abuse their power might prefer the more dangerous, illegal version."

"Indeed." Eadric stood. "It's time I paid my part of the bargain, Ms. Rhoswen."

I got to my feet. "Paid?"

"Information. Follow me." He strode toward the double doors.

I signaled to Phoebe and we followed him out into the hall. A few doors down, he unlocked a nondescript oak door and held it open for us.

I hesitated, not at all sure I wanted to enter a room he kept locked.

"Trust me, Ms. Rhoswen, you want to see this."

Phoebe brushed past me with her eyebrows raised. I steeled myself and followed her. The room was really a suite with two overstuffed chairs and a matching couch, not at all like Eadric's private rooms with the fancy Louis XVI style furnishings.

A door slammed in another room, and a small strawberry-blond toddler came running out, holding a stuffed elk and shrieking with delight.

"Beau," a female voice called from the other room. "Come back here, you monster."

My heart skipped a beat, then pounded so hard I thought it would jump out of my chest. I knew that voice. And when she appeared in the doorway, she froze, staring at me with her mouth open.

"Carrie?" I looked from the small, curvy witch Beau had intended to marry to the little boy now clutching her leg.

"Willow." She seemed to recover and smiled tentatively. Glancing down at the toddler, she put a hand on his head. "I guess it's about time you met your nephew, Beau Junior."

Chapter 31

I sank down into an oversized chair and clamped a hand over my mouth. Beau had a son. I had a nephew. And Carrie never told us.

"Beau," Carrie said. "This is your auntie, Willow."

The toddler clutched his mom's leg and peered at me shyly.

I ignored all the questions straining to escape my mouth and moved to crouch in front of Beau. "Hi, sweetie."

He tucked his head behind his mom's knee, one eye peeking at me, and giggled.

I smiled. "You're a charmer, just like your daddy." Oh my God. Had Beau known? Why had Carrie kept him from us? And why the hell was she living with vampires? I glanced up at her, my heart aching for Beau and for myself. Neither of us knew his child.

"I have some explaining to do." Carrie bent down and smoothed Beau's hair. "Can you give your auntie a kiss?"

I held my arms out, and the toddler wobbled into my embrace. Hot tears burned my eyes. I blinked them back and turned my face, tapping my cheek. "Here."

"Mwah!" He made a loud smacking sound, laughed, and ran back into the other room.

I stood. "He seems happy."

Carrie nodded. "He is."

"Did Beau know?" I held my breath, not sure what answer I wanted to hear.

She nodded again and sucked in a shaky breath.

Relief washed through me. Only a small hole remained in my heart. He'd kept this secret from me, and while I understood it was between him and Carrie, if I'd known, I could have been in his son's life the past three years. Phoebe took a place beside me and silently clutched my hand in hers. I squeezed, grateful for the support.

Eadric sat on one of the plush chairs and gestured to the rest of us. "Let's all take a seat."

Phoebe and I shared the couch, and Carrie perched on the chair next to Eadric. She stared at her fidgeting hands.

"You said you were going back to Washington to be with your family after we lost Beau," I accused Carrie. "Was that a lie?"

She bit her lip and shook her head. "No. I did go home for a few months. I wanted to stay with my sister, have Beau there, but I couldn't." Her voice wobbled. "It wasn't safe for either of us."

I tensed and grabbed the arm of the couch. "What does that mean—not safe?"

Allcot leaned forward, hands clasped. "You already know someone inside the Void is watching you."

"Well, yeah. They've wanted to control me for some time because of the Influence, and now there's the sunwalking thing." I waved my hand, indicating I didn't know what to make of the situation.

He shook his head. "No. They're interested in your creation, but there are other ways to control people. Spells, blackmail, other illegal magic. This isn't about the Influence. They're much more interested in your abilities. Specifically the ones relating to vampires."

I nodded. He was right about the Influence, of course. The Arcane had always been interested in it, but they hadn't gotten serious about *me* until I started sensing vampires. "Yes, but what does any of that have to do with Carrie or my nephew?"

Phoebe sucked in a breath.

"What?" I asked her.

She gave me a pained expression and turned to Allcot. "Did her brother have the ability to sense vampires?"

"Of course not," I said before Allcot could answer. "He would've told me. Besides, my abilities didn't start showing up until months after we lost Beau. If they were the same, then it makes sense they would have shown up around the same time. We *are* twins."

Carrie shook her head, her eyes full of sorrow and regret. "I'm sorry. He was going to tell you…" She wiped a single tear from her porcelain face. "But he never got the chance."

"What…?" Beau had weird vampire abilities?

It's not that I didn't believe it was possible. It had happened to me, after all. But he hadn't told me. And we told each other everything. A nagging seed of doubt tugged at my mind. He hadn't told me his girlfriend was pregnant. "Phoebs? You knew something about this?"

She shook her head. "I guessed."

I glanced from Eadric to Carrie. "Maybe you should start from the beginning."

"Yeah. I think that's a good idea," Phoebe said and glared at Allcot. "And don't leave anything out this time."

He'd definitely known more than he'd let on. A lot more. I glanced toward the bedroom where Beau Junior had disappeared to. Allcot had been keeping my family from me.

Phoebe's tone didn't seem to register with Allcot. He rose and moved gracefully to the wet bar. Using a key from his pocket, he opened a cabinet and removed a bottle that looked suspiciously like wine. But when he poured the thick red liquid, it was clear the main ingredient wasn't grapes. I wrinkled my nose in disgust.

"The beginning," he said, corking the green bottle, "actually starts many generations ago." He held up another bottle, this one presumably actual wine, in offering. We all shook our heads. No way was I drinking anything that could impair my comprehension.

He took his seat again. "The firstborn males in the Rhoswen line are quite unlucky. If you look closely at the family tree, you'll find none of them make it past twenty-five years."

"That's not true," I said automatically, even though doubt plagued me. My dad and Beau certainly hadn't. But what about my grandfather? He was still with us, living out in Montana somewhere. "Gramps did," I challenged.

Allcot shook his head. "I assume you mean Charles Rhoswen."

"Yes. He's still alive and well, working for the forestry department." Being fae, he knew every inch of the backwoods and was often called when hikers went missing.

"I'm sure he is. But he wasn't your father's father, and not the firstborn. That was Erwin Rhoswen, and when he died, his younger brother Charles married your grandmother and raised your dad."

Stunned, I sat back. How come no one told me that before? Then I narrowed my eyes and studied Allcot. "How do you know all this about my family?"

He lifted one shoulder in a tiny shrug. "Since Carrie came to us, I've done a lot of research."

I'd have to look into that. If what he said was true, it meant Beau Junior was in serious danger. I inched forward on the couch. "And that's why you're watching over my nephew? To keep him alive?"

Allcot lifted his chin in acknowledgment.

"Why?" It's not that I didn't appreciate his protection, but at what price? Would Beau Junior be beholden to him the rest of his life?

A tiny flash of irritation flashed over his features and then vanished. Was he irritated I'd questioned him, or just tired of being under constant suspicion? I shook off the thought. He'd created the situation; he could live with it.

"Carrie is Nicola's cousin. She's family." Allcot got up to refill his glass.

The hair stood up on my neck. That meant they thought of Beau Junior as family. And Allcot would be a permanent fixture in his life. I rubbed at my throbbing temple, trying not to think too much about the implications. Then a slow terror gripped my gut. "The person who killed Beau knows about Beau Junior? That's why you came here?"

Carrie shook her head. "Once Eadric figured out what was going on, we faked a miscarriage. As far as we know, he has no idea Beau Junior exists. But if he found out…"

She didn't need to continue. No wonder she lived in hiding.

"There's still the question of why." Phoebe said, breaking the silence. "Why are all the firstborn Rhoswens murdered?"

I sucked in a sharp breath. I'd long believed Beau's death wasn't an accident. But to hear the words spoken so plainly, it was like a jagged knife right in my chest. Phoebe clutched my hand again. It didn't help.

"Because," Allcot said carefully. "They all have the power to turn vampires into daywalkers."

My limbs went numb. I sat frozen on the couch, staring at Allcot as he poured another glass of thick red liquid.

"Willow?" Phoebe waved and scooted closer. "You all right?"

My chest started to ache. What had happened with David hadn't been a fluke. But how did I possess that power? I wasn't a male or the firstborn. Beau had arrived two minutes before I had.

"We think once Beau died," Carrie said, answering my unspoken questions, "his power somehow transferred to Willow through their twin connection. And that's why Asher is stalking her."

My head started to spin, and I sucked in a deep breath. Someone named Asher was after me?

Allcot took his seat again and concentrated on me. "Asher's the vampire you met in the cemetery the day you got home from California."

"But if he's a vampire, why would he want to stop such a thing?" Phoebe asked.

Eadric angled his head toward a painting depicting a family from what looked to be the sixteenth century. There was one man and three grown women, all very pale and all dressed in layers of ornate clothing, jewels at their throats. "That's Tobias Sleford and his mistresses. He was the King of the Vampire Royal Court at the time."

Some sensation returned to my fingers as I dug them into my palm. One thing I had learned during my run as a Void agent was vampire history. Sleford had been a man of the cloth before he'd been turned. His reign had largely consisted of instilling order in the vampire community—until he'd disappeared one hundred and fifty years later. It was suspected he'd been murdered, and the vampire royalty line was abolished. He'd been responsible for setting the groundwork for vampires, fae, witches, and humans alike to coexist peacefully.

"And?" Phoebe tapped her foot.

"Asher used Sleford's teachings and twisted them into his own perverse reality. He believes he's a prophet sent back by Sleford to segregate humans and vampires. In other words, he feels humans are superior to every other race and it's his job to keep humans safe. Naturally, Asher feels daywalking vampires are a mortal threat to humans. His band of followers has been taking out all fae who are known carriers of the sunwalking magic."

I gasped. "There are more of us?"

He shook his head. "Not that anyone's aware of. It's an extremely rare gift. I only know of one other family, and unfortunately that line was terminated about sixty years ago."

Terminated. Goddess above.

"And he knows about Willow?" Phoebe started to pace, nervous energy flowing off her in waves. "We have to get her out of here. Out of the country, maybe."

"Now wait just a minute—"

Allcot put his hand up, stopping me. "According to our intel, he's only keeping an eye on you as a person of interest. If you have a son, Asher would want to know about it. Since you're Beau's twin and he's unaware of Beau Junior, he has reason to believe you could pass the gene to your offspring. As long as he's unaware of your ability, you should be able to keep living a normal life."

"But what about the one that tried to jump me that night outside my shop?" He had been a vamp, after all.

"I suspect he's one of Asher's people. He may have been trying to impress his master or you might have snuck up on him. No way to tell. What we do know is if Asher finds out about your abilities, he will come after you."

Phoebe stopped pacing and balled her fists on her hips. "She can't stay here. It's too dangerous."

I stood, meeting her toe to toe. "I'm not going anywhere. I have a life here. I won't live it hiding out somewhere. Plus, Beau Junior is here. He's my family."

Phoebe glanced from me to Allcot and gritted her teeth. "Fine. But first thing tomorrow I'm signing you up for those self-defense classes."

"Deal." I smiled. This time I'd go. After the week I'd had, I was dying to. Literally.

Phoebe eyed Allcot. "If you don't think Asher will kill her, then why did you have David tell Maude there was a death threat?"

"It's not a total lie. If he learns the truth he will kill her." Allcot raised his crystal glass to his lips. "And I had my reasons for wanting one of my people on the inside."

Phoebe snorted. "I bet."

I started pacing again. "But you didn't know about my ability then."

"Willow." Carrie grabbed my wrist, stopping me. "We knew about your ability to sense vampires. I was afraid for you. It was my idea to have Davidson look after you."

I dropped to my knees in front of her, betrayal and hurt taking over my logical mind. "Why didn't you just tell me?" I demanded. "We were close. As close as sisters." I couldn't stop the tears from streaming down my face. "You just...left, and took little Beau with you. How could you do that?"

Her eyes glistened with her own tears. "I was afraid. For my child, for you, for all of us. I knew about Beau's ability. He told me, and deep inside I knew his death wasn't an accident, but I didn't know what to do about it. So I went to Nicola, knowing she had access to Eadric and his protection. That's how I ended up here. They've been watching over us ever since. And now you. Since the day David walked into your shop a year ago."

Eadric clucked his tongue in disapproval, and I gaped. I glanced back at Phoebe. "Did you know any of this?"

She shook her head, appearing just as surprised as I was. Though I don't know why. As soon as we'd walked into the room I should have made the connection. It was too much of a coincidence to believe I'd ended up with David by accident. He'd lied to me for over a year. *Bastard!*

This was all too much. "I have to get out of here." I turned to Phoebe. "Let's take Maude home." I glared at Allcot, daring him to protest. But he didn't.

He inclined his head. "I trust you will not speak of Carrie or Beau to anyone?"

"I need to tell Talisen." There was no way I was keeping this from him. Better Allcot understood that. "He's been searching for answers to Beau's death. If he keeps digging, he'll call attention to himself unnecessarily. I can't have that."

The vamp leaned back, crossing his arms over his chest. I almost thought he'd argue, but then he said, "That's acceptable if you put a silencing spell on the information."

I cringed. Tal would hate that. No one ever volunteers to have their free will taken away. But there were other people's lives on the line. "Fine." He'd understand. I hoped.

I moved to the open door leading into Beau's bedroom. He sat in the middle of the room, playing with a giant soft puzzle. I met Carrie's eyes and waved a hand toward him. "Is it okay?"

She gave me a small smile and nodded.

Thank you, I mouthed.

Joining my nephew, I sat next to him, handing him puzzle pieces as he worked out where they should go. His eyes and chin were the same shape as Beau's, but his nose was wider and cheeks puffier. I wondered if he'd grow into Beau's rugged good looks. I hoped so. Hoped with all my heart.

"Auntie!" he cried in exuberance, jumping to his feet.

"Yeah?" I laughed at his sheer joy as he ran around me in a circle.

He held out a brown-and-white plush dog. "Kiss."

I clasped my hands around the softest stuffed animal ever made and gave it a hug. "What's his name?"

"Mama named her." He moved in, snuggling me close.

"Oh? And what name did Mama give her?" I smoothed his unruly red-blond hair.

"Willa."

"Willa?" I parroted.

"No, like Auntie. Willa!"

"Willow?" I asked, choking back the emotion in my throat.

He laughed. "Yeah, like Auntie."

Chapter 32

When Phoebe and I returned to Allcot's office, Maude was resting on a couch and other than visible exhaustion, she appeared as good as new.

"Looks like Talisen worked his magic," I said, sitting next to her.

She placed a hand on my leg. "He did. Thank you for asking him to come here."

"Of course." I glanced around at the deserted room. "As soon as he gets back from wherever he went, we'll get you home."

She sat up, fluttering her newly healed iridescent wings. "He already left. Said he had somewhere to be."

He left? What the heck was so important he'd leave without even checking on me? We were in a vampire den, for God's sake. Was he that angry? Had I pushed him away with my no-dating mantra? I suppressed a frustrated sigh. I'd only been trying to protect our friendship. Looks like I failed.

"It seemed important." Maude patted my leg. "You'll work it out."

"It doesn't matter," I lied. Rolling my tense shoulders, I turned to my aunt. "But we do need to figure out what we're going to do about Felton." I paused. "Maude?"

"Yes?" She met my gaze with tired eyes.

"Why is he so obsessed with studying me?" What I really wanted to know was why she'd been so mean for three years, but now wasn't the time to discuss my hurt feelings. In all likelihood the prolonged use of the tainted Influence was the main cause. "I mean, I've worked for the Arcane for the last two years. Why now?"

"Oh, honey. He's always been obsessed with your abilities. It was my job to explore and exploit them to best further his cause."

"Which is?"

She shook her head. "Eliminating vampires. Your ability to sense them is an odd, but useful, trait. As long as you were helping our agents track down their suspects, he was happy to leave it alone. But when he found out a vampire was interested in protecting you, he went a little crazy and started investigating our family history."

"And he found out about my family line?"

She nodded gravely. "Yes. I'm sorry."

"Who told him?"

"No one. He found top-secret records, I think. I'm not sure. After his discovery, he ordered me to take you in for extensive testing. And by then you'd already transformed David. He couldn't stand the thought of any more daywalkers. If your friends hadn't broken you out, I'm certain you would have been incarcerated for good."

I sucked in a breath.

"Do you have any incriminating evidence we could use to bring charges against him?"

She nodded slowly. "Yes, I think I have some memos written in his hand, and I could be drug tested. The Arcane Influence leaves traces."

"And modifies personalities?" I couldn't help myself.

She frowned. "Yeah, but it was more than that. I was controlled for so long, eventually Felton's evilness started to weave its way inside me." Tears glistened in her stormy eyes. "I was lost." She took my hand. "Thank you for freeing me."

I choked out a laugh. "I was trying to free myself. But I'm glad you're back. Mom is going to be ecstatic."

"Me, too, sweetie. Me, too."

I stood. "Okay, then let's go so we can start the legal process. The longer Felton's out there, the easier it will be for him to manipulate the situation."

"That won't be necessary," Nathan said from behind me.

I reeled, finding him lounging in the open doorway, one foot hooked over the other. How long had he been there? It couldn't have been long. I would have sensed him. I shifted to stand in front of Maude. This was the vamp who'd tortured her. I'd be damned if I let him near her again. "Get out of here."

Nathan raised his eyebrows and his lips quirked up in amusement. "I live here."

I glanced back at Maude. She was staring at him with hate pouring from her blazing eyes. Every muscle was tensed and she appeared ready to pounce. I had to get him out of there before she snapped.

"What do you want?" I asked through clenched teeth.

"Nothing. But you should know we have Felton locked up. He won't be an issue."

Realization dawned. "He was captured when they broke David out, wasn't he?"

He nodded. "He won't be a problem for you again."

I stalked up to him. "I want to see him."

"Why?"

"To find out..." Did Nathan know about all the details? I had no idea, but I wasn't telling him. "I need to ask him some questions."

"No one else knows. He only told Maude."

I narrowed my eyes. "Knows what?"

"Your family history."

My eyes went wide. Did everyone know? How was I going to keep this a secret when the entire vamp population was on to me? "Allcot told you then," I stated in a flat tone.

"I'm part of Carrie's security team. Only a handful of us know what's going on."

"Oh." Well, wasn't that peachy? "I'd still like a word with Felton. Take me to him."

He leveled me with his neutral stare. "Sorry. Eadric's ordered the prisoner isolated. You can request a formal visitation, but it probably won't be granted."

Shit. I glanced at Maude, now standing. I wasn't sure if she wanted to back me up or bolt. The vamps had definitely tortured Felton, just as they had Maude. The thought made my stomach roll. Not that *he* didn't deserve it. Felton would've done unspeakable things to me, and he'd kept Maude under the Influence for years. Still, I hated that the vamps had taken matters into their own hands as if we didn't have a legal system in place.

Oh Lord. The legal system. This *was* New Orleans. On second thought, it was probably better if Allcot kept him in the dungeon. Or wherever they had the bastard chained up.

I stretched and winced, forgetting my wings needed time to heal. "Fine. Maude, let's go."

No one paid any attention to us as we left. Outside, I spotted Phoebe crushing a cigarette with the toe of her shoe. I swallowed the automatic admonishment poised on my tongue. It had been a bad week. Just as I approached her car, David appeared.

"Willow." He stood behind me with his hands stuffed in his jeans pockets.

"What?" I demanded, so angry I could stake him right there. He'd known about Beau the entire time we'd been together. Listened to me talk about how awful it was to not know what happened to him. Knew how much it hurt. And he'd had the answers the entire time.

Asshole.

Everything had been a lie. He'd used me. Dated me after being assigned to me. Spent time in my bed. My skin crawled with the now-tainted memory. I couldn't even look at him. "Go home, David. I don't need your *protection* anymore."

"Wait." He glanced over at Phoebe, either not catching the venom in my voice or choosing to ignore it. "I'll take her home."

Phoebe met my gaze, her eyes raised and amusement tugging at her lips.

"No, you most certainly will not." I scowled and pulled the car door open, glaring at David. "I'm not your property. Stop acting like you own me."

He held his hands up in surrender. "I never thought you were." He sighed. "Please, Willow, I have a few things to explain."

I huffed. "I don't want to hear it." Though I was more than mildly curious how he planned to explain away a whole year of our lives, a sudden breakup, and secret orders to keep an eye on me.

My aunt leaned in and whispered, "It might be better to get this over with now, rather than later."

I stared at her, my mouth open. Was she kidding?

She shrugged. "It's been my experience vampires don't give up easily. If you let him have his say and then tell him to stick a stake where the sun doesn't shine, he might start to get the picture." Smirking at David, she climbed into the front seat of Phoebe's car.

David shifted to move in front of me, blocking Phoebe and Maude from my line of sight. Regret and something close to shame flashed through his tortured eyes. "Please, Willow. One car ride, and if you tell me to get lost, I will."

"Wil?" Phoebe asked, poking her head around David's frame.

I stared at my ex, anger coursing red-hot beneath my skin. But when I gazed up at him, a piece of me softened. And I hated myself for it. I waved a hand at Phoebe. "Go on. I'll be right behind you."

"You're sure?" She glanced up and down the street, eyeing the traffic jockeying for her spot. "We could wait."

"And have that car block traffic for ten minutes?" I gestured to the red Mustang hovering behind us. "I don't think so. Go on home. I'll be right there."

"If you say so." A second later, the car squealed away from the curb, leaving a rubber trail on the road.

I turned to David. "Where's your car?"

He started to say something, but my expression must have made him change his mind because he closed his mouth and started walking. "This way."

I stayed a few steps behind him as I followed him down the block and around the corner to a small parking lot.

He pushed a button on his remote. A silver Mercedes beeped twice and then he opened the passenger door for me.

I wasn't impressed. No amount of chivalry was going to salvage this fake relationship.

Once inside the car, David sat there, staring out the windshield, hands wringing the wheel.

"It'd help if you put the key in the ignition," I said.

He clutched the wheel tighter. "It wasn't a lie."

"What wasn't? That you happened to wander in my shop that day? Or that you were just a regular guy working the oil rigs? Or maybe that you weren't close to your family and that's why you never talked about them? Or was it that you were being transferred to Texas, and it was better we broke it off rather than have a long-distance relationship?" I sucked in a breath. "No, it's none of those. Because clearly, those were all *lies!*"

He turned to me, his eyes swimming with regret. "I know I owe you an apology."

"An *apology?* Do you think I could ever forgive the fact that our entire relationship was fabricated? That you knew the answers to my past but you hid them from me?"

Pain flickered over his features, then in one blink, he was stoic and controlled, exactly the way he always was. "I love you." His voice came out strong and sure.

I jerked in my seat, ready to explode at the audacity of his statement, but he cut me off before I could get the words out.

"That was never a lie. The rest...Well, you know why I didn't tell you the rest." He shoved the key in the ignition. "I'm not asking forgiveness. I'm not asking anything. I only wanted you to be certain of that one thing." He turned to meet my frozen gaze. "I never lied about loving you."

Stunned, I sat there, speechless while he put the car in gear and finally took me home. I stayed silent the entire ride. I had nothing to say. What could I say? I'd loved him. More than I wanted to admit to myself. Even if he hadn't turned vampire, his lies had canceled out everything we'd shared. Trust was everything, and he'd broken mine. Not to mention he'd turned into something I didn't understand. Sadness slowly melted away the rage that had been feeding my resolve. When he came to a stop, he killed the ignition.

"David," I said tentatively.

He watched me, waiting patiently.

"You bit Maude against her will, and who knows who else." I gazed out the window, focusing on nothing. "I can't…I mean, it's not right."

I could feel his eyes on me, and the silence stretched out in front of us. When I couldn't stand it any longer, I turned to say goodbye, but he caught my hand, resignation lining his tired expression.

"That was Nathan. It's his job to coerce cooperation from our enemies." His voice was low, but not apologetic.

"And you just happened to be there? I saw the blood on your shirt."

"What do you want me to say?" His controlled, emotionless mask slid back into place. "I was there. I didn't stop it. We believed she was working for Asher. What did you expect us to do?"

"I don't know. Maybe find some proof before you tortured innocent people," I snapped.

He frowned. "Torture was the fastest way to get answers."

I shook my head. "And you got nothing, right? Other than finding out Felton was the real director. And where's he now? In another torture chamber?"

David closed his eyes, clearly not wanting to discuss this. But when he opened them, he met my determined gaze. "He's been eliminated."

Fear made my blood run cold. Goddess above. "He can't be. Nathan said I could request a visitation."

"Nathan has not been told of Felton's fate. Father made the decision a short while ago."

Of course he had. Felton had messed with Nicola. Son of a bitch! He should've stood trial. Every time the vamps took the law into their own hands, the rest of us lost a tiny bit more of our personal rights. Their disregard for all authority was so common it had become accepted, expected even. How long until the vampires had complete control of the city? They almost did now.

I stared at David as if really seeing him for the first time since he'd changed. He was vampire. A product of Allcot's upbringing. We were polar opposites in every way. One life, one death. Physically and spiritually.

"This," I said, waving a frustrated hand to indicate the two of us, "can't happen. Besides the political landmines, I can't stomach what happened tonight." *What you've become.* I let out a hollow laugh, realizing I'd known the whole time whatever was between us had died the moment he'd turned vampire. The David I'd known had never been real.

"I know, Wil. I know." He got out of the car and came around to open the door. He held out his hand. I hesitated out of habit. He hung his head. "I can't change what's happened. I respect your decision, but you should know, I'll always be here, ready to stand by your side. I'll always be your friend, whether you want me to be or not."

My heart cracked a little, and I slid my hand into his large one. The coolness numbed my fingers, but I didn't care. This was the last time I'd let him touch me. I was still pissed as hell, but vulnerability wasn't something I'd seen in him before. All it did was make me sad.

I moved up the front walk, and our hands disconnected in slow motion. "Good night, David."

"Good night." He waited for me to get inside and then sped off into the night.

I leaned against the closed door, catching my breath. So many emotions in one day.

"Did you cut off his balls?" Phoebe asked from the living room couch, lying under a cream-colored throw. A cup of what I'd bet my last dollar was Chimney Bark sat on the end table next to her.

I smirked. "It's over."

"Good. Talisen's waiting for you in the kitchen."

The tension instantly drained from my shoulders. Then guilt and trepidation took over. What would he say? The temptation to hole up in my bedroom was strong, but I couldn't put off talking to him. And right then, I needed my best friend. I started up the stairs and asked Phoebe, "Where's Maude?"

"Resting in my room. I offered it to her for the night. Talisen said she might need some restorative fae thing later. He said he wanted to keep her close for a few days, then she's going to go back to her place. But not before I search it for all evil-director paraphernalia or tampered edibles."

I smiled. "That's kind of you."

She shrugged. "She's your aunt."

"Thanks, Phoebs."

"Yeah, yeah. It's what I do."

I grinned.

Nervous energy trickled its way through me as I slowly climbed the stairs to the second floor. What would Talisen do once he knew the truth about Beau? Would he go back home? The mystery was solved. There was really no need for him to stay. A hollow ache filled my chest. I didn't want him to leave. Not yet.

I rounded the corner and stopped in the doorway, watching him scoop varying sizes of cookie-dough balls onto a baking sheet. Link was curled up close to his feet. I smiled, noting the batter covering the counter. "Looks like you could use a baking lesson," I said, keeping my tone light.

He glanced down at the mess in front of him, then grinned. "They're definitely not Martha Stewart style, but wait until their chocolaty goodness is melting on your tongue."

My mouth watered. And not from the thought of eating his cookies. His easy charm combined with the flour gracing the front of his jeans made me want to…I shook my head. Never mind. I'd basically just broken up with David for good, and here I was thinking about undressing Talisen. I took a seat at the table. "I can't wait."

Watching him work, I said, "I thought you had something important to do. You left The Red Door awfully fast."

"I did." He scooped another large mound of dough into his spoon. "University business. I had to meet one of the professors for the project we're working on. I'd already canceled twice. One more time, and I'm pretty sure he'd have cut me loose."

Yikes! This was his career, and the only reason he'd miss an appointment was because of me. "I'm sorry. I hope everything's okay."

"It's fine. Don't worry about it." A couple of minutes later, he popped the dough in the oven, set the timer, and rinsed his hands. He grabbed a couple of beers from the refrigerator and joined me.

I took a swig of the Turbo Dog he handed me. "I'm sorry about earlier. The way I bailed on our conversation and calling you to Allcot's place. I know I put you in a tough position."

His smile vanished. "Forget it. I shouldn't have brought it up. Bad timing." Reaching out, he grabbed my left hand, caressing my fingers. "But don't think that conversation's over."

My heart did a flip-flop in my chest.

"And don't worry about calling me to Allcot's. The way I see it, I owe you an apology. I was still pissed you'd left, but after I saw your aunt…Well, you obviously had your priorities in order."

"Tal, I—"

He held up his other hand. "Really. Let's forget about it. Now, Phoebe says you have news."

Right. I cleared my throat. "It's about Beau."

He stopped drinking mid-sip and slowly lowered his bottle. "I'm listening."

I stared at our joined hands and took a deep breath. "I have something to tell you first."

When he didn't answer, I glanced up and met his patient eyes. He nodded.

My breath caught as a lump formed in my throat. Talisen always knew what I needed. Knew I didn't need to be pressured, that I'd explain everything as soon as I found the words. He *knew* me. Sometimes better than I did. I swallowed. "I talked with David tonight."

His eyebrows pinched in anger and he pulled back, releasing my hand.

A sharp pain tore through my heart. I wanted his hand in mine. But I had to get this out first. "I won't be seeing him again."

Surprise flickered over his face and he sat back, waiting.

"I mean...son of a...This is hard to tell *you*, you know." I bit my lip and searched his face for some clue of what he was thinking.

He nodded slowly. "I guess it would be."

It wasn't much, but enough to keep me talking. "When David and I broke up, I was blindsided. I mean, I had no idea it was coming. Usually girls can sense when the relationship is going south. But I got none of that. Everything was fine, and then the next day I get a Dear Jane text message. I mean, talk about the worst way to break up with someone."

"Brutal," Tal agreed.

"Yeah," I huffed out a laugh. "Anyway, then I was called home, and I had such a great summer hanging with you, I hardly even thought of him. I *was* doing fine."

"Until you came back and found out he was a vampire?" His brows pinched again. "Wasn't that enough? He'd turned vamp, for fuck's sake, Wil."

"I know. If you'd asked me four months ago if I'd ever get involved with a vampire, I would have scoffed. Laughed in your face. But..." I paused. "I wasn't over him. I still loved him despite the changes."

Talisen's face fell, and a dark shadow clouded his deep green eyes. "Do you still…love him?"

The words hung in the air between us. Slowly, I shook my head. "I care about him. It's hard not to. We have history, and I changed him into a daywalker." I suspected because of that, we'd be tied to each other whether I wanted it or not, but I couldn't tell Talisen that. Not right now. "But do I love him? No. The things I've seen him do make it impossible to be part of his world. Not to mention the lies. I can't give my heart to someone like that."

Talisen's shoulders eased, and he reached for my hand again. His long fingers wrapped around mine, bringing warmth back into my being. "He hurt you."

"He can't anymore. I told you, his touch doesn't affect me."

"No, Wil. He hurt you." Tal pointed to my chest. "You trusted him and he let you down."

"Oh, that. Yeah." He had, but it was more than that. The violence and the unjust way his father treated people. The way he thought nothing of human life if he thought someone wronged his family. And David accepted it. Went along with whatever Allcot said. It was disturbing and wrong. "I think he thought he was doing the right thing. Heck, maybe he was. I don't know. I just can't be part of his world. It isn't me. You were right. I need life and he's death."

Tal squeezed my fingers. "I'm sorry."

I chuckled. "No, you're not."

His lips twitched. "You're right. I'm not sorry to hear you've come to your senses. But I am sorry about the way I acted. I'm also sorry you've been hurt." His intense green eyes locked on mine and for a second, I swore I saw a flicker of joy. Love even.

My heart soared. "There's one more thing."

He pulled back again, but this time he didn't let go of my hand.

"Nothing happened between me and David." Much. "Not after he turned, anyway." For some reason it was important to me that Talisen knew I hadn't shared a bed with David.

Talisen's smile came back in full force. "That's good to know. I'll keep it under advisement."

I laughed at his obvious pleasure, then sobered.

Talisen's grin faded and all seriousness returned. Once again, he understood me like no one else. "You need to tell me something about Beau."

I took a deep breath. "He was murdered."

Tal stared at me, his face suddenly blank of emotion. "That's what we've always thought."

"Now I know why." I let the words hang in the air until Talisen leaned forward and grabbed my other hand.

"Why?"

"I'm sorry, but I can't tell you unless you agree to a silencing spell."

His eyes narrowed with suspicion and then understanding smoothed out his features. "Allcot's request?"

Sighing with relief, I nodded. "I know it's awful."

"It's all right. Do what you gotta do."

I jumped up and ran to my supply cupboard. A pinch of augmented dill and thyme would hold his tongue. "Everything we say for the next thirty minutes or so after you swallow these will stay between you and me." I strode back to the table and handed them to Tal. "Okay?"

In answer, he swallowed the concoction and chased it with his beer.

I sat across from him, taking his hands in mine once more. Then I explained everything Allcot had told me, about the family history, Beau's ability, Asher's psychotic religious beliefs, and Allcot's theory that the ability somehow transferred to me because I was Beau's twin.

Talisen's eyes went wide with disbelief. "Beau was killed because he could sense vampires? Feel them like you do?"

"Yes, but he also would've been able to turn vamps into daywalkers." I pulled one hand back and started to pick at the label on my beer bottle.

"But he never said anything about it to me." His brow furrowed.

"Me neither. But Carrie knew."

"Carrie?" He straightened and his confusion turned to surprise.

"She's here."' I filled him in on the rest of the story, and by the end, silent tears leaked from the corners of my eyes. "My nephew's name is Beau."

"Oh, baby." Talisen got up and pulled me to my feet. His arms came around me, holding me tight to him. He rested his chin on my head and lightly stroked my spine. "It's been a really rough week."

A laugh got caught in my throat and came out as more of a sob.

"Shh. I know it's hard. But we have answers now," he soothed.

I nodded, clutching his shoulders, willing him to stay there with me, forever. But I knew deep down he'd go home now. My fragile heart started to rip in two. He'd come to help me find out what happened to Beau, and now we knew.

"Did Carrie seem open to letting you spend time with Beau?" Talisen asked gently.

"Yeah." I sniffed. "But we need to be careful. His life is at greater risk than mine if anyone finds out he exists. I can't let anything happen to him."

Talisen hugged me tighter, understanding this was all I needed.

Eventually the oven timer buzzed and pulled us apart. I took the oven mitt from Talisen, needing to distract myself for fear I'd burst into tears again. I set the cookies on a cooling rack and turned to face him. "What happens now?"

The worry left his face, replaced by serious eyes and a raised chin. "I'll watch Maude tonight to make sure she doesn't suffer any lasting effects from that piece of shit Nathan. You'll finally take those self-defense classes Phoebe's been harping about. I'll finish what I started with the university here and then we'll go back to our normal lives. We'll figure everything else out as we go along."

My heart sank. Go back to our normal lives. Mine here in New Orleans and his in Eureka. I was too chicken to ask how long he planned to stay, but he'd already been here a week. It couldn't be much longer. "You're right. Back to normal."

It's what I wanted. Right?

Tal gave me one more hug, kissed my temple, and headed out of the kitchen. "I'll be in Phoebe's room watching Maude if you need me."

After he left, I scraped the biggest cookie off the sheet and stuffed it in my mouth. Despite the presentation, the warm chocolate melted on my tongue, and I decided they were the best damn cookies I'd ever tasted. Or maybe I was too distraught to notice the difference.

After scraping half a dozen cookies onto a plate, I snapped my fingers and Link and I headed off to bed. I only hoped my oak could heal my tattered heart while it rejuvenated my tired limbs.

Chapter 33

Over the next three days, between the catch-up needed at The Fated Cupcake and Talisen's meetings at the university, we only spent about twenty minutes together. And that had been while rushing around the house getting ready for our respective days. Absolutely zero time to discuss the future.

"I'm sure he'll let you know when he makes his plans to go back to California," Maude said from a stool in the middle of my lab. We were at The Fated Cupcake, working on an antidote to the modified Influence the Void had been producing under Director Felton.

"Yeah," I agreed absently. I wasn't at all sure he would. I'd tried bringing it up that morning but he'd brushed me off, dodging the question altogether. It was classic Talisen avoidance when he didn't want to tell a girl he'd moved on. A hollow ache formed in my chest right where my heart should've been.

I suspected now that David really was out of the picture, his interest in me as more than a friend had vanished. Of course it had. The challenge was gone. And an invisible wall now stood between us. Exactly why I hadn't wanted to cross that line.

I rolled my shoulders. "It doesn't matter that much anyway. He can't stay forever. He has a job in Eureka."

Maude used a paring knife to chop up dandelion roots in a rapid motion. She paused. "You had a job there before you moved here. That didn't stop you."

I ignored the remark. Talisen had never shown any interest in leaving the redwoods. He was fae. It was in his blood. "I just want to know when, so I'm not surprised one day when I wake up and his duffel's gone."

"Understandable." Maude glanced at the clock on the wall. "I've got to get to the Arcane building. President Fischer's coming today to appoint the new Director of Ops."

I pushed a piece of hair behind my ear. "Are you in the running?"

She shook her head. "I doubt it. Not after Felton managed to control me. Makes the entire Void branch look vulnerable." She smiled, but it didn't reach her eyes. "I'll continue to be a field agent, which is all I ever was to begin with."

"Except everyone thought you were appointed after Felton supposedly stepped down." The Arcane was keeping a tight lid on recent events, just as they always did, except this time Maude had made many enemies while being controlled and hardly anyone knew the real story. "You won't have nearly as many resources to fight back if anyone comes after you as a field agent."

"I have you." She stood. "Don't worry, little one. We'll handle it." She gave me a kiss on my cheek and headed to the door. "I'll see you in the morning."

"I'll be here." I waved and the door shut with a soft click.

I spent the next thirty minutes moving the dandelion stems, blossoms, and leaves to separate jars and cleaning my work table. Tomorrow, I'd work on the first test batches of antidotes. It wouldn't do me any good to start with a distracted mind. I logged the augmented plants, made a to-do list, and tacked the sheet of paper to my corkboard.

It was just as well Talisen was too busy to spend any time with me. I was way behind on business. We were completely out of Truth Clusters and Mocha in Motion. The Truth Clusters could wait, but not the Mocha in Motion. I grabbed a tray full of already augmented dried cocoa pods and a gallon of my hand-roasted coffee beans. After a trip through the industrial grinder, the mixture was ready to be brewed, using my secret blend of caramel-and-vanilla-infused liquid. I was bottling the concentrate when a soft knock sounded at the door.

"Come in," I called, twisting the cap on a glass bottle.

"Willow?" Tami poked her head in. "You have a visitor."

"Okay, I'll be out in a minute." I put the prepared drinks in the walk-in and wiped the counter down one last time. Back in the storefront, Tami was busy helping a customer and pointed to my office.

Who the heck would be in my office? Phoebe? No, she was busy delivering the new agent Maude had tried to saddle her with to the Baton Rouge office. She couldn't be back already. Oh, no, David? It was still light out. He shouldn't be visiting me, especially so blatantly. I scowled and yanked my office door open, letting it crash against the inside wall.

Talisen sat in the seat across from my desk, his eyebrows raised in amusement. "Tough day?"

I stopped short in the threshold. "Hey."

He got up and gently pulled me into the room, closing the door behind us. "Hey, yourself."

I let him lead me to the old, comfortable couch against the wall. "It's been a while," I said and sat next to him, stiff with anxiety.

"Just a few days." He leaned forward, his hands clasped lightly.

Right. A few days after I'd told him my life was in danger, and I'd heard barely a word from him. "Yeah. Only a few days. Are you leaving?"

Surprise flickered through his eyes. "What makes you ask that?"

I shrugged. "You've been working hard to finish your business with the university. I figured you needed to get back to California."

He sat back, studying me. "Do you want me to leave?"

I shrugged again, avoiding his gaze.

Talisen was quiet for a moment, then he chuckled. "You've pegged me all wrong. Again."

"Huh?" I jerked my head up. "What's that supposed to mean?"

His face turned serious, almost angry. "It means you're thinking the worst of me, as usual. Do you really think I'd leave you now? After finding out about Asher?"

"But…" I rubbed a hand over my eyes. "Where have you been the last three days?"

"Interviewing."

"What? Here?" My heart started to hammer against my ribcage.

He nodded. "And apartment hunting."

I sat up straight, hope and fear fighting for dominance in my chest. A tiny smile tugged at my lips. "You're staying, then?"

He nodded, his eyes crinkling as he tried to hold back a smile. "Yes."

I flung my arms around him, burying my head against his shoulder. Tears of happiness burned my eyes. His strong arms came around me and we sat together, holding on to each other as he stroked my hair. "Thank you," I said, my voice muffled by his shirt.

"Shhh, there's no need to thank me. After Beau died, I made a promise to myself I'd protect you. No matter what. That's what I intend to do."

Protect me? I pulled back and got to my feet, my fists on my hips. What was I, a charity case? "I don't need a freakin' baby-sitter."

He gritted his teeth in clear exasperation and stood toe to toe with me. "Jesus! Stop that. I don't want to be your damned baby-sitter."

"Then what do you want?" I yelled, hurt and beyond frustrated.

He stared at me, shaking his head, and then laughed. Actually laughed at me. "I want to be with you. And only you." He cupped my face with both his palms, his intense gaze boring into mine. "Don't you get it? The reason I never stay with anyone is because I'm meant to be with someone else. It's you, Wil. It's always been you."

Speechless, I gazed back.